Praise for Sara Poole's *Poison*

"A fascinating page-turner as delicious and deadly as the poisons brewed up by its heroine." —Lauren Willig, bestselling author of
The Secret History of the Pink Carnation

"A riveting historical thriller . . . Sara Poole's brilliant debut novel presents a race to the finish between good and evil that will leave you breathlessly awaiting what is surely the birth of a series."
—Sandra Worth, award-winning author of
The King's Daughter

"Five hundred years before the Sopranos and their hit men, there were the Borgias and their poisoners. . . . The heroine Francesca may be the mistress of poisoning, but in my book, Sara Poole is the new queen of historical suspense."
—Robin Maxwell, author of the award-winning
The Secret Diary of Anne Boleyn

"*Poison* presents the most unique heroine I have ever seen in a mystery series (a complex, angst-filled Renaissance Dexter). . . . The plot is as much a fast-paced thriller as a compelling mystery."
—Karen Harper, *New York Times* bestselling
author of *The Last Boleyn*

"*Poison* delivers a fast-paced, gripping look at the wages of sin under the Borgias, as seen through the eyes of a troubled female poisoner. The seductive danger of Rome, lethal sanctity of the Vatican, and bitter taste for revenge all combine to produce an intoxicating brew that keeps us turning the pages, even as we glance fearfully at our fingertips for signs of residue."
—C. W. Gortner, author of *The Last Queen*

ALSO BY SARA POOLE

Poison

THE BORGIA
BETRAYAL

A Novel

SARA POOLE

ST. MARTIN'S GRIFFIN

NEW YORK

THE BORGIA BETRAYAL. Copyright © 2011 by Sara Poole. All rights reserved. Printed in the United States of America. For information, address St. Martin's Press, 175 Fifth Avenue, New York, N.Y. 10010.

www.stmartins.com

Library of Congress Cataloging-in-Publication Data

Poole, Sara, 1951–
    The Borgia betrayal : a novel / Sara Poole.—1st ed.
        p. cm.
    ISBN 978-0-312-60453-0 (hardcover)
    ISBN 978-0-312-60984-9 (trade paperback)
    1. Women poisoners—Fiction.   2. Alexander VI, Pope, 1431–1503—Fiction.
3. Borgia family—Fiction.   4. Intrigue—Fiction.   5. Conspiracies—Fiction.
6. Church and state—Fiction.   7. Renaissance—Italy—Rome—Fiction.
8. Rome (Italy)—Fiction.   I. Title.
    PS3569.E43B67 2011
    813'.54—dc22

                                                          2011000008

First Edition: June 2011

10 9 8 7 6 5 4 3 2 1

THE BORGIA
BETRAYAL

Prologue

I see . . . ," the woman said. She walked a little distance across the room to glance out the small window facing the river. Moonlight fell across her face. A young woman, pleasing enough in appearance though hardly remarkable in a city where beauty was common currency. Someone who would have aroused only passing interest were it not for the whispers that swirled around her.

"You never knew their names?" she asked.

The man who was about to die shook his head. He was kneeling on the bare wood floor in just his shirt, having been preparing for bed when she arrived. Come morning when the gates opened, he would have been gone from the city, taking the road north to Viterbo, to safety. Too late now.

His hands were clasped tightly in front of him, the knuckles showing white. "Why would they tell one such as I, lady? I am nothing."

She smiled faintly. "You were almost something. The killer of a pope."

Bile rose in the man's throat. He wondered how long she would make him suffer and what methods she would use. He had heard terrifying stories.

"Why would you do such a thing?" she asked. "For God?"

If he told her the truth, perhaps she would spare him a little. "For money."

Behind him, the man she had come with snorted. He had the look of a grizzled soldier but he wore the broad sash and other insignia of a high-ranking condottierre. A self-made man then, proud of it.

"I hope you got a good price," he said. "It was your own life you haggled for, whether you realized it or not."

The man's voice cracked. "I knew the risk."

"But you thought—what?" the woman asked. "That you could outwit me? That I would not realize what you had done until it was too late?"

"I hoped—" That they were cleverer than she, as they claimed. That what they gave him to put in the wine would not be detected. Yet she had found it all the same, the woman who bent down closer now to get a better look at him. He shivered, desperately afraid, praying not to wet himself. He had been reduced to that: Please God, don't let me piss.

"You wanted money that much?" she asked.

Had he? He couldn't seem to remember now. But he had looked at the gold they offered, more than he had ever imagined, and saw his life transformed. Wealth, comfort, ease when he had never known any, the best foods, lovely women. The promise of all that and more had shattered his wits. He thought that he must have been mad, knew that it would do no good to say so.

Instead, he said, "I was tempted into sin."

The woman sighed, almost as though she sympathized with him. Not so the condottierre.

"We can take him to the *castel*," he said. "Put him to the question."

She stood, looking down at the man for a moment, then shook her head. "There's no point. He doesn't know anything."

"How can you be sure?"

"He would have told us by now," she replied, and pointed to the puddle spreading across the floor.

The man's lips moved frantically in prayer. He stared up into her face, luminous in the moonlight, not unkind, almost gentle.

"Drink this," she said, and held out a wineskin made from the hide of a young goat, topped with a smooth wooden valve that slipped easily between his lips.

"I don't—" Tears slid down his cheeks.

She touched his hair soothingly and lifted the bag, helping him. "It will be easier this way. A few moments and it's over. Otherwise—"

The *castel* and hours, perhaps days of white-hot suffering before his life would end. Had already ended though he had not realized it, in the moment when he had allowed himself to hope for more.

It was a rich, full-bodied vintage fit for a pope, what he would have drunk in his new life had he been given the chance. He had a moment to wonder how she could possibly have known what the wine concealed. What if she was wrong? What if it had all been a trick and he was not going to die—

Scarcely had the thought formed when fire exploded in him, burning down his throat into the pit of his stomach and beyond. He cried out, convulsing. The woman stepped back, watching him closely, almost as though she was curious to see what effect the poison had on him. No, exactly like that.

He heard a great buzzing sound, a thousand insects swarming inside his skull. His eyes opened wide, bulging, even as his vision narrowed down, racing toward pinpricks of light before blinking out. He was blind and deaf save for the buzzing, and none of that mattered because of the pain. He would have cried out but the muscles of his throat were paralyzed as very quickly was the rest of him so that his last breath barely reached his lungs before his heart ceased to beat.

When it was over, the condottierre went to find the innkeeper who had been roused from his bed and stood quaking in the great room. A few coins in his hand, a quick word, and the grateful man learned that he had only to dispose of a body and keep his mouth shut, which he would do to the end of his days, he swore, and give thanks unceasingly to be shown such mercy.

Outside, in the pleasant coolness of the early spring night, Francesca waited. She pulled her cloak more closely around herself, for comfort more than warmth, and tried not to think too much about the dead man. She was very tired but she knew that she would not sleep. Not then, not yet.

The condottierre returned. Together, they walked toward the horses. "How many does that make this year?" he asked.

"Three," she said as he cupped his hands to give her a boot up. She disliked horses and preferred not to ride but as with so much in life, sometimes there was no good alternative.

Settled in the saddle, she added, "There will be more until we can put a stop to this."

"Or until one succeeds," her companion said.

She nodded grimly and turned her mount toward the river, anxious suddenly to be done.

1

The fate of the world rests upon a piece of paper set in front
of a man who puts down the freshly cut quill pen he has
been toying with for far too long and calls for wine.

The moment is suspended in my memory, caught like an insect
in amber as though some power beyond our ken stopped time at that
instant.

Of course, nothing of the sort happened. Time went right on,
bringing with it great events involving great personages. But beneath the glittering scaffold of history imagine, if you will, the lives
of humble people hanging in the balance. For truly, they did so
hang, and more than a few found their necks stretched unbearably.

I could have done with a drink myself just then. On this pleasant
day in early May, Anno Domini 1493, Rodrigo Borgia, now Pope
Alexander VI, had spent most of the afternoon considering the papal bull *Inter caetera,* decreeing the disposition of the newly discovered lands to the west. I had been in attendance throughout, for no

good reason; what man needs his poisoner to help him decide how to divvy up the world? But since I had played a role the previous year in hoisting him up onto Saint Peter's Throne, His Holiness had fallen into the habit of keeping me nearby. I would like to believe that he saw me as a talisman of sorts but the truth is that he thought it prudent to keep a close eye on me lest I do who knows what.

My name is Francesca Giordano, daughter of the late Giovanni Giordano, who served ten years as poisoner to the House of Borgia and was murdered for his pains. I succeeded to his position after killing the man originally chosen to take his place. I also slit the throat of one of the men involved in my father's death. Ultimately, I tried to poison the man I believed—incorrectly, as it turned out—to have ordered his murder. Only God knows if Pope Innocent VIII died by my hand.

Before you recoil from me, consider that I had good reason for all I did, at least by my own lights. Yet there is no denying that a darkness dwells within me. I am not like other people, although I can pretend to be when the need arises. I am as I am, may God have mercy on my soul. But then we can all say that, can't we?

Beyond the high windows overlooking the Piazza San Pietro, the day was fair. A northerly wind blew the worst of the stink off the city and bathed us in the perfume of the lemon groves and lavender fields for which every good Roman claims to yearn. That is a lie; we can barely spend a few days in *la campagna* without longing for the filth and clamor that is our beloved city.

Popes come and go, empires clash, new worlds arise, but Rome is eternally Rome, which is to say that its people were busy as always sweating, swearing, working, eating, fornicating, occasionally praying, and without surcease, gossiping.

How I longed to be among them rather than where I was, in an uncomfortable window seat under the censorious eye of Borgia's secretaries, both men, both priests, both despising me.

Not that I blamed them. My profession alone provokes fear and loathing without any additional effort on my part, but there is no escaping the fact that as a woman in a man's world, I discomfited many a male. I was then twenty, auburn haired, brown eyed and, although slender, possessed of a womanly figure. That, too, makes some men, especially priests, prickle with disapproval—or with something. Men prickle for so many reasons it is often impossible to know what provokes them on any given occasion.

Borgia being Borgia, a young woman of any degree of attractiveness could not be in his company without suspicion arising that she shared his bed. Disabuse yourself of any such notion regarding me. Borgia and I shared much over the years that would be thought unlikely between a man of his stature and a woman of mine, but bed was never one of them.

As for his eldest son, Cesare, that is a different matter. Thoughts of the son of Jove, as Cesare's more overwrought admirers styled him, distracted me from the endless, interminable moment. He had been away from Rome for several weeks, attending to his father's business. In his absence, my bed had grown cold.

Cesare and I had come to each other's notice as children in Borgia's palazzo on the Corso, he the Cardinal's son and I the poisoner's daughter. What began as wary glances progressed over the years until the night he came upon me in the library. I was reading Dante, ever my favorite; he was drunk and in pain after yet another argument with his father. I could claim that, having taken the *virgo intacto* by surprise, he had his wicked way with me under the benign gaze of the portrait of Pope Callixtus III, the family uncle and patron who had set them all on the road to glory. Yet the truth is that I had my way with Cesare as much as he had his with me, perhaps more. The darkness within me was drawn to him, constructed as he was of raw appetites that left no room for morality or conscience. He was without sin in the sense that he recognized none. With him, I came as close to being myself as I could ever hope in those years.

In his absence, I had considered taking another lover, but the only one I truly wanted other than Cesare I could not have. I was forced to fall back on the canard that self-denial is a virtue even as each passing day—and night—made eminently clear that it is anything but.

Does all this shock you? I hope so, for in truth, I am remembering how exquisitely bored I was just then and would do almost anything to liven things up.

"Are you going to sign it?" I asked finally, because really, someone had to. He'd been at it all afternoon, reading, rereading, groaning, complaining, insisting it be rewritten to change this word and that, and finally just staring at it. The pigeons that alit from time to time on the windowsill and pecked at the handfuls of grain I put out for them seemed more purposeful than did Christ's Vicar on Earth.

"Do you think I should?" Borgia asked. Despite the pleasant day, a faint sheen of sweat shone above his upper lip. He was then sixty-two years old, an age by which most men are in the grave or at the very least occupying a chair in Death's antechamber. Not Borgia the Bull. The office he had fought to possess with such vigor and guile had aged him, yet he could still be said to be a man near his prime. Even on his worst days, he projected an aura of indefatigability that sent opponents scrambling like so many ants seeking shelter from the burning sun.

Not for a moment did I believe he wanted my opinion. The question was merely one more excuse to delay disposing of what he feared might prove in time to be of greater value than he had yet perceived.

But then who knew how to put a price on a new world?

Unless it really was the Indies, as the instantly revered Cristoforo Colombo, hero of the hour, was claiming. In which case, there would be Hell to pay.

The wine he had called for arrived. Borgia leaned back in his chair, swirled the claret, and stuck his nose into the goblet. Let no one say that he was a savage. He could, when he chose, enjoy the bouquet of a noble vintage as well as any other great prince.

I watched him with hard-earned confidence. Since coming into the papacy, Borgia had collected an even greater assemblage of enemies than he had possessed as a cardinal. Fresh though the year still was, there had been three serious attempts against his life thus far. I had my own thoughts as to who might be behind the attacks but without proof my actions were of necessity constrained. Under any circumstances, nothing came near Il Papa—not food nor drink nor any item he might touch—without my scrutiny. The greater part of my job involved such efforts. Only occasionally was I called upon to do anything more, despite what you may have heard. Truly, people hear far too much.

"The Portuguese will not be happy," Borgia observed, whether to the air or to me I could not say. Perhaps it was the pigeons he addressed.

"You're giving them the other half of the world," I reminded him. He was doing just that with the help of his geographers, learned men if somewhat dour now that they had to remake all their maps. West to Spain, east to Portugal, and the Devil take the hindmost.

"I have to do something," he said a tad defensively, but who could blame him?

Just about anyone, as the situation was of his own making, but I forbear mentioning that. Let no one claim that I am entirely without diplomatic skills.

"Their Most Catholic Majesties will be pleased," I pointed out, meanwhile staring at the pen he had abandoned, willing it to leap of its own accord and sign the damn decree.

Ferdinand and Isabella of Spain would be delighted, hopefully enough to help Borgia in his present difficulties with the Kingdom of Naples. Difficulties he had provoked by—let me see if I recall—oh, yes, trying among other things to steal land from Naples to give to his second son, Juan, who he fancied to make into a great prince. People can be so very sensitive about such matters.

We would have war or we would not. The outcome hinged on the ability of the Spanish monarchs, once sufficiently paid, to purchase peace. Would a new world be enough to inspire them?

"Or not," Borgia said with a wave of his beringed hand. "This will have to wait." He tossed down the pen and rose from behind his desk.

"You are going?" I asked as I, too, stood. Given the seriousness of the situation, you might have thought that Il Papa would be focused solely on business. But Borgia never did anything without a reason— or several, sometimes seemingly contradictory purposes that managed nonetheless to come together in the end to further his vaunting ambition.

"I have promised to counsel a troubled soul," he said, suddenly in better humor.

I heard the secretaries groan and could not blame them. He would slip away to visit his mistress, Giulia Farnese Orsini, justifiably known as La Bella and, so far as I knew, not in the least troubled in her soul. Meanwhile, it would fall to the secretaries to deflect the questions of anxious ambassadors and courtiers trying to determine what, if anything, the Holy Father intended to do.

"Well, in that case—," I said, and made for the door. It being ever necessary to maintain appearances, Borgia would take the strictly private passage that linked his office with the adjacent Palazzo Santa Maria in Portico where he housed both his young mistress and his slightly younger daughter from an earlier affair that had also produced Cesare and two other sons. I would have to use the more public route, which meant running the gauntlet of hangers-on clustered just beyond the inner office. Fortunately, as I was both a woman and a figure of some considerable apprehension, I would be spared the worst of the interrogation about to afflict the hapless secretaries.

I got as far as the first antechamber before a nervous, ferret-faced fellow sidled up. Do not be misled by my description of him for, although it is accurate, I had a certain fondness for Renaldo d'Marco, formerly steward of Borgia's palazzo when he was a cardinal and now elevated to his service within the Vatican.

"Has he signed it?" Renaldo inquired, eyes darting furtively, which of course only made him more likely to attract undesired attention to himself—and by extension to me.

I seized his sleeve and drew him off a little into an inglenook where we could be less readily observed. The pounding and sawing from the nearby wing of the Vatican Palace where Borgia's grandiose apartment was under construction offered cover for private conversation. Even so, I kept my voice low.

"Not yet, but he will."

"Are you certain?" Renaldo was not asking idly. Like almost everyone, he had bets placed with one or more of the hundreds of touts in Rome who took such wagers. He might also have entrusted funds to various of the merchant houses whose profits could be affected by the papal decree. In this, he and I were no different. Borgia had been more than generous—any sensible man is with his poisoner. I had no complaints, but I would have been thought a fool if I failed to make sound use of the information that came my way.

"He has no choice," I said. "He must have Spain's favor and their Majesties have made it clear that there is no other way to gain it."

"But if Colombo is right—"

I nodded brusquely. All knew the problem that had so far stayed Borgia from signing the decree.

"If the Holy Father gives Spain what turns out really to be the Indies," I said, "there will be war with Portugal. Everyone knows that. But all the scholars, the geographers, the mapmakers, all of them still say what they said when the great captain was peddling his crazed scheme to every court in Europe and being sent away empty-handed: The world is too big for him to have reached the Indies."

In the weeks since the battered caravel *La Niña* limped out of an Atlantic storm to find shelter in the port of Lisbon, few had been able to speak of anything other than the astounding news she brought. Scarcely had the first reports reached Rome than Borgia set to work to determine how he might take advantage of whatever it was that had just happened.

To help him decide, we had endured a seemingly endless parade of sages who explained to him over and over exactly why, all claims to the contrary, Colombo could not possibly have reached the Indies. By all rights, he and his crew should have run through their provisions and perished at sea long before ever making landfall. That they had not could mean only one thing—they had found not the Indies with its great spice wealth coveted by all, but an entirely new, previously unsuspected land—Novi Orbis.

"What if they are wrong—?" Renaldo began but I would have none of it.

"The ancient Greeks knew the world's girth and so do we. Colombo has found something else, something entirely new, whether he wants to admit that or not. It may be a place of unimagined riches or it may offer nothing but death and ruin. Spain will find out soon enough."

The steward looked comforted by my reassurances yet something still troubled him.

"Have you heard the rumors?" he asked, bending a little closer so that I smelled the anise on his breath. It was not an unpleasant scent but it could not fully mask the nervous sourness emanating from his stomach.

"Which rumors? Each day, each hour brings new claims wilder than the last."

"I don't know how wild these are. Indeed, I fear they may be all too true. It is being said that man, Pinzón, captain of *La Piñta,* is dying of a disease no one has seen before. He is covered in strange pustules and consumed by fever."

I had heard the same rumor and shared Renaldo's fear, though I was not about to admit it. Sailors frequently returned home with all manner of ailments, but this was different. By all reports, no one had ever seen the scourge that was killing the subcaptain of Colombo's fleet. Nor was he alone; several other men who had sailed with the great discoverer were similarly stricken. There were even reports, as yet unconfirmed, that the same symptoms were appearing among the whores of Barcelona, the city to which many returning crew members had gone.

"We must pray for him," I said solemnly.

Renaldo paid that no more mind than I intended. "Of course, of course," he said. "But about the decree—you are quite certain?"

I assured him that I was and pleaded a pressing need to be elsewhere, which was true enough. Moments later, I was crossing the vast piazza, crowded as usual with all manner of tradesmen, gawkers, priests, nuns, pilgrims, dignitaries, and the like. The Vatican was, as always, open for business.

The sun, drifting westward, was warm on my face and I felt as though I could truly breathe for the first time in hours. Even the muscles in the back of my neck that had become so tense as I waited upon Borgia unclenched, if only a little. Behind me, the crumbling hulk of Saint Peter's lurked, more than a thousand years old and in dire danger of collapse. I did not look in its direction but as always, I was vividly aware of its presence.

Certain events the previous year haunted me still. Waking and sleeping, I relived the desperate search through Saint Peter's for a lost child in the hands of a madman bent on ritual murder. What I had seen in the corpse-clogged catacombs was nightmarish enough but it faded to inconsequence when compared to the terror that had followed in the vast, abandoned garret under the basilica's crumbling roof.

As though all that weren't enough, I had gotten it into my head that one of my dark calling should not go out of her way to attract divine attention, as I surely would do were I ever foolish enough to face God again on the very rock where His Church was built.

Fortunately, there had been no need to do so. Borgia himself despised the dreary pile; he had visited it only a handful of times since becoming pope and spoke regularly of pulling it down. He had some scheme in mind to build a new, more glorious basilica that would stand as a tribute throughout time to his papacy. Sadly, the funds for such an ambitious enterprise did not exist and were not likely to anytime soon.

It was just as well that no one seemed to notice, far less care, that I avoided setting foot inside Peter's Church. I could not remember when I had last made the prerequisite confession for the cleansing of one's soul. There had been that night the previous summer when I broke down and admitted to Borgia that the possibility that I had killed Pope Innocent VIII, the Vicar of Christ, God's chosen representative on earth, troubled me. He insisted on giving me absolution and I, weak as I am, accepted. We were both rather drunk at the time, which perhaps helps explain it.

Since then I had killed no more than three times, always in response to the attempts on Borgia's life and always as mercifully as I could, if that counts for anything. I told myself that to kill in defense of His Holiness did not constitute sin, which was not to say that I was without transgression. Relatively smaller offenses aside—fornication, alas on too rare occasion; lying, of course, as is always necessary in our world; working on the Sabbath, if the private studies I pursued for my own benefit could really be considered work—all that aside, the truth was that a day rarely went by when I did not contemplate murder.

I say contemplate in the sense of taking out an idea, turning it this way and that, considering how better to burnish and refine it, all in an exercise intended to give me some relief from the implacable reality that the mad priest Bernando Morozzi, the true mastermind behind my father's death and, I suspected, the instigator of the attacks against Borgia, remained very much alive.

Unsatisfied with the expulsion of the Jews from Spain the previous year, the priest with the face of an angel and the soul of the Devil had plotted to secure a papal declaration banning them from all of Christendom. I had played my role in thwarting his evil ambitions but I had failed to avenge my father's death. Thus far.

It would hardly do to explain any of that to some hapless cleric, who would then have to scramble about for an appropriate penance when there was none, since I was most definitely not contrite and I had absolutely no intention of mending my wicked ways.

Even so, the shadows cast by Peter's crumbling rock still had the power to make me shudder. I quickened my pace, eager to be gone, if only for a little while, from the Vatican and everything it represented.

2

The clouds had drifted off to the east, leaving Rome bathed in the clear, golden light all painters nowadays strive to capture but few ever can. I skirted the crowd and headed for the river, crossing by the Ponte Sisto. At the bankside just beyond the bridge, I engaged a grizzled boatman who, once satisfied that I had the coin to hire him, agreed to take me upriver several miles. Say what you will about Borgia, he had brought a far greater degree of order to Rome than the city had seen in many years. Ordinary women, that is to say without armed escort, could be out and about once again without fear of molestation. Not that there still weren't problems, no city is entirely free of crime, but all agreed that this was one thing Borgia had done well and for that most Romans were duly grateful.

The house I was bound for lay just outside the northern reaches of the city near the pleasant village of Cappriacolla. I left the boatman at the river's edge and walked a half mile or so along a lane shaded by oak and linden trees. Brief excursions to the country suit me well enough; I was enjoying the fragrance of wild rose and honeysuckle heightened by a deep note of manure as I came upon my destination.

It was a two-story residence built around an inner courtyard with a gate on one side wide enough to accommodate a carriage or wagon but narrow enough to be secured quickly in case of trouble. The stuccowork and other exterior details were very plain, as had been the style several decades before when the house was built. Overall, a visitor could be pardoned for mistaking it for the home of a prosperous country family content with its fields and vineyards.

As I approached, half a dozen oversized mastiffs ran out, cords of drool streaming from their floppy jowls. Individually, the mastiff can be among the most affectionate of dogs. In a pack, they will not hesitate to tear a strong man apart. The leader, a male who stood as high as my waist, threw back his immense head and barked deeply in warning. I stood where I was and extended my hand with the palm up. After a moment, the leader approached and sniffed me delicately. Satisfied that I was known to him, he barked again, more of a gentle woof to signal the others, and allowed me to proceed.

I entered through the single gate and crossed the courtyard to the ground-floor loggia. In the relative coolness there, I paused for a moment. Several of the floor-to-ceiling windows stood open. I could hear the hum of conversation competing with the somnolent drone of insects in the bushes outside.

Brushing aside the billowing white curtains, I stepped over the threshold into a large, well-proportioned room with a slate floor and a high, barrel-vaulted ceiling. The far wall was dominated by a stone fireplace above which hung a tapestry said to have belonged until recently to King Charles of France. How exactly the tapestry had come into the possession of the house's owner was a matter for conjecture.

Had I wished to do so, I could have asked him about it. Luigi d'Amico was standing nearby as I entered. He smiled and came forward.

"Francesca, how good to see you!"

It was impossible to doubt the warmth of his welcome or to fail to return it in kind. D'Amico was a big, ruddy-faced man whose gruff good nature masked a brilliant intellect. He had grown up in humble circumstances but early on had shown a knack for understanding the arcane workings of money. On that basis, he had gone into banking and, what seemed like a very short time later, found himself in possession of a large fortune. Whereas most men in his happy situation become art patrons, paying to have themselves immortalized, d'Amico turned his attention to his true passion—natural philosophy. He told me once that he wanted to understand how nature works as thoroughly as he understood money, which would have been very thoroughly indeed.

"How is our dear friend, your employer?" he inquired after we had exchanged the usual pleasantries.

"Tolerably well." Somewhat to my surprise, d'Amico had never tried to use our association to obtain information about Borgia. There were only two possible explanations for this—that he possessed a character of unique nobility seen nowhere else on earth or that he had sources within the Vatican better than myself. As much as I liked him, I was reasonably certain that the latter was the case rather than the former.

"That is good," he said as we went to join the others. That day there were a dozen of us. Almost all were men, but with my arrival, the group included two women. We had each made our way separately to the house. It was one of several locations where we met, taking care not to frequent any one place often enough to attract attention.

Our caution was necessary because we had all committed ourselves to a life in pursuit of knowledge, even when that put us at odds with the dictates of Holy Mother Church. If that is not exciting enough for you, if perhaps you had hoped that I was on my way to an amorous encounter to be described in salacious detail, let me remind you that for our efforts to plumb the secrets of nature we risked being accused of heresy and condemned to the flames burning throughout Christendom. I am all in favor of the moans and even occasional screams that accompany passion's fury. It is those wrung from the unfortunates condemned to the agony of death by fire that keep me awake at night.

But I digress; it is a habit of mine.

We called ourselves Lux, for the light we hoped to bring into the world. I was the youngest and newest member of the group, to which my father had belonged before his untimely death. The others were gathered around a table at the far end of the room. Only one I had expected to see there was missing—Rocco Moroni, a glassmaker of extraordinary skill who had brought me into Lux. Two years before, Rocco had been so misguided as to my nature as to approach my father with an offer of marriage. He knew me considerably better now, and I fancied he was glad of his escape, but he remained my true friend and the unknowing object of my amorous fancies. Before I could contemplate his absence, my attention was riveted on the large map that was the subject of the group's scrutiny.

"Juan de la Cosa drew it," D'Amico said, naming the captain of *La Santa Maria,* the vessel wrecked upon the reef of what Colombo was calling Hispaniola. "One copy is on the way to Their Most Catholic Majesties, Ferdinand and Isabella. The other is here."

"I will not ask how you managed to acquire it," I said.

Hearing my voice, a woman at the table looked up. "I think we can all surmise how he did it," she said with a smile. "La Cosa is said to be very unhappy with the great Colombo's treatment of him. He is determined to claim credit for himself."

Sofia Montefiore was a middle-aged woman with a sturdy build and a cloud of silver hair pinned up haphazardly around her plain but pleasant face. She was also an apothecary and a Jewess. We had become friends the previous year, drawn together in part by the bond of both being women working in a man's profession.

I bent forward as she spoke, studying the map. La Cosa had depicted a coastline that looked nothing at all like the Indies as it was known to those who had ventured so far in search of spices worth more than their weight of gold in Europe. His was an alien shore different from any seen before. If he was right . . . Mother of God, how much hung on his veracity.

"Is La Cosa in good health?" I asked.

"No pustules," Luigi responded cheerfully with unspoken reference to the dying Pinzón. "So far as we know. He seems to be in his right mind. Besides . . ." He dropped his voice, engaging all of us in his confidence. "Let us not forget the cod fishers."

Therein lay the crux of the matter. I am assuming that you eat cod, are heartily dependent on it for your well-being as is everyone I know, and therefore you understand its importance. But in case you are some species of being unknown to me, let me say that for hundreds of years the fishermen of Portugal have gone out to a vast northern fishery, which they are loath to discuss in any particular, and from there they have brought back cod in quantities sufficient to feed the greater part of Europe.

Some of the Portuguese, in their cups, have claimed to know of landfall west of where they take their cod. Some even claim to have encountered wild Norsemen with tales of other lands still further distant. Lands that it was said had been settled in centuries past only to fall victim to fierce savages who expelled the Norse, a rather startling thought given their own well-earned reputation as marauders and warriors.

None of which would have mattered had not Colombo and his brother been rumored to have made a voyage north many years ago during which it was said they almost froze, ate a great deal of cod, and drank a clear and potent liquor with the Norse, who told them tales of the westward lands, which they claimed stretched farther than a man could walk in many days.

So it was said.

I bent closer still, studying the map. La Cosa had crafted it intricately, showing such isles as he had encountered but setting them apart from what he clearly believed to be a true coastline.

If he was right . . . how much hung on that.

"It is amazing," I said. "If the calculations are correct—"

I was referring to the measurements made by the ancient Greek Eratosthenes, his work being well known to the Arabs, rediscovered by ourselves and confirmed many times over. As a result, any intelligent person with a mind to discover it can know the girth of the world. Only a very few, Colombo among them, have insisted that the world is much smaller and the Indies, therefore, must lie within westward reach.

"If they are correct, Colombo truly has found Novi Orbis, the New World."

I looked up at the man who had just spoken. He was in his late twenties, a few inches shorter than d'Amico, with a dark, neatly trimmed beard and mustache. His expression was almost childlike in its innocent curiosity. This despite the fact that he wore the black and white habit of the most feared order in Holy Mother Church, the Dominicans.

Friar Guillaume could scarcely contain his excitement. He traced a finger above the coastline, careful not to touch the parchment, and sighed with delight.

"A new world," he said. "It defies imagining. Truly, Creation holds far more marvels than our poor minds can encompass."

If it surprises you that a Dominican should have been a member of Lux, let me assure you that Guillaume was an exception to much of what you no doubt have heard about "God's Hounds," those baying hunters of the Inquisition. Recall that for every Torquemada and other lover of the stake and the rack, the Dominicans can also claim to have fostered the likes of Saint Albertus Magnus, who argued that science and faith could exist side by side in accord and, supreme above all, the great Saint Thomas Aquinas, upon whose shoulders the Church can fairly be said to stand. How far the order had fallen from such heights of brilliance into the fevered passions of the Grand Inquisitor I will leave you to judge for yourself.

We lingered a little while longer over the map, which continued to exercise an almost irresistible fascination for us all, before moving on to an early supper. Of necessity, we had to be gone from the house before dark so that we could make our way back to our various homes without undue difficulty.

The meal was, as always when d'Amico provided it, excellent. The conversation ranged from the map to the latest experiments and inquiries being carried out by various of our members. I was able to report on the results of my efforts regarding the precipitation of nitrate of silver from solution. I will not bore you with the details except to say, in all modesty, that the company found my presentation of considerable interest.

We were enjoying a *dragée* of spicy hypocrase accompanied by figs and oranges, intended to close the meal and promote digestion, when the conversation around the table was interrupted by the fierce barking of the mastiffs, followed quickly by the shouts of men.

Attackers!

I can see us still as we were at that moment, frozen around the table in the instant before the full import of what was happening shocked us into action. Luigi leaped to his feet and seized the map, rolling it tightly as he ran. Friar Guillaume acted as quickly, hastening to pull aside the tapestry that concealed a door leading from the hall. A few chairs were knocked over in our haste but otherwise there was no sound save for the continued shouts of the men, closer now, and the howls of the dogs. We had all known such a moment might come and had prepared ourselves as much as was possible. That, as well as Luigi's sensible precautions, no doubt explained our seeming calm.

Even so, my heart beat frantically as we crowded into the passage that slanted downward, running between walls until it reached the villa's basement. From there a second concealed door gave access to a low, dank tunnel. Luigi struck a flint, giving us just enough light to see where we were going.

Sofia was right behind me; I took comfort from her presence even as the knowledge of our shared peril propelled me forward. I imagined the men crashing into the hall, finding evidence that we had only just gone, and redoubling their efforts to capture us. If we were caught, a quick death would be the best for which any one of us could hope. Far better that than the torture cells of the Inquisition.

"Hold," Friar Guillaume directed, raising his hand. We were near the end of the tunnel. Up ahead, I could see a glimmer of fading daylight behind a screen of bushes. Sweat trickled down my back. I reached behind and grasped Sofia's hand. If the attackers knew about the tunnel . . . if they had posted men at this end of it . . .

The friar edged forward cautiously until he came to the grille blocking the entrance. He peered out in all directions before finally stepping back and motioning us forward.

"The way is clear," he said with a smile. I exhaled in relief as around me, I heard the others do the same. Guillaume eased the grille open and stepped aside. "Go swiftly and with God."

We went in pairs, Sofia and I together, parting from the others with quick words of reassurance and hasty embraces. As the attackers were likely to have come by the river, we avoided that and struck out across the fields ripe with summer wheat. The setting sun gave us our direction but we went quickly all the same, mindful that it would soon be night.

We had gone some little distance when Sofia glanced over her shoulder. She stopped and touched my arm.

"Look," she said.

I turned and saw black smoke rising against the darkening sky. Having failed to find us, the attackers had fired the villa. By morning, it would be nothing more than a charred ruin. But our bones would not lie within it, like the poor cracked remains I had seen on the funeral pyres of the condemned. For that, I struggled to be grateful.

We could not afford to tarry. By then, the concealed door in the hall surely would have been discovered, along with the passage behind it. That would lead our pursuers to the basement, where they would have greater difficulty finding the tunnel but would conclude that we were at large. We could expect them to launch a search of the surrounding area without delay.

With that uppermost in mind, Sofia and I stumbled onward. She fell once, tripping over an exposed root, but quickly regained her feet with my help.

"I am fine," she insisted when I expressed concern. "It takes more than a little tumble to rattle these bones."

In the face of her courage, I could offer no less. We hurried on, helped by the light of the quartered moon, and came finally to a stream where, out of breath and exhausted, we knelt to drink. The villa was miles behind us and we heard no sound of pursuit. For the moment at least, we seemed to be safe.

With that realization, the shock of what had happened crashed down on me, worsened by the implications that lay behind it. I sagged to the ground. Beside me, Sofia did the same but she, at least, still had the strength to put an arm around me.

Softly, she said, "We are alive, Francesca. Later, we will deal with what has happened, but for this moment, let us give thanks that we have survived."

She was right, of course, and I knew it, but dread weighed me down. Against her shoulder, I said, "Guillaume and the others . . ."

She patted my back gently, like a mother soothing a fretful child. I had never known my own mother's touch, for she died giving me life. Yet there were times when I imagined that I heard her voice singing to me softly, and glimpsed a face lost to me forever.

How foolish the fanciful longings of our hearts.

"They have gotten away safely, I am sure," Sofia said, "and Luigi is far too clever to let the villa be traced to him. Lux will endure, have no doubt of that."

I prayed that she was right but I also understood, as I lay there in the gathering night, that we had been betrayed. Someone who knew Lux well enough to be aware of the carefully hidden time and place of our meeting had acted to destroy us.

Someone who would act again unless I, Francesca Giordano, the Pope's poisoner, stopped him.

3

S ofia and I remained in hiding outside the city until just after
dawn. A light rain was falling as we joined the stream of merchants, travelers, traders, and gawkers flowing along the Via
Flaminia toward the city gate. The rain did not keep down the dust
churned up by the passing of so many horses, carts, and boots. It lingered as a reddish mist several feet above the ground, thickening as
we drew nearer to the city.

The road ran straight and true, as the old Roman roads do, between slender poplars and tangled hedgerows giving way to fields of
ripening grain and vines laden with grapes that would be ready for
pressing in a few weeks. Crows cawed over the creak of wagon wheels,
the jangle of harnesses, and—rising sweetly on the air—the strum
of a lute accompanying a troubadour not shy about sharing his skill.
He was singing a tale of love, of course, something involving the
doomed Troilus and Cressida, when I smelled the city.

How to describe the aroma of Rome? I have heard it spoken of slightingly by those intent on displaying their refinement but who succeed only in making themselves out to be asses. For myself, it is a perfume like no other, comprised of equal parts wood smoke, tidal flats, manure, sweat, and a tantalizing high note I cannot identify but know in my dreams. On those occasions when I have been required to leave the city—usually mercifully brief—I can ease the inevitable homesickness by holding up some item of my own clothing that, even when washed, still retains the olfactic memory that is uniquely *Roma*.

Since the healing of the Great Schism a few decades before, the city had been restored as the rightful center of the Christian world. The place old men and women remembered as a tumbled ruin of hovels and shanties was being rebuilt at dizzying speed into the greatest city in Europe. The results were marvelous, of course, with magnificent *palazzi* of travertine marble springing up seemingly overnight, transforming the drab palette of wattle and daub into a glorious array of rose, purple, and gold. That the air was choked with dirt and grime, the streets all but impassable, and the cacophony virtually deafening was of no matter in the larger scheme of things.

Sofia and I parted near the Ponte Sant'Angelo. "Go safely," she said as she embraced me. Despite our travails, she looked strong and resolute, but I could see the worry in her eyes. We both knew that our reprieve was no more than temporary. The new spirit of learning and inquiry to which we of Lux had dedicated ourselves was fiercely opposed, then as now, by forces determined to keep the world shrouded in ignorance and superstition. It was only a matter of time before they struck again.

"You as well," I said, and hugged her back, not for the first time wishing that she was bound elsewhere than to the Jewish Quarter. The influx of refugees expelled from Spain by Their Most Catholic

Majesties, King Ferdinand and Queen Isabella, had overwhelmed the small warren of narrow streets and twisting alleys built on marshlands flooded regularly by the Tiber. The resulting outbreaks of disease and the all-pervasive sense of despair had put me in mind of my beloved Dante's *Divina Commedia*.

With Innocent VIII's timely death, the Jews had struck a bargain with Borgia. In return for a payment rumored to be as great as four hundred thousand silver ducats, which he used to buy his way to the papacy, he agreed to tolerate their presence in Rome and by extension in Christendom.

In the months since, conditions in the ghetto had improved somewhat as many of the refugees moved on to other destinations and those left behind allowed themselves to enjoy a fragile sense of security while remaining mindful that it could prove to be all too illusory. I had offered to use what influence I had to find Sofia accommodation in the larger city but she had demurred, pointing out that she was unlikely to be able to run her apothecary business anywhere the Christian guilds held sway.

Even so, she remained in my thoughts long after she was out of sight, as I made my way to my own apartment on the edge of Trastevere. Upon his ascension to the papacy, Borgia had arranged for me to be housed along with his daughter, Lucrezia, his mistress, Giulia, and their servants within the Palazzo Santa Maria in Portico. That lasted only a few weeks, until I convinced him that while a pope could flaunt his daughter and his mistress to his heart's content, his poisoner should remain cloaked in a modicum of discretion. I know he agreed, although he never said so directly, because he raised no objection when I moved into the newly constructed building, one of many in the city owned by Luigi d'Amico, who had suggested it to me.

For the first time in my life, I was living on my own, a condition that I found agreeable. I had an older woman who came in to clean and do the washing. As for the rest, I enjoyed visiting the markets, the sheer number and variety of which make up one of Rome's greatest treasures. Preparing meals for myself was both pleasant and practical, and not only because I needed to guard against attempts on my own life as vigorously as I protected *la famiglia* Borgia. The surest path up the ladder of professional success for those of my dark calling is to poison a renowned poisoner. Nothing assures one's reputation as swiftly. I had taken that same route myself the previous year when I killed the man Borgia had intended to replace my father, claiming that position for myself instead. No doubt there were some in Rome or beyond who would have done the same to me, had they dared.

I had another reason for wanting solitude. The nightmare that had visited me for as long as I could remember lost none of its terror through repetition. I woke from every encounter in the grip of fear greater than any I can express. It was not uncommon for me to cry out and to be distraught for some time after waking. I preferred that there be no witnesses to that.

I approached the building with caution, still on the lookout for anyone who might be lying in wait. But activity on the street seemed entirely normal—the usual assortment of harried clerks, high-nosed clergy, liveried retainers, cheeky apprentices, stolid merchant wives, and the occasional enterprising thief all jostling along despite it being Sunday, the supposed day of rest.

Like many buildings in Rome, the three-story structure roofed in red tile presented an almost blank façade to the street, punctuated only by a scattering of small, barred windows and a low, arched doorway through which I entered. Immediately beyond, everything changed as a spacious loggia gave way to a courtyard that served as both garden and open-air kitchen. It was still early enough that the *portatore* was not yet on duty. Relieved to be unobserved in my disheveled state, I took the closest steps and reached my apartment quickly.

It consisted of three rooms on the first floor above street level—a salon where, as I rarely entertained, I had set up the apparatus I used in my work, and my books; a bedchamber with an adjacent space for bathing; and a pantry equipped with storage cabinets lined in sheeted metal to discourage the inevitable vermin, a stone sink with a drain to an outer wall, a small coal stove with its own chimney drawing off smoke to the outside on which I could cook simple meals, and a thick wooden worktable kept clean with vinegar and sand.

The apartment was graciously designed with high windows that provided excellent ventilation and a balcony that ran the entire length of each floor. My furnishings were more than adequate for my needs. I had the large bed with the acantus-carved posts inherited from my father, as well as his puzzle chest with the lock meant to foil any would-be thief and my mother's wedding chest carved with scenes of the Sabine Women. These, along with my worktable, apparatus, books, and clothing, were my sole possessions when I moved into the apartment. But as is the way of such things, in the few months I had lived there I had accumulated an ever-expanding assortment of belongings.

Lucrezia had sent a quartet of benches in the newly fashionable Roman style. Each *lectus* was carved from mahogany inlaid with chestnut, the frame supporting crisscrossed leather straps covered with a feather mattress with pillows at either end, the whole ornamented in the finest deep blue velvet with gold tassels. Had I been inclined to entertain, my guests would have been more than comfortable. Further, several curved chairs with scrolled arms and a table set on a wide pedestal also arrived, the gift of His Holiness himself. Cesare, claiming disappointment that I already possessed a bed, as he would have liked to provide me with one—recall that he was shy of eighteen years at the time and still very taken with his manhood—made do with extravagant rugs in the Moorish design, so glorious that I hesitated to spread them over the floors as they were intended. Only the very rich customarily enjoyed such luxury, but I must admit that every morning and night when my bare feet sank into them I spared a grateful thought for my sometime lover.

For myself, I found the murals of bucolic gods and goddesses already decorating the walls to be pleasant enough, but that did not prevent me from acquiring several small works by the renowned Pinturicchio—recently hired by Borgia to decorate his new apartments in the Vatican, and by my beloved Botticelli, whose work had fascinated me since I first encountered it adorning the Sistine Chapel. I indulged my passion for books when and where I could, determined as I was to add to the library my father had left me. I even added sparingly to my wardrobe in recognition of my status and because Lucrezia nagged me mercilessly until I did so.

On the balcony, I planted various flowers useful to my trade. With the coming of spring, the iron railings overflowed with blooming foxglove, oleander, aconite, and more. On occasion, I amused myself wondering if my neighbors ever noticed what I cultivated. Those same neighbors kept their distance from me, although not, I think, solely because of my profession. The building tended to attract residents who, for one reason or another, valued their privacy. I asked no questions of them and they posed none to me.

While I waited for water to heat in a copper basin set over a brazier, I stripped off my clothes. The hem of my overdress was encrusted with mud, and small leaves and twigs bore evidence of the frantic scramble Sofia and I had waged while escaping the villa. Reluctant as I was to encourage gossip, I folded the garments away carefully at the bottom of the wardrobe, intending to see to them myself when I had time.

Having washed and drunk a restorative tea of willow, chamomile, and nettle, I dressed in a fresh shift and a simple overdress of light blue linen, both cut just fashionably enough to assuage Lucrezia. Despite her best efforts to outfit me more modishly, I clung to sensible clothes that would not impede my work. Not for me the absurdly long sleeves, tight bodices, pointed shoes, and ever more elaborate headdresses that seemed designed to ensure that a woman could not take a step or lift a hand without difficulty.

As I readied myself, I considered what to do next. I would be expected at the Vatican but it was early yet and unless Borgia asked for me directly, my absence was unlikely to be noticed for at least a few hours. If questioned later, I could always say that I was inspecting the provisions, gifts, offerings, and outright bribes intended for His Holiness that flowed like a river at floodtide into the Vatican every day. In point of fact, a great deal of my time was spent doing exactly that.

You may wonder why, in the aftermath of the attack on Lux, I did not seek out Borgia at once and entreat his protection. Do not think the omission signified a failure of trust, for I had absolute confidence in my employer; I knew he would always and unfailingly act in his own interest. When that happened to coincide with mine, *bene.* When it did not, I preferred to rely on myself alone.

Accordingly, I set off across the river to the Campo dei Fiori, the city's most important market and the place where it is said everyone in Rome eventually comes, if only for the frequent executions. As always, the narrow, cobblestoned streets of the Campo were crowded with shoppers taking advantage of the Church's dispensation, effective on all but a handful of holy days, allowing the sale of goods deemed to be "essential." But in a change from the previous year, there were fewer thieves and correspondingly less evidence of the cudgel-wielding patrols hired by the merchants to discourage them.

There were those, the wiser among us, who said that the relative peace Borgia had brought to the city would not last, that inevitably it would be crushed under the weight of his insatiable ambitions. As it turned out, they were right, but I was blind to that at the time.

Indeed, I was sufficiently preoccupied making certain that I had not been followed that I passed by the streets of the cloth merchants, goldsmiths, leather workers, scriveners, and the like with scant notice until I came finally to the Via dei Vertrarari, the street of the glassmakers. There I slowed and took a moment to smooth my hastily donned garments and touch a hand to the braid encircling the crown of my head. It was a practical hairstyle, as I was forever reminding Lucrezia when she urged me to wear my hair down on the absurd claim that it was one of my best features. I am no slave to vanity but I confess to caring how I looked to the man who, had I been a normal woman, would have been my husband.

From this you will, no doubt, conclude that I am a contrary creature, and there is some truth to that. Drawn to Cesare as I was, I was still entirely capable of longing for Rocco—for the man himself, for the life I might have had with him, for the woman I could not be.

As I approached the modest timbered building that, unlike its neighbors to either side, offered little to draw interest, the thought pierced me that had I been free to accept Rocco's proposal two years before, I could be sitting in front of that shop with a baby on my knee. It was not the first time that I was tormented by the vision of what might have been, nor would it be the last. I took a swift breath against the pain in my heart and proceeded, only to stop abruptly when a small bundle of spitting fury launched itself at me.

Several things happened all at once: the kitten, for such it was, dug its claws into my skirt and proceeded to climb up me, all the while mewing fiercely; two large dogs of the foolish sort who always look as though they are about to tumble over their own paws loped after it, stopped only by my stern look; and a small boy of seven years with a mop of dark hair, a sprinkling of freckles, and an engaging grin burst from the shop shouting, "Don't let her go, Donna Francesca, she's already clawed their noses to ribbons and she'll do worse!"

By this time, the kitten had nestled into my arms while continuing to spit warnings at the dogs. She, for perhaps not surprisingly the animal turned out to be female, seemed to have no sense of her own size or the ease with which either of her victims could have made a meal of her. On the contrary, she appeared to be merely using me as a perch upon which to catch her breath before launching herself back at them.

"Perhaps we should go inside," I said, a little breathlessly myself, for just then a tall, powerfully built man in his late twenties with the same brown eyes and hair as his son stepped from the shop.

What shall I say of Rocco? That he was a good man and my friend? Such should be self-evident. That the thought of what we might have shared had I been an entirely different person haunted me? I have told you that already. Shall I admit that his eyes were not merely brown but flecked with gold and that when he smiled, the world stopped? You will think me a giddy girl, a gross deception to inflict on so good a reader who has yet to recoil from the shocking revelations of my true nature.

Unless, of course, you are secretly drawn to them, which is entirely your affair.

Strictly speaking, Cesare was the more classically handsome of the two, not to mention having all the advantages of great wealth and social standing. But Rocco . . . he was the calm center of the storm that was my life, my place of refuge and, however tenuously, of hope I could not bring myself to abandon even as I believed it to be futile.

"Francesca?" He smiled as he took in my efforts to restrain the tiny pile of fur and grime who threatened to best me as readily as she had the dogs. "What have you there?"

"I'm not sure." I could only hope that he ascribed my heightened color to the efforts needed to contain the cat and not for self-consciousness at seeing him. "She looks like a kitten but she doesn't seem to know that she's one."

Rocco laughed and looked at me warmly. He had never shown the slightest resentment toward me for rejecting him as a husband. To the contrary, he had been all that was kind and good. There were times when I suspected that he was only waiting for me to come to my senses and agree to wed him. A woman better than myself would have done the decent thing and disabused him of any such notion.

Mercifully, Nando squeezed between us. He held the door to the shop open. The dogs continued to circle, tails wagging even as they bared their teeth.

"Hurry before they get her," the child said.

4

I stepped into the shop with Rocco close behind me. The single ground-floor room set beneath a low loft was typical of those found in the homes of craftsmen and traders save that it was tidier than most, being occupied only by Rocco and his son instead of the more usual sprawling families. The floor was stone covered with woven rush mats, one of the few outward indications of the glassmaker's growing affluence, belied by the deliberately plain exterior. A fireplace with a pair of swing hooks for holding iron pots provided warmth in winter but was swept clean of ashes and left empty at this time of year. What cooking Rocco did went on outside, where he also did most of his work. There was also a table surrounded by stools, shelves that held samples of the glassmaker's art, and a ladder that gave access to a sleeping loft. Less obvious but known to me all the same was the false wall near the back door. Opened, it revealed the more specialized work that Rocco did for particular customers, myself among them, including the glass stills, retorts, sublimatories, and other devices required for the practice of alchemy.

While it is true that Venice still claimed the finest glassmakers as her own, the craft had long since spread beyond that watery city where Rocco himself had been born. Rome boasted a firm of glassmakers to the pope, the d'Agnelli, whose wares were sought as far away as Ingleterre and, it was even said, eastward to Constantinople. Of late, they had fallen on sad times, having suffered the death of their only son, but they remained a force within the city. The family head, Enrico d'Agnelli, continued to dominate the glassmakers' guild. Yet sensibly he left room for newer men to make their mark.

Rocco had occupied the shop for all the half-dozen years I had known him. In that time, he had achieved a quiet following among both connoisseurs of glass and the growing community of alchemists. Had he chosen to do so, he certainly could have afforded more spacious accommodations. But he was by nature a modest man who also had a sensible appreciation for the protection of anonymity. The simple shop nestled among seemingly more prosperous competitors suited him well.

He secured the door behind us, shutting out the noise of the street. At once, I was aware of the relative coolness and quiet of his home, of the pleasant scent of fresh rushes and herbs drying in the rafters above, and as always, of the longing in me for what could not be.

In my preoccupation, I must have held the kitten too tightly for she hissed and stuck out a tiny paw, as though to rake me.

Nando grinned. "She's not afraid of anything, is she? Like Minerva, always ready to do battle."

"Minerva, indeed," Rocco said with a smile. He looked at me as he added, "The goddess who never surrenders. An apt name, wouldn't you say, Francesca?"

I turned away, all too aware that there had been times when I would gladly have surrendered to the glassmaker who spun works of astounding beauty from sand, wood ash, and fire. Call it wickedness, call it hypocrisy, but the truth is that being certain that I could never be wife to Rocco only increased my desire for him. My reluctance to lower myself in his estimation stopped me from acting on my natural tendencies, but only just.

"If she must have a name," I said, looking down at the kitten that, still in my arms, set about washing herself with admirable industry. "Are you going to keep her?"

"Can we, Papa?" Nando asked.

Rocco hesitated. "I thought you wanted a dog."

"I do, but—"

"Why don't you keep her, Francesca?" Rocco prompted. "She seems to like you."

I stared at the creature, ready to explain why that was impossible. A deep rumbling, surely too vast for so small an animal, came from her. She blinked startlingly blue eyes and opened her tiny mouth in a yawn.

"I've never had a pet." My father had discouraged fondness for any particular animal, the better to steel me for the practice of testing new poisons on stray cats and dogs. It pained him to use them in such a way but he saw no alternative. He was horrified when I insisted that people should be used instead but ultimately he found merit in my argument that a man or woman condemned to torture and the stake would welcome a quicker and more merciful death. The discreet arrangements he made with various prison officials have served me well when needed, which, lest you think too badly of me, I assure you is not often.

"Then it's time you did," Rocco said, for thankfully he had no notion of my dark thoughts. That quickly it was settled. I could say no to Rocco on a matter as fraught as marriage, but when it came to the small things—upon which some say life truly depends—I was helpless to deny him.

He pulled a stool from the table and invited me to sit. As I did, Nando presented himself before us and stuck out his hand with the palm up. I noted that his fingers were ink-stained. Several months before, his father had begun teaching him to read and write. Getting the boy to concentrate on his lessons was something of a chore, as Nando saw little use for paper and pen except to draw. I had seen several of his sketches and thought he showed true promise.

"I know, Papa," he said with a grin, "tell Donna Maria that you want an especially good loaf."

When Rocco looked bemused, Nando eyed us both and laughed. "Every time Donna Francesca comes to visit, you send me to the bakery for fresh bread."

I am certain that we both flushed then but Rocco did not disagree. He drew a coin from his pocket and sent it spinning through the air. Nando caught it and hurried off.

Except for the kitten, who had gone to sleep on my lap, we were alone, if only briefly. Rocco wasted no time. He took the stool across from me and said, "I've had a cryptic note from Luigi, something about postponing further business until the weather clears. Do you know what that's about?"

I breathed a small sigh of relief that the banker was safe and quickly said, "I came to tell you that the villa was attacked while we were meeting. Sofia and I got away and I think everyone else did as well. You've had no trouble here?"

Rocco had paled the moment I began to speak. Now he shook his head and said, "Nothing . . . I had no idea. You are unharmed?"

When I assured him that I was, he said, "Tell me all that happened."

As I finished describing the events of the previous evening, Rocco took a deep breath and let it out slowly. I could see that he was struggling with himself, torn between anger over what had occurred and deep concern as to what it portended.

"Do you know who the attackers were?" he asked. "Did you see their faces?"

I shook my head. "The dogs alerted us and we fled too quickly to see anyone. Nor did they see us. They may not know our identities." I was hopeful that was the case but precautions had to be taken all the same.

"If they do, we will hear from them again soon," Rocco said. His face was grim as the full weight of the problem we confronted sank into him. "You could have been killed."

Along with Sofia, Luigi, Guillaume, and the rest, but it was of me he thought and for that I admit to being pleased. Even so, I replied bluntly. "I would have been fortunate to be killed rather than captured and subjected to questioning. But enough of that. Someone betrayed us; there is no other explanation. We must find out who was behind the attack."

Rocco's gaze lingered on me a moment longer before he nodded. "Guillaume may be able to help. He should be able to learn if the Inquisitors are involved."

I am no coward but the thought of confronting the black-robed arbiters of souls made me shudder. Although we had been spared—thus far—the crazed spectacle of heresy-hunting that had become the fashion in Spain, here, as there, the Dominican Order was entrusted with making what are so blandly called "inquiries" into suspected lapses of faith. They delved anywhere they chose and were free to use torture as a means of getting at what they considered to be truth. I had already helped to foil a plot involving the Grand Inquisitor of Spain, the loathsome Tomás de Torquemada, who sought to provoke an anti-Jewish outbreak in Rome at the time of the papal election the previous year. It was not beyond the realm of possibility that he knew of my involvement and might look to his brethren to revenge him. But he was far from alone in having cause to strike against those seen as challenging the power of Holy Mother Church.

"If it was God's Hounds," I said, "someone has unleashed them."

"Borgia?"

"Hardly, for he despises them. Il Papa is not above using those he loathes for his own ends, but he considers the Inquisitors to be a dangerous element in need of restraining. I don't think he would do anything to encourage them."

"Then who?" Rocco asked. He appeared about to answer his own question when I interjected.

"We were examining a copy of the map La Cosa made. Perhaps someone knew it would be there and seeks to suppress what it shows. Someone who is interested in hiding evidence that Colombo really did not discover the Indies. And then we should not overlook the possibility that some other of us in attendance might have enemies. Luigi, for instance; he has risen very far, very fast. Such men frequently sow ill will behind them."

If you suspect that I interrupted Rocco because I did not want to hear what I was certain he would say, you have the right of it. But even I knew that the reality of our situation could not be long ignored.

He reached over and covered my hands with his. "No possibility should be overlooked. I know it is hard for you to speak of him, Francesca, but if Morozzi still lives—"

"He does," I said. "To my shame." In Rocco's presence, I had even more reason to regret my failure to kill Morozzi. The previous year, the mad priest had come terrifyingly close to killing Nando. That I had managed to save the child's life did not absolve me of responsibility for bringing such danger near to him.

"If it is Morozzi," Rocco said, "or the Inquisitors or anyone else, is it likely that Borgia will know? More to the point, can you find out from him?"

"I can try, but information is to Il Papa as gold is to other men. He may be willing to trade it for something else of value but he will never simply give it away."

Nando returned just then, curtailing our discussion. We spoke of far more pleasant things over wine, bread, and good cheese from the Piedmont. It was only after I left that I realized I had not thought to ask Rocco why he had missed the meeting at the villa.

Nor had he offered any reason.

After leaving Rocco's, I returned briefly to my rooms, stopping on the way to purchase a small piece of cod for Minerva from a fish vendor in the Via dei Pescatori. As I stepped through the archway of the building into the loggia, a tiny woman appeared in the open top of the half door from which a view could be had of all comings and goings between the building and the street. She was no bigger than a child—and thus required to stand on a stool to see above the lower half of the door—but she had an air of authority that would have done a giantess proud.

"What have you there, Donna Francesca?" she asked, gesturing at the kitten.

Portia, the only name I knew her by, was our *portatore,* a position poised somewhere between servant and tyrant. She and she alone heard complaints, settled disputes, arranged for repairs, and—clear testament to Luigi d'Amico's trust in her—collected the quarterly rent. She also directed guests, accepted packages, and kept a discreet eye on things in general. In her youth, rumor had it, she had been one of a troupe of acrobatic dwarfs who were very popular in Rome for a time. How she came to be in Luigi's employ is unknown to me, but given his sagacity in all things practical, I assume he knew what he was about when he hired her.

"Her name is Minerva," I said, indicating the kitten, who appeared to have gone back to sleep.

"Do you mean to keep her, *donna?*"

That Portia knew of my profession was beyond doubt, although she never alluded to it. For that, if nothing else, she had my gratitude. I moved quickly to disabuse her of any concern regarding the animal's fate.

"Apparently so. She seems to have taken a liking to me and I to her."

"Well enough." From one of the many pockets in her immense apron that covered her almost from chin to toe, Portia withdrew a folded paper and handed it to me. "This came for you a short time ago."

I juggled Minerva in one arm while I broke the seal and quickly scanned the message. It was from Vittoro Romano, the captain of Borgia's personal guard. He inquired as to my health and suggested that we speak at my earliest convenience. Given that *il capitano* was a man of consummate discretion, I concluded that he would not have taken the unusual step of sending a written message unless something of importance was afoot.

"I must go," I said, tucking the note away. With an apologetic smile, I indicated Minerva. "If you wouldn't mind getting her settled for me?"

The *portatore* took both kitten and cod with only a small sigh. "Of course, Donna. Am I not here merely to serve?"

"I'll look for more of those cherries you enjoy," I offered. "His Holiness is fond of them as well. We just got a new shipment in from Vignola. Nothing but the best."

Placated, Portia bestowed a smile and rubbed Minerva behind her ears, eliciting a throbbing purr that followed me as I hastened back out onto the street.

The day being mildly warm with a pleasant breeze from the sea, I decided to walk rather than be ferried along the river or avail myself of one of the sedan chairs that thronged the crowded streets. Rome is a great city for walking, assuming one does not mind hills. Beyond being virtually guaranteed of encountering something new and interesting, being on foot gave me the opportunity to gauge the mood in the streets, always of concern to one charged as I was with protecting a noble family.

I admit to paying even more than usual attention to my surroundings, on the lookout for anything that might give a clue as to who was behind the attack on Lux. Were there truly more of the black-robed Dominicans present in Saint Peter's Square or was that just my imagination? Did the golden-haired priest I thought I glimpsed at a distance bear more than a passing resemblance to Bernando Morozzi or were my eyes playing tricks? Was there more security evident in general or had a bad scare and a sleepless night so frayed my nerves that I was jumping at shadows?

I breathed a small sigh of relief as I approached the Vatican barracks, housed in a long, low stone building constructed only a few decades before and kept in excellent repair. The papal guard, including many of the men who had served Borgia when he was a cardinal, enjoyed an array of comforts reflective of his dignity. In addition to the barracks, they had their own kitchens, expansive stables, a spacious training field and, it was said, access to some of the better brothels in the city, all courtesy of His Holiness.

Despite the latter, they maintained an admirable level of discipline and readiness thanks in no small measure to the man charged with leading them. Vittoro Romano was in his fifties, of medium height and build with the straight spine and firm stance of a much younger man. He had been a soldier almost all his life but had also found time to become a husband and father to a boisterous family, all daughters who had married well and graced him with grandchildren he adored.

He was speaking with one of his subordinates as I approached, giving me an opportunity to observe him. The two might have been talking of the prospects for rain, the capabilities of a new recruit, or the imminent likelihood of war; it was impossible to tell which. Vittoro was always and unfailingly a man of great calm with seemingly no capacity for excitement. An astrologer would ascribe his temperament to having been born under the sign of Saturn, although as to whether that would be correct I could not say. Like almost all of us, he had no notion of the date of his birth, far less the time. I wonder if it is such ignorance on the part of ordinary people that allows astrologers to appear so wise.

Seeing me approach, Vittoro dismissed the man he had been speaking with. Before I could say a word, he shook his head and gestured toward the nearby stables where deep shadows offered concealment. Even there, he kept his voice low. Intrigued despite myself, I gave him my full attention.

"I am glad to see you looking so well, Donna Francesca. I thought we might have a word before you are swept into the day."

I took the compliment for what it was, the kindness of a friend. After the events at the villa and a sleepless night, I was hardly looking my best.

"Of course, Capitano. What can I do for you?"

He glanced around to be sure we were not observed, then leaned a little closer.

"Cardinal della Rovere has reached Savona. Word has it that he is gathering forces there and intends to make for France."

I inhaled sharply. Ever since the conclave the previous year that resulted in Borgia becoming pope there had been rumors that the bitter rivalry between His Holiness and the much younger but no less ambitious della Rovere was about to break into open warfare. At Savona, family seat of the della Roveres, the Cardinal would be as a hawk in its aerie, inviolate. And if he did make for France and the welcoming arms of its young, war-hungry king, not all Borgia's scheming might be enough to save us. Coming on top of the trouble with Naples, this boded very ill.

"What does His Holiness intend?" I asked.

"He has ordered security here increased. I am bringing men in from the other papal properties. Of course, the task of protecting His Holiness would be simpler if he hadn't acquired a troubling new habit."

Given all of Borgia's myriad peccadillos, I was hard-pressed to imagine what new vice he could have acquired, and said as much.

"He has taken to disappearing," Vittoro said.

My initial reaction was disbelief. Granted, there were long stretches of time when His Holiness was *in camera,* not to be disturbed. But there was no mystery as to why. Everyone knew that Christ's Vicar was blessed with a robust carnal appetite.

"He is with La Bella or some other woman," I said. There was no reason to assume that Il Papa restricted himself to just one mistress, lovely though she was, when so many appealing women in Rome would be happy to receive him.

"Not so," Vittoro said. "He isn't in La Bella's apartments or his own or any guest accommodation and he hasn't left the precincts of the Vatican. He is somewhere else, somewhere I don't know about."

"There are any number of discreet ways in and out of the Vatican—"

"Forty-seven ways—tunnels, passages, and the like. Or at least there were. I had forty-five of them sealed up shortly after Borgia was elected, with his approval. The remaining two are closely guarded."

"Then where is he?"

"His secretaries claim not to know. They say that he is disappearing from within his private office. Two concealed doors lead from there but they connect either to his own apartment or to the passage through the Sistine Chapel that comes out in the Palazzo Santa Maria in Portico, near to La Bella's quarters. Neither solves the mystery of where he is going."

"Or what he is doing," I said slowly. The implications were considerable. Borgia was at heart an inveterate schemer. Partly that was a necessary by-product of his lust for power but also I think he simply enjoyed what was for him something of a living chess game but with much higher stakes than to be found on any board.

"Precisely," Vittoro said. "How am I to protect him if I do not know what he is up to?"

"I will learn what I can."

The captain nodded, clearly relieved that I had grasped the importance of the matter. After a moment, he said, "When His Holiness got the news about della Rovere being in Savona, he called for you. You weren't to be found."

I shrugged, hoping to convey the impression that my absence was of no particular significance.

"It's probably to the good that His Holiness has had time to reflect."

Vittoro understood as well as I that there are occasions when the most faithful servant has to turn a deaf ear. Otherwise what is said in the heat of the moment can take on its own momentum. Even so, he was not so easily put off.

"Is everything all right, Francesca?"

Such informal address did not surprise me. He had known me since I came as a child to Borgia's palazzo on the Corso. When I succeeded to my father's position, far from condemning my methods, Vittoro had offered me support and more. I knew that I could rely on him absolutely and yet I still hesitated to confide in him. Lux was that important to me and, I feared, that vulnerable.

"Well, let us see," I said with a smile. "Il Papa may or may not be about to give the Indies away to the Portuguese, prompting Spain to arms. Unless, of course, he's giving it to the Spaniards, which would put the Portuguese at our throats. There is the matter of Naples . . . and the multiple attempts on His Holiness's life by unknown sources . . . and now his bitter rival seems to be positioning himself for war. In the midst of all this, our master has taken to disappearing mysteriously. All in all, I would say matters lie about as we who serve *la famiglia* must expect."

Vittoro chuckled. "Don't forget Madonna Lucrezia, whose nuptials will be soon upon us."

"Quite right, let's not forget that." Privately, I gave odds of no better than five to three that Borgia would allow the marriage to take place. Lucrezia had already been betrothed formally once or twice, depending on which rumor you believed. What would another broken pledge mean?

Except that this particular betrothal and the marriage to follow involved the peacock-proud house of Sforza, whose support had been key in securing Borgia's election to the papacy. On that basis alone, he might feel called upon to honor it.

"Sometimes I imagine that in my old age," Vittoro mused, "I will sit in a garden and watch my grandchildren at their play. The sun will be shining, but not too brightly, there will be a gentle breeze smelling of lemons and lavender, pigeons will coo in the cote, and I will have no thought save for whatever tasty dish my dear wife is preparing for our dinner."

"And you will not be bored? You won't miss all this?"

"As I said, I will be old."

We did not speak of what I imagined for myself, for Vittoro knew better than to ask. The past haunted me too vividly to leave much room for the future.

I lingered a little longer before going off about my duties. There were always new supplies arriving in the kitchens, sides of beef and baskets of fish, heaps of fruits and vegetables, rounds of cheese, vats of wine and ale, and all that without regard for the provisions that were beginning to come in for the wedding feast.

I sampled everything, delving to the bottoms of sacks and baskets, prying open carcasses, and so on. Fresh food is notoriously hard to poison, any agent leaving traces of smell, taste, and color for the experienced eye. For the same reason, it is difficult to taint wine or ale without making either liquid cloudy, although sometimes the visual evidence is very slight indeed, discernible only to the most experienced eye, which, grace to God and my father's excellent training, I have. Prepared foods are a different matter—sausages, smoked meats, dried fish, anything with a great quantity of spice all offer the promise of concealment. For that reason, I required that anything of that nature be manufactured under my supervision.

That left only the matter of contact poisons, the rarest and most difficult to handle of all substances in the poisoner's arsenal. I had some considerable familiarity with them, having accomplished the rare feat of applying a contact poison to the outside of a glass carafe, the method by which I had killed my father's successor and claimed the position for myself. With that incident always in mind, I inspected anything that could come into contact with Borgia or his family—every scrap of fabric but also other materials including glass, gold, silver, and the like. With the wedding fast approaching, gifts were beginning to arrive and each of these also had to be checked.

Despite all these demands on my attention, I was at work only a little time before a page came to fetch me. His Holiness required my attendance. I washed my hands in a copper basin, dried them on a length of cloth offered by a kitchen maid who kept her head down and fled the moment I was done, and followed the page up the stone steps from the kitchen, through flagstone passageways, up a gilded flight of steps, and finally into the presence of Christ's Vicar on Earth, Il Papa Alexander VI.

C hrist's blood!" Borgia bellowed. His voice shook the gilded walls and threatened to crack the high windows looking out over the square. Secretaries, clerks, and hangers-on alike quaked and looked about wide-eyed for some means of escape.

"Blessed Mary and all the Saints tell me why I did not kill that man when I had the chance?"

Abruptly, his attention swiveled to me. My hope that his anger would have been defused by now was not to be fulfilled.

"You should have convinced me to do it," Borgia declared. "That's your job, isn't it?"

As our avid audience looked on, relieved no doubt that someone had taken the brunt of his displeasure, I came a little farther into the room. My face was schooled to calm despite the knot in my stomach and the dampness of my palms that had nothing to do with the sultry morning. Borgia was not given to such outbursts of temper, reserving them solely for those occasions when he felt particularly provoked. But when he was so roused, truly he was a force to behold. In the interest of candor, I will also say that there were times when I suspected his anger was more artifice than actual emotion, but on this occasion, he seemed genuinely enraged.

In light of the news Vittoro had given me, there was no mystery as to who had so provoked Borgia's ire, nor could I pretend to misunderstand him. That being the case, I had no choice but to fall back on the semblance of candor. True candor would be a shocking breach of decorum, raising all sorts of problems of its own accord. But the semblance of it was a well-practiced art within the hallowed walls of the Vatican and, for that matter, wherever those with an appreciation for power gather.

"Is it?" I asked lightly, as though it were really no great matter, certainly no reason to explode in fury and burn all before him, starting with my own poor self. "I thought my job was to see to your safety." Almost as an afterthought, I added, "And on occasion perhaps remove some encumbrance. I don't recall you mentioning the Cardinal in that regard."

"More fool I," Borgia muttered but he was calming already, the admirable intelligence and order of his mind once more in evidence. He glanced round as though suddenly aware that we were observed. "Out! Out! Worthless dregs, all of you! Out!"

They went. Borgia and I were left alone, as no doubt he had intended, for now there would be great speculation about what he had to say to his poisoner in private. I admit to being curious myself.

Without ceremony, he slumped in the high-backed chair behind the vast desk of burled wood and inlaid marble, and gestured me into one of the smaller chairs across from him. It was a signal honor to be seated in his presence and one he did not accord me except when we were alone or as good as. You may wonder at such intimacy, as I did myself from time to time, but over our years together I came to at least some understanding of what drove Borgia to confide in me. La Bella and other women who came and went had their place in his life but I don't believe he ever allowed them to see into the darker reaches of his soul. As for his confessor, some hapless priest held that nominal position while no doubt thanking God daily that Il Papa felt no impulse to bare his conscience to him.

But great men, for all their armor of invincibility, are still only men, and something in them all cries out to be known by at least one other who can, at the end of days, attest to their humanity. Typically, it is an outcast who takes such a role—a jester, a dwarf, or, though it was painful for me to acknowledge, one such as myself, set apart and isolated by my dark calling.

All the same, I did not fool myself. Whatever the needs of his soul, Il Papa played a deep game in which I was only one more pawn.

"That turd, della Rovere, plots to bring down my papacy," he said. "Moreover, he may be behind the recent attempts on my life, the source of which you still have failed to discover. Whatever he is up to, I want the problem he presents resolved once and for all."

"Holiness—" I intended to mention the practical difficulty of getting to della Rovere now that he was over three hundred miles away in his family's stronghold, and perhaps even my own doubts that he had a hand in the attempts to kill Borgia, but Il Papa was having none of it.

Before I could speak further, he declared, "You've come up with creative solutions in the past. Do not disappoint me now."

Having written *fini* to the discussion, at least so far as he was concerned, His Holiness reached for a flagon of wine set on a silver tray on his desk, filled a Venetian goblet studded with gems, and took a long swallow of claret. He was drinking earlier and more of-

ten than had been his custom before coming into the papacy. La
Bella had told Lucrezia, who had told me, that he slept poorly and
sometimes woke in the grip of night sweats. I wondered if what he
had plotted and schemed for decades to attain was proving to be both
more and less than he had anticipated.

I was about to stand, assuming myself to be dismissed, when he
spoke again.

"What do you hear from Cesare?"

Still struggling to come to terms with the order I had just been
given, I replied noncommittally. "He seems well."

I assumed that letters from Cesare were intercepted and read before they ever reached me. What Borgia wanted was not so much the
content of the letters as my interpretation of them, but that I was
hesitant to give.

"Happy with his lot, is he? Content to follow my orders?"

Cesare happy? Content? His was a mercurial nature ruled by
passion and ambition. Happiness did not enter into it. Surely his father, who was not far different, knew that?

"He is loyal to you," I said, because in the end wasn't that all that
mattered, at least to Borgia?

Il Papa passed a hand over his jowls wearily. An observer might
have been forgiven for thinking that he was an old man resigned to
the foibles of the young. Nothing could have been further from the
truth.

"Is he? He rails against the life I have given him. Claims he'll go
off and become a *mercenario* for whoever will hire him. Says he'll
make his living with his sword before he'll put on red skirts."

"He is young yet—" Although to be truthful, I had difficulty
imagining Cesare in the vestments of a cardinal of Holy Mother
Church. Aside from the very few old men still clinging to their

missives, the princes of the church were cunning, ambitious schemers best suited to wield power from behind their expansive desks. Cesare, on the other hand, was made for the field of battle. Anyone who had been in his presence long enough to say a single paternoster ought to have known that.

"He is my son! He will damn well do as I tell him."

My father had wanted me to marry and give him grandchildren but he had the good sense to recognize that I was my own self, for better or worse, and not a mere extension of his will. Perhaps it was because he had afforded me such regard in life that I was so determined to honor him in death.

"Then what difference does it make to you how he feels about it?" I asked.

Borgia took another swallow of his wine. He set the goblet down and appeared to study it for a moment before looking at me. Without warning, he said, "Will he betray me? Tell me that, poisoner. The son of mine you take into your bed, does he whisper to you of patricide?"

I was aghast, plain and simple. That he should entertain the notion of betrayal at the hands of his eldest son was bad enough but that he should consider me as a coconspirator was unthinkable in all its ramifications, not in the least for my own survival. An only child of a doting father, I claim little understanding of the inner workings of families, but even I knew that there could be only one possible answer.

"Did you sleep at all last night?" I was bidding for time, of course, time for my frantic mind to frame the necessary response in a way that would be believable. But in some flickering corner of my thoughts, I was also genuinely concerned for him, God help me.

"Is Giulia prattling?" he countered, scowling.

"She cares for you. We all do. If you go around talking like that, people will say your wits have addled."

Harsh words to hurl at a pope, but they seemed to soothe Borgia. He had claimed in the past to like my audacity although I always doubted that. I think rather that he ever weighed me in the balance, looking for the moment when I would become more trouble than I was worth. But just then I still had use, not only to preserve his life but also as a means of communicating with his wayward son.

Relenting slightly, he said, "I know I can depend on Cesare when all is said and done. Whatever else he is, he is no cuckoo, slipped falsely into my nest. Were he, I would be forced to expel him even though he fall to earth and be crushed, which, I am assured, he most certainly would."

"How fortunate then," I said with a perfectly straight face, "that he is an eaglet, the true son of his father."

Borgia chuckled; he was as mercurial as his son in his own way, his moods ever ready to be shifted. But I never made the mistake of thinking him capricious. Anyone who did think so quickly had reason to regret it.

"You worry needlessly," I said. "Would you be happier if Cesare was a milksop to meekly accept whatever you decree for him? He has strength and spirit. Be glad of both but know that in the end, he will always do as you wish."

Borgia belched softly behind his beringed hand. "I could do with a decent night's rest."

Which was as close to apologizing for his suspicions as he would ever get.

"I know a good apothecary, should you want something more effective than wine."

He pretended to be startled. "You surprise me, Francesca, as ever.

Part of being a good Christian is to refrain from providing others with opportunity to sin."

It was my turn to sigh. Sometimes I truly feared that he knew every nook and cranny of my life even as I still clung to the belief that Lux remained hidden from his scrutiny.

"Sofia Montefiore has no reason to harm you, Holiness."

"Indeed not, the Jews love me. Have not I offered them the hand of tolerance?"

A well-greased hand, to be sure, but I refrained from saying so. Borgia eyed me a moment longer before he said, "When next you see my son, remind him to behave himself at the wedding. I will brook no nonsense there."

"I don't expect to see Cesare any time soon." Indeed, I had no idea when I would see him at all, as in his present mood, it might be best if he stayed away from Rome until Lucrezia was well and truly wed.

Borgia merely smiled and waved me off. I left still struggling to come to terms with what I had been ordered to do. The practical hurdles aside, I was not convinced that sending Cardinal della Rovere from this world would accomplish anything of real value. The Church would still be riven by ambition and steeped in venality. And the ordinary people, what of them? They would still be distracted by the day-to-day struggle to live, too wearied to care much about the doings of their "betters." Unless something happened to pierce the fog of apathy and seize their attention. The death of Cardinal della Rovere, for example? Would that be sufficient to send the mobs into the streets?

I had no time to dwell on the matter. Renaldo was waiting for me in the antechamber. The steward bent his head toward the inglenook where we had spoken the day before. I joined him there. Borgia's mood had been such that I hadn't dared to try to discover what he knew of the fire at the villa but Renaldo was another matter. I would not hesitate to sample whatever tidbits he had to offer.

Barely had he gained my attention than he confided, "He signed the bull." This was said with the air of a man well satisfied with the bets he had placed and not a little relieved to have the matter settled.

I nodded, glad myself of the information but determined to acquire much more. "Well and good but, as you will already know, he is troubled."

The steward looked at me sharply, no doubt hoping that I would reveal what had required a private conversation between Borgia and his poisoner. The betting on the subject would be fierce, one way or another. Indeed, it was likely that the touts of Rome were already setting odds on whether I would be sent to dispatch della Rovere and, considerably steeper, if I would succeed.

"I wondered if you knew why," I said, deflating Renaldo's hopes while at the same time flattering him with my apparent faith in his wisdom. In point of fact, the steward could have become an immensely wealthy man, as opposed to being merely very well-off, had he chosen to sell what he knew about Borgia's dealings. The presumption is that secrets are to be found hidden in ciphered letters or overheard in whispered conversations, but the truth is that the best place to learn what a great man is really up to is to look at his household accounts. Know where and how he spends his money and you will know all that really matters.

Renaldo kept those accounts and did so with scrupulous care. He knew what Borgia spent on porridge for the boys who turned the spits in his kitchens and what he spent for little toys of a lascivious sort for La Bella, not to mention everything in between.

"There has been a flurry of payments," he murmured. Like any good custodian of his master's wealth, it pained Renaldo to disperse it. Of late, he seemed to have suffered more than usual.

"To someone in particular?"

The steward shook his head. "A host of someones. Argus had fewer eyes than does our master."

I smiled at the reference to the many-eyed guardian of Greek legend. But at the same time, I wondered whom Borgia was watching—and why.

"He had a visitor this morning," Renaldo said. "Before he was even out of bed, one of his 'eyes' came to report. La Bella was disgruntled, so I heard. Word has it she is with child again."

I had not known that and was grateful for the information, not to mention simply glad to hear it. La Bella had lost a baby the previous year and I held myself partly responsible, although I had managed at least to save her life.

"What was so urgent?"

Renaldo leaned a little closer. He spared a quick glance over his shoulder to make absolutely certain that we could not be overheard, then murmured, "Il Frateschi are in Rome."

I restrained a shudder. The "Brotherhood," as it was known, was a group of fanatical followers of the friar Girolamo Savonarola, the scourge of Florence who had appeared in that city three years before and had not stopped ranting since. According to reports Borgia received almost daily, the fiery Dominican's sermons were attracting ever larger crowds drawn by his ravings against the rich and powerful, whom he blamed for every evil under the sun, and the Jews, who he claimed were allied with them. In particular, he decried the glory of the Medicis and their golden city where art and tolerance reigned supreme, calling it the Devil's crucible. Their inability to silence him thus far only added to his aura of divine authority.

Most important, from my perspective, Savonarola and his *frateschi* were fierce enemies of everything to which we of Lux were devoted. Should they ever prevail—God and all the Saints forbid it—we would be the first to go to the stake.

"Surely they would not dare to come here." Even as I spoke, I weighed the likelihood that I was wrong. If Savonarola believed that Borgia might truly be on the verge of being deposed, he might well want his followers to be as close as possible to the seat of papal power, the better to assure that one of their own would claim it.

And that would mean the end of everything—most particularly of any chance that the light of knowledge would lift humanity out of the mud in which we had been mired for so long. We would sink back into the darkness, possibly never to emerge again. For all his failings— and I was only beginning to suspect how vast those were—worldly, rapacious Borgia was our strongest bulwark against that.

Moreover, as much as Il Papa suspected that his rival della Rovere might be behind the attempts on his life, Il Frateschi could also be responsible. There was no telling how far such fanatics might go or what assistance they might acquire.

"Who knows what they dare?" Renaldo replied. "I know only that our master is beset by many challenges, some of his own making to be sure but others pure villainy by lesser men who would bring him down the better to prop themselves up."

I could not have put it better myself. Truly, Borgia created many of his own difficulties, but his enemies were too often men who would see the world in ruins, if only so that they could harvest the wreckage.

"Then we must make sure they do not succeed, Master d'Marco."

For all that he went about twitching like a nervous ferret, Renaldo had a spine. He straightened, looked into my eyes, and said, "Indeed we must, Donna Francesca. He depends on us."

"Speaking of—" I dropped my voice another notch, causing the steward to lean closer. "Do you have any idea," I asked, "where His Holiness has been going?"

"I'm not sure I follow you—"

"His secretaries have reported that there are times when he slips out of his office and effectively disappears."

"La Bella—"

"He isn't with her or anywhere else that can be discovered. You understand this is not good for his security."

I trusted Renaldo understood that and more. It would not do for Borgia to be involved in anything that we, his faithful servants, did not know about. How then could we assure his comfort and well-being?

Not to mention our own.

"I will see what I can find out," the steward assured me.

I just had time to assure him of my gratitude before a secretary appeared to summon the steward into the inner sanctum. He bustled off with a proper air of importance. I made my way more slowly back in the direction of the kitchens, where I continued my inspection of the newly arrived provisions. It was all well and good to contemplate how della Rovere could be poisoned, but with the circumstances so dire, I had to take greater care than ever before to assure that Borgia would not be.

It was late afternoon when I finished. Weary as I was, I considered returning to my apartment for some much needed rest. But my conscience pricked, reminding me that while I lack the instinct for friendship that some enjoy, I make up for it with diligence. Duties too long neglected commanded my attention. With them in mind, I made my way to the Palazzo Santa Maria in Portico.

7

Lucrezia sat among a nest of jeweled brocade, shimmering velvet, cloth-of-gold, and spun silver, like a glorious bird of paradise in her natural habitat.

She was crying. Her complexion, normally likened to alabaster tinged with rose, was mottled and tear-streaked. Her golden hair, usually arranged in ringlets around her heart-shaped face, was uncombed and in disarray. Her expression, indeed the entire disposition of her slender form, bespoke acute misery.

Her ladies hovered nearby in various degrees of anxiousness and ennui. Borgia had decreed that as the daughter of the reigning pope, Lucrezia must be properly attended. The great families had proved reluctant to offer up their daughters, widows, nieces, and so on for such service, but the second tier of social climbers and eager merchant clans had been happy to oblige. So far as I could gather, between them they had not mustered a single female who was useful in even a minor domestic crisis.

"He hates me!" Lucrezia cried when she saw me. "I cannot bear it! How can he be so cruel, especially just now when he knows how anxious I am?"

I did not attempt to answer but knelt in the shambles of exquisite fabrics and hugged her. She cried all the harder for several minutes as I patted her back and murmured soothingly.

"There, there," I said, or something to that effect.

If all this strikes you as strange given my nature, let me say that the Pope's daughter and I had known each other since I was an artless girl of nine years and she little more than a babe. Despite the difference in our social status, we had been drawn together in the shared experience of being only daughters of powerful men who, each in his own way, instilled fear in most people while showing us what we wanted to believe was only love and care. That was a bond that not even the greatest exigencies of our lives ever managed to break.

At length, her distress gave way to small, hiccupping sobs that fell finally into silence. She straightened a little and stared at me, her eyes swollen and red-rimmed.

In a whisper filled with bewildered despair, she said, "How *can* he? Only tell me that."

A letter, its red wax seal broken, lay on the floor beside her. I picked it up with one hand and, after a quick glance, crumpled it away into the pocket of my underdress. The few lines I had read angered me greatly, but I was not about to reveal that.

"For pity's sake," I said as lightly as I could manage, "surely you know how Cesare can be? Your brother is as feckless as the fickle wind, blowing hot as Hades until he blows himself out."

And in the process scorching all those foolish enough to care about his good opinion.

"He says that I am a traitor for marrying where our father says I must! He says I will rue the day I set eyes on Giovanni Sforza! He calls him a weakling, a drone, and a sodomist!"

My eyebrows rose at that last part for it was the first I had heard that the Lord of Pesaro liked boys. Indeed, I suspected Cesare had made the slander up out of whole cloth. But as to the rest . . . there was something to that.

"He even calls him a bastard," Lucrezia concluded, a little more calmly. "Has it escaped his notice that so are we?"

"Cesare only notices what suits him," I said, and summoned a smile. Gently, I wiped her tears away with my fingertips, then stood and held out a hand.

"Come now, you will make yourself ill. And look what you've done to all this lovely cloth. Your maids will be forever smoothing out the wrinkles and dabbing up the water spots."

She rose and, glancing down at the mess she had made, had the grace to look abashed. "It was foolish of me—"

My point made, I moved to soothe her. "Anyone in your position would be upset. But you must understand, Cesare is a man—" In fact, he was a few months short of eighteen and, in my eyes at least, still very much a boy for all that he had risen to the occasion the previous year when I most needed his help. Apparently, he could not manage to do the same for his sister.

"—and men," I went on, "have no understanding of what it means to be a bride."

Neither did I, having done my utmost while my father was alive to convince him that I was unfit for matrimony. Not that I don't appreciate men; as I have already revealed, I have a weakness for certain of them. But I value my independence above all else, in large part because it is only by keeping some distance between myself and others that I can hope to conceal the darkness within me, that which leads me to my peculiar trade.

"He says he won't come to the wedding," Lucrezia said with a final sniff. I took it as a good sign that she lowered her voice. Now that the worst was over, her ladies were hovering closer. No doubt they hoped to pick up some indiscreet remark from either of us that they could bear off in triumph and bray to the world.

"Of course he will come," I assured her. "We both know that he would never hurt you like that."

"But what if he causes a scene?" she asked with sudden consternation. "What if he even . . . *attacks* Giovanni?"

The possibility was not as outlandish as it might seem. And not, whatever you may think, because there was anything unnatural in the love Cesare and Lucrezia had for each other. Yes, I know the evil things that have been said about them. I also know that they were both incapable of acting as they have been accused of doing.

Besides, I shared Cesare's bed often enough to be certain that no thought of his sister lingered there.

"He may be tempted to do something unforgivable," I admitted, equally softly. "But in the end, he will not dare to set himself against Il Papa."

Clasping my hand, she drew us both out of the disheveled room and into the walled garden beyond. At the same time, she gestured the ladies to stay behind, to their visible disappointment.

We walked a little distance along one of the gravel paths set between beds overflowing with spicy carnations, heavy-blossomed geraniums, climbing passion flowers, and delicate pansies stretching toward the sun. The paths intersected at the center of the garden where a stone fountain topped by a naked cherub sprayed a fine mist of water filled with miniature rainbows.

"How I pray you are right," Lucrezia said as we settled on a stone bench near the fountain.

"But you must know that Cesare is very unhappy with Papa. He is furious that it is our brother Juan and not himself who is made a duke, and promised an army to lead as well as a grand marriage. That is the life Cesare wants for himself, not the life our father plans for him."

Borgia intended for his eldest son to become a cardinal, never mind that he had yet to take holy orders. In due course, he meant for Cesare to become pope, leader not only of Christendom but of a Borgia dynasty ruling a unified Italy in which the great families and the powerful city-states would be shackled to Saint Peter's throne.

All this may seem now like no more than a fever dream but I assure you it was entirely real. Borgia—Il Papa—may have been the one man with the vision and will to conceive so vast a reordering of our world but no one with any sense discounted the possibility that he could succeed.

Except for Cesare, who, though he deferred to his father in public, seemed bound and determined to defy him everywhere else.

"Even so," I said, "he will do nothing to spoil your wedding day."

However impetuous Cesare could be, I was reasonably certain that he could control himself for a handful of hours. But as to what would happen after that . . . I preferred not to think.

Lucrezia seemed to be of like mind for she mustered a smile. "I am sure you are right. At any rate, I must stop worrying about Cesare and think of happier things." She leaned closer, confidingly.

"I finally know the date upon which I will become a wife, if only in name."

This truly was valuable news. The date for Lucrezia's wedding to Giovanni Sforza had been debated for weeks. Bets had been placed on when the ceremony would take place, with a sizable number of side wagers being placed on the chances that the wedding would never occur at all.

I had refrained from speculating in this particular area but I was still interested to know the final outcome.

"When is it to be?"

"Cardinal Sforza's astrologers have determined that the twelfth of next month is the most auspicious day."

"Have they . . . ?" That would not please Borgia, who had wanted the marriage to take place later, when he hoped to be in a better position to determine if he wanted it to take place at all. Further, he could not abide astrologers. Il Papa had difficulty enough accepting that our heavenly father had any say in his personal fortunes. The notion that the alignment of the stars at the moment of his birth somehow shaped his destiny offended him mightily.

Lucrezia nodded. She seemed genuinely pleased.

"Giovanni will arrive two days before then," she said. "There will be great celebrations to welcome him—a Mass in Saint Peter's, a feast, followed by horse racing and other games. Of course, absolutely everyone will be there except me but Papa has said that I can be on my balcony to glimpse my husband as he rides past."

From beneath the silver filigree bodice of her gown, she withdrew a small locket, opening it to reveal the portrait of a young man. With it cupped in her hands, she offered it for my admiration.

"Don't you find him handsome?"

This was not the first time I had been invited to comment on the appeal of Giovanni Sforza—nor the tenth. I stifled a sigh and said what I always said on such occasions.

"He is very fine."

In fact, at the age of twenty-six, the Lord of Pesaro and Gradara was almost exactly twice Lucrezia's age and a widower in the bargain. The bastard son of Costanzo Sforza, he had succeeded to his natural father's honors by virtue of the lack of a legitimate heir. Completely dependent on the far more powerful branch of the Sforza family in Milan for his advancement in this world, he was hardly the great lord Lucrezia might have dreamed of marrying. But he did have pleasing enough features, including a long, straight nose, a fashionable beard, and dark, flowing hair. He was also said to have an amiable nature, although that is said of all bridegrooms who are not outright ogres.

"Pesaro is said to be quite charming," Lucrezia remarked as she returned the portrait to its place close to her heart.

"So I have heard."

Her betrothed's seat was a pleasant enough little town on the Adriatic coast, famous for its festivals. It was of interest only because of its strategic location on the Via Emilia, the ancient road of the Romans linking the eastern coast with the agriculturally rich north. At Rimini, it connected to the Via Flaminia, leading directly into Rome. None of which would interest Lucrezia in the least. Of far more importance to her was what Pesaro was not—not Milan, or Florence, or Naples or Venice or Rome itself. It was, in plain fact, a provincial town ill-suited to a young woman who had lived all her life at or very near the glittering heights.

I was mulling that over when a page approached, arms folded behind his back, eyes averted yet watchful, ready to be of use should Madonna Lucrezia require anything.

She waved him off, a signal that she had more concerns.

When we were alone again, her golden head bent closer to mine as she murmured, "Has my father said . . . anything?"

I understood at once what she was asking. Had Borgia said anything about whether or not this was to be yet another broken betrothal. Not that he confided in me—although, to be entirely truthful, there were nights when we sat together over a flagon of wine when he had been known to unburden himself. But Lucrezia knew that I was often in her father's company and she was asking if he had said anything I had overheard.

In point of fact, nothing needed to be said; the problems were that obvious, centering as they did on the refusal by the head of the House of Sforza to yield control of the rich duchy of Milan to its legitimate ruler. As that young man happened to be the grandson of the King of Naples, the stage was set for a bloody clash between two of the most powerful families in Italia. Borgia, nominally allied with Milan but not eager to face the wrath of Naples, which he had managed to annoy in his own right, was counting on the Spanish monarchs to arrange a solution that in effect allowed him to have his *torta* and eat it, too.

"It seems clear," I said carefully, "that your father values his alliance with the Sforzas."

A less aware young woman might have been satisfied with that but Lucrezia knew her father better than almost anyone else, although I do not think he ever realized the extent of her understanding.

"Today he does," Lucrezia said. "But I fear he is like Cesare, believing that no man will ever be good enough for me."

My private theory was that it was more a matter of Borgia being uncertain that any man was good enough for himself. Having achieved the papacy, he might have been expected to settle back and survey the

world from the lofty heights of Saint Peter's Throne. Instead, his restless mind sought even greater victories—and the alliances he would
need in order to achieve them.

Tact did not come easily to me but I tried all the same. "A year may
seem like an age but it really is not. It will pass before you know it."

Lucrezia cast me a sideways glance redolent of skepticism more
suited to one far older than herself. But then I was forgetting that
for all her tender years, she had grown up in a household that left
very little room for innocence.

"Come," she said, rising from the bench. "I have an adorable new
monkey I want to show you and you will stay for supper, of course. I
will be desolate if you do not."

More likely she would be bored and lonely. Until her marriage,
and its consummation, by agreement not to occur until a year hence,
Lucrezia lived as did all young women of high rank, sequestered in
a beautiful cage. Because of the ambitions of her father, she had to
guard her every word and look even from her own ladies. I was one
of the very few of her acquaintance with whom she could experience
the freedom to be herself.

Her tacit acknowledgment of this was flattering, of course, hinting as it did at a friendship of equals that ignored the very real differences between us. A lesser mind than my own might have been
gratified by it. But I saw past myself to a young woman, alone and
anxious, whom I was, by virtue of my distinctly unvirtuous profession, engaged to protect.

"I would be delighted to stay," I said, which was overstating the
truth considerably but seemed worthwhile all the same for the smile
it prompted from Lucrezia.

I stayed. I admired the monkey—a dirty little animal, in my
opinion, better left to run wild wherever it is they come from. We ate

supper together at a small table in her private chamber. Her ladies, to their consternation, were excluded.

Over partridge flavored with fennel and apples, I teased, "You know there will be great speculation as to why you insisted on dining privately with one of my peculiar calling."

We had, by then, drunk a fair amount of wine, enough so that we both giggled at the prospect of what the gossips would say . . . or were already saying. It was all a little blurred.

"They will wonder," Lucrezia ventured as she sucked on a partridge wing, "if I am seeking your professional advice. Perhaps I want to know how to deal with my soon-to-be husband if he proves less than pleasing."

She had drunk as much as had I, I swear, yet for just a moment her gaze was disconcertingly sober. And serious.

"Are you asking me how to be rid of a tiresome husband?" I asked, half jokingly, praying that she could not possibly intend any such thing. She wasn't even wed yet. Surely she could not already contemplate the need to free herself from matrimony's bonds?

But she was Borgia's daughter, as I would do well to remember.

"Of course not," she said quickly. "I have only the greatest affection for Giovanni, or I'm sure that I will once I finally meet him. It is merely that one hears things. That there are ways to prevent children from coming, ways to render a man so that he cannot perform, and even ways to—"

She broke off then, perhaps seeing from my expression that she should go no further.

"I have disturbed you, dear Francesca," she said as she refilled my glass. We were entirely alone, without even servants.

"Believe me," she said with all apparent sincerity, "I would not upset you for the world."

75

Say it was the wine, if you will, but I say it was the memory of Lucrezia as a little child, toddling toward me in perfect trust, that was as a balm to the spirit of one set apart from all others by the darkness she had only just begun to recognize within herself.

"There are ways to accomplish all sorts of ends," I said. "Obviously they exist and I know of them, or I would be of no use to your father."

Such were the remnants of her innocence that she flushed and for a moment could not meet my gaze.

Such was her strength of purpose—or perhaps her desperation—that she overcame her qualms and looked at me squarely.

"If I ever need to know what they are, will you tell me?"

What would Giovanni Sforza have given to know that his betrothed had asked such a question?

What more would he have given to know my answer?

"I will do whatever is needed to keep you safe."

I lingered awhile longer in Lucrezia's company but declined her invitation to stay the night. By then, I was so exhausted that I barely felt able to put one foot in front of the other. Instead, I indulged and hired a sedan chair to convey me back to my apartment.

Only one last task remained to me before I could tumble gratefully into bed and hope no nightmare visited me. Stopping at Portia's door with the basket of cherries I had filched for her, I raised my hand to knock only to discover that the door swung open at my slightest touch. From beyond, in the darkness of the apartment, I heard a faint moan.

I set the basket of cherries down outside the door and entered cautiously. Uppermost in my mind was the thought that if whoever had been behind the attack on Lux had come looking for me, Portia might have gotten in his way.

I slipped a hand beneath my overdress to grasp the knife worn in a leather sheath near my heart. The blade was a gift from Cesare, who gave it to me because of what he insisted was my known propensity for getting into trouble. I have no notion how he came by such an idea but on several nights when we were both a little tipsy and temporarily sated with lovemaking, he had instructed me in the knife's use. I will not distract you with the image of him, naked, by candlelight, demonstrating the proper way to gut a man, but I will say that he claimed I showed alarming aptitude.

Closing around the hilt, my fingers trembled. I almost called out to the *portatore* but before I could, a movement to my left alerted me to danger. I turned, the knife drawn, and saw in the obscurity of the shuttered room the shape of a man coming stealthily but swiftly toward me. I had only a quick, blurred impression of him—taller than myself, broad through the shoulders, agile. The cold sheen of steel in his hand blocked out all else.

The attacker came closer, emerging out of the gloom. I caught a quick glimpse of a young face grimly set and then . . .

I was no longer myself save so far as I am the darkness and the darkness is me. As a wave will surge up suddenly out of a storm, driven by unseen forces deep below, so did the darkness awaken within me. It came with irresistible fury sweeping away all else. The woman I can pretend to be vanished beneath the ravenous hunger I could neither deny or defeat.

I heard the measured beat of my heart resounding as a solemn cadence deep within me. The dim light rippled as though I could see the faintest movement of the air. I pivoted on one foot, instinctively mimicking what Cesare had taught me, and thrust out my arm, the elbow locked in place exactly as I had been instructed. In the throes of the darkness, bright clarity beckoned. I was above and beyond fear in a realm where nothing existed save for the single, perfect moment of release.

I saw my hands and the knife that had become an extension of them as though both were far removed from me and I no more than a spectator observing a contest, the outcome of which seemed already decided. Certainly, I experienced no hesitation as I plunged the blade into the soft tissue of the lower belly and felt the echo of its entry reverberate up my arms.

The man made a strangled sound, almost a grunt, more of surprise than pain. With both hands still clasping the hilt, I drove the knife upward, digging the razor-sharp edge through skin and muscle. Dark blood gushed from the ripping wound. My victim howled and grabbed for my throat only to miss when, instead of trying to elude him, I thrust in even closer, as a butcher will the better to split a carcass.

So much blood, hot and rank with the stench of copper, flowing over my hands, my arms, spraying my face, pooling at my feet. So many screams but none my own, for the darkness within me had burst all bounds, fed by a fierce elation that blotted out all else.

A neighbor, entering the building, heard what was happening. He moved out shortly thereafter, before I had an opportunity to speak with him, but, as I pieced it together, he summoned the patrol, which took one look and retreated, calling for the nearest condottierri. Vittoro was still in the barracks when the summons came. Recognizing the address as my own, he led the guard. I will not speculate about what they confronted when they burst into the room save to say that none of those men, excepting Vittoro, has ever looked me in the eye since. As for me, I was lost in the red womb of death where light does not penetrate and conscience, mercifully, does not exist.

When next I recalled myself, I was sitting in a chair in my own salon. Minerva was nearby, observing me. Looking at her, I was surprised to see that her fur was white, not gray as I had presumed. The discovery of the kitten's true color assumed the utmost importance in my mind. I concentrated on it to the exclusion of all else and was still mulling it over when Vittoro touched my shoulder gently.

"Francesca?"

I looked up, meeting his eyes, and memory returned. "Portia?"

He appeared relieved to have me back again, more fool he. "The *portatore?* She was beaten but she'll recover. I spoke with her briefly. The trouble started when she opened the door to the man. He was there to ask about you, she was reluctant to answer, and apparently he thought he could persuade her."

"Is he——?"

"Dead? Yes, he is. How are you feeling?"

I looked down at my hands, noting only a few lingering traces of blood around my nails. My overdress was gone; I never saw it again. I wore only my shift. There was no sign of the knife.

"I am very thirsty."

Vittoro went away for a little time and returned with a goblet. I drank greedily. My hand shook on the cup, so that he had to hold it steady for me. When I was done, I let it go and sat back with a long sigh.

"Do you know who he was?" Vittoro asked. He had taken the stool beside me. I opened my eyes a slit and noted that he was watching me carefully.

"I barely saw his face." The thought occurred to me that I should steel myself to look at what was left of the attacker. "I could——"

"Best not," Vittoro said quickly. "I've a good memory for faces and he was unknown to me. We'll hold off putting him in the ground if you insist, but I really don't see the point."

To my horror, a tear slipped down my cheek. Seeing it, Vittoro clucked his tongue. That good man—husband, father, grandfather, never mind that he could not count the number of men he had killed—said softly, "Francesca, you protected yourself and the *porta-tore*. There can be no sin in that."

I clenched my hands so that the nails dug into my palms but could not prevent the tears that fell, hot and stinging, offering no balm. I did not look at Vittoro, afraid as I was of what I would see in his eyes. Fear? Disgust? Or worst of all, pity? I could bear none of those. Indeed, just then I thought I could endure nothing more.

My eyelids were almost unbearably heavy but I snapped them open. If I slept, the nightmare would come in all its fury. I feared that I would drown in blood before I could awake. But if I did not sleep, I would be unable to function and with danger so evidently at hand, it was vital that I retain my faculties.

"There is a small packet in a drawer in the table beside my bed," I said. "Would you bring it to me, please?"

When I had told Borgia that there was a sleeping remedy more potent than wine, I spoke from personal experience. Although I tried to use it sparingly, the powder Sofia provided gave me surcease from dreams of every sort. For that, I both treasured and feared it.

At my direction, Vittoro mixed the powder with warm water. I drank it down in a single gulp. When it was gone, I rose, leaning on his strong arm. "Unless you mean to carry me, I should get to bed now."

I last remember Vittoro spreading a light cover over me. As though from a great distance, I heard him say, "Don't worry about Borgia. I'll keep him at bay."

And perhaps he could, but not entirely and not for long. I slept, thanks be to Sofia, but with the certain knowledge that time was flowing like the implacable drips through a water clock, their measured fall ever a reminder that chance favors the ready hand, outstretched to catch the moment.

The next morning, I woke feeling considerably better than I had any right to do. Minerva had clawed her way up onto the bed sometime during the night and was curled beside me. The deep rumble of her purr as she washed herself woke me. Having seen to my own toilette, I gathered her up for a visit to the garden, where she seemed to understand what was expected of her. When we returned, the day's milk had been delivered. I gave her some along with a portion of dried cod that I soaked in it. By the time I was ready to leave, she had perched herself on a windowsill from which she could survey her new domain.

I paused on the way out to check on Portia, steeling myself for what I was certain would be her reaction to the monster she had seen emerge from within me. Yet she sounded perfectly cheerful when I called to her and she replied.

"Entrato!"

I entered as she bid, finding her stretched out on a padded bench beneath a window opened to receive the soft breeze. Her small apartment was as tidy as ever; there was no trace of the deadly struggle played out within it scant hours before.

Seeing the direction of my gaze, she said, "Captain Romano sent some people over. They took care of everything."

I nodded and turned my attention to her, relieved to see that despite the bruises darkening on her face and the sling in which her left arm rested, she looked surprisingly well. The cherries I had brought were in a bowl on the small table beside her. She gestured to them.

"Would you like some?"

The thought of eating made my stomach roil but I took one for courtesy's sake. "How are you feeling?"

Her broad face crinkled in a smile. "Surprised to be alive, if you want the truth, Donna. I owe you that."

A solid, practical woman, she appeared undismayed by what I had done, and for that I all but sagged with gratitude. Even so, I felt compelled to point out what surely must have been obvious. "You would not have been in danger but for me."

She did not deny it but said only, "You've an enemy, all right, but I suppose you already know that."

"I would like to know more. Captain Romano didn't recognize the man and he didn't think I would, either."

"He looked like a hundred men you pass in the street every day. Not exceptionally young or old, tall or short, fat or thin, handsome or ugly, just ordinary. Nothing to distinguish him at all except . . ." She broke off, hesitating.

Her description ruled out Morozzi, who had the face of an angel to conceal his demonic nature, but left the possibility that he had sent someone in his stead.

"Except what?" I urged. "Anything you can remember could prove helpful."

"You understand that I was in a rare state? I can't really vouch for anything I think I saw."

By which I hoped she meant what she had seen of me as well.

"Even so . . . ," I prompted.

"He was wearing a drab sort of doublet—brown, I think—and there was nothing to notice about his hose or shoes. But under the doublet, his shirt . . . I only got a glimpse of it but even so—"

"What did it look like?"

83

"It was blue, a very bright blue and gold. There was a design on it, I couldn't quite make it out but it might have been a tree."

Not for a moment did I doubt that Portia understood exactly what she was telling me. The most ordinary Roman can recognize the coats of arms emblazoned with the crests of our noble families. Being able to do so is useful when dealing with men-at-arms who may or may not be bent on mayhem depending on their master's current state of mind. Borgia's crest, for example, was mulberry and gold, emblazoned with a bull, until he became pope and incorporated the original design within the crossed keys and crown of his new authority. Cardinal della Rovere's, on the other hand, remained a blue field surmounted by a golden oak.

"You won't speak of this to anyone else, will you?" I asked.

For the first time since I had entered her rooms, Portia frowned. "I'm not a fool, Donna. With all respect, I hope you won't be, either. This is serious business."

On that we were in full agreement. I stayed a little while longer to make sure she was comfortable and had everything she wanted, then took my leave. The day was fair but promised to be hot. The sweepers were out scrubbing the streets and also scrubbing away at graffiti that had appeared overnight. Rome is a great place for graffiti, the more graphic and ribald the better. I caught a glimpse of what appeared to be the naked rump of a woman being penetrated by a male organ that could only be described as improbable in size before both disappeared under lather and bristle brush.

To settle my stomach, I stopped long enough to buy a honeyed *cornetto* from the tray of the boy peddling them and ate it as I made my way toward the Vatican. The walk, short though it was, gave me time to absorb what I had learned and decide how best to proceed.

I had finished my breakfast and brushed the crumbs from my

bodice by the time I spied Vittoro just leaving the apartment he shared with his wife adjacent to the Vatican Palace. Donna Felicia waved to me from the open ground-floor door and gave me a warm smile, by which I concluded that the captain had said nothing to his spouse of what had required his attention the previous evening.

"When were you planning to tell me?" I asked as we walked together across the piazza.

Vittoro made no pretense of not understanding. "I thought to wait until you were more yourself, as I am glad to see you are."

I accepted his explanation and went on. "What do you make of it?"

"To be frank, I have a hard time believing that della Rovere was behind the attack on you. He has motive, of course, especially if he is responsible for the attempts on our master's life or he suspects that you may be sent to kill him. But surely he would have gone about disposing of you more subtlely."

I agreed. "He's made mistakes in the past, to be sure, but he's far from a fool. Really, what assassin wears his master's colors to do the deed?"

"My thoughts exactly, but before you jump to the conclusion that—"

"It was Borgia?" A conclusion that Vittoro surely must have dreaded, as it would have transformed me at once into His Holiness's most dangerous enemy.

"I've already considered that," I said. "If he did send the assassin to inspire me to want to kill della Rovere, he would have had to be certain that I would survive the attack."

In which case, His Holiness knew even my darkest secret, a possibility I could not bear to contemplate.

"Our master values your services far too much to put you at such risk," Vittoro countered.

"He is at least toying with the idea of sending me to Savona, where I surely will die nastily."

"He can't be serious about that. You realize," he added quietly, "that leaves only one other possibility."

Thus for the second time in as many days I heard the name of my father's killer on the lips of a friend.

"Morozzi."

9

I knew of only one person who could tell me for certain if the mad priest was back in Rome. The distance from the Vatican to the Jewish Quarter was not far, being less than a mile. I walked swiftly, stepping around the piles of waste, animal and otherwise, that cluttered the streets. Despite the looming threat of upheaval, war, and even schism, Rome was a thriving city. Her hearty citizens appeared ever ready to follow the old adage of *carpe diem* and seize the day. However, I would have been very much surprised if a goodly portion of those I passed did not already have a bolt-hole in the countryside in the form of a bumpkin relative who could be cajoled or forced to take them in. At the first sign of serious trouble, the roads would clog with wagons and the river with barques as everyone who could flee did so. Only the old, the very poor, and the despised would be left. I was on my way to visit the last of those.

Sofia Montefiore's apothecary shop was on a narrow lane not far from the Via Portico d'Ottavia, the piazza at the heart of the ghetto that still contains the remnants of an ancient forum named in honor of the sister of the great Augustus. Although no wall surrounds the ghetto—one is always being proposed by someone or other—many of the streets leading out were blocked by the piles of stone and rubble designed to limit access for any seeking to enter or leave the area. Borgia had promised to have the streets cleared but nothing had been done about that so far.

Situated so close to the river, the streets of the ghetto were swept regularly by tidal floods, invading many of the shops and tenements, and bringing with them swarms of mosquitoes that made life a misery. Only the wealthy—and they did exist—fared any better, residing as they did on slightly higher ground in what amounted to fortified *palazzetti*. Whether to protect their wealth or simply because they saw no alternative, the merchants had long since joined forces with the senior rabbis to enforce a policy of cooperation with the authorities. Not everyone agreed with them.

Sofia was bandaging the arm of a young boy when I arrived. "Sit down," she said. "I'll be done in a moment."

I smiled at the boy and did as she bade. The front of the shop was sparsely furnished with a few stools and a simple wooden counter behind which Sofia dispensed the powders, tinctures, lotions, and poultices that offered some relief for the conditions that plagued so many. Unlike others of her calling, she prescribed only those remedies that she knew to be effective. Many of these were not even in evidence, being confined to cabinets in the back room for discretion's sake.

The air smelled pleasantly of the mingled scent of thyme, rosemary, lavender, and the like drying in the rafters above. Several large barrels of vinegar stood along one wall. Sofia believed vinegar to be most helpful in preventing infection in wounds and in maintaining cleanliness in general. She used great quantities of it but at the cost of her skin, her hands being always red and hardened.

Yet her touch was unfailingly gentle, as I could see with the boy who, though pale, remained calm under her ministrations. As she finished, she bent close to him and whispered a few words in his ear. He nodded and sprang up, pausing only to thank her before running off.

When we were alone, she washed her hands in the basin and dried them before she looked at me. Her dark eyes were unfathomable. I resisted the impulse to squirm under her scrutiny.

"How are you?" she asked.

"Fine. I saw Rocco yesterday. He is concerned about what happened at the villa but there is no indication that anyone was caught—"

I would have preferred that no one else know of the events in Portia's apartment but that was not realistic. The hard truth was that the danger to Lux might begin and end with me. I, not anyone else, might have been the target of both attacks. If that were the case, the other members had the right to know, if only the better to protect themselves.

Sofia heard me out in silence. A look of dismay crossed her face when I spoke of killing the assailant but she waited until I was finished before she said, "Are you certain that you are unharmed?"

"Completely. I even slept last night, thanks to your powders." Not for the world would I speak of the creature I became *in extremis,* when the darkness within me howled for blood and could scarcely be sated.

"Look at me," I said and, having stood, I threw out my arms and twirled around like a heady girl showing off a new gown. "Do I not look perfectly fine?"

It was an absurd thing to do, as I think I realized even in the midst of doing it. Yet I could not seem to stop myself. I was that set on acting as though the events of the previous night had left me unscathed or, better yet, had happened to an entirely different person.

"I am sorry to say that you do."

I stopped in mid-step, my arms falling to my sides, and stared at her. Why would she, above all, wish ill for me?

Seeing my expression, she seized my hands in hers and spoke most earnestly. "I have seen others do what you are doing, try to cope with a terrible experience by denying that it has any power to affect you. But what we think buried and forgotten can return tenfold to harm us."

What could I say to her? That she need have no such worry for me because I had enjoyed killing the attacker? That far from being dogged by terror, I still basked in the lingering pleasure of what I had done?

No, I did not think Sofia wanted to hear that.

Instead, I said, "I thank you for your concern but this is far from over. I must remain strong to deal with what may be coming."

That at least she seemed to understand. "Your courage is admirable but please, heed what I say. I count you among my dearest friends and I will be glad to listen whenever you need to talk."

Oh, ho, she would not be! What, after all, would we discuss? The surge of power and release that overcame me when I killed, as though a demon buried deep within had broken free? The various and imaginative ways in which I contemplated ending Morozzi's time in this world? The nightmare that I knew, in the aftermath of recent events, had to be upon me again soon?

I could never let my mask slip, not with Sofia or anyone else. To the world, I had to be simply Francesca Giordano, a poisoner to be sure and therefore to be feared. But still not that different from all those who make the hard bargains needed to live in a hard world. Let any discover otherwise and I was certain they would turn on me like ravening dogs and tear me asunder.

I was fumbling for something, really anything to say that would divert her when the door at the back of the shop opened. The man who entered was young, only a few years older than myself, tall and broad-shouldered. With his dark, curling hair, strong features, and black eyes, he could easily have been mistaken for a Spaniard. But David ben Eliezer was a Jew, one of the first I had met after discovering that my late father had himself been born into that tribe. Until recently, David had made his home in Rome but he had left the city the previous year in pursuit of Morozzi. At the sight of him I tensed, knowing as I did what his presence likely meant.

David pulled out a stool from beside the worktable and sat down. He looked tired but resolute. Nodding to us both, he said, "Should I be worried that the boy found me so quickly?"

"I told him where to look and he's a good lad, he won't say anything," Sofia replied.

By which I gleaned that the leaders who oversaw the Jewish Quarter were not aware that David was back among them. As they considered him a dangerous rabble-rouser, that was just as well.

"Donna Francesca," he said with a faint smile, as though we had been apart no time at all. "You look tired."

Before I could reply, Sofia took it upon herself to say, "Someone tried to kill her last evening. It was the second attack in as many days."

David's eyebrows shot up. "I have heard nothing of this. What is happening?"

I made short work of telling him, minimizing the details as much as possible. Even so, he grasped the whole of it without difficulty, putting it together with his considerable knowledge of larger events.

David made it his mission to know of anything and everything that might affect the safety of the Jews in Rome and throughout Christendom. The simmering conflict between Borgia and Cardinal della Rovere was no secret to him.

"Could Borgia be responsible?" he asked. "Would he go that far to convince you to kill della Rovere?"

Carefully, I replied, "It seems a little extreme, even for him. I think it more likely that Morozzi is behind what is happening. That is, if he has returned to Rome?"

David sighed and for a moment I had a glimpse of the toll the past months had taken on him. He had lost weight from a frame that had been spare to start and there were deep shadows under his eyes. But he rallied quickly and said, "He may have, I am not certain. Since his flight from Rome last year, he has kept busy cultivating those who share his hatred of us and are eager to work with him to bring about our extermination. He slipped out of Florence a fortnight ago. I tracked him as far as Ostia before he eluded me."

"Does he know you have been watching him?" I asked, struck by the sudden thought that David himself could be in danger from the mad priest.

"Despite my best efforts, I think he may. He has made powerful allies among Il Frateschi. I have no doubt that they are helping him now. At any rate, by the time I lost him, I was convinced he had to be making for here so I came on in the hope of discovering his whereabouts. So far I have been unsuccessful."

"If he is here," Sofia asked, "what does he want?"

"I don't think there is any mystery to that," David replied. "He wants what he has always wanted—a pope who will destroy the Jews."

"Then he has a problem," I said. "Della Rovere has no love for you but if he achieves the papacy, he will have greater matters than the Jews to concern him."

Had he become pope the previous year as he had sought, della Rovere likely would have signed the edict condemning all the Jews and thought little of it save what advantage he could gain by seizing their property. But circumstances had changed since then. The discovery of what truly might be a new world had given everyone pause. Few sovereigns would be eager any longer to expel those who included many of the men capable of financing the exploitation of virgin lands. Worse yet, those same men would likely find a welcome in the embrace of the Turkish sultan, who, with their encouragement, could decide to take an interest in the new world himself. How ironic it would be if, in an effort to "cleanse" Christendom, the Church handed Novi Orbis to Islam.

Whatever his failings, della Rovere was at least smart enough to understand that.

"Morozzi may well be thwarted yet again," I added, hoping that it was true.

"Who could he hope to make pope in della Rovere's stead?" David asked.

Even as he spoke, the same thought seemed to occur to all three of us. It fell to me to voice it, reluctant though I was.

"From what I understand, Savonarola is a true fanatic."

David nodded. "He is that and more, and he has the support of the common people because he claims to want to purify the Church of its venality."

"Perhaps he does," I said. "How better to cleanse Holy Mother Church than to take control of it?"

"Surely the cardinals would never elect him?" Sofia asked. The idea clearly horrified her, and for good reason. Venal popes bathed in corruption could at least be bought. But a true fanatic, imbued with the conviction that God moved through him . . . There was no telling what that sort might do.

"They will if they feel that they have no choice," I said. "Let him bring big enough mobs into the streets, as he has been doing in Florence, and anything might happen."

Papal conclaves were notorious under the best of circumstances. Crowds streamed into Rome from all points, most normal business was suspended, and the potential for mischief was always in the air. Add to that the inevitable tension people feel when a matter so touching on their own welfare is being decided and it does not take much to set match to tinder. Had the Church and her princes been better respected . . . had ordinary men and women seen them as anything other than venal hypocrites, it might have been different. But as it was—

"They must be stopped," Sofia said. Her hands were clasped so tightly in front of her that I could see the knuckles gleaming white. "We cannot let this come to pass."

"Indeed, we cannot," I said. "But if we are to have any hope of preventing Morozzi from carrying out his designs, we must learn his whereabouts."

We spoke for some time about how that could best be accomplished. With the rapid growth of Rome since the healing of the Great Schism almost eighty years before, the city had become even more of a warren of neighborhoods, streets, and alleys. Morozzi might be hiding anywhere. The three of us could not hope to find him on our own; we would need considerable help.

"Rocco will have to be told," Sofia said.

With the memory of what had happened to Nando the previous

year, I agreed. "And a safe place must be found for his son. I will see to that."

I did not have to explain the necessity of finding a sanctuary for the boy before I could focus on the business of stopping Morozzi. Sofia and David were both well aware of my lingering guilt over the danger I had placed the child in.

We spoke a while longer about how best to find the mad priest, ending our discussion shortly before sunset when the streets leading into the Jewish Quarter would be closed. David departed a little ahead of me. He exited through the back door of the apothecary shop into the warren of alleys that made it possible for anyone so inclined to move about the ghetto unobserved. I knew he would find ready shelter with others who believed as he did that any people, Jews included, had to be prepared to fight for their own survival rather than rely on purchased tolerance.

Sofia saw me out through the front door. As we walked a short way together, she asked, "Do you have any idea why Rocco wasn't at the meeting?"

"He didn't say, but I'm sure he had a good reason." In truth, I had not had any chance to think about that, what with one thing and the other.

We walked a little farther to the edge of the piazza. With David's departure, Sofia's concern for my well-being returned. Before we parted, she said, "You will remember what I said, won't you, Francesca? If ever you wish to talk of matters weighing on your mind, I would be glad to listen."

Reluctant to give her any false assurance yet equally unwilling to hurt her, I could offer only a smile and an embrace. Leaving the Quarter, I resisted the urge to turn around and see if she was still watching me.

10

I stopped on the way to my rooms to pick up the ingredients for a simple meal—a little *culatello,* the ham we soak in wine until it emerges rosy red, a small loaf sprinkled with rosemary, a handful of the good, meaty olives of Puglia, and a decent bottle of wine. Outside Portia's door, I put my burdens down and knocked softly so as not to disturb her if she was asleep. To my pleased surprise, the top of the door was flung open. Standing on her stool, Portia grinned at me.

"There you are then, Donna. How has your day been?"

For reasons I could not begin to guess, Portia looked like the proverbial cat that had swallowed the canary. Her dark eyes glowed and her cheeks, beneath the bruises, were pleasantly flushed.

At a loss to understand her manner, and more than a little envious of it, I said, "Fine, I suppose. . . . I wanted to see how you are."

"Have no worry for me, Donna. I'm fit as a fiddle. You just go on up now and enjoy your evening."

As I intended to spend it alone, save for Minerva, I could only nod. Having gathered up my purchases, I made my way upstairs still puzzling over Portia's mood. To add to the mystery, I heard her chuckle behind me.

I opened the door, eased my way in, and made for the small pantry, where I deposited my packages with a relieved sigh. Minerva was sitting beside the stone sink. She blinked and moved aside when I tried to pet her, her blue gaze fastened on something behind me.

I think I knew before I turned, feeling him in some way I could neither define nor deny. Perhaps I smelled him. At once, my body tightened and I felt a rush of warmth.

"Cesare," I said in a futile effort to sound stern, for truly what right did he have to cajole his way into my apartment, as he had obviously done with Portia's connivance. How daunting to think that not even the sensible *portatore* was proof against the charms of Borgia's eldest son.

He had a drink in his hand—one of my best goblets, I noticed when I turned to face him. His dark hair with a slight reddish cast was loose and brushed his shoulders. In features, he resembled his mother—the redoubtable Vannozza dei Catannei—far more than his father, having her long, high-bridged nose and large, almond-shaped eyes. He had been in the sun even more than usual and was deeply tanned. In public, he wore the expected raiment of a high-born young man but that night he was dressed for comfort in a loose shirt and breeches.

Apparently, he had been in my apartment long enough to make himself at home. Besides finding the wine, he had removed his boots and was barefoot.

"Let me see you," he said, and put down the goblet.

He undressed me there in the pantry, stripping my clothes away garment by garment. I did not help him but neither did I offer any hindrance. Women's clothing held no mysteries for him; he made short work of the task. When I was naked, he stepped back and scrutinized me slowly from head to toe.

"You are bruised."

"Am I? I hadn't noticed."

"Lucrezia says you killed the bastard."

I did not question how the Pope's daughter knew of the attack on me. Young though she was, Lucrezia understood the value of information and cultivated her own sources for it.

Cesare's hands were shaking. Hard, sun-darkened hands made to hold a sword or lance unflinchingly, but they trembled against my pale skin.

Something broke within me. Sofia believed that I did not allow myself to feel but she was wrong; I felt far too much. Terror when the nightmare came upon me as it so often did, pleasure when I killed, and always wrenching longing for the life that might have been mine if only I were an entirely different person, so that I was locked in a paradox where I could never have what I yearned for without my own extinction.

All of that rose up in me in the moment that I touched Cesare, ran my hand down his muscled arm, curled my fingers around his, and went forward quickly, without thinking, to take his mouth with mine. He allowed this, my dark lover, because hunter that he was he seemed to understand and accept my need.

In truth, I think a part of him gloried in it. You may assume that life came to him easily by virtue of his unvirtuous birth but in fact everything he valued he took for himself through the sheer force of his will. Everything except me. Even that first time under the gaze of Callixtus, I took him.

Some while later, I remember him laughing as he picked me up from the slate floor of the pantry where we had lain oblivious to discomfort and carried me across the salon to my chamber. We tumbled across the bed, limbs entwining, mouths searching. Drugged by pleasure, I scarcely felt the tears running down my cheeks until Cesare caught them on his tongue and touched the saltiness to mine.

"Will you ever tell me what haunts you?"

I turned my head away, letting my tears fall onto the pillow at the same time I tightened around him, drawing him deeper. He groaned and closed his eyes, the question and all else forgotten, if only for the moment.

Later, while I lingered in the bed, my breathing slow and regular, my mind mercifully mute, Cesare rose and went into the pantry. He came back with wine, bread, cheese, sausage, and Minerva. This man, who had lived all his life with hosts of retainers waiting to serve his every need but who to the end of that life preferred a simple meal whether in a camp of soldiers or in the bed of a lover, waited upon me.

We ate, feeding each other and sipping from the same goblet, laughing at the kitten's antics until she fell asleep curled in a white ball at our feet.

"Do you know who did it?" Cesare asked at length. He lay propped up on his side, the palm of his hand cupping his cheek. He looked young, as he was, and disingenuous, as he most certainly was not.

I had been expecting the question. What bound us together all those years was not merely bedsport. Make no mistake, for all his volatile temperament, Cesare possessed rare intelligence. The praise of his tutors who taught him Latin and Greek while he was still a child and his performance at the universities of Perugia and Pisa where he distinguished himself attest to that. I will not claim that the clarity of his mind was chief among his attributes where I was concerned, however it did make all our dealings at once more appealing and more satisfying. When all was said and done, we were allies. Almost to the very end.

"He was wearing della Rovere's colors," I said.

He raised a brow, challenging me to draw the obvious conclusion. "You see your father's hand?"

"Who wants della Rovere dead more than he?" Cesare challenged. "They've been rivals for years but it's worse now, much worse."

Indeed, it was, but I was not about to tell Cesare that his father had ordered me to find a way to solve the problem. Let him discover that for himself.

"There's another, more likely explanation," I said.

By the time I finished telling Cesare about Morozzi, the languor of our interlude was gone. He was all keen attention and honed instinct, this man Il Papa was determined to make into a desk-bound redskirter.

"Are you certain about this?" he asked.

I nodded. "He was followed to Florence and observed there, then followed on the way here. Apparently, he has allied himself with Savonarola."

Cursing under his breath, Cesare rose and walked naked from the chamber. He returned moments later carrying his clothes and mine.

"Get up," he said, tossing the garments to me. "My father must hear of this. He will have questions for you."

I had some experience in not bringing information to Borgia's attention in a timely manner and I had no intention of making that mistake again. I threw off the covers, rose, and began quickly to dress.

"I can't say I'm eager to tell him—" Accepting that the task was necessary did not make me relish it. I had been subject too recently to Borgia's wrath to want to experience it again so soon.

Pulling on his trousers, Cesare grinned. "Don't worry, I'll tell him. He'll hear it from me and he'll realize that he needs me at his side."

My dark lover was relishing the situation, I realized, pleased with the opportunity to be of service to Il Papa on his own terms, as though Borgia might yet be persuaded to let his eldest son have the life he longed for. That would not happen, of course. I knew it, and perhaps in some way so did Cesare. But just then he was still hopeful enough to try.

As I have said, Rome was safer in the early days of Borgia's reign than it had been for some time. Even so, I would not have ventured out alone after dark if I could possibly avoid it. Cesare had no such hesitation nor did he seem to see the need for any sort of escort. He suffered himself to wait only until I had myself more or less in order, then we were off.

For the sake of his dignity, Cesare ordinarily would not have risked being seen traversing any part of the city on foot. He kept a stable of splendid horses, all lavishly cared for, and never looked more at ease than when he was mounted. But the present circumstances required discretion, hence his willingness to forgo the usual trappings of his rank.

The night air stirred heavily under the weight of a late season sirocco blowing out of the distant desert far across the sea. It brought with it the usual oppressive mugginess that clogs the head while still managing to sting the skin with a thousand tiny pinpricks. Some say that the incessant wind also brings madness borne on the breath of foreign devils but I am skeptical of that.

It being that hour when the last sot has sought his bed and the first peddler has yet to leave his, nothing moved in the streets save the ubiquitous rats, scurrying here and there. I imagine them as the descendants of their kind who saw Augustus and Constantine, who watched civilization rise and fall, and who now see it rise anew for however long the Almighty allows us before we are struck down again. Truly, Fortuna betrays us all in the end.

It was well past midnight when we climbed the steps to the Vatican Palace. A drowsing guard leaned against the entrance with his halberd all but slipping from his grip. He straightened up abruptly when Cesare kicked him in the shanks.

The guard's expression of righteous outrage turned to horror when he recognized the Pope's son. Shocked to attention, he muttered, "Sorry, sir, very sorry, didn't realize it was you."

With one hand on my elbow, Cesare brushed past the guard and up the wide marble stairs to the papal offices. Even at that hour, several hapless secretaries were loitering, half asleep on their stools, in case Il Papa should require them as the insomniac Pope was known to do even in the depths of night.

Cesare roused one with another well-placed kick. "Where is my father?"

He was not, as we had expected, with La Bella. To the contrary, he was in his office and he was not alone.

The moment I saw the dark head in the seat opposite his desk, my instinct was to leave. I had met Borgia's second son only a handful of times and had no particular opinion of him save that he lacked his elder brother's wit. But he and Cesare together in the same room was never a good idea and especially not when matters were already so fraught.

Cesare, however, seemed of a different opinion. He strode into the room with a broad smile and exclaimed, "What an unexpected pleasure! Brother, you are well, I hope?"

The Borgia charm seemed on full display but the appearance was deceptive. Whereas his father was genuinely outgoing, boisterous, and high-spirited, Cesare's nature took a much more secretive and inward-looking turn. He was inclined to suspicion and the nurturing of grudges, although he did his best to conceal both inclinations. Over the years, he had mastered the trick of reflecting back upon his father what Borgia most wanted him to be—a young version of himself, ultimately his means of cheating death and assuring his own immortality.

But the cost of maintaining this simulacrum was high. I was one of the very few who knew that Cesare was prone to episodes of lethargy and despair during which he lacked even the energy to rise from his bed.

Juan, lately made Duke of Gandia, stood. His tone was cool, if superficially cordial, but he did not have either the good sense or the will to fully conceal his enmity. It shone too clearly in his eyes, all the more so when he glanced at me, only to avert his gaze quickly.

"Well enough, brother. We were just speaking of you."

I stepped back a pace, unwillingly fascinated to see these sons of Borgia together. They both had their father's height although Cesare had the better form, even allowing that I was prejudiced in his favor. Chance had graced them equally with the looks of their mother, who it was said had dallied with the young Giulio della Rovere in the days before he became a prince of the church. Their affair supposedly ended when Vannozza came to Borgia's notice, though some still say that the rivalry between the two men had its origins in her bed.

That lively lady's sons stood, backs erect, shoulders squared, hands reaching for but not quite touching the hilts of their swords. Had they ever been friends? Perhaps as very young boys; there was little more than a year between them, they naturally would have been drawn to the same games and pastimes. But not for most of their lives, pawns as they were in their father's great game.

Unhappy, rebellious pawns, I saw, and not just Cesare, for the same tension shimmered in Juan. Having come second since the day of his birth and now tasting what it meant to be first, if only in his rival's eyes, he would be reluctant to yield the smallest part in the struggle that seemed inevitable between them. Almost I could believe the rumor then circulating in the city that Juan had gone so far as to threaten his brother's life should Cesare lay claim to any of the honors and benefices that Juan regarded as his right.

Borgia did not appear to see that or, perhaps more correctly, he did not care. They were his sons; they would obey him. To remind them, his voice snapped as a whip cutting through the fragrant night air wafting off the terraces lined with orange and lemon trees.

"Sit down, both of you." When they had obeyed, however reluctantly, he turned his attention to me. "And you, Francesca, don't be shy, join us." As I took the chair he indicated, he demanded, "Have you come as surety for my wayward son's behavior?"

Before I could reply, Cesare said, "She has come to answer the questions you will have when I tell you what I have discovered."

A bubble of exasperation rose up in me. It was not that I begrudged Cesare taking credit for what I had learned, or at least not entirely. Rather it was more a case of being weary of the constant jockeying for position that went on all around Borgia. I was guilty of that, too, on occasion, but I liked to think that at least in that regard, I was one of the lesser sinners.

"Remember that priest," Cesare continued. "Bernando Morozzi, who caused us so much trouble last year? He's returned to Rome and he's working for Savonarola."

Borgia sat back in his gilded chair, steepled his fingers, and regarded his eldest son over them. "Yes, I know."

I released my breath slowly. Until that moment, I had hesitated to let myself truly believe that Morozzi was in the city. After all the months of chastising myself for staying in Rome rather than pursuing him, he really had come within my grasp. It was almost too much to hope for.

"You know?" Under other circumstances, Cesare's expression would have been comical. As it was, I was too involved in my own thoughts to feel more than passing sympathy for him at being so deflated.

Not so his brother.

"Of course, he does," Juan said. He made no attempt to hide his pleasure at Cesare's chagrin. To the contrary, he clearly relished it. "Our father has the finest spy network in Christendom. How did you imagine that he would not know?"

"Did you?" Cesare demanded of his brother. To give him credit, he rebounded quickly. Perhaps overly so. Although he remained seated, I saw his hand creep again toward the hilt of his sword, his fingers flexing as avidly as he ever touched me.

"Did you?" he repeated.

"Enough," Borgia said. "I have no patience for this." He turned to me. "I assume you will want to be involved in stopping him."

I did not answer at once but only stared at my employer. Thoughts that had swirled in the back of my mind since the attack on Lux came to the fore, gelling suddenly as certain substances will when presented with the right conditions.

"I thought I already was involved," I said. "The only question is how much?"

Ever choleric, Juan demanded, "What is that supposed to mean?"

I ignored him and addressed Borgia. "How long have you known that Morozzi was back in Rome? Did you, for example, know before an assault took place on a certain villa?"

I was daring greatly by challenging him, but whether it was the late hour, the influence of Cesare's presence, or my own contrary nature, I was no longer willing to sleepwalk my way across Borgia's chessboard. He knew what Morozzi was to me. *He knew.* His failure to tell me at once of the mad priest's return so that I might take matters into my own hands and do what I had to was inexcusable. And led to only one possible conclusion: He had kept silent so that he could use me to his own purposes.

It was not in Borgia's nature to offer explanations for his actions. That he did so now suggested that he knew how deeply he had offended me.

"Given that Morozzi blames you for thwarting his effort to defeat me last year, you were the most obvious way to draw him out. I used you as bait to lure him to the villa in the hope that he would be captured or killed. It was never my intent that you come to harm. Why would it be? We both know that I have need of your services now more than ever."

That being self-evident, I could hardly dispute it. There was a great deal more I would have liked to ask—how he had known that I would be at the villa; how he had gotten word of my presence there to Morozzi? But I judged that I had gone as far as was prudent for the moment.

"You have not asked me about the second attack on you," he said.

Nor had I had any intention of doing so. The attack on the villa had been bad enough but the circumstances there—the warning provided by the dogs and the availability of the escape tunnel—gave reasonable assurance that I would have every opportunity to elude Morozzi.

The second attack was a far different and more serious matter. But for the dark turn of my own nature, it could well have ended with my death. If I truly thought for a moment that Borgia would countenance that—

"There is no need to ask you of it, Holiness. The assassin was wearing Cardinal della Rovere's colors."

"And that persuades you that he was responsible?" He looked amused by the notion that I could be so naïve.

"It persuades me that Morozzi is attempting to drive a wedge between us. Your conflict with della Rovere is hardly a secret. No doubt the priest thought that I would blame you."

Juan sucked in his breath and turned toward me, his face darkening. "Are you suggesting that my father would—?"

"For pity's sake!" Cesare interrupted. "She's saying that she knows Papa wasn't behind it. Neither was della Rovere. The Cardinal would never be so stupid. Can you at least try to listen or, better yet, just keep quiet?"

Juan's hand twitched to his sword and he began to rise again but Borgia cut him off. "It's a sad pass when the only words of wisdom in this room are coming from a woman. Cesare, explain yourself. What are you doing in Rome when I ordered you to keep watch on Savona?"

This was an interesting bit of news, as Cesare supposedly was rusticating in the papal castle at Spoleto, his presence there taken as an indication that Borgia intended to continue his policy of discretion regarding his children and not advance them beyond all tolerable limits despite having attained the crown jewel of the papacy. As I had never noted any such capacity for self-restraint on Borgia's part when it came to the fortunes of *la famiglia,* I was pleased to have my skepticism justified.

However, I had also assumed that Cesare would have some ready-made explanation to excuse his presence and was caught off guard when he said, "I received word that Francesca had been attacked."

Jesus, Mary, and all the Saints! Scant hours before, Borgia had been wondering out loud if his son and I were conspiring to commit patricide. Now to find out that Cesare had abandoned the mission his father had sent him on out of concern for me—

"Holiness, he does not mean—," I began, all too aware of Juan's triumphant smile.

"Which is not to say that I wasn't already on my way here. Had I remained near Savona, you would be blaming me for putting too much trust in couriers."

"What is so urgent that you had to bring word of it yourself?" Juan demanded, swallowing his disappointment at not seeing his brother crushed beneath their father's anger.

Cesare ignored him and addressed Borgia.

"Della Rovere is meeting with emissaries from the French king. Rumor has it that Charles will agree to support the Cardinal's bid for the papacy in order to undermine the influence of Spain, which you are considered to favor above all else. To that end, the French are prepared to invade the papal states with forces sufficient to depose you."

The face of Christ's anointed vicar reddened. He slammed his fist down on the top of the desk, sending the large gold-and-silver ink set bouncing into the air and almost tumbling the pile of papers waiting his attention onto the floor. I flinched as, I noted, did Juan.

Cesare, on the other hand, did not react at all but took the wave of patriarchal rage with admirable stoicism.

"*Bastardo!*" Borgia shouted. "We have scarcely recovered the unity of Holy Mother Church and he wants to rip us apart again! What does he think? That I will go quietly? By God, I will not! If he wants a war, he will have such a one as Christendom has never seen!"

That was partly bravado, of course, but there was enough truth in it to send a shiver up my spine. Della Rovere had a powerful ally in the French king but Borgia could call on the assistance of both Spain and Portugal, assuming the monarchs of each believed that he had given them the Indies. With their help, he could wage all-out war that would convulse the Italian peninsula and beyond. And not just any war. Inevitably, given the nature of the struggle, any such conflict would take on the cloak of holy war with both sides proclaiming that God was on their side. Armies would march, men would die, and cities would burn along with their precious libraries and universities. All the dreams that I and the other members of Lux had for a better world would lie in ashes.

Unless, Borgia seemed to be telling me, I found a way to stop it by removing della Rovere from the board. Better that one man die rather than many.

The discussion went on, Cesare and Juan arguing over which of them Borgia should trust to solve the problem, with Juan, seemingly intent on demonstrating his lack of wits, insisting that his brother must have misunderstood della Rovere's intent regarding the French. My thoughts wandered to matters nearer to my own heart, namely the question of where Morozzi was hiding. Mad though he was and quintessentially evil, I had learned to my sorrow that he was at least my equal in intelligence. He would not do the expected; of that I was certain, but of very little else.

It was late, I was weary. The argument, for it had become that by then, showed no sign of winding down. Cesare and Juan both seemed fiercely determined to win their father's favor by denying any shred of it to the other. As for Borgia, I could not escape the conclusion that he both encouraged and enjoyed his sons' rivalry.

Seeking distraction, I glanced around the papal office. Filled as it was with gilded furniture, marble columns, paintings—all of worldly subjects in keeping with His Holiness's preferences—it would have suited the noblest king or emperor, which, of course, was exactly how Borgia saw himself.

Along one of the brocade-covered walls, near the carved double doors through which we had entered, there was a *spioncino,* a small concealed hole through which the occupant of the office could be observed discreetly, the better to avoid disturbing him at inopportune moments. The existence of the *spioncino* was not generally known but neither was it a secret to those of us who served His Holiness. Similarly, I knew the location of the two concealed doors that Vittoro had mentioned. If Borgia really was not using them, how exactly was he managing to elude the vigilance of his secretaries?

And why?

Pleading fatigue, I left Cesare with his father and brother a short time later and accepted an escort back to my rooms. Even at so late an hour, I considered seeking out Rocco, but exhaustion dogged my steps and clouded my mind. Before I could tell him of the possible threat to his son, I had to have a plan for dealing with it. Besides, so far at least Morozzi had directed his attentions solely toward me. I had no reason to think that would change quite yet.

Once in my chamber, I wasted no time disrobing, and crawled into bed next to Minerva. Sleep was elusive, as always. I lay awake thinking about the mad priest, trying to anticipate where he might go and what he might do. Above all, I was determined that this time when we clashed, as I was certain that we would, those I cared for would be protected.

At length, I slept. As I knew it would, the nightmare came.

11

I am in a very small space behind a wall. There is a tiny hole through which I can see into a room filled with shadows that move. The darkness is broken by flashes of light but I cannot see their source. Blood is everywhere, a veritable ocean of blood rising against the walls and threatening to drown me. I try to scream but my throat is paralyzed; no sound comes from me. My hands push against the wall but it will not yield. I am trapped alone with the blood and my own terror.

I awoke suddenly, covered in sweat with my heart pounding. My fists clutched the sheet as though it were a lifeline thrown into the roiled sea of my mind. From long practice, I forced myself to lie still and breathe steadily. In time, I calmed enough to get up and stumble into the pantry, where I stood with my head over the stone sink, waiting for the waves of fear-induced nausea to pass.

When at last they, too, were gone, I poured water from an ewer and drank while staring out the high windows of the salon. The gray hint of dawn was just beginning to spread over the city, revealing red tiled roofs sprinkled with terra-cotta chimney pots. From its nest under the eaves, a lark offered tentative song.

There was no question of my being able to go back to bed. Fortunately, I have never needed more than a few hours of sleep in order to function properly, or so I choose to believe. I dressed quickly, saw to Minerva's needs, then left the apartment. At such an early hour, Portia's door was closed. I resolved to visit her later to see how she did.

Outside in the coolness of early morning, the street sweepers were busy sprinkling water over the paving stones and brushing them down with long-handled brooms. They followed the dung collectors at work with their shovels and wheeled barrows. An advantage of living in one of the better parts of Rome was the relative cleanliness. Elsewhere, filth piled in the open sewers or collected in the rubbish middens beloved of the city's army of rats. Sofia thought such conditions bred disease and I saw no reason to disbelieve her.

Cleaners were also scrubbing away at more lewd graffiti that had appeared during the night. They worked under the scrutiny of condottierri, suggesting that the scribblings had given more than the usual offense to some august personage.

I joined the stream of early risers making for the Campo dei Fiori. There boys were raising the wooden shutters over shop fronts while girls, standing on stepstools, reached high to water the trailing baskets of flowers that lent the market a festive air. The aroma of fresh bread wafted from the Via dei Panettieri, where the bakers could be found. My stomach rumbled but I ignored it and went on, anxious to reach my destination.

Rocco's shop was not yet open. I tapped lightly at the door. It was opened promptly by Nando who, seeing me, smiled broadly.

"Good morning, Donna Francesca. Did you bring Minerva?"

"Alas, I did not. But I will tell her that you asked after her."

He laughed at my whimsy and went to tell his father that I had come. In his absence, I reflected on the mystery that children represent, their spirits at once so fragile yet so stalwart.

There were times when I wondered what I had been like as a child. My father had rarely spoken of the years before he entered Borgia's service, and for myself, I remembered little of them. I had what I took to be a vague memory of a small house where we may have lived when I was perhaps six or seven but I could not even tell you what town it was in. My first clear memory of living anywhere was the apartment we occupied in Rome not far from the Campo dei Fiori for several years before we moved into Borgia's palazzo on the Corso.

Apart from that, there are only flashes—a window from which I could see sparkling water; a cupboard with the painted images of birds; the sound of a woman singing softly. And sometimes, when I am on the very edge of sleep, the scent of lavender and lemon mingling in an aroma I find oddly soothing.

I have the impression that other people remember more but I could be wrong as I have never really discussed it with anyone. I preferred to live in the moment or, better yet, to anticipate the future in which I would finally kill Morozzi and be free. Although I could not have told you what I expected to be freed from.

Rocco returned with his son and was about to greet me when I drew a small box and a notebook from my pocket and held them out to Nando. "I thought you might like these."

Wide-eyed, he took them both, turning the notebook over in his hands before opening the box. The delight that filled his eyes when he saw what was inside made me forget for a moment the seriousness of my purpose.

"The charcoals came from the studio of Master Botticelli. I have no skill at drawing, but I understand that they are among the finest made."

"You are too generous—," Rocco began, but stopped when he saw the quick shake of my head.

"Perhaps you could go and draw something now?" I suggested.

Good son that he was, Nando looked to his father. "Papa?"

"Of course," Rocco said quickly. "You can sit outside if you like—"

"But don't go from in front of the shop," I added.

Nando shot me a puzzled look. Young though he was, he understood that his father had the ordering of his life, not I.

Rocco glanced at me and his face tightened. "Stay in front where I can see you, lad," he said.

Scarcely had the boy run out than I took a deep breath and said, "Morozzi is back in Rome. I know how to keep Nando safe but I must have your agreement."

Rocco paled. I had no difficulty recognizing the fear that swept over him because I shared it in full measure.

"Are you sure?" He managed, despite everything, to retain control of himself. Terror, no matter how well justified, would serve no good purpose.

I nodded. "He has allied himself with Savonarola and is under the protection of Il Frateschi. I must find him, but in all honesty, I have no idea where to begin looking."

"I will give you all the help I can but first—"

"I didn't come here for that," I said quickly. "It isn't my intent to involve you in such dangerous matters ever again. I only want to make sure that Nando will be safe."

Rocco stared at me for a long moment before abruptly nodding. "How do you think to accomplish that?"

He listened carefully as I explained. When he nodded, I let out my breath in relief. What I had proposed might seem to run against all good sense, yet I was convinced it was the only possible course.

"This man, Captain Romano, has he agreed to help?"

"Not yet. I came to see you first but I know he will not hesitate. Although Borgia may very well be Morozzi's ultimate target, right now no place is safer than within the precincts of the Vatican. The papal guard has been increased and no one is allowed beyond the square and the basilica without special permission."

He looked toward the doorway and beyond to where Nando sat in the sun, bent over a drawing on which he was working industriously. He was a sturdy child and tall for his age but for all that so very vulnerable.

On impulse, I slipped my hand into Rocco's and squeezed gently. "No harm will come to him, I swear."

An oath that I knew full well I could keep only if I killed Morozzi—quickly.

So absorbed was he by worry for his son that I wasn't certain Rocco had heard me until he turned and met my eyes. In them I saw anger at the threat to his son and fierce resolve to deal with it.

But as is so often the case, one sort of passion leads on to another.

"I believe you," he said, and raised my hand to his lips.

Confusion filled me. The single kiss we had shared months before had assumed in my memory the sense of a corner not turned, a path not embarked upon. But my sudden, vivid awareness of the heat and texture of his mouth, his breath against my skin, our closeness and our relative privacy, all combined to shake my certainty. And to remind me most forcefully of what a stubborn creature she was, that other self I could never be, who insisted from time to time on acting as though she actually existed.

The moment passed. I drew my hand away and, with greater difficulty, my gaze. The mundane sounds of the street—the creak of wagons, the bark of a dog, a man's hearty laughter—gave me something safe to pin my attention on until such time as the ragged seam of my composure stitched itself back into the semblance of normality.

Rocco rose, pushed back his bench, and strode outside. I did not hear what he said to Nando but I was relieved by the boy's quick smile and the eagerness with which he hurried back into the room.

"We're going to visit the Vatican, Donna Francesca. Are you coming with us?"

"Of course." My false brightness might fool the child but I could not hope to conceal my feelings from Rocco unless I found a way first to control them within myself. There was only one way I knew to do that; I had to turn away from the light he brought into my life and allow the darkness free rein.

And so we went out into the day—a man, a woman, a child. Anyone might be pardoned for assuming that we were a carefree little family, except that one of us moved through scarlet shadows, busily conniving at bloody death.

The streets were considerably more crowded but I did my best to take careful note of all those around us, the better to determine if we were being followed. I saw no one in the least suspicious but that did not necessarily mean that we were unobserved. Any of Morozzi's allies among Il Frateschi might be watching. For that matter, so might Borgia's "eyes."

Vittoro was about to depart for the barracks when we arrived. His wife, Donna Felicia, was just smoothing his doublet over his shoulders as they stood together at the open door.

"Donna Francesca," Vittoro said, his gaze going to Rocco and Nando. "Moroni, is it, the glassmaker?"

"I am, sir," Rocco said, and extended his hand.

While the men assessed each other, I put an arm around Nando's shoulders. As I had hoped, the boy's wide-eyed stare and shy smile drew Felicia's attention. She bent down to look at him.

"Who would this fine lad be?"

"My son." Rocco drew him forward. When the introductions were done, he said, "Nando, I'm going to speak with Captain Romano for a few minutes, all right?"

The boy nodded, happy to go with Donna Felicia, who held out her hand to him with the suggestion that he might like a fresh-baked *boconnotto* filled with sweet cream. The three of us stepped into the small room Vittoro kept just beyond the front door where he conducted business. Once there, I wasted no time explaining why we had come.

Before I had finished, the good captain was nodding. "Of course, the boy can stay with us. Felicia will be delighted. Our grandchildren are here almost every day yet she still complains that the house is empty." To Rocco, he said, "Be assured he will be well cared for."

After we had both thanked him, we spoke a little longer about the situation with Morozzi before Rocco went off to talk with Nando. I don't know exactly what he said to him to explain what was happening but the boy seemed to take it all in stride. Donna Felicia had him at the long wooden table in the kitchen where the Romano family—grandparents, daughters and sons-in-law, and grandchildren—still supped together most evenings. His face was smeared with cream and he looked well contented.

When father and son had taken leave of each other—hopefully only for a very short time—we stepped outside accompanied by Vittoro. Rocco stood silently, taking in the bustle of activity as the Pope's guards drilled under the eagle eyes of their officers. I had the impression that training had been stepped up of late and appreciated that Vittoro was leaving nothing to chance.

"I know that you are doing everything possible," Rocco said. "But hundreds of people come and go here each day. If Morozzi is determined enough, you may not be able to keep him out."

"That is true," Vittoro said readily. "A sufficiently committed assassin can penetrate anywhere. But remember, Morozzi has never shown any tendency to sacrifice his own life. That being the case, the riskier I can make it for him, the better."

Turning to me, he added, "I am more concerned about your well-being, Donna Francesca. I trust you will take every care."

I assured him that I would, fully aware that I lied. I would take every *reasonable* care but the fact remained that in seeking to kill Morozzi, there was every likelihood that I would be giving him the opportunity to kill me. I had to trust to my own skill, and possibly to the shade of my father who I hoped watched over me, that I would prove to be the more deadly.

Any comparison of myself to Morozzi inevitably risked rousing the darkness within me. I feared it was a matter of like calling to like, a possibility that brought with it unspeakable dread. To distract myself and because I was determined to let no weakness of my own intrude on what had to be done, I thanked Vittoro again for his help and bid him a quick farewell.

Rocco and I walked a short distance away when I felt compelled to say, "I am sorry to have brought such trouble on you. Hopefully, Nando will be able to come home soon. I will send word to you the moment the problem is resolved."

Given that he had just been forced to leave his child in the care of people he did not know, I expected his mood to be grim. But I was unprepared when he stopped suddenly and faced me. His eyes glittered with a hard light I rarely saw in them and his face had darkened ominously.

"What do you think, that I will hide from this? That is all well and good for Nando, he is a child. I am a man. You would do well to remember that, Francesca."

I was taken aback. Far from failing to think of Rocco as a man, I thought of him that way far too often.

"I know perfectly well who you are. You are a good and decent man who has the misfortune to be caught up in events not of your making but—"

"I cannot protect him by doing nothing!" His face twisted and for just a moment I caught a glimpse of the full extent of his fear. "My own son, and I must entrust him to strangers to keep him safe. And I cannot protect you either. You won't allow it."

Without warning, he took hold of both my arms and drew me closer. "Do you have any idea how that makes me feel, Francesca? Any idea at all?"

I truly did not, but only because I never allowed myself to think in such terms.

"You . . . do not like it, clearly. But none of this is your fault save that you have befriended me. The blame is mine for involving you. If I were as other women—"

"We are as God makes us. If only you would accept that, you would find—"

Accept it? Accept that I was just as the all-knowing and all-merciful God wanted me to be? How could I accept such a possibility, hinting as it did at cosmic cruelty beyond any mortal's capacity to endure?

"What is God, then?" I demanded. "A puppet master pulling the strings for His own cruel amusement?"

Fortunately, no one else was standing close enough to hear me, for my words were heresy, plain and simple. For them I could—many would say *should*—burn. Even Rocco, the very soul of tolerance, appeared taken aback.

"God is never cruel, Francesca. When we falter, He weeps for us."

"So you believe and so I would like to but—"

The anger went from him as swiftly as it had come. Without a word, he gathered me into his arms. A wave of longing rose up in me so powerful that for a moment, I could not breathe. I gasped and leaned my head against his chest, letting his strength enfold me.

The sweet balm of Rocco's embrace drove away all else. My awareness of the world around us—all the bustle of Saint Peter's Square and the nearby looming wreck of the basilica that still so haunted me, and beyond the turbulent city baking in the late spring heat—faded to nothingness. We stood, the two of us alone, in a stolen moment of time all the more precious for having come so unexpectedly.

Perhaps God truly does show us His mercy if only we allow ourselves to receive it.

But whether by divine compassion or merely the hungry yearning of two souls, the world would not be held at bay forever.

In a heartbeat, it returned . . . with a vengeance.

12

"*What is this?*" Cesare strode toward us as though out of a thundercloud, scattering dust, pigeons, and hapless passersby in every direction. He came with a hand on the hilt of his sword and an unholy gleam in his eyes. The boy/man filled with arrogance and pride and, worse yet, whatever demons the confrontation with his father and brother had raised in him.

Without waiting for a reply, he turned on Rocco. "You're the glassmaker, Pocco Somebody? What are you doing here?"

I was tired to the bone, having slept little and badly. Worries crowded my head, leaving scant room for yet another. It was there all the same—in black velvet, a froth of lace at his throat, a flash of ruby in the ring on his left hand that caught the sun as he gestured.

"Why are you holding my father's . . . servant in the middle of Piazza San Pietro in front of hundreds of people and why is she letting you?"

This was the moment for Rocco to step back, bow his head, and murmur something conciliatory. Surely, he knew how volatile noble sons are, how easily stung in their vanity, how quick to take offense for any reason or none at all. He was an intelligent man and no stranger to eloquence. He easily could have put the matter to rights.

Which made it all the more alarming when he thrust me behind him, took a step toward Cesare—entirely the wrong direction!—and said, "What I do is not your business, signore. I am not answerable to you."

Aiiee, Blessed Mary and all the Saints! The man I had thought the soul of good sense and stability chose that moment to reveal himself as a raving lunatic. Moreover, I was not alone in realizing what he had done. Already an avid crowd was gathering. What better entertainment than to watch the Pope's son hack some presumptuous commoner into tidy tidbits?

Another moment and the touts would be upon us, laying odds and collecting bets. Cesare would be favored, to be sure, but only for the most obvious and practical reasons: He had been trained from tenderest youth to kill. Rocco would be the sentimental pick by far although I was sure that anyone betting on him would lay off side bets to balance the risk. Round and round it would go until it ended the only way it could—with gore and sorrow and Morozzi off somewhere laughing as his adversaries bloodied each other.

I have no particular skill in the womanly arts but even I knew what had to be done.

"Where are you going?" Cesare demanded as I turned on my heel and began to walk away. I let my back speak for a moment before I stopped and glared at them both over my shoulder.

"To see to business. Obviously, one of us has to."

They both gaped at me in a most satisfactory fashion, which served to embolden me further.

To Rocco, I said, "*If* you could manage to tear yourself away, perhaps you would inquire of Guillaume whether he has discovered anything of use."

Rocco frowned, uncertain how to deal with my refusal to play the passive female. He should have known better.

Cesare did, however loath he might be to admit it. From the corner of my eye, I saw his reluctant grin. A little of the tension in me evaporated as he said, "And do you have instructions for me as well, Donna Francesca?"

I answered as diplomatically as my lingering ire would allow. "For you, signore? Surely you do not believe that I would be so presumptuous. However . . ."

"However?" Cesare repeated. Mercurial as he was, his good humor was returning. I suspected that I knew the reason why. For all his often overweening pride, Cesare respected nothing so much as audacity. Thanks be to God, I had that in abundance.

"If you would be so kind, Captain Romano is doing his best to strengthen the defenses hereabouts. I am certain that he would be grateful for your help."

I did not speak lightly in that regard. Cesare was a born warrior with all the instincts of such. Vittoro, being of the same mind, knew his worth better than Cesare's own father did.

Mollified and, I think, not a little amused, Cesare nodded to me, spared Rocco a slighting glance, and took himself off. With his going, the disgruntled crowd, disappointed at being denied a show, dispersed.

I exhaled in relief but did not linger. Before I turned to go, I said more gently, "Send word, if you will, if Guillaume knows anything. In the meantime do, please, try not to get yourself killed."

Far from looking grateful for my intervention, Rocco merely shrugged. He seemed inexplicably pleased with what had transpired.

"If I'd gotten that sword away from him, he would have found out what it is to eat dust."

As it was beyond my capacity to imagine how Rocco thought he could have disarmed Cesare Borgia, I did not reply. But as I walked away, I could not resist a glance over my shoulder at the man who truly did not seem to have any sense of his own limitations. Rocco was looking after me, his expression thoughtful and, to my way of thinking, far too perceptive.

Later, perhaps, I would consider the significance of the two men who unknowingly shared my affections actually having met—and so nearly come to blows. But just then I had more important matters to consider. Borgia had left certain questions in my mind that I intended to resolve without further delay.

I hurried on and shortly reached the Palazzo di Fortuna, Luigi d'Amico's principal residence in Rome. Like most people of exalted means, he had private accommodations scattered about the city, places he could slip away to in times of trouble or simply to conduct confidential business. But this being a Tuesday, I knew he would be at home and receiving.

Even so, after entering the gilded hall at the front of the palazzo, I made no attempt to join the line waiting for admission to the main salon. Instead, I lingered, pretending great interest in the wall paintings drawn from Greek and Roman allegory until Luigi's steward saw me and approached.

"Donna Francesca," he said, "if you would be so good as to accompany me."

I was led to a small room in a nearby wing where I was bid to wait.

The room was graciously furnished with couches in the Roman style, small marquetry tables, and tall, padded chairs. High windows looked out over the gardens. Scarcely had I entered than a servant slipped in carrying a silver tray upon which rested a carafe of chilled lemonade and a dish of *biscotti*.

"Signore d'Amico will be with you as soon as possible," the steward said as he left me.

I slaked the thirst brought on by my hasty walk to the palazzo and nibbled on a *biscotto* as I gazed out the windows. Time passed slowly. I wondered if I might slip out to Luigi's ample library without being seen. Reluctant to abuse his hospitality, I settled instead in one of the chairs and schooled myself to patience.

Sometime later, I awoke with a start to find myself no longer alone. Luigi was just entering the room. The banker closed the door behind him and regarded me somberly. Although I had seen him only a few days before, he looked suddenly much older, as though weighed down by cares I could only guess at.

"You must be very tired to sleep sitting up," he said.

I straightened myself, struggling to throw off the fog of Morpheus. My tongue felt thick and I had difficulty getting my bearings.

"I heard what happened," Luigi said. I had presumed as much, trusting that Portia kept him informed. Silently, I waited for what I suspected would come next. Since Borgia had admitted his role in the attack on the villa, my mind had turned over the question of how he had known that I would be there. In my estimation, one explanation was far likelier than any other. It was for that reason that I had come.

The banker walked a little farther into the room. His face appeared strained and he seemed to be weighing his words heavily. Finally, he said, "I am very sorry."

Out of respect for our friendship and, to be fair, no small measure of sympathy for the predicament he must have faced, I did not pretend to mistake him. Instead, I asked, "Do you want to tell me how it happened?"

Luigi sighed heavily. He looked like a man caught between anger and apprehension, with the latter predominating.

"His Holiness can be most persuasive. But I swear to you, I had no idea that he would go so far. He said only that he wanted to flush out Morozzi."

I was not surprised that the banker knew about the mad priest; Luigi had the Pope's confidence in the way that only the man who knows where the money is can.

His face tightened. "He certainly never suggested that my villa would be burned to the ground, much less that you would have to fight off an assassin."

"He didn't have anything to do with the second attack, but tell me how the first came to pass."

Luigi sighed as he lowered himself into the chair opposite me. Leaning forward, with his hands clasped between his knees, he spoke with the eagerness of a man needing to unburden himself.

"His Holiness summoned me a week ago. He knew that you were in the habit of meeting with me and others."

"Then he knows about Lux?" I did not try to hide my alarm.

"Up to a point. He honestly doesn't seem to care what we do so long as we restrict ourselves to natural philosophy and steer clear of politics. In that regard, I suppose we are fortunate."

"But he still put pressure on you?"

Luigi nodded. "He said that it was up to me whether he helped Lux or harmed us. He wanted to know the time and place of our next meeting. He said only that every precaution would be taken to assure no one came to any harm. He seemed completely confident."

"He always does. You must not blame yourself. His Holiness has a rare gift for discerning vulnerability and making use of it."

Certainly, he understood how readily I could be manipulated when it came to the matter of making Morozzi pay for my father's death.

"You are uncommonly kind," Luigi said. He blinked and for a moment I caught the sheen of tears in his eyes. That so brilliant and successful a man could be so humbled by his dealings with Borgia made me consider the cost of my own association with the pontiff, but only briefly. This was not the time for such doubts.

"I wonder . . . ," Luigi ventured. "Do the others have to know about this?"

I had not considered that but as I turned the question over in my mind, I saw no good purpose in alarming all of Lux. At least not immediately.

"Events are presently in turmoil," I said. "Let us see where we are when matters are more settled before we make any such decisions."

He nodded gratefully. "It is a difficult situation for all of us but for you more than any. Given the danger, I cannot help but think that you would be better off out of the city. I have any number of residences where you will be safe. You might like Capri, for example. It's lovely this time of year."

The island was also almost two hundred miles from Rome. Luigi was not merely suggesting that I seek a place of greater safety; he was suggesting that I give up the battle entirely.

"That is good of you but I am not about to flee. Morozzi's return to Rome gives me the chance I have longed for to avenge my father. But beyond that, we need Borgia's strength and cunning to stop Savonarola and others of the same ilk. To that end, I am determined to protect His Holiness at all costs."

Luigi looked unconvinced but he did not attempt to argue the point further. Instead, he said, "That may prove difficult. There are times when I think our pope is his own worst enemy."

I frowned. The banker had contacts from the Grand Duchy of Muscovy in the frozen north to Constantinople and the inner circle of the Ottoman Turks. If anyone was in a position to know what dangers might be stirring in the shadows, he was.

"What do you mean?" I asked.

He glanced toward the windows as though to be sure there was no one nearby in the gardens who might overhear us. Even then, he pitched his voice low.

"Their Most Catholic Majesties are not happy with the bull His Holiness signed. They want more."

I swore softly under my breath. "He must have their support in the matter of Naples."

"He must indeed," Luigi agreed. "Rumor has it that they are sending an emissary who will lay out their demands but who will also"—he lowered his voice yet further—"who will reproach His Holiness for tolerating the presence of non-Christians within his borders. They will cite the Moors in particular but it is understood that privately they will tell His Holiness that he should follow the will of his predecessor, Pope Innocent VIII who, they will claim, was preparing to order the expulsion of the Jews from all of Christendom."

This was worse even than anything I had imagined. If Ferdinand and Isabella were willing to make such a demand, they must be certain indeed of how precarious Borgia's position was and how desperately he needed them. Even so, no one could expect him to take such a humiliation well.

"He will be enraged," I said.

Luigi nodded. "Likely so, but what can he do? As you said, he must have their support."

Which raised the possibility that the danger to Sofia, David, and all the Jews was even greater than I had thought. If Borgia decided to sacrifice them against all good sense—

"We must do everything possible to strengthen Il Papa so that he may withstand the challenges he faces. In particular, Morozzi must be stopped before this gets completely out of control."

Leaning forward a little, I added, "It occurred to me that you might be able to help find him. His Holiness may have the finest spy network in Christendom, so it is said. But I doubt that much of anything can happen in Rome without your knowledge."

To give Luigi credit, he did not indulge in any false modesty. Grasping my meaning at once, he said, "You are referring to my *portatori?*"

I nodded. Portia and all the others like her were the banker's eyes and ears throughout the city. They knew better than anyone who was coming and going, who had secrets, who was committing indiscretions. I had no doubt that Luigi made good use of such information for his own ends but now I wanted him to put it to work for a higher cause.

"If they could be alerted," I said, "to take note of newcomers to the city, particularly any who may have come from Florence, and most especially to be on the lookout for Morozzi, that would be a great help."

"Of course," Luigi assured me. "But you realize, he could be staying anywhere. Il Frateschi has sympathizers here. Unfortunately, we don't know who they are."

I had thought of that but it did not discourage me. "Wherever he is, he is not invisible. Someone, somewhere has had contact with him. Perhaps it has only been a matter of delivering food or carrying what seems like an innocent message or observing an encounter without understanding its significance."

Luigi was nodding before I finished speaking. "It will be difficult but you may be right. I will see what can be done."

I thanked him and lingered a little while longer as he was eager to speak of other matters, less touching on his shame. Having managed to save Juan de la Cosa's map in the escape from the villa, he showed it to me again. Together, we marveled at what, more than ever, I hoped truly was Novi Orbis, the New World.

Tracing the novel coastline with one finger, Luigi said, "Colombo claims that all the men and women in the islands he visited were handsome beyond compare and that all went naked except for leaves covering their privates. They were of gentle demeanor and had few weapons, but dwelt in a state of sin nonetheless, lacking as they do all knowledge of the One True God."

I was skeptical that any place could be such a seeming Eden but however well-disposed its people might be, I did not envy them their encounter with us. In my observation, we are all too adept at clothing the most venal acts in righteous intent.

I left the palazzo a short time later, intending to return to the Vatican. It was all well and good for Vittoro to increase the guard around Borgia but that would afford us little if poison managed to slip through. I would have to redouble my vigilance.

Thinking about the best way to do that, I came around a corner and walked into a crowd gathered in front of a building. Men and women alike were pointing and laughing at some recent piece of graffiti. I squeezed closer to get a look, only to regret instantly that I had done so.

The artist—I am loath to call him that but he was undeniably skilled—had done an all too credible job of depicting a naked young girl with golden hair arranged in ringlets around a heart-shaped face. She was smiling over her shoulder at an unmistakable figure arrayed in the crimson and gold raiment of a pope, his chasuble pulled open to reveal an enormous penis aimed at her raised rump. Lest anyone be left in any doubt as to the object of His Holiness's attentions, the young girl wore a pendant dangling between her small breasts in the shape of the entwined letters *L* and *B*.

Shock roared through me, followed hard by disgust so intense that I feared I would vomit. A shrill whistle sounded in the distance. The crowd began to scatter as a troop of condottierri came on the run. I managed to slip away and continued on toward the Curia but with every step the bright day seemed to fade further. A chill stole over me. In the chatter and laughter of passersby, I feared that I heard the stirrings of a mob only waiting to be unleashed upon the bidding of the fanatic Savonarola, who concealed within his bosom the viper I was sworn to crush.

13

Several days passed during which I busied myself checking every item of food and drink intended for Borgia or his family with even more than my usual care. So, too, did I inspect every object that might come into contact with them. The work was tedious but necessary.

I was occupied with this task one afternoon about a week after my encounter with Luigi when I received a message from him. It was delivered by Renaldo, who found me in the cavernous kitchens beneath the Vatican Palace. The day was warm verging on hot and the kitchens, their immense fires lit for preparation of the evening meal, were sweltering. I had worn the lightest clothing I possessed, a thin shift and a simple linen overdress, but even so I could scarcely breathe.

In the past, it had been my custom to pass on food under my seal to the kitchen staff, confident that every member had been thoroughly vetted and understood the dire consequences that would befall them should any dish engender illness. But given the attacks on Borgia as well as the nearness of the wedding, I thought my presence a useful reminder of the need for meticulous care.

The kitchen stretched the entire width of the palazzo but was divided by broad archways into separate sections. At the far end, bread was baked in beehive-shaped brick ovens tended by *panettieri* who wielded their long-handled wooden paddles with grace and agility. Besides the flour that tended always to cling to him, a *panettiere* could be recognized by the smoothness of his arms, the hair having been singed from them by repeatedly reaching deep into the hot ovens to place and retrieve dough.

In the next kitchen over, apprentices worked diligently preparing the vast array of fish and shellfish brought to the palazzo daily from the boats that docked in the nearby port of Ostia. Several were laboring over a pile of squid, carefully removing the ink sacks while others filleted trout, plaice, and whiting, and still more scrubbed the mussels and oysters that would shortly be simmering in a nice broth.

Nearby, in the *cucina di carne,* skinny, sweat-drenched boys turned rotisseries heaped with capons intended for the evening meal. The birds' golden skin dripped fat into the fire below, often sending up bubbles of hot oil that burned the boys even as they were stoically ignored. Above their heads pungent Spanish hams, introduced to Romans several decades before by Uncle Callixtus, the first Borgia pope, hung from rafters as they awaited the carving knife. His Holiness's fondness for the heavily salted flesh of pigs fed solely on acorns and allowed to age several years escaped me. I found the flavor overwhelming and avoided it whenever possible. But then my taste in food has always been very simple, influenced as I am by professional concerns.

I made my way through each of the kitchens in turn, greeted politely by the *maestro della cucina* even as the lesser cooks, apprentices, and kitchen boys scrupulously avoided looking at me. I understood their reluctance, especially considering the rumors about me—that I was *strega,* of course, for how could a young woman endowed with the dark knowledge of the poisoner's art be anything other than a witch? But it did not stop there. The more imaginative claimed that I could kill with a single look—the times I wished that I could! Or that I could judge the guilt or innocence of a person simply by looking into his eyes. Again, if only that were true. Inevitably, there were also whispers about the exact nature of my relationship with Borgia, the role I had played in his ascension to the papacy, and so on. I ignored them as best I could and tended to my duties.

I had finished at last and was sipping chilled lemonade and wiping my brow when Renaldo appeared.

"There you are," he said on a note of exasperation. "I've been looking everywhere for you."

"I can't decide whether I'm working or hiding," I admitted as I lifted the beaded carafe and poured a glass for the steward. Borgia had been incessant in his demands of late, seemingly requiring my presence half a dozen times a day. It had been all I could do to slip away long enough to see to my actual duties.

And that did not even take into account the matter of Cesare, who, unless I was very much mistaken, had moved in with me. Officially, he was still supposed to be in Spoleto, but he had a house in Trastevere not far from where Juan also resided, and there was talk of an apartment in the Vatican being prepared for him adjacent to his father's. Even so, he showed no inclination to go elsewhere. His clothes were all over my chamber, his guards stood duty outside my door, he continued to charm Portia at every turn, and Minerva—shameless hussy—ignored me completely when he was present, preferring to crawl into his lap and have her ears rubbed.

Ah, well, I could understand that urge readily enough.

"I can't say that I blame you," Renaldo said when he had emptied his glass and held it out to be refilled. "These are hardly the best of days."

"God willing," I said, "we will see better. What brings you here?"

"A message came for you from Signore d'Amico." He held out a folded paper.

I broke the seal and read swiftly, only to sigh with disappointment. Luigi was making every possible effort to help me but so far his *portatori* had discovered nothing of use. No one had seen so much as a hint of Morozzi. Nor had Guillaume been able to discover any trace of him, although he did say that the Dominican chapter house was in an uproar over the disappearance of a friar. Whether that had anything to do with Morozzi, he could not say. I was beginning to fear that my foe truly was invisible.

To distract myself, I asked, "What is the mood in the city?" Between spending so many hours at the Curia each day and being occupied with Cesare each night, I had no opportunity to judge the disposition of Rome's citizens.

"Tense," Renaldo said succinctly. "His Holiness has men out scrubbing every inch of wall but they can only do so much." So did he delicately refer to the continuing proliferation of obscene graffiti libeling Borgia as an incestuous father and Lucrezia as his whore. Grace to God, she seemed to have no awareness of what was happening, or so I concluded from our conversations during the rare moments I was able to visit her.

"Has anyone been caught?"

He shook his head. "Not that I have heard. Rumors abound, each wilder than the last. Della Rovere is on the outskirts of Rome. He has raised an army of angels. Borgia has fled and sought refuge among the Moors. Or he has been caught in the arms of an incubus sent straight from Satan." His voice dropped a notch. "Or he is Satan, sent to torment us in the end of days when the pure shall be separated from the sinful."

I rolled my eyes but as much as I would have liked to dismiss all that as the ramblings of the ignorant, I suspected that they were far more. Someone was embarked on a deliberate campaign to paint Borgia as a figure of unrivaled evil, the better to justify his expulsion from the papacy. I had no doubt as to who that was.

"What are the touts saying?" I asked.

Renaldo shrugged. "Around the Campo, odds are five to three that Borgia will survive. But in Trastevere, it's three to two that he'll be gone by autumn."

"Isn't that unusual? I mean, aren't these things typically decided ahead of time?" By which I meant the general understanding that the touts of Rome formed an unofficial guild, in which they did not compete against each other in the matter of setting odds.

"People may just be responding differently to what they are seeing," the steward suggested. "Some of the graffiti has been particularly . . . imaginative."

I did not care to think what could be worse than what I had seen. Moving on quickly, I asked, "Is there any news of the Spanish envoy?"

Don Diego Lopez de Haro had yet to arrive in Rome, but if Luigi's information was correct, and I had no reason to think otherwise, he could not be far off.

Renaldo glanced around to be sure no eager ears lurked nearby. *Sotto voce,* he said, "He is en route but seems to be in no great rush. Perhaps Their Majesties are giving our master time to think things over. That may be working. When His Holiness is not raging against their effrontery, he is considering ways to placate them."

That was as I had feared. What with one thing and another, I had not managed to slip away to speak with Sofia or David. Nor had I heard anything from either of them. Such a state of affairs could not continue. If Borgia did intend to sell out the Jews in return for the support of the Spanish monarchs, something would have to be done to stop him.

Sadly, I was at a loss just then to imagine what that might be.

"Can you do something for me?" I asked Renaldo after we had finished the lemonade. Matters seemed to be well in hand in the kitchens and I had no real reason to think that there was any danger from that corner. It was vital that I get away for a few hours unobserved.

"If His Holiness asks for me, would you tell him I am—" I was what? What excuse would be sufficient to hold off Borgia the Bull when he wanted, nay demanded attention?

"Tell him I am attending to a gynecological matter but will return shortly."

Renaldo turned beet red, so much so that for a moment I feared for his immediate health. In an effort to soothe him, I patted his hand and said, "My thanks, Master d'Marco. I know I can rely on you."

Before he could inform me otherwise, I made my escape. Saint Peter's Square was packed as always, even more so because Vittoro had so many guards stationed about. As always, I averted my gaze from the basilica as I made my way toward the river. My mind was occupied with thoughts of the task Borgia had laid on me. The plain fact was that I had yet to make any progress in the matter of determining how to kill Cardinal della Rovere. The combination of the practical difficulties and my own disinclination was proving a formidable stumbling block. I resolved to work harder on the problem.

I had not gone very far before a prickling at the back of my neck made me turn. The street was crowded with shoppers, tradesmen, wide-eyed visitors, and the like. A faint ripple of movement caught my eye. Not twenty feet away, a man emerged from beneath an arch, stepping out into the light for just a moment. In that fragment of time, I saw him clearly. He was bathed in the soft light of a Roman afternoon, his somber garb in no way detracting from the startling beauty of features that were the classical expression of masculine beauty—straight nose, square chin, high brow, and chiseled cheekbones. His eyes, even at that distance, were large and of the purest blue. His hair was a nimbus of golden curls clinging to his perfectly shaped head. He looked like an angel.

He was, in fact, the devil Morozzi.

You will say that I was tired, preoccupied, worried, and you will be right. But there was not an instant's doubt in my mind as to whom I saw, who had been following me. Morozzi himself did not leave room for any such uncertainty. He stepped a little farther into the street so that I could have a better view of him. As I stood frozen in place, he smiled at me.

I had my knife. Cesare had seen that it was restored to me, cleaned and keenly honed. It nestled in the leather sheath near my heart.

Twenty feet, a handful of steps. He would not expect me to attack him in public, in the midst of a crowd, with no hope of escape. It did not matter. I wanted only to kill, after which I would gladly proclaim to the world why I had done it.

The darkness stirred within me but too slowly, like a poor chained beast hampered by the weight of its own yearning. I took a step through air so strangely thick that I had to push against it as though it were a wall. It occurred to me suddenly that he might be using a charm against me. Not that I believed in such things but with Morozzi all facets of evil seemed possible.

His smile deepened. He watched me a moment longer before he turned back into the archway through which he had come, and vanished.

Scarcely had he done so than my limbs unfroze. I sprang across the intervening distance, heedless of those I shoved aside. Beyond the archway was a wooden door. I thrust it open, startling a young boy who jumped at sight of me. Ignoring him, I raced through the fabric shop, finding myself facing a blank wall on the other side of a narrow lane that led toward the river. Frantically, I looked in both directions but there was no sign of Morozzi. Long moments passed before I finally acknowledged that my adversary had vanished into thin air.

I staggered the rest of the way to the Jewish Quarter without clear memory of getting there. Sofia took one look at me as I entered the shop and hurried to help me into a chair.

"Francesca, what is wrong!"

I tried to speak but my chest was so tight that I could not seem to catch my breath. That good woman pressed a cup of water—she filtered and boiled every drop before allowing anyone to drink it—into my hand. I drank and the tightness eased. After a moment, I was able to speak.

"I cannot believe . . . He was there, in my sight and I did— nothing. Nothing! Merciful God, what is wrong with me?"

Sofia bent down so that she could look at me directly. Her hands grasped my shoulders. "Who, Francesca? Who was there?"

I took a breath, forcing myself to think clearly, but the image of the mad priest smiling at me continued uppermost in my mind, threatening to block out all else. As though throwing off a yoke, I forced it away and concentrated on Sofia. Her face was creased with worry even as her eyes assessed me carefully. She had more knowledge and more good sense than any I knew who posed as physicians and were as likely to do harm as any accidental good. I knew that I could rely on her.

That knowledge eased me further so that finally I was able to answer her. "Morozzi. He was in the street, following me. I saw him clearly. But when I went after him, he vanished as though he had never been."

Sofia continued to regard me steadily. "Morozzi? You saw him but he vanished?"

"Like smoke. He went through an archway that led to a shop. I followed but I couldn't find him. He was gone!"

To my horror, sobs welled up in me. I tried my best to contain them but could not. With a cry, I buried my head in Sofia's shoulder and clung to her.

"I failed! He was right there, I could have killed him and been done with all of this! What is wrong with me that I could not do it?"

Sofia held me tightly until the worst of the storm had passed. Softly, she patted my shoulder and said, "You carry a terrible burden. It is bound to affect you in ways you cannot imagine. Do not berate yourself for what happened. Perhaps it was only an illusion—"

I straightened with a cry wrung from my heart. "No! He was there, I know it. Morozzi is in Rome and he is so emboldened that he showed himself to me in broad daylight. What am I to make of that? What power protects him?"

In the grip of my despair, ancient fears stirred within me. Was it possible that the man who sought the destruction of an entire people was not merely mortal? Did a demonic force move through him? And if so, how then could I ever hope to stop him?

Sofia was having none of that. Looking me squarely in the eye, she said, "You know as well as I that human beings need no special encouragement to do evil. We are all too capable of it entirely on our own. Morozzi is a man, plain and simple. As sure as you and I are both in this room, there is a straightforward explanation for what you saw."

Thanks be to God for her sensible nature. It drew me back from the brink of panic. I took a breath, another, and nodded.

"You are right, of course. I am forgetting, Rome is a warren of underground passages. He must have used one of them."

Sofia nodded. "I will send for David. He will know what to do."

I was sipping tea that Sofia had brewed for me when the young Jewish leader arrived a short time later. He did not come alone. A fresh-faced boy with a mischievous grin scampered at his side. I had not seen him in several months and was struck by how much he had grown, though his chin still looked soft as a baby's bottom.

"Benjamin," I said with unfeigned pleasure. We had become acquainted the previous year when he had tried to pick my pocket on my first visit to the ghetto. Since then, we had become fast friends. "Attending to your studies, I hope?"

"Whenever I can get him to sit still long enough," Sofia said with a smile. She riffled his dark hair. "At least he claims to have given up his former trade, isn't that so, Binyamin?"

Her insistence on using the Hebraic pronunciation of his name wrung a groan from the boy but it vanished as quickly as it had come. "I make more money carrying messages and running errands anyway."

"I'm glad to hear it," I said. With a glance at David, I said softly, "We need to talk."

He nodded and laid a hand on Benjamin's shoulder. "Do us the courtesy of pretending that you don't hear what we have to say, all right?"

The boy shook his head at the folly of adults but went over to the side of the room and slid down against a wall. He drew a cat's cradle from his pocket and made a show of occupying himself with the string.

After I had described my brief encounter with Morozzi in considerably calmer terms than I had managed with Sofia, I said, "Clearly, he is using underground passages to come and go as he pleases. If I could get a better idea of where they lie—"

"They are everywhere," David said. "Rome is crisscrossed with catacombs, buried streets, tunnels, sewers, everything imaginable. No one knows the full extent of them."

"But Morozzi must have some considerable knowledge," I persisted. "Otherwise, he would not be relying on them. If he knows that much, someone else must as well."

"We can make inquiries," Sofia offered.

"Please do so quickly. We have little time. An envoy is coming from the Spanish monarchs to tell Borgia that in return for their support he must withdraw his from you."

"So we have heard," David said quietly.

I was not surprised. Although thousands of Jews had been forced to flee Iberia the previous year, others managed to stay on by declaring themselves *conversi,* converts to the "one true faith." Such men and women lived under a pall of suspicion but so long as they gave no evidence of backsliding, Their Most Catholic Majesties had to tolerate their presence or risk discouraging all conversions to Christianity.

"Don Diego Lopez de Haro," David went on, "is expected to reach Rome in ten days. He intends to enter into negotiations with Borgia regarding several matters, of which we are regrettably one. However, the primary purpose of his visit is to reconcile His Holiness with the King of Naples."

"Reconcile how?" I asked. This was crucial. That Borgia sought an end to his troubles with Naples was unquestioned, but there was only so far he would—or could—go. He was counting on the Spanish monarchs, once sufficiently bought, to devise a solution he could accept.

"By convincing Borgia that his interests do not lie with Naples's enemies, namely the Sforzas."

The family to which His Holiness, in recognition of his debt to them, was about to give his daughter.

"The Spanish want to stop the wedding," I said. It was an appalling thought, raising the specter as it did that by so doing, Borgia would not only be stripped of a vital ally just as the trouble with della Rovere was heating up but that in the process of disappointing the Sforzas, he would acquire them as a powerful enemy.

Carefully, I said, "His Holiness expects a more helpful approach from Their Most Catholic Majesties in return for his very generous gift of whatever it is that the great Colombo has found."

David shrugged. "He can expect whatever he likes but the plain truth is that, now that they've gotten a look at him as pope, the Spaniards are appalled by Borgia. They don't expect the Vicar of Christ to be a saint but he goes too far even for them."

"Are you saying they want to see him deposed?" If that was true, worse was piling on top of bad. When that happens, catastrophic usually isn't far off.

"Not necessarily," David said. "For all their religious posturing, Ferdinand and Isabella want what will best serve their own power. A weakened Borgia in thrall to Spain for his very survival would suit them well enough."

Sofia had been listening with care to everything we said. Now she broke in. "We cannot allow that to happen! As Borgia goes, so do we."

"I despise the man," David said. He had never been one to stand on ceremony but now anger fueled his candor. "However, I don't see that we have any choice. The merchants and rabbis can yabber over this all they want, trying to figure out where to throw their money, but we have to act."

"If Borgia's position could be strengthened," I said. "If he was not under threat from Morozzi and through him from Savonarola—" And if the threat from della Rovere could also be removed. I would not speak of what His Holiness had charged me to do but it was uppermost in my mind. Della Rovere's death could resolve a great deal, so long as it was not laid at Borgia's door.

"We have less than a month to the wedding," David said. "If Morozzi and Il Frateschi aren't defanged by then, I fear the worst."

"We must find where they are hiding," I said.

From the corner of my eye, I saw Benjamin look up. He carefully removed the cat's cradle from around his fingers, tucked it back in his pocket, and stood.

"I think I know a way," he said.

14

The who?" I asked. In the quiet of Sofia's apothecary shop, empty of customers at the hour between late afternoon and the first stirring of evening, I thought I must surely have heard Benjamin wrong.

"The king of the *contrabbandieri*," he said in a tone that suggested my ignorance of so august a personage was difficult to credit. "You must have heard of him?"

We adults glanced at one another with mingled uncertainty and incredulity.

"I don't think so," I said finally.

"Well, perhaps that is not so strange," Benjamin said, brushing off the lapse with a wave of his hand. "A man in his position has to be careful who he trusts."

"What exactly is his position?" David asked.

"He is king of the smugglers, or at least a lot of them. It's like a guild, of sorts. Alfonso the First—that's his name—had the idea of starting it so that they weren't all competing and fighting with each other. At first there was a lot of skepticism but Alfonso is clever; he didn't try to force anyone but instead let them come to their own conclusions when they saw for themselves that he treats everybody fairly. Now most of them wouldn't want to go back to the old ways, even if some still grumble from time to time."

Now that I thought about it, I supposed that made sense. With excise taxes high and every lordling eager to take advantage of them, it is no wonder that enterprising individuals find ways to buy and sell goods more economically. Indeed, the more taxes and other difficulties mount, the more the business of the city is forced underground. And in Rome, it is literally underground, as goods of every description come and go through the very passages I wished to discover.

Even so I remained hesitant. "How is it you know of him?"

Benjamin's grin split his face from one side to the other. "Because he used to be one of us—a pickpocket, I mean. We're his *fratelli*. He still trusts us more than anybody else."

He—whoever he was—might also judge that children were inherently more trustworthy than adults and in that regard, I could not disagree with him. On the other hand, I was concerned that Benjamin remained a part of the world I thought he had left.

So, apparently, was Sofia, for she said, "Don't you mean that you used to know this person, Binyamin?"

To give the boy credit, he had an explanation ready to hand. "If I worried that everybody I do errands for is obeying every law, there are two nuns in Santa Maria Maggiore who I might be able to work for. And you, too, of course. That's about it."

He was exaggerating—slightly, but I took his point. Besides, this was no time to stand on niceties.

147

"I should meet this man," I said.

Immediately, David said, "I'm going with you."

"He might not like that," Benjamin cautioned. "It would be better if Donna Francesca and I went alone."

I saw the boy's point—a child and a woman were bound to appear less threatening than would a man of David's stature and manner. But at the same time I was relieved when he rejected the idea.

"Neither one of you is going alone," he said. "If the great Alfonso has a problem with that, he can take it up with me."

I was more concerned about what the smuggler king would think of Benjamin for daring to bring strangers into his domain. Out of respect for the boy's pride, I did not say so but I resolved to make sure that he came to no harm.

Taking leave of Sofia, who urged us to have every care, we made our way to the Piazza di Santa Maria in front of the ancient church dedicated to the Virgin, although some say far more ancient deities are also worshiped there. The usual crowd of women was gathered around the old octagonal fountain, drawing water and, far more important, exchanging gossip. They glanced at us as we passed. I averted my face and was relieved when no gust of chatter erupted behind us. In those days, there were still places that I could go unrecognized, although increasingly they were rare. Idle apprentices—lingering unnecessarily over errands set them by their masters—passed the time of day leaning against the walls of the stone houses framing the square and watching the girls go by. A few young noblemen, always on the outlook for trouble, ambled through. The silliest of them strutted with their hips turned out to emphasize the size of their genitals displayed beneath snug particolored hose and short doublets. More than a few made use of the horsehair wadding that had become all the rage among a certain class of males. Truly, it was a wonder they could walk without continually bumping into whatever happened to be in front of them.

As we crossed the piazza, David found a moment to put a private word in my ear. "Take no unnecessary chances with this fellow. I have never heard of him, whoever he really is, and there are others we can turn to for help."

Why it is that seemingly everyone I know believes that I rush into danger without a second thought bewilders me. Rather than argue about it, I assured David that I would be cautious. We proceeded down a narrow lane that constricted further into an alley before seeming to end at a blank wall draped in ivy.

"Are you sure this is the way?" I asked.

Benjamin grinned at me over his shoulder, reached under a swath of the ivy, and lifted it to one side. Beyond I glimpsed a black opening just large enough for a single person at a time to enter.

"There are many entrances to the underground," he said as we followed him within. From the sack that dangled at his waist, Benjamin drew a flint, iron pyrites, and a small bundle of rushes set in a steel lamp to which he set a spark with such ease as to make me wonder exactly how often he ventured into the stygian depths.

"You can find them all over Rome but you have to know where to look."

I nodded but did not speak. The narrowness of the passage and the weight of the darkness relieved only by the faint glow of the rushes pressed in on me. I am not one of those unfortunates susceptible to acute unease in small places but even so I was relieved when I saw, before we had gone very far, a faint glow up ahead.

It proved to come from a shaft cut toward the surface, admitting the slanting light of late afternoon. We encountered other such openings as we continued on. I felt a slight breeze stirring air that would otherwise have been stale at best and possibly too spent to sustain life.

"It's not much farther," Benjamin said.

True to his word, we came shortly to a wider passage lit on both sides by torches set in brackets along the walls. At its end, the stone and brick walls widened out into a broad chamber that, at first glance, appeared to be filled with a haphazard jumble of crates, barrels, chests, and objects of indeterminate shape. Only as my eyes adjusted to the light did I realize that a cluster of people were gathered at the far end around a raised platform.

"Come on then," Benjamin said. "But both of you let me do the talking, all right?"

We assured him that we would as I tried to comprehend my surroundings. The walls bore the faint tracings of murals in which men and women in the garb of the old Romans gazed out at us with varying degrees of solemnity and amusement. The floor showed a scattering of mosaic tiles that had covered it in the distant past. The air smelled of old stone, dust, earth, and wood smoke. I concluded that I was in a villa long since covered over by the layers of the city built above it and reoccupied by those with reason to stay out of sight.

Benjamin urged us forward toward the dais. The two dozen or so people gathered there were all young, some no more than children, and garbed in a motley collection of garments that paired the brocade waistcoat of a nobleman with the miter of a bishop and the leather jerkin of a soldier. Some of the boys had shaved their heads, giving them the look of fierce hatchlings. A few sported star- and crescent-shaped brandings on their cheeks that I knew to be the marks of Roman gangs. The girls, some very young, had attached themselves to these boys, several of who had gathered two or three to his side while others had to be content with one. All gazed at me with frank suspicion bordering on hostility.

Alfonso the First, *il re dei contrabbandieri,* lounged at the center of all this, on an ornately carved chair covered with gilt such as Borgia himself would not have despised. He was little taller than myself with close-cropped hair, gangly limbs, and raw-boned features. I made his age to be about seventeen or eighteen years, testament to the hard life of Rome's poor in which fewer than half saw twenty. Added to that the dangers of a smuggler's existence and I was not surprised that older rivals had fallen by the wayside.

Two girls of no more than fifteen years stood to either side of him, leaning close to display their pippin-sized bosoms. Each had a hand on one of his thighs. They were both blond and at first look appeared to be at least sisters, if not twins.

Nothing in the appearance of *il re* explained his rise to power over the others, save for the hard gleam in his eyes that bespoke at once intelligence and will.

"Who's this then?" he demanded, his voice slightly high and strident but lacking nothing in authority.

"Friends, *padrone,*" Benjamin said with no sign of the fear he must have been feeling, for I certainly was. We were surrounded by brigands, all no doubt willing to do their chieftain's bidding in an instant. No one in the world above knew where we had gone. If we did not return, our fate would become one more of those enduring mysteries in Rome, trotted out from time to time over the years and mused about before being forgotten again.

Bowing his head with every indication of true deference, Benjamin approached the throne.

"They have come to ask for your help, if you would be so gracious as to give them audience?"

"You mean they've come to try to buy it," the smuggler king said. His acolytes laughed though none smiled.

I shot a quick glance at David, who did not appear amused but who was, grace to God, holding himself in check.

Alfonso studied us for a moment before affording us a single nod. I took that as an indication that I could speak. Choosing caution as the wisest course, I addressed him as I would Borgia when he was in a middling good mood but still required careful handling.

"It is true, sir, that we do not expect something for nothing. However, we are hoping to convince you that our interests align with yours in a matter of great importance."

Whether because I had spoken instead of David—it is always assumed that a man will take the lead—or whether *il re* was simply innately cautious, he took a moment to think this over. At length, he said, "What matter?"

"We are hunting a man lately come to Rome. We believe he is using the underground passageways to move around the city undetected. This man is highly dangerous. He must be stopped."

"He sounds like some kind of criminal," Alfonso said, to appreciative guffaws.

"Would that he were. He is, in fact, a madman who puts us all at peril."

At the mention of madness, the mood sobered. Madness, as every sensible person presumes to know, is a sign of the Devil's possession. The afflicted either have committed some act so sinful as to open the way for evil to possess their souls or they have fallen to such misfortune by failing to follow the dictates of Holy Mother Church— obeying her priests, tithing to her, and so on. The idea that madness might be a sickness like others of the body is entertained by only a very small circle of scholars, namely those who have read the texts of

Arab physicians and others who have dissected the brain and speculated as to its function.

I had no particular opinion one way or the other as to what drove Morozzi to his vile actions. My interest extended no further than putting an end to them by killing him.

The smuggler king's eyes narrowed. "What danger does he pose to me?"

I was reluctant to answer within hearing of his followers. Instead, I inclined my head and asked, "May I approach?"

He hesitated, no doubt suspicious of my intent. But I was, after all, only a young woman whose garb suggested some degree of standing and affluence but who certainly gave no cause for alarm.

With a flick of his hand, he dismissed the blondes and in the same motion beckoned me to his side. I bent closer and dropped my voice so that only he could hear me.

"What do you pay Borgia, *signore,* two parts in ten?"

He frowned, possibly at the ease with which I spoke of His Holiness, Christ's Vicar on Earth, and his propensity for having a finger in every pie. But likely also because I seemed better informed than my appearance would account for.

"Less than that."

I made a show of being impressed though I doubted he was telling the truth. Since becoming pope, Borgia had tightened his hold on every aspect of life in Rome. Nobody could do business without paying him what he regarded as his due, not even the wiliest of smugglers.

"What do you think his successor will demand?"

"You're talking about that prig, della Rovere. Word has it he's starting to take religion seriously."

"We can't have that, but forget him. What about Savonarola?"

Alfonso looked at me in surprise. So close to him, I could see the pockmarks of childhood disease on his face and note that one eye squinted while the other appeared healthy.

"That hound who's always yapping about purifying the world?"

I nodded. "The man we seek is working for him. If he succeeds, he will bring Savonarola's cause to Rome, perhaps even bring him."

He sucked in his breath and leaned forward. "Who are you?"

"My name is Francesca Giordano."

Il re dei contrabbandieri paled. He pressed himself into the high back of his chair and stared at me in disbelief.

"You can't be her. She's old and has warts."

"Because she is *strega*? Ask yourself, why would any self-respecting witch go about looking old and with warts?"

Il re contemplated this without ever taking his eyes from me. Slowly, he nodded.

I smiled and made my offer. "I would like to be your friend."

We all want to have friends, the more useful the better, and the smuggler king was no exception. He needed only a scant moment to consider his options. Why risk the enmity of a powerful witch who has the ear of the Pope when you can have her on your side?

"And I wish to be yours, Donna Francesca. Tell me more of this man who troubles us both."

When I had done so, including providing a detailed description of Morozzi and warning that he might be accompanied by members of Il Frateschi, we took our leave with promises that I would hear as soon as anything was discovered. Satisfied that searchers were looking high and low for the mad priest, I could only hope that word would come from some source before too long.

The soft light of evening clung to the city as we emerged onto the surface once again. David insisted on seeing me home and I accepted gratefully. The attacks on the villa and my residence had heightened my sense of danger. I took some comfort from the knife in its leather sheath tucked under my gown but I was also glad of his company, and Benjamin's as well, of course.

At that hour, most citizens of Rome were hurrying to finish their business and retire for the night. Shopkeepers were closing up, lowering large wooden shutters down over windows that fronted onto the street. Light shone in the windows above where families would be gathering soon for supper. The last retainers of the mighty were making their way back to their masters' palazzos, their horses' hooves clattering over the cobblestones. The pushcart men were trundling off accompanied by the squeak of wooden wheels. Pigeons sought their roosts while the gulls bold enough to venture inland from the port of Ostia made one last circle of the sky before departing for open water. In another hour or so, after darkness descended, the denizens of the night would begin to emerge—the pimps and whores, cudgel men and tricksters, the purveyors of opium for those who could afford it and wine that had scant acquaintance with a grape for those who could not. All those and more would claim the night city for their own. So, too, would come the rats, which I particularly abhorred.

At the corner of my street, I bade farewell to my companions but not before I said, "We will find Morozzi, one way or another. I am certain of it."

David mustered a smile but it faded quickly. He put an arm around Benjamin's shoulder, a simple gesture of protection and comfort such as I knew he would offer, if only he could, to all the children threatened by fanatics like Morozzi and Savonarola but equally at risk from the della Roveres of this world who blindly assume that whatever is good for them serves the greater good. Beside them, Borgia seemed almost benign.

"Let it be soon," he said.

I watched them go before turning into my street. Portia was still at her post. She raised an eyebrow at sight of me.

"Think you're smart to get him riled up, do you?"

I pretended not to understand her but she was having none of that. "How you expect to keep such a man when you're off doing who-knows-what is beyond me."

Did I expect to keep Cesare? The question took me by surprise. We had known each other for so long and had fallen into being lovers so readily that I gave scant thought to what lay ahead. Unlike silly girls who sigh over *le canzoni di amore,* I had no interest in such things. How could one such as I when love is difficult enough, not to say impossible, for normal people to achieve?

But there was another reason why I gave no thought to what future I might have with Cesare. I gave little thought to any sort of future at all. My plans extended no further than the day, hopefully soon, when I would kill Morozzi. Of what came after that, if anything, I had no notion.

On that thought, I climbed the steps to my rooms and opened the door to find the son of Jove glaring at me.

C esare stood with his hands on his hips and an unholy look
    in his eyes.

"You haven't harmed it, have you? Tell me you haven't.
There's no need for that. I like children, I have two that I know of
and I take good care of them as well as their mothers. You shouldn't
think that I would do otherwise with you. On the contrary, I—"

By which I gleaned that Renaldo had offered up the feckless explanation for my absence that I had so impulsively suggested and that
Cesare, hearing of it, had leaped to entirely the wrong conclusion.

Even so, I confess to being touched. Exasperated, to be sure, but
also moved in a way I could not quite grasp.

"There is no child." I entered and closed the door behind me. "And
no, I don't mean now; there never was. I told Renaldo to tell your
father what I did so that His Holiness wouldn't fuss about my being
away for a few hours. It never occurred to me that you would hear
and be concerned."

"You're not pregnant?" He managed to look both relieved and chagrined at the same time.

"I take precautions."

"That is against God's will."

"For Heaven's sake, Cesare, do you hear yourself?"

I was too weary to debate the matter, thinking only of a bath, something to eat, and bed. But I had not counted on my dark lover. Whether it was the thought of progeny or some other impulse that had stirred him to thoughtfulness, he had filled my private chamber with roses and caused a table covered in white linen to appear laden with what he knew to be my favorite delicacies.

What could I do but throw off my weariness and give myself to the fleeting moment? We dined after a fashion as Cesare insisted on feeding me choice tidbits rather than allow me to feed myself. After a bit more of a hearty Umbrian red than sense dictated, I did the same until his insistence on licking every crumb from my fingertips before sucking each clean proved too distracting.

You may find it unlikely that one born to so great a life of privilege would be determined to make more of himself, but Cesare was a great believer in the ability, not to say the duty of a man to forge his own destiny. To that end, he had examined his nature and concluded that while there was much to be admired, he was lacking in one particular virtue:

Patience.

His choice to cultivate it in passion's bower may seem unorthodox but it worked—too damn well.

"Enough!" I cried at last. For emphasis, I dug my fingers into his broad shoulders.

He raised his head from between my thighs and grinned wolfishly. "Just a little more."

Teetering on the precipice, held there by his too-talented tongue and his uncanny knowledge of my body? A puppet pulled this way and that at his pleasure. I didn't think so.

My hips bucked, trying to throw him off. Never mind my shortcomings as a horsewoman. If I could get him on his back, he would be well and thoroughly mounted before he could draw breath. "I'll do the same to you if you don't—"

"Don't what, Francesca?"

That easily, he slid up the length of my body and into me. My gasp turned to a groan as I tightened around him. Whatever fancy I had entertained of tormenting him in turn vanished as quickly as it had come.

"Now," I urged, and clasped him fiercely.

"Restraint is its own reward," he murmured, but that did not stop him from moving just as I longed for him to, so smooth and sleek, devilishly good for all that he was still in some respects a boy. A strange consortium of sensation overcame me: pleasure, of course, shattering in its intensity but hard on it a wave of tenderness that caused me to wrap my arms around him and hold him close, as though I might shelter him from all the perils beyond our private world.

It was a foolish notion to be sure for Cesare himself represented just such peril to any foolish enough to cross swords with him. Yet in the aftermath of release that left my bones limp, I cradled him and smoothed the dampened curls from the pale nape of his neck, that hidden place where the sun scarcely ever reached and he remained spotless as a babe.

Some time later—pale dawn was edging up over the roofs of the buildings I could see out the open windows of my chamber—I stirred in Cesare's arms. He muttered something I could not make out and turned over, dragging the covers with him. I extricated myself and sat up. My body was pleasantly quiescent but my mind, that was another matter entirely. It was restless and in need of occupation.

I saw to my ablutions, fed Minerva, and wandered out to the table where I kept my apparatus, including an array of glassware I used in my experiments and the hourglass by which I timed them. Nearby were the shelves holding my books, some of recent vintage but many handwritten manuscripts passed down to me by my late father.

My mind, ever restless, turned toward the matter of how to kill della Rovere. The task remained a tantalizing puzzle. As Vittoro had suggested, an assassin with no thought to his—or her—survival could kill anyone. But since that did not describe me except in the matter of Morozzi, I had to find another way.

How to penetrate the layers of security around the Cardinal formed by his guards and his own poisoner? How to assure that he ate, drank, or touched something that would prove fatal? How to do all that without directly pointing the finger of guilt at Borgia and thereby undoing any good that might come from the Cardinal's demise? Or, of concern only to my own conscience, unnecessarily endangering others?

I confess, it was a problem to which I could find no ready solution. All the tried and true methods of poisoning rely on some degree of proximity to the victim, some opportunity to slip a lethal powder or potion past the most vigilant protection. But, on the other hand, poisoning is used to instill fear and ultimately obedience. Generally, whoever has ordered the victim dispatched wants to be known or at least suspected, if only to reap those rewards.

Not so in this case. Borgia could not afford to give the French king any cause for war. If della Rovere died, His Holiness had to be able to decry the tragic loss of a respected prelate, admittedly with whom he had disputes but who, in the spirit of Christian charity, was mourned all the same.

How then might it be done? Any poisoner worthy of the name can spot tainted food or drink. Contact poison is more difficult to discern but with due care it, too, can be discovered. What could I possibly slip into della Rovere's household undetected with reasonable expectation that it would reach him before it killed someone else, thereby alerting him to the danger?

Only one answer seemed possible. I had to find a poison that did not work at once. One that required an accumulation of exposure to have its effect. Arsenic would do for that except that it would take far too long. I had to find another way.

I was attempting to do so when a sound from the door to the salon caused me to turn. Cesare stood there, as he had arisen from bed, naked and in the usual state of arousal that came on him in the mornings.

"What are you thinking about?" he asked, idly scratching his chest.

"You, of course," I replied, and went to him.

An hour later, he was off to attend on his father. I stayed behind to collect myself, which mainly involved having a bath while I considered what needed to be done next. A walk always being useful in clearing the head, I set out and shortly found myself in the Campo dei Fiori near Rocco's shop.

Lest you think ill of me for going from my lover's embrace to the man I might have married, let me remind you that the fate of men and nations hung in the balance. Besides, I had never claimed to be other than contrary when it comes to affairs of the heart.

With Nando staying at Vittoro's, where he was fussed over by

Felicia, the front of the shop was empty. I found Rocco in the yard behind the building. He was working bare-chested in the morning sun, bent over a table on which he had set a small grinding wheel propelled by a foot pedal. I had a few moments to observe him unnoticed. The sun had laid a patina of gold over his skin, reddening along the curve of his broad shoulders. His hair was tied back and secured by a leather thong to keep it out of his eyes. He worked steadily and with great concentration. Even seated, moving only his hands, he looked the image of grace.

I cleared my throat. At once he stopped, letting the wheel run down, and turning, saw me. Only then did I notice that he had a cloth pulled up over his nose and mouth.

He lowered it and smiled. "I was just thinking about you."

Heaven help me, I blushed like a girl and for a moment was at a loss for words.

Rocco stood up and dusted off his hands. "Guillaume has caught a whiff of something but he isn't sure what it is."

"Has he?" Of course, I wanted the particulars, but first I needed a moment to recover what dignity I possessed. To that end, I made a show of interest in his occupation.

"What are you doing there?" I asked, indicating the worktable.

"I'm learning to grind lenses. There's an increasing demand for them and I thought they'd make a good sideline. They are glass, after all, so I thought with a little effort I should be able to manage them."

"And are you?"

He shrugged. "I'm getting better. Diamond powder seems to give the best polish by far."

"Is that what you're using? It sounds expensive."

"It is," he agreed, "but the results can't be equaled by any other method. With practice, I should be able to turn out lenses you wouldn't mind using."

"I'll look forward to trying them. Now tell me, what does Guillaume say?"

We walked together into the relative coolness of the shop, where Rocco poured us both goblets of chilled water. Like Sofia, he never drank anything that had not been boiled and strained first. It was all well and good that the ancient Aqua Virgo aqueduct had been restored to operation some forty years before by Pope Nicholas V. The water it carried into Trevi was sold throughout the city by men and boys balancing immense barrels on barrows that creaked and squeaked at all hours of the day and night. But most people still had to depend on cisterns that were full or dry at the whim of the rains, or wells that could never be counted on not to bring up clay in place of water. For the poor, there was only the Tiber, a disgusting broth of every imaginable kind of filth that made my stomach twist even to think of drinking.

"Guillaume reports dissension among the Dominicans," Rocco said. "A monk who went missing some time ago was fished out of the Tiber, dead with his eyes and tongue cut out. No one seems to have any idea of what happened to him but some of the friars are saying that the actions of Il Frateschi have created a sinful atmosphere in which any evil thing could occur."

"They blame the Brotherhood for the graffiti?"

"They do. Guillaume says that even many of those who dislike Borgia do not believe that any good can come of such vileness."

"I am glad to hear it. Perhaps one or more of them can be persuaded to help us."

"Guillaume hopes the same but he must choose his moment carefully. Push too hard and they are likely to close ranks."

"He will do his best, I'm sure."

"As will we all, but—"

He hesitated and I could see that he was wrestling with himself. "Francesca, about yesterday—"

About Cesare, I feared he would say next. About why Borgia's eldest son had taken such umbrage because Rocco and I embraced.

"You were foolish to put yourself in danger," I said, preferring as always to take the offensive. "You could have been seriously hurt or worse."

"How was I to know that spoiled popinjay would come strutting over and—"

"Forget about him, he doesn't matter." At least I did not want him to, not where Rocco was concerned. "Everyone around Borgia is on edge right now."

"If that's all it is—"

"What more could it be? What are you saying?"

I was a fool to press the matter, especially since I had so recent a reminder that Rocco was not a man to back down in the face of a challenge. He looked at me squarely.

"You are a free woman, Francesca, beholden to nothing save your father's memory. I understand that."

"But—?"

"There is no 'but.' I am in no position to judge you or anything you do."

"Yet you think I could be judged were you not so magnanimous as to forgo the exercise?"

"We are all judged. You, me, every last one of us whether we want to acknowledge that or not. God judges every moment of our lives."

"How loving of Him. Perhaps He would do better to help instead." I held up a hand, cutting off whatever Rocco might have said in response to my latest bit of blasphemy. "And don't talk to me again of free will. Nothing is free that comes at the cost of being constantly weighed in the balance and found wanting."

"Who finds you wanting? I do not."

But I did; every day with every breath I was not the woman I longed to be. The woman who had the right to take the hand of the good man who stood there, refusing to berate me for what he surely must suspect was the truth about my relationship with Cesare. Who, instead, only looked at me sadly.

"Let us not argue, Francesca. As you said, everyone is on edge. Giovanni was a good man who loved you dearly. Grieve for him, by all means. Bring his killer to justice, if you can. But leave vengeance to God. The weight of it is too great to be borne by any man or woman."

"You see so clearly," I said, not without a hint of bitterness. I could argue that Rocco, good man that he was, stood in the light and was blinded by it. Whereas I . . . I had to sharpen my every instinct in order to survive in the dark.

But for all that, I could not bring myself to be at odds with him. Instead, I touched his arm, a gesture of reconciliation, and received a quick smile in return that did not reach his eyes.

We spoke a little while longer, cordial words, nothing important. I walked away from the shop knowing that both of us meant well but only the sadder because of it.

In the way of my mind, before I had gone very far my thoughts veered in a new direction. Or perhaps I should say in a very old one. Inexplicably, or so it seemed at first, I found myself thinking of Pliny, not the young one who left us that riveting account of the destruction of Pompeii but Pliny the Elder, whose death beneath Vesuvius his nephew witnessed from the safety of the sea.

The elder Pliny was a great one for cataloguing everything and sundry, compiling it all into his *Naturalis Historia,* that vast encyclopedia upon which we remain far too dependent even now. He is best known to those of my ilk for his claim that a diamond, placed in a goblet or other container to which poison has been added, will neutralize the deadly effects. Believing him, some have gone so far as to swallow diamonds whole in an effort to protect themselves.

My father had been so impressed by the breadth of Pliny's wisdom that he had actually tested this claim, only to discover that it had no apparent merit.

I could not have told you why I fled from thoughts of Rocco to those of a long-dead Roman and his fascination with diamonds. Or why, as I went about my business the rest of that day, I kept returning to the image of Rocco bent over his worktable, using pulverized diamond to grind down the tiniest imperfections in glass.

It was only late that night when I lay alone save for Minerva—Cesare having been sent by his father on an errand to Siena, where Borgia kept some of his money rather than entrust it to the Medicis—that my seemingly random thoughts began to coalesce into a possibility. Once grasped, it caused me to rise from my bed, wrap a shawl around my shoulders, and sit the remainder of the night in the window seat looking out over the slumbering city where so many plots were hatched and so many deaths plotted, all in the name of Christo et Ecclesiae.

16

nother week passed, during which I managed to visit
Lucrezia frequently enough to allay my fears about her
mood. She was calmer than after the upset brought on by
Cesare's cruel letter and she no longer seemed to feel any need to
strike out at him in turn. This was explained the third time I called,
when I found her in the garden feeding crumbs to the pet finches
kept in wicker cages.

"He says he only spoke out against the marriage because he does
not believe our father has any intention of allowing it to endure. Cesare
thinks Papa is only upholding his promise to the Sforzas in order to
keep them on his side long enough for him to come to an arrangement
with Spain and Naples, after which he will no longer need them."

Although I doubted that Cesare had been so temperate in his
explanation, I saw the sense of what she said. Borgia was capable of
using his young daughter as ruthlessly as he used his sons, and he
certainly had no illusions about the sanctity of marriage.

I stayed a while with her, nibbling on strawberries and listening to her talk of her intended. Privately, I thought she was building up the Sforza by-blow to such a degree that he could not possibly meet her expectations. But perhaps time would prove me wrong.

"He will be here two days before the wedding," she told me. "Papa is planning a grand reception, even a special Papal Mass at Saint Peter's, the only place big enough to hold all the guests. I will be allowed to see him but only from a distance."

"I am sure you will not be disappointed." Despite my doubts, I still hoped for the best.

She was very lonely just then, having little use for her ladies, who she knew were no more than spies for their own families. La Bella visited her as often as she could but His Holiness's mistress was pregnant again and said to be having a difficult time. I lingered longer than I should have because of that, not leaving her even as the afternoon aged.

To be fair, I had another reason for remaining sequestered with Lucrezia. The time had come to tell Borgia that I might have found a method for killing della Rovere. I was reluctant to do so for many reasons, not the least being my continued concern that any attack against the Cardinal would not be limited to him alone but would also kill those unfortunate enough to be near him when it came. Of course, those could be the French emissaries, whose loss might only serve to convince their king that God did not favor his enterprise. But what of others—chance guests, hapless servants, and the like? So far as I knew, della Rovere had no mistress at the moment; he was making that great a show of his propriety to contrast himself to Borgia. But there were always women coming and going through secret doors and hidden passageways. Boys as well, but let us not dwell on that. My point is that I was far from reconciled to killing della Rovere and I most certainly saw no reason to kill anyone else.

So I delayed, refining my plans, considering this and that until finally time ran out. Borgia sent for me, going so far as to dispatch a messenger to Lucrezia's apartments, where he found us playing cards in the garden fanned by blackamoors in satin pantaloons and shaded by broad awnings.

"I have to go," I said, rising with reluctance. Fortunately, I was not unprepared for the summons, having been anticipating it for several days.

She must have sensed my mood for she caught my hand and gave me a smile that showed a flash of her former mischievousness, before she donned the sober mantle of wife-in-waiting.

"Come back and we will have sorbet," she said. "Lemon, if you like, or plum. I know you like that."

I assured her that I would and set off for the Vatican Palace. Shortly, I was shown into Borgia's inner office. His Holiness was seated behind the wide sweep of his desk. He was not alone. Once again, Juan was with him. I wondered if they were discussing the grand marriage rumored to be in the works. Betting was running about evenly between a Spanish or a French bride for Borgia's second son. The choice could determine whether we had war or peace. I would have withdrawn and waited in the antechamber for a more propitious moment but His Holiness beckoned me forward.

"There you are, Francesca. I was beginning to wonder if perhaps you'd gone off for a little holiday somewhere."

I did not make the mistake of taking him seriously, being all too aware that my employer kept himself well apprised of my movements. But I did stand patiently while he pretended to survey me.

When he appeared satisfied that his point was made, I said, "I have been seeing to my duties, Holiness."

He waved a hand, as though dismissing any suggestion otherwise. "Oh, I'm certain you have been, but to what result?"

"May I point out that you remain in the peak of health?"

"Thanks to you, is that what you mean? Well, I suppose there's something to that, but it's not enough. I thought I'd made that clear."

"So you did, Holiness."

I glanced at Juan, who was making no effort to hide his distaste, although whether that was because of my occupation or because the brother he loathed and had threatened to kill shared my bed, I could not say.

"If we might speak alone, Holiness?"

Borgia's gaze narrowed as he assessed my request. "Alone?"

"If you please."

Juan appeared about to protest but before he could do so, his father waved a hand toward the door. "Give us a few minutes."

The duke reddened and glared at me with what I can only describe as hatred. If I had not already had an enemy in that quarter, I acquired him then.

"As you wish, Father," he said, and took himself off stiffly, making a show of closing the gilded door hard behind him.

When he was gone, I said, "I have been giving the matter that you laid before me considerable thought and I think I have something that will interest you."

I withdrew a small pouch from a pocket of my overdress. Having approached his desk, I unfolded a black cloth about a foot square, spread it out, and poured the contents of the pouch onto it.

Borgia leaned forward and studied what I offered. He frowned. "It looks like salt."

"It is salt, of the finest quality, taken from your personal supply." I laid a second black cloth on the desk and set on it a small packet that I unwound carefully. "Now, if you would be so good as to look at this."

"More salt," Borgia said after a moment.

I shook my head. "Not so. This is pulverized diamond. It is very expensive; I had to borrow it from a friend." I had visited Rocco again a few days before, asking for the loan of the diamond powder. He had graciously assented despite my failure to offer any explanation for why I wanted it.

"If you look through this lens," I said, offering it to Borgia, "you will see that while the two appear virtually identical, they are in fact very different. The powdered diamond contains many more sharp edges that cannot be seen by the unaided eye."

"What is the point of all this?" Borgia asked even as he did as I bid.

"Diamond in this form is used to grind and polish. In effect, it lacerates surfaces very finely. It has occurred to me that it might be possible to mix a quantity of diamond powder with finely ground salt and have the presence of the diamond escape undetected. Once ingested, the diamond would come into close contact with the soft tissues of the gut where, I believe, it would do considerable harm."

"I thought it was understood that diamond protects against poison. Indeed, I've wondered why you didn't advise me to use it."

"Because I have a care for your health," I said. "It is true that there are those who swallow diamonds whole and pass them without difficulty, but there is always a risk that they will lodge in the lower body. When that happens, the result is acute pain until the object finally comes loose. On the other hand, there is no evidence whatsoever that diamond protects against poison, despite what Pliny claimed. My father tested the proposition thoroughly enough to be convinced of that."

"All right," Borgia said slowly. "You say that even finely ground, diamond will cut enough to do real harm. Is that it?"

I nodded. "The smallest particle retains all the characteristics of its source but can be multiplied thousands of times over. Additionally, it can be mixed with the finest grind of salt in such a way as to mask its presence. Then it would only be a matter of getting that salt to Savone, where, because of its quality, it would be reserved for della Rovere's table."

"The Cardinal is making a great show of his personal piety. When he dines in public, he eats very little."

That could put a crimp in my plans but I sensed a qualification in Borgia's wording.

"In public?"

"Indeed. In private, he remains quite the gourmand. Not really the best for him given that his bowels are unreliable."

"You are saying that when he eats, he is alone?"

The Pope shrugged as though it were of no import, when I was certain he knew otherwise. So did he toy with what passed for my conscience.

"As I said, he is making a show of his piety."

"All the better. We would have only to wait for him to ingest a sufficient quantity."

"How long?"

"I don't know. It depends on how much he takes. But if he uses it regularly, say several times a day, and there is enough diamond present in the mixture, I believe the effect would be fairly quick."

"The moment he is ill, suspicions will be raised that he is being poisoned."

"Of course," I agreed. "Suspicion of poison is raised whenever an eminent person dies in any way other than falling off his horse or being run through with a blade, and even then it has to happen in front of a multitude of witnesses to be believed. But it is well known that della Rovere is heavily protected, making poisoning him very difficult and unlikely. Even if everything in contact with him was inspected over and over, I don't believe anyone would think of the salt, much less examine it under a lens."

"Once he's ill," Borgia said, "the Cardinal may stop eating."

"He may," I agreed, "but I believe that there will be so many fine cuts as to make it impossible for his body to heal. Additionally, physicians know well that injury to the lower bowel brings on sickness very swiftly, even if they do not know why. That is what will actually kill him."

Borgia thought for a few moments. He examined the salt again, as well as the diamond. Finally, he said, "This is the best you've been able to come up with?"

"Given the difficulties involved in getting past della Rovere's poisoner, it is."

"Yet you've hesitated to bring this to me. Why?"

"I only just recently—"

"You were fully prepared with everything to hand. Clearly, you've had ample time to think this through."

He had me there. Not for a moment did I consider revealing to him that I had been concerned about killing anyone in addition to della Rovere. Far less that I had hesitation about killing the Cardinal himself.

"It is expensive," I said.

"How expensive?"

"Extraordinarily, given the quantity of diamond I believe will be required. Indeed, I think it is fair to say that there has never been a poison as expensive as this."

Borgia sighed. He ran a hand over his jowls and looked at me. "You are asking me to decide how much della Rovere's death is really worth to me."

"That is what it amounts to." I gathered up the salt and, with greater care, the diamond powder. When I had returned both and the lens to my pocket, I said, "Perhaps you would like to consider the matter?"

"Perhaps I had better. Does anyone else know about this?"

"Not so far as I am aware. That is why I asked to speak with you privately."

"You didn't read about it in one of those books your father left or hear about it from him?"

I shook my head. "So far as I know, I am the first to think of it. Of course, that may not be true. The ancients had great knowledge of poison, much of it now lost to us. At any rate——"

"Have you figured out how to protect against it?"

I understood his concern. Though I might well be the first poisoner—at least of my own day—to realize how diamond powder could be used, that did not mean that I would be the last. While the price would be prohibitive for almost everyone, all that was needed was one ambitious prelate—or monarch—willing to kill at literally any cost.

"I have discovered that while salt dissolves in water, pulverized diamond does not. I do not know why this is but I think it has something to do with the hardness of diamond that remains unchanged even when it is finely ground."

"And it won't occur to della Rovere's poisoner to test it in that way?"

"Salt is notoriously hard to poison, at least until now. Without knowledge of this method, there would be no reason to examine it with such care."

He seemed satisfied by that but not enough to come to any decision or to dismiss me. I remained standing where I was while Borgia appeared to sink into deep reflection. Finally, just as I was wondering if I should slip away, he roused himself to notice me again.

"You don't think I should do it, do you?"

"I have carried out your instructions—"

"And presented me with a ruinously expensive method that might or might not work. Hardly encouragement to get the deed done."

"I'm sorry if my efforts do not meet your expectations, but—"

"It isn't that," he said, brushing aside my concern. "What you've come up with is ingenious. As I said, you have a gift for finding fresh solutions. No, you're not the problem."

I was glad to hear it. So, too, was I relieved that he did not rush to order della Rovere's death. The price might be deterring him but I hoped there were other considerations as well.

"You know about the Spanish envoy who is coming?" Borgia asked.

"There are rumors."

"I'm sure there are. Have you talked to your Jewish friends? I'm assuming they still have decent enough sources in Spain. Do they understand the predicament I face?"

"You need the support of Their Most Catholic Majesties to prevent war between France and Naples, a war della Rovere hopes to use to depose you. But the price for their help seems to be going up."

"Novi Orbis is no longer enough," Borgia said with palpable disgust. "Now they want the Sforza alliance broken and, for good measure, the Jews expelled. They would leave me stripped of allies and

175

beholden to Spain for everything. But worse yet, they don't think. How is it possible for people to have so much power yet be so stupid?"

I did not presume that he really wanted my opinion but a response seemed called for all the same. "In what way are they failing to think, Holiness?"

"About the Jews, of course! They go on and on about the need to expel them but do they ever ask themselves what purpose the Jews serve? Yet the answer is obvious. Whenever something goes wrong who do ordinary people blame? The Jews. At the first sign of plague, crop failure, drought, anything at all, it's the fault of the Jews. But what if there weren't any Jews? What if they were gone? Who do you think would be blamed then?"

"I don't know, Holiness."

"Holy Mother Church, that's who, for failing to prevent the ills of the world. How long then do you think people would obey our laws, tithe to us, bequeath us their property for their souls' sake? The whole business would come crashing down in the blink of an eye."

He sighed deeply and fell back in his chair. "If the Jews didn't exist, we would have to invent them."

I will admit I had never considered what he was saying but it did possess a certain logic. Since the conclusion of the *reconquista* of Iberia the previous year by Ferdinand and Isabella, there weren't enough Moors in Europe to take the blame for everything that went wrong. As for witches, really, how many of them can you burn before ordinary people finally object to their wives, daughters, sisters, mothers, aunts, and the like meeting such a grisly fate?

No doubt Sofia and David would be interested to hear Borgia's views on why the Jews were necessary. I would have to remember to tell them when next we met. For the moment, my sense was that I would be wise to stay close to His Holiness. In his present mood, he bore careful watching.

I worked through the remainder of the day within the Vatican Palace and went home with a purloined leg of lamb, part of the perquisites—big and small—of serving His Holiness. This I entrusted into Portia's capable hands. Cesare still being off on his father's business, she and I enjoyed it together in her rooms accompanied by fresh asparagus and a nice claret. Minerva had a share of the lamb and seemed to enjoy it.

I slept better than usual and might have gone on doing so for some hours after dawn had not I been awakened at the first hint of light by a banging on my door.

Wrapped in a robe, I stumbled out to find half a dozen condottierri, the leader of whom held out a large leather pouch. Placing it in my hands, he said, "With the compliments of His Holiness."

The condottierri left, marching down the stairs loudly enough to rouse any other tenants still trying to sleep. Portia emerged in their wake, blinking sleepily. I called down the stairs that everything was fine and withdrew back into my rooms.

Having taken the pouch over to my worktable, I opened it and peered inside. In the faint light of the new day, I beheld a seeming infinity of stars that burned with cold, inhuman light. Borgia, it seemed, had made up his mind.

17

The Spanish envoy, Don Diego Lopez de Haro, arrived with due pomp, bearing flowery declarations of Their Most Catholic Majesties' filial obedience to the Supreme Pontiff. Negotiations commenced; at once the rumors began to fly. His Holiness was exhibiting coolness toward de Haro. He had cut short one of their scheduled meetings and missed another entirely. His Holiness was becoming irate. He had suggested that de Haro's lineage was insufficiently noble for so significant a mission. He had taken to interrupting de Haro and seemed disinclined to let him speak. He had raised his voice . . . he had shouted . . . he had broken a blood vessel in his eye shouting . . . he had hurled a vase of inestimable value at de Haro and thrown the man out of his office. De Haro had said that he would not return without proper regard for his safety.

Some of this was true, some was not. (The vase incident was exaggerated; it was a goblet.) In the end, it wouldn't really matter how angry Borgia was; he would have to strike the best deal that he could and let the rest go.

In the interest of giving him wider options, I occupied myself in turning the king's ransom worth of diamonds into finely pulverized powder, still valuable to be sure but worth only a fraction of what they would have commanded while whole.

Before I began, I will confess to considering what else I might do with the gems. They were sufficient to buy a life of luxury anywhere, as well as the force necessary to protect it. I could flee to Constantinople, where the Ottomans seemed set on establishing a great center of learning. How welcoming they would be to a woman I could not say but wealth always smooths the way. Or I could make for Paris, disguise myself as a boy, and penetrate the university there. And then there was Bruges or Basel, both centers of light in our world of darkness. With due care, I could escape Borgia's vengeance and make a good life for myself as that rarest of creatures, an unmarried woman of independent means.

I might have given more serious thought to such a course had I not been tethered to the life I already had. Aside from the matter of vengeance for my father, never far from my heart, I would also have to leave people for whom I truly cared and who might face Borgia's retribution in my stead—Rocco, Sofia, David, and others. Under no circumstances could I allow that to happen.

With His Holiness's grip on my life in mind, I took firm hold of the steel-tipped hammer bought from a blacksmith in the Via dei Fabbri, where the forges burn all day and night and the air rings with the clang of metal on metal. I inhaled deeply and, before I could think too much of what I was about to do, struck a blow against the leather pouch laid on my worktable. I really had no idea what to expect but I reasoned that if the gem cutters of Bruges so renowned for their craft could score facets into diamonds using a fine steel wedge carefully tapped, the stones had to be susceptible to dividing. The hammer was a brute-force method, but unlike a master cutter, I was not looking for precision. Crushed would do well enough.

I worked at the task for several days, going slowly and checking often to make sure that the results could not be detected when mixed with the finely milled salt I kept nearby for comparison. In between bouts of hammering, I secured the diamonds in the secret compartment of the puzzle chest that I had from my father. The chest itself was an ingenious mechanism designed to keep a false bottom in place. To free it, the right sequence of steps had to be carried out on the four outer sides of the chest itself, a procedure that involved sliding separate sections of wood in different directions until at last the hidden lock was released. Only then would the bottom tilt slightly, revealing itself. One misstep and the lock would reset.

I had put the diamonds away and was preparing to leave for the Vatican when I remembered that Minerva was overdue for a visit outside. When I went in search of her, she was not to be found. Well aware that cats take frosty pleasure in watching humans scramble about on their behalf, I refused to worry but made a show of departing anyway. Before I could do so, she emerged—I'm not entirely certain from where; like every building in Rome, mine had its secrets— appearing in the center of the salon, where she sat washing herself with admirable unconcern.

We returned from the garden to find Benjamin waiting for me. He bopped up and down and launched at once into his purpose in coming with great urgency.

"Donna Francesca, Padrone Alfonso wants you to know that the man you seek may have been seen in a tunnel under Trastevere in the early hours of this morning. It's not certain but based on the description you gave, it sounds as though it could have been him. *Il re* asks what you want him to do?"

My heart beat a little faster as I strove to remain calm. After all my efforts, this was the first real indication I had received of where Morozzi might be hiding. I set Minerva down in the salon as I strove to gather my thoughts.

There really was very little to think about.

"Tell him to meet me in Trastevere just after sunset, at the fountain in front of Santa Maria."

"You're going into the tunnels?"

"I must. Tell him also to make sure his people know how dangerous this man is. They should do nothing to draw his attention to them."

"I will go with you," Benjamin said stoutly.

I grimaced and gave him a little shove out the door. The thought of another child coming within Morozzi's reach— "Don't think for a moment to do any such thing. Sofia would have my head, and that's only if she got to it before David did."

"Even so—"

I bent down—though not very far, for he had grown inches in recent months—took him by the shoulders, and spoke earnestly.

"Benjamin, hear me, I know that you have a great deal of experience on the streets and that you can take care of yourself in most situations. But Morozzi is . . . different. He has something inside him, a kind of darkness that makes him extremely dangerous."

"How do you know that?"

What could I say? That I understood Morozzi in a way others could not because we were alike to some degree? The mere thought of that filled me with such horror that I was hard-pressed not to scream out in denial of it.

"I just know. You have to promise me that you will be with Sofia tonight or somewhere else safe. Otherwise, I won't be able to concentrate. I'll be distracted worrying about you and who knows what that could lead to."

"I don't want you to come to any harm," he said with sincerity that touched my heart.

"Good, then promise me you will do as I ask."

He needed a moment to think it over but finally Benjamin nodded. "I promise, but you have to promise, too, not to take any crazy risks."

I tried a look of bafflement but he was having none of it.

"I know some of what happened last year," he said. "You're lucky to still be alive. You have to be more careful."

More affected by his concern than I cared to admit, I assured him that I would take every precaution. As usual in such circumstances, I was lying.

When Benjamin was gone, I delayed my own departure long enough to make the necessary preparations for the night to come. That done, I walked briskly toward the Vatican, being sure to keep my wits about me and maintain a sharp eye for any sign of trouble. Along the way, I noticed more condottierri than usual in the streets. Despite the gathering warmth of the day, they wore full armor and the plumed helmets of the papal household. I wondered if the show of power wasn't Borgia's way of sending a message to a populace too well amused of late at his expense. Of the graffiti, I saw no sign at all, although I did notice that quite a few walls appeared freshly scrubbed.

The sun was bright, the day all but cloudless. The incessant wind that had plagued us of late had died away, if only temporarily. In its place was a light, fresh breeze that smelled of the distant mountains

to the north where the ice we Romans love to eat flavored with lavender and rose petals has its birth.

I was crossing the Piazza San Pietro—noting as I did that the
crowd appeared sparser than usual and the guards more numerous—
when I saw Rocco coming from the direction of the barracks. He had
not yet seen me and for just a moment, I was tempted to dart into the
kitchens until he had passed. But although my vices are manifold,
cowardice is not among them. I stood my ground and found a smile.
Glimpsing me, his brow knit together and in the moment before he
spoke, I sensed that the reluctance I felt was not mine alone.

"How is Nando?" I asked after we had exchanged stilted greet-
ings. I assumed Rocco had come to visit his son and in that I was
correct. Nonetheless, his reply surprised me.

"He is . . . happy." A rueful grin forced its way past his guarded
manner. "Donna Felicia is the soul of kindness. She pampers him
unabashedly, as do her daughters. I swear he has been more cosseted,
more admired, and generally made more of in these few days than I
have managed to do since he was placed in my arms."

Having had the benefit of a loving father myself, I knew full well
that Rocco was a devoted parent—caring, patient, and wise. No
child could have asked for more.

But when I said as much, he passed a hand through his hair in
which buried gold glinted and replied, "I don't know whether I am
or not but I do know what I am not—and cannot be. A mother."

It was then I noticed that his eyes, usually so clear and candid,
were focused somewhere over my shoulder. He was not looking at
me directly.

"Francesca—"

Did I know? Did some secret sense warn me that the ground was about to shift beneath my feet and assumptions I had made unknowingly come tumbling down? I have wondered that from time to time but have never really found an answer.

Suffice to say that I was not prepared when, having fortified himself with a deep breath, Rocco said, "I have been wanting to tell you . . . that is, I think you should know . . . there was a reason why I wasn't at the meeting at the villa."

That had been more than three weeks ago and a great deal had happened since. I had long since ceased to wonder at his absence; indeed, I had never given it more than passing notice. Such was my trust in Rocco that I assumed he had a sound reason for his not being there.

But Sofia had asked after it, hadn't she? She had wondered, even if I had failed to do so.

"I had planned to attend," Rocco said. Something fascinating must have been going on in the direction of the stables because he was still looking toward them and not at me. "I'd arranged for Nando to stay with Donna Maria at the bakery. But at the last minute, a visitor turned up."

"A visitor?" I heard my own voice—cool, polite, moderately interested—as though from a distance.

"Signore Enrico d'Agnelli. He came himself . . . alone. I was almost out the door and suddenly there he was."

The memory of Rome's most renowned glassmaker's visit seemed to fluster him. He reddened. "As you may know, his only son died last year. A fever of some sort, I believe."

"Did he?" I had heard of that, for Rome was—still is—a chatty city in which everything is grist for the gossip mill. I had never known the young d'Agnelli or any of the family, for that matter. Why then the sense of dread that was growing in me?

"D'Agnelli has a daughter. Her name is Carlotta. She turned eighteen last month."

"Did she?" I was parroting myself but could not help it. Eighteen was an interesting age for a young woman, a time when even the most indulgent father will feel compelled to turn his attention to the subject of marriage. Mine had.

For the first time since he had begun to speak, Rocco looked at me directly. He appeared torn between conflicting—and irreconcilable—realities.

"D'Agnelli has a notion that I should come into his business. I told him I was flattered but not interested, and that was the truth . . . until just now. Seeing Nando with Donna Felicia and her daughters . . . it made me realize what he has missed by not having a mother to love him."

I did not have to ask how the man who had lost his only son envisioned joining forces with the most gifted young glassmaker in Rome. Obviously, the fair Carlotta—already I tormented myself with thoughts of her beauty—would have a key role to play in any such arrangement.

"Not all women make good mothers." I regretted the words the moment I spoke. The acrid taste of their bile stung my throat. I knew too well that it was not of Carlotta that I spoke, but of myself.

"Even so—" His eyes darkened. He reached out a hand—square, blunt-tipped at the fingers, scarred here and there from the fire he wove into wonders. For just a moment, I thought he meant to touch me.

We are all of us balanced on Fortuna's wheel, clinging as best we can lest we tumble heedlessly into Fata's dark maw. Yet we can, if we dare, let go and in that golden moment find the strength of our own wings unfurling.

But I did not know that then.

A single step toward him, likely nothing more would have been needed. Had I taken it, everything else, the entire course of my life from that moment on, would have changed. Or so I imagine.

A cloud drifted across the sun. In the sudden gloom, I froze. But for the slow beat of my heart tolling in my ears, I might have been a statue.

Rocco stared at me a moment longer. "Even so—," he repeated, and dropped his hand.

I watched him walk away, the sight of him wavering like a reflection in a pond rippled by the fall of a stone. He disappeared into the crowd and was gone before I could move again.

The day passed with unbearable slowness. I cannot tell you what I did although I must have done it well enough, for no one commented on my behavior or so much as looked at me askance, at least not within my viewing.

I was alone, Renaldo being off somewhere or other, the secretaries occupied as usual, and the rest of Borgia's vast staff being disinclined to seek my company. In the midst of the busy stream of comings and goings, moderated by Vittoro's increased vigilance but still significant, I felt my solitude more keenly than usual.

That being the case, when I had finished with the necessary inspection of goods, I sought diversion until that hour when I had engaged to meet Alfonso. It did occur to me that I should visit Lucrezia but the thought of yet another conversation about her anticipated wedding just then filled me with such disquiet that I could only make a silent promise to remedy my neglect as soon as possible.

Instead, I turned my attention to the lingering mystery of Borgia's disappearances. Where was he going and how was he managing to get there?

At that hour—it was by then midday—His Holiness was scheduled to be hosting a performance by the papal choir in honor of the hapless Spanish envoy, after which the two men would adjourn for further discussions, free, it was to be hoped, from any more flying tableware. As always, Borgia's secretaries would be in close attendance upon him. His office would be empty.

One advantage to being held in fear and dread is that scarcely anyone ever thought to question what I did. The guards on duty throughout the Curia knew of my friendship with their captain but they would have avoided challenging me strictly on the basis of my own dark reputation. The same could be said of the various clerics scurrying back and forth, all burdened with armfuls of ledgers, reports, correspondence, and the like, without which no large institution, certainly not Holy Mother Church, can function. These priests made a particular point of averting their eyes as I sallied up the marble steps, down the long gilded corridor, through the antechamber, and to the very door of Borgia's inner domain within the Vatican Palace.

There I paused, but only briefly. While it is true that an excess of audacity can lead to disaster, more often than not it will carry the day, or so has been my experience. A quick glance through the *spioncino* confirmed that the office was empty. I eased one half of the double door open and slipped inside. Leaning back, I let my weight close the door behind me and surveyed the room.

Partly, my intent was to make sure that I did not inadvertently displace anything and thereby leave evidence of my intrusion. But mainly I was curious to see the office without Borgia's overwhelming presence. Most people leave touches of themselves in any place they inhabit. Surely so outsized a figure as His Holiness would have an imprint larger than most. But the more I looked around the ornate space, the less I saw of him. The wide marble expanse of his desk was bare save for the elaborate ink and pen set. The shelves behind it held such objects—small sculptures and the like—as could have been found in the home of any wealthy man. In all fairness, Luigi d'Amico had better, but then the banker's taste was far more refined than was Borgia's. A few books were in evidence on the shelves but they appeared untouched. The paintings were good enough but again, nothing remarkable or any in way personal. The whole seemed designed solely to give the impression of great riches and power while concealing the man within. Of the religious nature of his office, there was no hint at all.

As Vittoro had said, two concealed doors led from the office, one to a corridor that led to the private papal apartments within the Vatican and the other to the Palazzo Santa Maria in Portico, where it came out near the entrance to La Bella's quarters. The doors were not so much hidden as discreetly designed so that they fit so snugly into the surrounding walls and so precisely matched their decoration as to be undetectable by any but the most observant eye.

Neither was what I was looking for.

Quickly, I made my way around the perimeter of the room, tapping lightly on the walls as I went. You may wonder how I knew to do so, but recall, a good poisoner must be constantly examining objects that may hold concealed compartments filled with hidden dangers. I simply applied the same techniques to the much larger container that was the office.

Initially, my efforts yielded no results. I was beginning to wonder if the very premise on which I acted, namely that Borgia had a secret means of leaving his inner domain, was wrong when my attention drifted to the shelves along an outer wall. The more I studied them, the more they seemed not quite right. Only after staring for several minutes did I realize that one edge of the shelves, where they fit into the recess that held them, was thicker than the other.

Swiftly, I ran my hand down that side. Nothing happened. For a moment, I felt the hollowness of defeat but then a thought stirred in me. I was moderately tall for a woman but Borgia was taller still; indeed, he towered over most men. He could reach a hidden lever far above my grasp.

Hardly breathing, I scrambled around for an embroidered stool of the sort offered to visitors whose rank did not quite merit a chair. Having located one, I dragged it over to the shelves and clambered up on it. Scarcely had I begun to examine the space higher up than my hand encountered a concealed lever. With great anticipation, I pulled it.

The shelves moved very slightly, bumping against the stool. I scrambled down and shoved it out of the way, then eased the shelves open farther. They were very heavy but swung on well-oiled hinges. I had no difficulty making a space large enough to fit through.

I will admit that at that moment, I hesitated. Borgia was unlikely to approve of what I was doing no matter how good a reason I might give him. While the claim that I was acting out of concern for his safety had some merit, the truth is that I was overcome with curiosity.

Because of my father's favored position in the household of then Cardinal Borgia, who also served as vice chancellor of the Curia, I had grown up more familiar with the environs of the Vatican than were all but a similarly privileged few. Not only had I been permitted to visit the Sistine Chapel, usually open only to the highest ranking clergy and noble guests, I had also visited the Vatican Library. It contains an astonishing four thousand or so works, mostly Hebrew, Greek, and Latin codices in addition to manuscripts acquired from the library at Constantinople. There is talk of commissioning a building solely to house the library, but so far nothing has come of that. In addition, I was aware of the existence within the library of certain archives said to contain the most sensitive correspondence, state papers, and the like. My father had seen them there, though I had not.

With all that, I was quite certain that the Vatican still concealed many secrets. No one person would ever know them all but I had the urge to discover at least a few.

All of which I hope makes clear why I left Borgia's office behind me and ventured down the hidden passageway toward a destination I could only guess at. To my surprise, initially I did not need a lamp to see my way. Narrow windows near the ceiling admitted sufficient light while also informing me that I was still within an outer wall. Further, unlike many of the passages I was familiar with in the Vatican and elsewhere in Rome, this one was dry, clean, and large enough that even a man of Borgia's height could walk without stooping.

I continued on for several minutes before noticing that the passage had begun to slant downward. A little farther on I came to a point where the outside windows ended and only darkness lay ahead. There I stopped, relieved to find several well-tended oil lamps along with flint and tinder on a shelf close to hand. I lit a lamp, lowered the wick to give a steady light, and kept walking.

A short time later I came to a heavy wooden door inset with brass strips heavily darkened by time. Despite its apparent age—the wood appeared wormy—and its considerable weight, the door yielded with only a light shove. Beyond lay a chamber—not large by any means but large enough that the light from the lamp only hinted at its farthest edges. An iron grille stretching from floor to ceiling and divided by a locked gate separated me from what lay beyond. I could see, but only remotely.

On the other side of the grille, I made out a large, high-backed chair of intricately carved wood padded with cushions, a footstool similarly fashioned, and a pair of small tables. Nearby were several lamps and, I could not help note, a wooden rack holding bottles of claret. The room was far enough below ground to be cool even on so warm a day. However, that, too, had been considered. A cooper brazier stood near the chair, ready to give warmth if needed, and more light.

Someone was making himself very comfortable in this hidden room below the Vatican Palace. Someone who could come and go at will from the pope's private office.

Of course, I realized at once that I likely had found the explanation for Borgia's mysterious disappearances. But what drew him to the room? What was hidden there? Try though I did to discern the contents by peering beyond the iron grille, going so far as to press my nose through it, I could see only obscure shapes.

However, I could just make out the words on the tarnished plaque set in stone above the grille.

MYSTERIUM MUNDI

The mystery of the world. And, it seemed to me, a play on the sacred words of the holy Mass in which the priest calls upon the faithful to rejoice in *mysterium fidei,* the mystery of the faith.

Above me, the life of the Vatican went on, the chanting of the hours, the saying of Mass, the buying and selling of indulgences, the confessions for the sake of the immortal soul. All that is required by God, so we are told, including the getting and keeping of power.

But here, beneath the surface, buried in the earth, here was the mystery of the world, the very reality that we of Lux sought to pierce not on the basis of faith but through reason. Where, it seemed, Borgia had been spending his stolen time.

Lacking a key, I could go no farther. Even so, I was reluctant to leave. I stood for some unknown time straining to get a glimpse of what lay just beyond my reach. Eventually, my eyes adjusted to the dim light sufficiently that I could make out pigeonholed racks of what might have been scrolls or possibly maps, as well as shelves of bound books, some of which appeared to be extremely old. I thought I saw slabs of carved stone covered with what might have been lettering. There were also chests of various sizes, and objects I could not make out at all.

Eventually, I returned to the surface but only with the greatest reluctance. The papal office remained hushed, devoid of activity save for a few dust motes dancing in the rays of sun that penetrated through the high windows. Beyond I could hear the quotidian noise of the day beginning to wind down as the sun dipped toward the chimney pots.

My hand strayed to the leather sheath holding my knife close to my heart. I had an appointment to keep. But I resolved that, assuming I was able, I would find a way to return to the secret room beneath the palazzo and discover what treasures it concealed.

I was at the octagonal stone fountain in the Piazza di Santa Maria in Trastevere just before sunset. A dozen or so local boys were gathered around, drawing water for their families or masters for the night. They lingered in the waning light, bragging of their exploits, pushing and mock-wrestling with one another until the great bell in the tower of the church di Santa Maria behind us rang out the call to vespers. Then they scattered, vanishing into the surrounding lanes and alleyways, leaving only puddles behind them.

Except for a handful of beggars bedding down for the night in front of the church, I was alone. Around me I could see lamps being lit in people's homes and in the nearby taverns, hear the clink of dishes and the murmur of conversation. Someone, probably in one of the taverns, broke into a song that was popular that spring—yet another ditty about a ripe young girl and the swain who loved her— and a second voice joined in. The heavy, fecund scent of the river vied with the aroma of wood smoke and the ever-present odor from the sewers.

I looked toward the church. It is said to be the oldest house of prayer dedicated to the Virgin in all of Rome, although the clerics at the church of Santa Maria Maggiore on the Esquiline will tell you otherwise. At any rate, it has the look of great age despite having been razed to the ground and entirely rebuilt by Pope Innocent II less than five hundred years ago. (It is a measure of the antiquity of Rome that anything a mere few centuries old must be considered young.) Innocent II used enough of the old building to preserve its venerable appearance but in the process destroyed the tomb of his rival, the Antipope Anacletus II, which was likely the point of the whole exercise. The victor lies there now, keeping company with the head of Saint Appollonia, yet another virgin martyr, and a piece of the Holy Sponge.

You can see why Santa Maria is a popular stop for visitors to the city, but only in daylight. With the gathering gloom, the piazza in front of the church rapidly filled with shadows. The moon, not yet quite full, had hovered as a pale daytime presence over the city during the hours of light and would not return until shortly before sunrise. In its absence, the cold stars offered scant company.

I had just begun to wonder if perhaps Alfonso had not gotten my message, or more likely was choosing to ignore it, when a stirring off to the side alerted me that I was no longer alone.

Shapes emerged out of the shadows, staying close to the walls, moving swiftly. Two . . . three . . . vanishing into alleys, reappearing, edging nearer. I saw a face—young, pale, caught in the sudden light from a window. It disappeared and another took its place only to vanish in turn. They came quickly but with care, not venturing out into the open piazza until they must have been certain that I was by myself and posed no danger.

Then three formed a perimeter around me. I spied the glint of steel in their hands and drew a quick breath. If they were not Alfonso's men . . . if Il Frateschi had somehow followed me . . .

I reached for the knife in the sheath near my heart and was about to draw it when *il re dei contrabbandieri* himself emerged from an alleyway and walked toward me. Previously, I only had seen Alfonso seated in the thronelike chair surrounded by his loot and his acolytes. Standing, he was taller than I expected and reed thin, with long, gawky limbs that for all his height, he seemed not yet to have grown into. He came with a cheeky grin and a sweeping bow as graceful as any young nobleman could manage.

"Donna Francesca, well met."

I took a breath to steady myself and got to business. "And you, Signore Alfonso. What can you tell me of the man who was seen?"

"He matched the description you gave—tall, blond-haired, face of an angel. My man only caught a glimpse of him but he was clear all the same. There is no doubt."

Perhaps not, but still I wanted to be sure. "What was he wearing?"

"A dark cloak, covering him from head to foot. It had a hood but that was pushed back. My man thought he caught a glimpse of a priest's cassock underneath."

I nodded, satisfied, and went on. "This happened in a tunnel near here, during the day?"

"In one of the passages, yes, a little after sext in mid-afternoon. My man was . . . making a delivery. You understand?"

I understood that the tunnels under the city were an excellent means of avoiding the attention of the condottierri who, while they might very well not stop the passage of untaxed goods, would certainly exact their own fee for looking the other way.

"Was the man he saw alone?" I asked.

"He was, and seemingly in a hurry. He disappeared around a corner and was gone from sight."

Frustration welled up in me. If not even the smugglers who knew the Roman underworld better than anyone could track Morozzi, what hope had I?

"Do you have any idea where he went?"

"*Sì,* of course, otherwise I would not have bothered you with this. Come, I will show you."

Alfonso led me up the steps to the church. I hesitated a moment before entrusting myself to the mercy of Our Mother, who always seems so much more inclined to accept us as we are than does the harsh and vengeful God men worship. We entered through the ancient stone porch with its sloping tiled roof beneath the fresco of the Virgin suckling her son and into the nave lined with richly carved capitals that some whisper bear the face of another Queen of Heaven, this one called Isis, the capitals having been taken from her temple on the nearby Janiculum. The great Pietro Cavallini's mosaics of the life of the Virgin infuse the interior with light and color despite now being two centuries old. I could just make them out in the dim illumination of the oil lamps reflecting off their gilded surfaces. Vespers had concluded but the lingering perfume of incense drifted on the air. The interior was empty save for ourselves. The Church fathers do not allow the poor to seek shelter within Holy Mother Church lest they pollute her glory, although they are allowed to huddle outside around her skirts.

We were about halfway down the nave when Alfonso touched my arm lightly and drew me off into one of the aisles. He pointed to a small wooden door all but hidden in the shadows.

"That's where I figure he would have come out, going by where my man saw him disappear. There's an old stone staircase in that part of the passage that leads up into the crypt right under here. From there, it's no trick to find your way out."

I was not surprised that Morozzi would use a church to come and go surreptitiously. He had done much the same the previous year with no less than Saint Peter's. But that raised the troubling question of whether he had allies within Santa Maria's ancient walls.

Far in the back of my mind, a memory stirred. Like every other great church in Rome, Santa Maria in Trastevere has a *titulus,* a cardinal-patron who holds the honor of the office—and reaps its considerable financial benefits—without being required to provide any personal service. The position was held at that time by His Eminence Cardinal Giorgio da Costa, Archbishop of Lisbon. Not surprisingly, the Portuguese prelate was no friend to the Spaniard Borgia. Even more important, da Costa was well known to be della Rovere's ally.

Was it possible that a priest or even several in service at Santa Maria would be confident enough about da Costa's sympathies to provide aid to one intent on dislodging the present occupant of Peter's Throne on the mistaken assumption that della Rovere would benefit?

Or was I becoming too caught up in the conspiracies that are mother's milk to Rome, suckling as we are at the teat of the she-wolf? Was I seeing treachery where none existed?

There was only one way to find out. I turned to Alfonso.

"How many men can you put in the piazza, in the nearby streets, around this church, and in the tunnels underneath?"

He hesitated. "Without disrupting business—?"

"Forget business. Borgia will pay you well." I was presuming much to say so but I was determined to convince His Holiness that my plan was sound.

"How well?"

I thought quickly. "Suppose he agrees to take only one part in ten for, say, a year?"

"Or better yet, he takes nothing for two years."

"That is a great deal of money." In point of fact, I had no idea how much Borgia would be giving up but I knew that he had vastly more to lose if he ceased to be pope.

"You are asking a great deal," Alfonso countered, reasonably enough. "But you may want to reconsider. Putting so many men on watch assures that they will be seen."

"That's exactly what I want." At his puzzled look, I explained. "If Morozzi suspects that I am on to him, he will be driven to act rashly and then I will have him."

Or so I believed. My confidence was born of arrogance, for which a terrible price would shortly be paid. But that night, standing in the hushed interior of Santa Maria, I thought only of striking the deal I was certain would put vengeance for my father within my reach at last.

Alfonso and I dickered a while longer before coming to an agreement. In sign of it, he spit in the palm of his right hand and offered it to me. I did the same without hesitation and we shook. We parted in front of the church, the smuggler king vanishing back into the shadows. I made my way to my apartment. I did so well aware that I was followed by darting shapes, moving swiftly, hugging the walls and flickering in and out of my awareness.

They would be Alfonso's men for the most part, keeping watch on his new "partner." But somewhere among them would be Borgia's own "eyes," for I did not doubt he was having me followed. I could expect a summons to explain myself before very long. Mindful of that, I sought my bed in the hope of a few hours' sleep only to drift in that halfway state between wakefulness and dreams wherein Rocco appeared again and again, turning from me toward a woman, strangely with the face of Isis, who opened her arms to him and smiled.

19

s I had expected, His Holiness was not pleased to learn of the arrangement I had made on his behalf with Alfonso. But after I had explained my reasoning, he grudgingly approved.

However, not without comment. "Between the diamonds and now this, you are costing me a king's ransom."

"In service of saving you a pope's treasure."

As he had no reply to that, I was banished from his presence until I had something "useful," as he put it, to tell him. He was not looking well just then; the talks with de Haro seeming to take their toll, but not on Borgia alone. Renaldo whispered that the envoy was suffering stomach pains despite refusing to eat anything other than food he had brought with him.

"All probably spoiled by now and making him ill," I said. It served him just as well since he was so foolish as to think that mere wagonloads of foodstuffs could protect him if Borgia directed otherwise.

Would I have killed de Haro? The question is purely hypothetical, of course. As frustrated as he became with the envoy, His Holiness never so much as hinted that he would welcome his demise. Nor would I have encouraged him to do so. But if there had been some compelling reason, something touching on the all-important matter of war or peace, life or death? What then would I have done?

A little henbane seed ground into bread, perhaps. Or a dash of young-leafed larkspur in the wine. Or failing that, a personal favorite of mine, oil of belladonna substituted for one of the many fraudulent chrisms the foolish believe can protect them from poison.

But enough of that; Heaven forfend that I provide you with occasion for sin.

Later that day, I returned home to find not the word from Alfonso that I was hoping for, but a package from Cesare. It contained a large quantity of sheer black lace of the sort Spanish women make into mantillas along with a note suggesting I might find a more intimate use for it. The gift raised my spirits, which had continued very low.

It also prompted a chuckle from Portia, who hovered while I opened the package.

"I always did appreciate a man with a good imagination," she said.

"Yes, well, I'll have to see what I can do with it." As I had precisely no skills as a needlewoman, I was at a loss where to begin.

"I can recommend a good seamstress," Portia offered. "She won't rob you, she doesn't gossip, and she does fine work."

Having secured the name of the paragon and thanked Portia for it, I hesitated. My mind had been very heavy of late, ever since Rocco sprang his news, although I tried hard not to admit that was the cause. I could not help brooding about the d'Agnelli *figlia*, try though I did to keep her from my thoughts.

"Would it be possible . . . ," I began. "That is, do you think . . ."

Portia rubbed the lace between two fingers and looked at me sideways. "Not like you to be so tongue-tied."

"I'm not, that is, I just wondered if I might ask you for a favor? Another favor, actually. I know you just did me one and you're always so good about looking after Minerva, but—"

Portia dropped the lace and stared at me. "What is wrong with you, Donna? And before you tell me, just let me say that the notion of you being so flustered by anything at all is terrifying. Has Borgia really gone and done it? Are we on the edge of catastrophe? Are the heavens about to split open and fire rain down?"

"No! Nothing like that. It's nothing, really. I just wondered . . ." I took a breath and let it out in a rush. "Do you know anything about *la famiglia d'Agnelli*?"

"The glassmakers? They lost their only son last year."

"Yes, I know that, but they have a daughter—"

"They may," Portia said slowly. "Although I can't say that I've heard any talk of her."

She paused a moment, looking at me far too shrewdly. I did my best to appear no more than mildly interested.

"Do you want me to see what I can find out?"

"Not if it would be any trouble. It isn't important, after all."

"Oh, well then—"

"But if you happened to— I'm just a little curious." I trailed off, feeling as ridiculous as I no doubt sounded.

Portia shrugged and returned her attention to the lace. "I'll see what I can do."

I did not imagine she was fooled for an instant. Sooner or later, I would have to tell her the truth, but until then at least I had other, some would say more pressing, matters to attend to.

I was doing so the following day when Vittoro sought me out. I was on my way to visit Lucrezia, having felt badly about neglecting her, when he intercepted me as I was crossing the piazza.

"What is this I hear?" he demanded without preamble. "You've enlisted the smugglers to look for Morozzi?"

"No one else has had any luck—not Borgia's own 'eyes,' or so I presume, for surely he would have said something by now. And not Luigi or the Jews."

I had sent word to Sofia and David of where I believed Morozzi was hiding, and had notified the banker as well. Certain though I was that they would all do their best to find him, my hopes rested most strongly with Alfonso.

"If I can force him to reveal himself—"

"You'll do what, Francesca? Go after him singlehandedly? This obsession of yours—"

Any doubt as to where Vittoro had acquired his information disappeared. Borgia, too, had referred to my obsession with Morozzi when I told His Holiness what finding the mad priest was going to cost him.

Because I genuinely liked Vittoro, I spoke softly. "Would you call it an obsession if it had been your father who was murdered?"

He had the grace to look abashed. "No, I suppose I wouldn't. I don't blame you for caring so deeply but at least don't try to do this alone."

"I have no intention of doing so. Morozzi will make a wrong move. When he does, there may not be much time to act, but be assured, I will welcome all appropriate help."

That was neither a lie nor entirely the truth. I had no particular wish to confront the priest alone, but I would take no risk of him being warned off by the presence of others. Most important, I intended that it would be my hand that sent him to Hell's domain.

Vittoro appeared less than satisfied but he let the matter drop. We walked a little farther together.

"The boy is doing well," he said after a few moments.

I did not have to ask whom he meant. There was only one boy so far as I was concerned. "I am glad to hear it. You were good to take him in."

Vittoro snorted. "It will be a harder task to give him back. Felicia adores him and so do the girls. He's a clever sort. Did you know he draws very well? He's done portraits of my daughters that look exactly like them."

I wondered if the d'Agnelli *figlia* would have the sense to encourage Nando's gift or if she would expect him, like his father, to take up her family business.

In a blatant bid to change the subject, I asked, "What impression do you have of the negotiations?"

"Is that what we're calling them? I thought they were some combination of shouting match—at least on Borgia's part—and sulking."

"That bad?"

"Who knows? It is clear, however, that His Holiness would have an easier time of it if he didn't have to worry about what della Rovere is up to."

The comment, accurate though it was, made me wonder if Vittoro also knew that I was devising a way to kill the Cardinal. It would not have surprised me. The captain of the condottierri had excellent sources of his own, as well as being in Borgia's confidence.

We talked a little longer before parting. I went on to Lucrezia's apartment. She was in her bath but called for me to come in.

The *bagno* was a spacious room with high windows overlooking the palazzo's gardens. Its floor was an intricate mosaic in the Roman fashion depicting dolphins at play. In the center sat an immense *vasca* in rosy pink marble, elevated on lion's paw feet with high scrolled sides. Such was its size that Lucrezia and all her ladies could have bathed in it together. However, she was alone except for an attendant who hurried forward with a stool for me. I sat, breathing in the thick perfume of hibiscus and jasmine rising as tendrils of vapor from the steaming water.

She made a pretty picture with her golden hair caught up and pinned to the top of her head, her face rosy from the heat, and the rest of her submerged beneath the milky water. Had I not known her quite so well, I would have missed the strain evident in her eyes and around her mouth.

"Do you want to get in?" she asked. "There's plenty of room."

I was tempted. Since moving out of the palazzo, I had made do with a tin hip bath. As much as I cherished my privacy, there were certain amenities that come with living among the rich and powerful that I missed. But with everything that was happening, I could not stay long.

"Another time. I just came to see how you are."

Lucrezia sighed and cast her eyes to the ceiling, where cherubs cavorted. "How am I? Let's see . . . I am impatient . . . anxious . . . excited . . . exhausted from standing hour after hour for the seamstresses *and* very tired of being poked with pins. How are you?"

How indeed? Closing in on the killer of my father, I hoped. Sore at heart over Rocco's news and loathing myself for such hypocrisy. Missing her brother and the hot, mindless coupling he provided. Doing my best to keep her father alive.

"Fine," I said. "Busy, of course, but that's to be expected."

"Tell me, among all the wedding gifts, which is your favorite?"

So did she discreetly allude to the fact that I had to vet each and every gift before it was allowed anywhere near her.

"That life-sized baby elephant done in silver with the jeweled trunk. A bit plain perhaps but—"

Lucrezia laughed and I had the pleasure of seeing her, if only for a moment, restored to the young girl she was.

"Where shall I put it, do you think? In the great hall of my husband's villa in Pesaro where all our guests may admire it? Or somewhere more private perhaps, just for our own enjoyment?"

"In the nursery," I suggested, for I knew this was a subject dear to her heart. "What little child wouldn't adore having his own elephant?"

Lucrezia clapped her hands. "Perfect, that is exactly what I shall do. Assuming I ever see Pesaro."

She did not wait for my reply but took a breath and submerged completely under the water. When she surfaced moments later, her hair had tumbled loose and drifted around her. She appeared, I thought, as a mermaid might, provided that a mermaid could be preoccupied with worldly matters. Even this close to the wedding, she still had her doubts whether it would occur. I wondered if she knew of the Spanish envoy's determination to stop it.

Our eyes met in silent understanding.

"Oh, dear," Lucrezia said, "I believe I am almost out of soap." At once, the attendant bowed and hurried off to find more. The moment we were alone, she asked, "What do you hear? Tell me everything."

That was out of the question, but I would tell her what she needed to know.

"Da Haro and your father are at odds. There is doubt that they can come to any sort of agreement."

"They must! The Sforzas will never yield Milan to the King of Naples, no matter that he has the better claim. The Spanish must use their influence to make him see that. Otherwise, my soon-to-be family will look north for help and we will have the French on our doorstep."

With della Rovere's encouragement and possibly that of other cardinals as well. But I did not say as much. Lucrezia grasped the situation well enough as it was.

"Have you placed your bet yet?" she asked.

I knew she was referring to the heavy load of wagering going on all over the city as to whether or not the marriage would take place. The last I had heard, odds were running seven to five against it.

"Certainly not. I never bet on such things. Besides, I did very well when your father signed the bull. It doesn't do to be greedy."

She squeezed water out of a sponge and let it dribble over her head before she said, "You are so fortunate to control your own life."

"Hardly that, but I am glad of what independence I have." Even if there were days when it seemed little more than a sham.

She lifted her pale shoulders and let them fall. "I will never know what that is like. My life is my father's to do with as he wills. I fear that even once I am married, that will continue to be so."

It would have been the rankest hypocrisy—more even than I was capable of—to try to persuade her otherwise. Borgia was determined to control the lives of all his children now and forever. He intended them to at once further his goals and assure his immortality.

But first he would have to wiggle out of the morass of conflicting ambitions, rampant greed, and venal corruption in which he had enmeshed himself.

"If you continue to worry so much," I said, "your bridegroom will think you are a poor, dour thing. He will flee all the celebrations meant to welcome him and ride hell-bent back to Pesaro as fast as his horse will go."

A girl less confident of her own charms might have been taken aback by that. Not so Lucrezia. She merely smiled.

"No, he won't. He will think me winsome and delightful. He will sprinkle rose petals at my feet and call me his beloved."

We were laughing over the antics of besotted males when the servant returned bearing a fresh box of soap. She set it down on a nearby table and faded back into the wall.

Lucrezia had no actual need for the soap; it had merely been a ruse. We resumed chatting about the wedding gifts, her clothes, all innocuous matters. My eye drifted to the wooden box. I recognized it readily enough for it was the same sort I had been examining for months. The box came from Venice and bore the seal of the manufacturer on its lid. It was large enough to hold a dozen hand-shaped soaps made with olive oil and various perfumes. The soaps were a favorite of both Lucrezia and La Bella. Between them they went through an astounding quantity.

I leaned forward a little and lifted the top of the box, in the process breaking the maker's seal. The same one that surely would have been broken had I inspected the soaps, as I inspected everything meant for any member of *la famiglia,* before replacing it with my own. The interior was separated into compartments, each holding a scented soap wrapped in different hues of silk to represent the various fragrances. I sniffed hibiscus, jasmine, rose, lavender, lemon, and thyme. There were two bars of each type of soap; every compartment in the box was filled.

"Is something wrong?" Lucrezia asked.

I let the lid drop back and smiled. "No, of course not, I was just admiring the soaps."

"You're welcome to them, if you like."

"That is very kind of you."

Still smiling, I turned to the attendant and asked, "Where did you get these?"

Deliberately, I kept my voice gentle and my tone light. It would not do to frighten her.

Even so, she paled and for a moment, I feared she would not be able to speak. Clearly, she knew who I was.

"Donna Lydia gave them to me," she managed to gasp finally. "She is in charge of Madonna's toilette."

"Would you ask her to step in here?"

As the attendant fled to do my bidding, Lucrezia leaned her head back against the tub and looked at me silently. She said nothing, nor did I. We waited, but not for very long.

Donna Lydia bustled in. She was about my age, pretty enough, with creamy skin and well dressed in the manner of a wealthy merchant's daughter not shy about showing off her fortune. Indeed, I marveled that she could move so gracefully, stuffed as she was into a confection of silk, velvet, and lace with a tightly boned bodice square cut above the breasts to reveal the transparent chemise beneath. All this was topped with a *templette,* fitted to the back of the head and coming forward at the sides, the whole edged with rosettas, the glass beads made in Murano that had become all the rage among those who could afford them.

"Do you require something, Madonna Lucrezia?" she asked, flashing a smile that revealed good teeth. She looked vaguely annoyed at being taken from her amusements but showed no concern whatsoever at my presence, thereby revealing her rank ignorance.

"Not at all, but I believe Donna Francesca does."

"Madonna Lucrezia has very kindly offered me a gift of soap," I said, indicating the box. "My favorite scents are hibiscus and jasmine. I would like to try both before deciding, but I don't want to confuse the perfumes. Would you do me the kindness of trying one so that I may smell it, too?"

Admittedly, as ploys went, it was weak. Had Donna Lydia possessed a mind attuned to more than her own pleasures, she might have sensed that. As it was, she merely shrugged, helped herself to a bar of the jasmine, and with an impatient sigh, raised her long sleeves sufficiently to place her hands in a nearby copper brazier filled with cool water. The soap, being of the finest quality, lathered quickly.

I waited, counting under my breath. When I reached ten, Donna Lydia began to scream.

20

I will have the entire family executed! No! Better yet, I will have them hung in chains in the piazza without food or water while the entire city watches them linger in agony and beg for death!"

So Borgia declared in mid-stride, halfway across his office, where he paced back and forth in a fury looking for something, anything upon which to vent his rage. He was still in the heavy formal garments in which he had come from his meeting with da Haro, their discussion interrupted when I sent word of what had occurred. Best he hear it from me rather than another, was my thinking. His broad face was fiercely red and gleaming with sweat. Nearby, his secretaries quaked, unable to leave without his permission but rightly terrified to be in his presence when he was in such a state.

I had maneuvered myself so that his desk was between us. From that position of relative safety, I said, "By all means do so if it will make you feel better. But they are guilty of nothing worse than having a daughter too stupid and careless to notice that my seal was missing from the box. If Donna Lydia had suspected for a moment that the soaps were poisoned, she would never have tried one so readily."

"It doesn't matter! My God, don't you realize, my only daughter, my precious Lucrezia could have been—"

I resisted pointing out that it was precisely because I had realized what could happen that it had not and said instead, "Donna Lydia has suffered severe burns to both her hands. If that isn't enough, she managed to touch her face and it is also affected. If I am right about the cause, her condition will continue to worsen for several days. Blisters will form and eventually break, leaving lesions behind. These will continue to be very painful as they crust over. Eventually, they will heal, but it is likely that scars will remain."

Borgia stopped, caught his breath, and looked at me. "She isn't going to die?"

I shook my head. "I believe the soaps were tainted with oil from one of several possible plants—oak perhaps, ivy, maybe sumac. People come into contact with these all the time and develop similar symptoms. But in this case, the oil appears to have been concentrated, probably by distillation, with the result that the effect was more severe, but in no case would it have been deadly."

"Then what is this about?" Borgia demanded. "If the intent wasn't to kill Lucrezia, what was it?"

I had considered that since the moment I first suspected that all was not right with the soap. There had been an outside chance that Morozzi had acquired—or worse yet created—a contact poison equal to my own but, in all modesty, I considered that unlikely. All the same, with access to Lucrezia's household, he could have slipped in poisoned food or drink that would have been far more devastating. The thought chilled me. Despite all my efforts, neither Borgia nor anyone else could ever be fully protected while the mad priest yet lived.

"He isn't interested in her," I said. "This is about you. Consider, if Lucrezia died suddenly, everyone would suspect poison and simply assume that one of your enemies had killed her. You might even get some sympathy for your loss. However, if she was suddenly overtaken by a dread scourge, seen to be in the state that Donna Lydia is now, wouldn't people be far more likely to consider that a sign of God's punishment for some grave transgression? Forgive me, Holiness, but it would be taken as evidence of your sins."

I did not have to spell out to what I referred; Borgia grasped my meaning for himself. His face darkened yet further, turning an alarming purple, and for a moment I wondered where the nearest foxglove might be found, that being a useful remedy for heart failure, although too much of it . . .

I digress. To my great relief, he took control of himself, albeit with a visible effort, and spoke almost calmly.

"If he has such reach, why didn't he just kill me instead and be done with it?"

"Because your servants, unlike Lucrezia's, are not foolish girls easily duped."

I left it to him to realize, as I had with the benefit of hindsight, that allowing his daughter to be served by such lack-wits was a serious mistake.

"I want them all gone," he decreed. "Every last one of them. She is to see no one but my own servants and whoever Vittoro judges absolutely reliable. Is that clear?"

"Completely, but her greatest safety lies in finding Morozzi quickly." Finding and dispatching him to the Hell he so richly deserved.

"Then damn well do it! The man is flesh and blood. He has to eat, drink, piss, maybe even whore if he has the *coglioni* for it. He is somewhere in this city—*in my city*—and I want him found!"

Vases rattled as this final pronouncement was made. The secretaries were white with fear and I confess that my hands, clasped at my waist and hidden within the long sleeves of my overdress, were more than a little chilled despite the heat of the day. Yet I understood Borgia's sentiment well enough. The hunt had gone on long enough. It was time for the kill.

Borgia continued to rant but I did not hear him. Thus far, I had dealt with the situation calmly and reasonably, but now fear and anger born of what had almost happened threatened to overwhelm me. Lucrezia scarred, Borgia weakened, perhaps fatally, and my own self shamed, my reputation in tatters while my father's murderer walked away laughing. And beyond that, Lux snuffed out, the world plunged into darkness, all hope for a world of light and reason extinguished.

Pain stabbed through my head. I closed my eyes against the sudden brightness, an explosion of light that turned the world white. A hot, urgent thrumming rose in my blood. Behind my eyelids, I saw darkness roiled by a red wave that moved before me, engulfing the room, the palace, the city, all of creation. I was drowning in it, unable to breathe. The wall was in front of me and the hole within it, admitting flashes of light that illuminated a landscape of sheerest terror and despair. Dimly, yet as close as a whisper in my ear, I heard a child whimper.

"Francesca."

A child who was—

"Francesca!"

The crimson wave receded. I opened my eyes. Borgia was staring at me. My chest was so tight that I could not speak. I was leaning back against his desk, a stunning breach of protocol by itself, never

mind anything else I had done or said. Had I spoken? Had the darkness? Had he heard it howling deep within me?

"Are you all right?" His Holiness demanded.

I managed a nod that clearly left him unconvinced.

"Get out," he ordered, waving a hand in the direction of the secretaries. They, too, were staring at me, but scrambled to obey and
fled, hardly delaying long enough to shut the doors behind them.

"Sit down," Borgia said, and pushed me into a chair near his desk.
I sat, overwhelmed with numbness, unable to move or speak. When
next I was aware of anything, he was pressing a goblet of chilled wine
into my hand and insisting that I drink.

I did so without tasting. My hands trembled. I grasped the goblet
between them to keep from dropping it and finished the wine. Slowly,
my senses returned. I was aware of Borgia's scent close to me—sweat
beneath brocade and velvet, the citrus soap he favored, and something
more, some mingling of the man's raw strength and ambition with an
undernote of creeping fear.

"What did you see?" he demanded.

I bit back a sigh. His Holiness was convinced that under certain
circumstances I was prone to visions. I had tried to dissuade him to
no effect. Suffice to say, he did not seem to care where such visions
came from—whether from God or the Devil—only what they could
reveal.

"Tell me," he insisted.

"I saw blood," I said, as much to make him stop as anything else.
"A sea of blood, drowning us all."

He frowned. "All of us, not just my enemies?"

"Drowning the world."

Clearly, this did not meet with His Holiness's approval. He was
silent for a moment before making his pronouncement.

"It was not a vision. You are overwrought, no doubt because of the danger you almost failed to deflect from my daughter. I forgive you for that. Now go and compose yourself. But don't take too long. I expect you to deal with Morozzi without further delay."

I nodded and stumbled to my feet, taking care how I set the goblet on the desk lest it fall and I shatter with it. Somehow I managed to collect myself sufficiently to walk from the room and out of the antechamber. I moved through a well of silence, acutely aware of the eyes on me from every direction. Every priest, every clerk, every hanger-on stopped and stared at me.

They might not have existed so far as I was concerned. The taste of copper lingered in my mouth. I waited until I had exited the Vatican Palace, then spit against a wall, discovering in the process that I had bitten my tongue. My blood stained the pale stone and dripped into the ground. I shuddered and moved on.

Despite Borgia's admonitions, I was not inclined to return to my apartment at once. In the aftermath of what had happened, a strange restlessness overtook me. I felt an irresistible need to keep moving.

On the Ponte Sant'Angelo, I stopped and stared out toward the southern bend of the river. At that time of year, the Tiber is a sluggish beast writhing its way through the heart of the city. Matters are different in winter when late rains can swell the river's banks to bursting, but just then a twig dropped from where I stood would have had a leisurely trip down the length of the river and out into the Tyrrhenian Sea less than a hundred miles away. When the wind is right, the scent of the sea overlaid with the perfume of the country it passes through fills the city. But just then hardly a breeze stirred the torpid air.

I watched as the ferrymen pulled their long, narrow boats up onto the muddy bank. During the day, vying for customers, they were as cutthroat as any competitors could hope to be. But with food and their beds beckoning, they worked together to hoist the boats up onto the road. There the ferrymen's children waited to help their fathers carry the vessels back to their humble dwellings. In the morning, the operation would be reversed. In another city—perhaps the city of Plato's Republican dream where all men dwell together in peaceful congeniality lacking even the need for laws, far less lawyers—in that city, the ferrymen would leave their boats safe on the riverbank and return with the dawn to find them still there. But Rome is a city of thieves or, if that seems unkind, of scavengers, many of who live in tumbledown wooden shacks huddled along the river where they find their livelihood trawling for anything they can sell. An unattended boat would be gone in the flick of an eye with not so much as a splinter to mark its passing.

But the Tiber takes even as it gives. Stand on the bridge below the looming hulk of Castel Sant'Angelo long enough and you are assured of seeing at least one body drift by. Daily, the dead inhabit the river. Whether the victims of violence or of their own hopelessness, they tend to look the same, bloated remnants of the souls who once possessed them. Very few of the bodies are those of children, and it is even rarer to find a baby, but that is because they tend to be so small that their remains lodge in the pillars beneath the city's bridges, where they escape notice.

I leaned against the stonework, grateful for its coolness in the day's lingering heat, and tried to forget what had happened in Borgia's office. No doubt he was right that I was overwrought, though I hated to think of myself in such terms. I was sleeping badly, as always. The Devil's wind that had blown through the city of late had robbed me of appetite. I longed for Cesare . . . ached for Rocco . . . worried that I would never be able to avenge my father properly . . .

and wondered, when I dared, why I could not simply be like other people, living a life of blessed ordinariness.

It was an affectation, of course. No one really wants to be ordinary. As much as they looked at me askance, more than a few women—and a great many men—happily would have exchanged their humdrum lives for the wealth and power that I possessed. No doubt they would laugh at me for longing after what they had.

Or perhaps not. Perhaps just a few were wise enough to appreciate the virtues of love and honor, faithfulness and humility. They might well pity me.

But I was damned if I would pity myself.

I went home. I fed Minerva. I changed out of the heavy formal clothing I wore within the Vatican into the boy's attire that I resorted to on those occasions when I wanted to move about the city unrecognized and unhindered. I awaited word from Alfonso and when very shortly I got tired of waiting, I left and walked across the river into Trastevere.

Twilight was fast approaching when I entered the piazza in front of Santa Maria. I took up my post a little off to one side and waited. The square and the nearby streets began to empty out. I watched the shapes in the shadows, tracking their movement. Soon enough, one approached me.

"I didn't recognize you at first," Alfonso said. He grinned cheekily at my boy's garb.

"Have you ever tried to chase someone while wearing a skirt?" I asked.

"Can't say that I have. There's been no sign of him, if that's what you're here to ask. He's gone to ground."

"No, he hasn't. He has sent a message. We cannot wait any longer."

Alfonso looked skeptical. "What do you want us to do?"

I told him. When I was done, he puffed up his cheeks and let his breath out in a rush. "You're sure about this?"

"I think it is the only way."

"Well, then . . . here." He reached into a pocket and withdrew a small wooden whistle, handing it to me.

"What is this for?"

"It's one of my ideas," Alfonso said proudly. "They're cheap and easy to make. I give them to all my crew. A single whistle means come on the run. That's good if there's somebody who hasn't got the word yet about my being in charge, maybe they're causing a problem for one of my boys. We gang up, let them know what's what, and more times than not, they fall in line. Two whistles means scatter, run. That's good when the condottierri show up and we want to avoid trouble."

It was an ingenious idea and I said as much. He preened, just a little, but quickly turned serious.

"I understand what you're saying about tightening the noose, flushing him down into the tunnels and not leaving him any way out except through the church. It's a good plan. But with all respect, why do you want to face him alone? Wouldn't it be better to have guards there with you?"

"Certainly, provided I could be sure that Morozzi would not realize that they were there until it was too late. I have learned to my sorrow never to underestimate him. The only way he will show himself is if he is certain that I am alone."

"You're the bait?"

I nodded. Borgia had sought to use me as such when he allowed the villa to be attacked. As distasteful as that was, it was too good a tactic for me to ignore.

"Morozzi wants to kill me for reasons that lie between the two of us, but also because I stand between him and his ultimate target, the Pope."

Such are the times we live in that the notion of someone daring to strike at the Supreme Pontiff did not surprise Alfonso. He merely nodded.

"And you think you can stop him by yourself?"

I did not blame him for being skeptical but—as Vittoro had said—Morozzi had never shown any tendency to sacrifice his own life. On the other hand, a sufficiently committed assassin can penetrate anywhere.

It was not that I wanted to die, not in the sense of seeking my own death as did those poor souls swallowed by the writhing Tiber. But the thought of being done with the darkness, the nightmares, the visions, the sense of being set apart from others and alone, which had grown so powerful since the murder of my father . . . all that had a certain seductiveness. Of course, against that weighed the teachings of Holy Mother Church regarding the hideous sufferings that awaited the apostate, murderess, fornicator, and possible *strega* in the Inferno below. But what had begun as a canker of doubt within me had blossomed into a thorny hedge wherein questions, outright disbelief, and growing contempt tangled impenetrably. Behind it, I sheltered, defiant and resolute.

"I will do what I must," I said.

For all his youth, *il re dei contrabbandieri* had not risen to his exalted position without understanding when a storm can be navigated around and when it must be gone through. He nodded and laid a hand lightly on my shoulder before vanishing back into the shadows.

I was alone in the gathering darkness. Before me, the stone bulk of Santa Maria loomed. I lifted my gaze to the mosaic of the Virgin suckling her son and, in defiance of all those who would condemn me, said a silent prayer that if there was anything out there, anyone to hear me and care, I would not die by Morozzi's hand.

Before fear could overcome me, I ran up the steps and into the church.

21

There was disagreement later about exactly who was responsible. Some claimed it was the apprentices, always suspected of running riot at the least or no provocation. Others declared that the culprits were imps from Hell who cavorted naked on cloven feet. A few insisted that it was the smugglers, but as no one could explain why they would behave in such a way, that was not taken seriously.

What is known is that Trastevere did not sleep that night. How could it when mischief-makers ran riot through its streets, singing loudly, bursting into homes and shops, upending tables, sending chickens and pigeons alike into a frenzy, freeing pigs into the roads, and all the while inexplicably chanting, "Come out, priest, come out! Come out, come out wherever you are!"

The plain truth is that there were more than a few priests in Trastevere that night—as any other. One or two may have been chastely in their own beds. Perhaps not; those numbers seem high. The rest were content to drink and carouse right along with a bevy of bishops, several archbishops, and at least one cardinal.

Some tried to flee when the trouble began only to be caught by what was rapidly turning into a torchlight parade drawing even decent people into a whirling bacchanalia where, amid pounding drums improvised out of kettles and staves and clashing cymbals thrown together from metal plates, liberated wine flowed freely and a general mood of good cheer prevailed.

Others of the cloth dove under beds from where they were rousted when the happy, singing mob threw open doors, dragging all into their midst with most—presumably not the members of the clergy—joining in the cry that resounded through every alley and lane: "Come out, priest, come out! Come out, come out wherever you are!"

It was even said that the cry was taken up in other neighborhoods, carried from rooftop to rooftop wherever people sought relief from the oppressive warmth. To this day on the anniversary of the Imp's Parade, as it came to be known, you can still hear the mocking admonition from the throats of all those brave enough to utter it.

"Come out, priest, come out! Come out, come out wherever you are!"

The goings-on in Trastevere meant nothing to me save that they should accomplish their purpose. I reasoned that the threat of discovery coupled with the mocking nature of the mob would compel Morozzi to seek safer ground. In hope of that, I took up my position in the church near the wooden door that Alfonso had revealed.

In my hands, I held the knife I had used to kill the assassin Morozzi had sent, likely a member of the Brotherhood, not that his identity mattered to me. I had gotten lucky with him thanks to the element of surprise and Cesare's coaching. But I could not count on luck again.

Accordingly, I had made a slight alteration to the blade. It was now coated with a contact poison that, unlike that encountered by the feckless Donna Lydia, I knew to be deadly. Of course, this meant that it required the most careful handling. I drew a deep breath to steady myself and kept my eyes on the wooden door.

I did not have long to wait.

Before I had barely settled myself, the door was flung open and Morozzi hurtled through it. He wore a black cloak that obscured him from head to toe, and moved as though demons were in pursuit, although I suppose that if they had been, he would have embraced them. At any rate, he took no more notice of me than he would have of a gnat.

So quickly did he come that he got beyond the door and into the aisle that traversed the church from apse to nave before I could react. He was running toward the altar when I leaped in pursuit. It was in my mind that there had to be many ways out of the old church and that Morozzi would know of them. He seemed to have spent all his time in the city investigating its hidden byways. I could not risk him vanishing into another of them.

"Hold!" I cried. "Bernando Morozzi, hold!"

He stopped and turned, looking toward me from the deep obscurity of his hooded cloak.

"It is I, Francesca Giordano. Will you run from me, coward? Or will we finish this now?"

I was counting on his hatred of me as well as the assumption made by every male that women are the weaker sex, unequal in any struggle. Sadly, that is too often true, but I had to believe that in my case it would be otherwise. I was prepared and I was determined.

All I had to do was draw him close enough to so much as nick him with the knife. That would be enough.

Lest he sense my intent, I kept the blade lowered at my side as I walked toward him.

"Not so brave when you are alone, are you?" I taunted. "You can send someone to try to kill me but you are afraid to do it yourself. It was the same with my father. You could not do that either but had to act through others."

He did not move or speak but I felt his eyes glaring at me.

I moved closer, propelled by the utter rightness of what I was about to do. Killing Morozzi would rid the world of a monster, avenge my father, protect the Jews, and help to preserve Borgia all at the same time. The certainty of what it would mean filled me with strength unlike any I had ever known.

I was so close. . . .

An arm wrapped around my throat from behind. In the same motion, I was yanked off my feet. I had only an instant to realize what was happening before the breath was squeezed out of me.

"Strega," a voice hissed in my ear. *"I will watch your bones crack in the fire."*

A witch. But far more important, a fool. I had fallen into the trap of my own arrogance, forgetting what I not only knew but had warned other people of—that Morozzi was far too clever ever to be underestimated. Like Borgia, he played a deep game, always think-ing many moves ahead. For certain, he had outmaneuvered me.

Desperately, I thrust backward with the knife but Morozzi was too fast. In an instant, he threw up his free arm and blocked my strike. Pain shot down through me. Only with the greatest effort did I manage to hold on to the knife.

At the same time, the other man, the one who had gulled me into thinking he was my quarry, rushed to assist Morozzi. He seized my wrist, intending to wrest the knife from me. His hood fell back and I saw a young man, not much older than myself, his eyes alight with the fire of a true believer.

Morozzi tightened his hold around my throat yet further. Black spots swam before my eyes. I knew myself to be only moments away from unconsciousness and death. With the last of my strength, I held on to the knife just long enough to nick the young man's chin. Scarcely had I managed to do so than the blade fell from my numbed fingers. At first, the wound meant nothing to him; I doubt he even noticed it. But the poison is among the fastest-acting I have ever created. In the space of mere heartbeats, he staggered back as all the color drained from his face.

Seeing him, Morozzi must have realized that something was wrong. He tightened his hold around my throat even more. I clawed at his arm in desperation but it was no use. The blackness closed in around me and I went limp.

Moments later—it could not have been longer than that—I recovered to find myself lying on the floor of the church against a column where Morozzi must have hurled me. He was bending over the younger man, screaming at him.

"What is wrong? What did she do to you?"

Distantly, I realized that in the tumult, Morozzi had no more idea of what had happened than did the younger man himself. So far as they both knew, I had managed to strike him down with, at most, hardly more than a pinprick.

I crawled upright, holding on to the column, and saw what Morozzi saw. His lackey was writhing on the ground, gasping for breath as his eyes bulged and his limbs convulsed.

As I said, the poison is fast-working.

Which meant that I had little time to finish the job. Frantically, I scrambled across the floor, trying to find the knife. If I could only get to it quickly enough—

The younger man was in his final throes. Black foam spewed from his mouth. Morozzi recoiled in horror. He turned away and saw me just as light from one of the altar lamps glinted off the knife's blade.

I lunged for it, sobbing with relief when my hand closed around the hilt. With the last of my strength, I struggled upright. I would meet Morozzi on my feet and, by God or the Devil—at that moment, I truly did not care which—I would kill him.

The mad priest froze, his face contorted in rage. He made to rush me only to halt suddenly as his gaze locked on the knife. To my despair, I watched as understanding dawned.

"*Strega,*" he said again, with fear and loathing. The raw instinct for survival took command. With a furious snarl, he turned and fled down the aisle.

At the same moment, the last of my strength left me. I slid to the floor. My throat felt constricted by fire and every breath I struggled to draw was agony. Later, I might be glad that I was alive but just then I could think only that Morozzi had escaped me—again. Poor weak creature that I was, I lay on the cold stones and wept.

Slowly, I became aware that I was not alone. Kind hands touched me. Voices murmured. I was lifted and carried some distance through shadow and flickering light, up a short flight of steps and into a room.

"Bring the lamp closer."

I winced and tried to turn my head away.

"It's all right, I just want to see your throat."

Sofia. I opened my eyes to find her bending over me, her face creased with worry. She leaned forward, listening as I breathed, then straightened and nodded to someone standing behind her.

"It's bad but she can breathe normally, thanks be to God."

Her hands moved over me gently. "Does anything else pain you?"

Only my heart, but I saw no reason to say that. Instead, I shook my head and struggled to sit up. At once, a familiar figure stepped forward to help me.

"David . . . how did you . . . ?" My voice emerged as little more than a croak, yet he still managed to understand me.

"Benjamin kept his promise," he said as he settled me against the bolster at the top of Sofia's bed. It was set behind a screen in the workroom at the back of her shop. I could smell the drying herbs and hear the soft hiss of the fire in a nearby brazier where water was heating.

"He stayed out of the way but he made sure to put me in touch with Alfonso. He sent word that you were in trouble."

"More fool I." Done with tears, I steeled myself for what had to be faced. "Morozzi got away."

"We know," David said, not unkindly. "We found the other man. He's been . . . taken care of."

I nodded, understanding that it was never good for the Jews for a body to be found in a church. Inevitably, they would have been blamed.

Thought of that reminded me of what Borgia had said regarding their purpose. My mouth twisted. Still struggling to speak, I gestured for Sofia to bend closer.

"I am sorry to have failed you," I whispered.

A tear slipped down her cheek, silver in the pale light. Her arms enfolded me. I inhaled the faint aroma of vinegar that always clung to her. But just beneath, rising up to replace it, I smelled lavender mingling with lemon, a perfume I had never associated with Sofia. I had only a moment to wonder at it before I heard a woman singing softly. An extraordinary sense of contentment washed over me. For the space of a heartbeat, I felt utterly safe and loved.

With my next breath, terror roared through me. It came without reason or warning. The faint thought struggled through my mind that it was some sort of reaction to what I had experienced in the church but it was quickly evident that this was far more. I was plainly and simply petrified. My heart pounded so frantically that it seemed intent on exploding from my chest and I was hard-pressed to breathe. Mewing sounds that I scarcely recognized came from me. I clung to Sofia even as I lost all awareness of her presence.

I was behind the wall but it offered no protection; a wave of blood poured in beneath, above, around, engulfing me. I heard screams and a voice pleading but the words made no sense, coming as they seemed to from some moment just before the world shattered.

"Stay very quiet, sweetheart. Don't make a sound."

Who spoke? Whose hands pressed me gently into the darkness?

"Please God, don't let her see . . ."

"Mamma!"

A great silence engulfed me. It went on for what seemed a very long time. I lay within it, curled deep inside myself, safe so long as I did not move. Some unknowable while later, I saw shards of sunlight, tasted broth spooned onto my tongue. A sparrow flitted within my sight. The sheets under me were cool. Someone spoke to me.

My father?

But he was dead and I had failed yet again to avenge his murder.

"Francesca—?"

I opened my eyes. Sofia still held me but it was David who had spoken. When I did not respond, he asked, "What is happening to her?"

"It is as I feared; the strain has been too much. She is remembering."

"Remembering what?" David asked, and I wondered myself, but I think in some way I already knew.

I slept then, deeply, and mercifully without dreams. When I awoke, it was morning. I smelled porridge cooking and heard voices nearby. I moved but tentatively, feeling as fragile as the glass I loved to watch Rocco create. Yet I managed to sit up and even to swing my legs over the side of the bed. From there it was only a matter of gathering enough strength to rise.

The world spun but I held on, waiting until it righted. When it had, I took one step, followed by careful others. Sofia and David were sitting at the table in the front of the apothecary shop. They jumped up at sight of me.

"I am fine," I said, but failed to fend them off. Truth be told, I didn't try very hard. In my weakened state, the notion of being taken care of was an irresistible temptation.

"Sit down," Sofia urged. When I had done so, she set a cup of tea in front of me and stood at my side until I had drunk the better part of it. The taste was faintly bitter but not unpleasant. Soon enough, I began to return more fully to life.

First and most important, I had to know, "Did you find my knife?" Although I had used it on Morozzi's lackey, it would still be coated with the contact poison, making it extraordinarily dangerous to anyone who might handle it carelessly.

Sofia moved quickly to reassure me. "We assumed, given the circumstances, that it had to be dealt with carefully. I have it locked away in a box."

Relieved, I nodded and pressed on. "What is happening in the city?" My voice sounded like gravel rolling around in a barrel but I was determined to speak.

"There is no sign of Morozzi," David said. "Alfonso has his people looking but to no effect, at least not so far. Borgia's men are at your apartment, asking after you. Rumor has it that you are dead."

Ah, Rome and its gossipmongers, ever ready to spin a good story.

"How do they say I died?" You may think my curiosity morbid but I was truly interested in knowing.

"Struck down inside a church," Sofia replied. She looked grim. "Opinion is evenly divided as to whether that was punishment for your wicked ways or Borgia's."

"Borgia's, of course. On my own, I am hardly worthy of so dramatic an end."

"You may jest, but this is a serious matter. You could have been killed. As it is, you—"

"I am fine," I said before she could continue. Fragments of memory were surfacing in my mind. Vaguely, I recalled being in a considerable state when I was brought to the apothecary shop. In truth, I remembered rather more than that but I was in no mood to acknowledge it. Not with matters of such import closing in around me.

"I must go," I said, and made to rise, only to be pressed back into the chair at once by both Sofia and David, each with a hand on my shoulder.

"Don't be ridiculous," Sofia said. "You aren't going anywhere until I am convinced that you can stand for more than a moment or two. In the meantime, you must eat."

To my surprise, my stomach rumbled. I was genuinely hungry; indeed, I was ravenous. I spooned the porridge she set before me into my mouth with unseemly haste, and not only because I was anxious to go. Truth be told, I often eat without really tasting the food, my mind being preoccupied with some other matter. But the porridge was creamy, sweet with a hint of salt, delicious.

"This is good," I said, and held out my bowl for more. As a child might.

Sofia and David exchanged a glance but neither spoke. When I had finished the second portion, I sat back with a huge sigh, a hand on my comfortably full stomach. For a moment, all seemed right with the world.

Of course, it was not. Morozzi was at large; Borgia was likely frantic, though he would never admit it; and I had tarried long enough.

"I really have to leave," I said. This time when I rose, they did not object but both looked concerned and, worse yet, uncertain. Plainly, they were at a loss as to how to deal with me. I could hardly blame them. Neither David nor Sofia had any familiarity with the kind of deception that I worked so readily upon myself.

Even so, my friends were determined to help me.

"I'm going with you," David said as he stood.

"We shouldn't be seen together," I cautioned. Bad enough if the leaders of the Hebrew Quarter learned of his return; if he was spotted in the presence of Borgia's poisoner, or worse yet her ghost, they would be beside themselves.

"We'll go the way we brought you here," he said. "Through the tunnels."

I was beginning to wonder why anyone in the city ever went about on the surface, being rained on, stepping in piles of manure, dodging horses and carts, and the like. Were it not for a tendency to collapse without warning, becoming instant tombs, Rome's hidden byways would have been even more popular than they obviously were.

"Take this with you," Sofia said as I prepared to leave. She pressed a small packet of herbs into my hand. "The tea has a reviving effect but it is also calming."

I nodded but said, "If you wouldn't mind, I could use more of the sleeping powder."

Given what had happened in the church and afterward, I feared that when the nightmare came, as it surely would if I was not drugged sufficiently to prevent it, it would so overtake my mind as to render me unable to escape it. I was willing to do anything to avoid that.

Sofia hesitated and for a moment I feared that she meant to refuse. Panic rose in me. With the benefit of hindsight, I should have taken it as warning of my true state. Instead, as I always did, I pushed it aside.

"I can give you a little more," she said finally. "But the powder is too dangerous to be used regularly. We must find other ways to help you sleep."

So great was my relief that I wasted no time assuring her of my heartfelt intent to do just that, when in fact I had no wish to do anything of the sort. Lest you think me utterly without conscience, let me say that I did feel a twinge of guilt at so misleading her, but it was far too weak to give me other than momentary discomfort.

Having received the powder from Sofia, and my knife as well, I took my leave with David. He led me back through the underground passages until we emerged into a narrow lane adjacent to the Piazza di Santa Maria. At that hour of the morning, the square around the fountain was thronged with passersby on foot and on horseback, as well as carts and wagons jockeying for position. No one took any notice of us. Still in my boy's garb, I looked no more remarkable than any young apprentice, but my anonymity could not last. Deliberately, I averted my eyes from the church where I had so lately confronted death, and bid David farewell.

"You will be careful?" he urged, his brow furrowed as he studied me. "Now that Morozzi knows you are hunting him, there is no telling what he may do."

The same thought had occurred to me but I did not say so. The mad priest was not likely to take my failed attack on him as anything other than a blatant provocation. He was certain to retaliate soon, making the urgency of stopping him greater than ever.

Having assured David that I would take every precaution—yet another lie to add to my ever-growing tally—I made my way to my apartment. I hoped for some brief period of respite in which I could gather myself but that was not to be. Scarcely had I turned the corner into my street than I realized that the inevitable reckoning for my failed attack on the mad priest was about to come due.

22

Vittoro would not look at me directly. He kept his eyes focused on the wall over my shoulder. His hands were clasped behind his back, his features set in an expression of studied aloofness. Were I his subordinate, I would have quaked with fear. As it was I had to remind myself that I had done nothing other than use my best judgment regarding how to keep Borgia alive. Granted, a case could be made that I had erred by not calling in more assistance to confront Morozzi. But had I succeeded in killing the priest, my audacity would have been applauded. I was not disposed to apologize for it, although in all candor that might have been the safer course.

The building was surrounded by condottierri who had taken up position in front and overflowed into the loggia. Apart from the soldiers, no one stirred along the street. My neighbors had the good sense to hide inside their residences, from which they peered out through shuttered windows at the goings-on below.

"Donna Francesca," Vittoro said when he spied me. "Alive and whole, despite what we have been hearing."

That seemed to give him no pleasure but I had to hope that my old friend still welcomed my continued presence on this earth.

"So it appears," I replied. "I need to bathe and change. Come up with me and we can talk."

Thus did I attempt to take control of the situation, insomuch as that was possible. I was counting on Vittoro's inherent goodwill to grant me time to explain what had happened and in that, thankfully, I was not disappointed.

"His Holiness is deeply concerned about you," he said as we passed Portia's door. The top panel was open and I thought I caught a glimpse of her hovering just within but I could not be sure.

I did not take that statement literally, nor could Vittoro have meant for me to do so. We both knew full well that Borgia's concern in any matter extended no further than his own welfare.

"He shouldn't listen to street gossip," I replied.

"You have been missing since yesterday. Much of the city has been caught up in an anticlerical riot that associates of yours are suspected of having provoked. There are reports of a killing within Santa Maria, although no body has been found. Now you show up, in boy's garb and hardly able to speak because of what looks like a serious attempt to strangle you."

I touched a hand to my throat self-consciously. "Morozzi escaped me, for which I take full responsibility. However, at least I have been able to confirm that he is in the city and the number of his followers has been reduced by one."

Il capitano raised an eyebrow. "By your hand?"

I shrugged in silent acknowledgment. "I understand that His

Holiness will hold me accountable for my actions but I don't think he would appreciate my appearing before him like this."

I was a sufficient source of scandal already without provoking yet more, but I also wanted some little time to prepare what I would say in my own defense before facing Borgia.

Vittoro did not disagree. He accompanied me up the stairs to my apartment and waited in the salon while I bathed and changed. Ordinarily, I paid little attention to what I wore, but under the circumstances I thought it prudent to take more than usual care. Accordingly, I chose a flowered Florentine silk that Lucrezia had pressed on me and even went so far as to let down my hair, brush the tangles from it, and secure it under a silver net snood.

When I emerged, Vittoro was standing by a window overlooking the interior garden. He was petting Minerva, who appeared to have taken a liking to him. Surveying me as he might have one of his own daughters, he appeared satisfied by what he saw.

Even so, he said, "I must warn you. I have rarely seen our master in such a state."

Harangued by the Spanish emissary, threatened by the demands of both the Sforzas and the King of Naples, with the specter of della Rovere looming over him, and now also confronted by Morozzi allied with the fanatic Savonarola, Borgia was indeed besieged on all sides. I knew that he had been in difficult positions before but there had always been a certain *brio* to him, a combination of enthusiasm and confidence that carried all else before it. More recently he had seemed merely angry or impatient, perhaps even disillusioned. After devoting the better part of his life to attaining the papacy, was our master discovering that Saint Peter's Throne was not quite so comfortable a perch as he had imagined it would be?

Rather than voice my concerns and in the process heighten them, I accompanied Vittoro largely in silence across the river to the Vatican Palace. The day marked one week to the appointed date for Lucrezia's wedding to Pesaro. The bridegroom was expected to arrive in the city two days before then. In anticipation of his welcome, crews were out scrubbing the Corso and surrounding streets; draping banners in the gold and mulberry colors of the House of Borgia and the white and gold of the Sforzas over balcony railings; and setting out pots of poppies, marigolds, and white lilies mixed with jasmine. Armed guards stood watch against any repetition of the obscene graffiti that, for the moment at least, seemed to have stopped.

In kitchens all over the city, preparations were under way for the vast public feast Borgia would offer up as tribute to the people of Rome. Ordinarily, anticipation of the festivities would have prompted a certain lightheartedness and good cheer but everywhere I looked, I saw faces set in sullenness, if not outright hostility. I had been so preoccupied with keeping Borgia safe that I had paid little attention to the mood growing in the city. Now I regretted not taking more notice of it.

Despite what their "betters" like to think, humble men and women pay keen attention to what is happening around them; how can they not when their very survival depends on the whims of those fate has raised above them? That is all the truer of the sophisticated citizens of Rome. They knew full well the danger approaching from all sides. If what I saw was a fair representation of the city as a whole, the goodwill Borgia had received upon his election to the papacy had evaporated like rain striking heated stone.

Our armed escort kept the crowds at a distance from us, but I caught more than a few, perhaps guessing who I was, make the horned sign to ward off evil. Much good it would do them.

Having seen me within the confines of the Curia, Vittoro did me the courtesy of going no farther than the foot of the grand marble staircase leading up to the first floor and Borgia's offices. I was spared the ignominy of being brought to His Holiness under guard. Yet I must admit that, distasteful though that would have been, I would have welcomed a strong arm to lean on as I climbed the steps.

The denizens of the Curia being no more immune to the lure of gossip and scandal than any Ostian fishwife, my arrival was an occasion of great notice. One by one those I passed fell silent, regarding me with various degrees of malicious pleasure and outright hostility from which I gathered that my odds were not considered good. I regretted having no opportunity to lay off a few bets before confronting my fate.

Only one friendly face awaited me and even that was guarded.

"Donna Francesca," Renaldo said as he darted into my path. "Praise God, you are alive."

"For the moment. How is His Holiness?"

Renaldo grimaced. "In a rare state. Signore Cesare has returned from— Well, I'm sure you know where he was."

The knowledge that the business in Siena had been concluded lifted my spirits. Had circumstances been otherwise, I would have had no thought but to be reunited with my dark lover. Unfortunately, at the moment I had other priorities.

Renaldo bent closer. In my ear, he said, "They are arguing worse than I have ever heard them. I fear they will come to blows."

"Right now?" I asked, surprised. "Cesare is here?"

Renaldo nodded, not even bothering to pretend surprise at such familiarity on my part.

"He arrived about an hour ago. He is enraged by the attacks on Donna Lucrezia's honor. He actually blamed Il Papa for using her as a pawn and thereby putting her in danger." The steward shuddered. "The shouting got worse after that. Frankly, I'm surprised the walls aren't cracked."

I listened intently but heard nothing.

"And now the silence—" The steward looked heavenward.

I understood his concern. Heated argument between father and son was worrisome enough; dead quiet was far more ominous.

"Has anyone—?" I began.

"Looked through the *spioncino*? They haven't the nerve. They've all fled to the farthest antechambers or beyond."

Where I would have been more than happy to join them, had I already not been in such disrepute with my employer that I did not dare risk more. Gathering my courage, I nodded.

"Perhaps I should let His Holiness know that I am here?"

Renaldo puffed up his cheeks and exhaled sharply, a sure sign of his agitation. "I think that would be a good idea."

For all that he approved my intention, he did not offer to accompany me. I could hardly blame him. Had I been the witch people accused me of being, perhaps I would have had a convenient spell for creating a simulacrum of myself to do my bidding while I remained at a safe distance. Unfortunately, I lacked such skill.

"Well, then," I said, and ventured forth.

The innermost antechamber directly next to Borgia's private sanctum was empty. I crossed it quickly, ignoring the murals of a lush Eve cavorting with the serpent. On the crest of a deep breath, I peered through the *spioncino*. I expected to see father and son in quieter conversation, having remembered belatedly the need for discretion. I would knock, announce myself, and hope against hope to be received with a minimum of outrage.

The office was empty. There was no sign of either Borgia or Cesare.

I cracked the door open, stepped inside, and peered around. No, they were not hiding in the corners waiting to leap out at me. They were nowhere at all.

There were only three possibilities: They had adjourned to Borgia's apartment, which I thought unlikely, as Renaldo would surely have known of their presence there. They had left the Curia and were in the adjacent Palazzo Santa Maria in Portico. I had difficulty imagining that in the throes of a serious argument, they would seek the company of either La Bella or Lucrezia.

That left the secret door and the passageway leading to the Mysterium Mundi.

I told myself that it was my duty to seek out His Holiness without delay, assuage his fears about my fate, and take responsibility for my failure to kill Morozzi. In doing so, I would reveal my knowledge of the concealed room beneath the Curia, but that was a price I was willing to pay to discover what lay within the hidden sanctuary, and what had drawn Borgia *padre e figlio* to it.

I inched open the hidden door behind the bookcase and proceeded along the passageway slanting downward into the bowels of the earth. As sunlight faded behind me, I hesitated to light a lamp, reluctant as I was to give notice of my approach. Waiting while my eyes adjusted to the darkness, I saw up ahead a glimmer of light, sufficient for me to continue on cautiously. Shortly thereafter, I caught the low murmur of men's voices coming from the same direction. A breeze carrying the scents of moist earth and the nearby river cooled my cheeks. I crept toward the long shadows of two men cast against the stone walls. Their backs were to me; I could hear them talking but could not make out their words. Gathering my courage, I stepped from the darkness.

Cesare saw me first. He was all in black, the somber hue accentuating the broad sweep of his shoulders and chest, the tautness of his waist and hips, the powerful muscles of his thighs. Truly, I was the most distractible creature. Yet I did manage to note that his garments were mud-splattered, suggesting that he had ridden for the city in great haste. The unguarded look of relief that flitted across his face startled me. Had we been alone, I might have responded without restraint, that glad was I to see him. Borgia's presence quashed any such possibility.

"The prodigal daughter!" Il Papa exclaimed. "Dare I ask how you come here? If there is any place more secret in all of Rome, I haven't heard of it."

I lied without hesitation rather than reveal my penchant for sticking my nose where it does not belong. "My father told me of this place."

Before His Holiness could question me further, I made a show of looking around with great interest. That, at least, was genuine. Whereas on my first visit, I had been able to make out very little from the far side of the grille, now I could see that the room was filled with floor-to-ceiling shelves stuffed with scrolls, illuminated manuscripts, loose sheaves of parchment, jeweled casks, crystal vials, and, most ominously, skulls that looked not entirely human. Larger oddities, too big to be shelved, took up most of the remaining space. I glimpsed statues of bearded angels that, upon closer look, appeared to resemble demons; curiously carved bas reliefs; a large black rock half the height of a man with a highly polished, smooth surface as though burnished by fire; and too much more for my mind to grasp.

"What is all this?" I asked. "Why is it locked away?"

Cesare answered me. "For centuries, treasures of all sorts have flowed into the lap of Holy Mother Church. Most she approves of and welcomes but from time to time something may raise questions or worse yet, doubts. When that happens, it comes here."

Given the fondness for burning people who dare to challenge orthodoxy, I had presumed that the Church destroyed anything that might be a threat to it, but apparently I was wrong. Excitement filled me. I happily could spend hours, days, weeks delving into every shelf and corner of the room. But my personal fascination did not explain why Borgia was there, particularly not given everything else he had to occupy him.

"Have you brought me the head of Morozzi?" Il Papa inquired. "If that's too much trouble, I would settle for his black heart, assuming you can find it."

I had seen him in many moods—triumphant, relaxed, drunk, thoughtful, scheming—but I had never seen him as he was then. His hair—newly blackened by an application of oak apple burned in oil and mixed with vinegar—was in disarray. His clothing was rumpled with stains across the chest as though he had eaten, or more likely drunk, without notice. He was unshaven and his eyes were bloodshot. But it was his mouth that worried me most, so tightly drawn as it was that I could make out the thin white line surrounding fleshy lips. Christ's Vicar was not a man to restrain his emotions, particularly not when they were so dark. At the most, I had minutes to convince him not to dispose of me there and then.

"I will do my best, Holiness. As you know, I am as eager as you are to see Morozzi dead, perhaps even more so."

My voice still rasped painfully but I managed to keep it steady. Cesare frowned and stared at my throat. He looked about to speak but was prevented by his father's quick rejoinder.

"Yet he lives because of your vanity," Borgia accused. "You don't want anyone else to kill him, only you."

It was true; Morozzi was responsible for my father's murder, in the name of justice he had to die by my hand. Of course, I was not about to say so.

"I could have taken men-at-arms with me into Santa Maria. But had I done so, Morozzi would never have come anywhere near. He would have been warned off."

"I told you she had a reason," Cesare said. "You should have listened to me. And now you don't even bother to notice that she's injured."

He cast me a look at once all too perceptive and boldly intimate. Heat crept over me even as I struggled to give no hint of it.

Borgia brushed that aside with a flick of his hand. "You'd defend her no matter what she did."

That was both flattering and worrisome. I had hoped that the doubts Borgia had voiced about Cesare's loyalty, and by extension my own, had been put to rest. Apparently, that was not the case.

"You're too quick to condemn," Cesare countered. "We have enough enemies without you manufacturing more."

Borgia's face darkened. Instinctively, I glanced over my shoulder, seeking a quick route of escape but finding only the dark corridor fading away into blackness.

"Don't tell me what I should or shouldn't do, boy! The day you understand the world half as well as I, I'll—"

"You'll what? Admit that I'm capable of thoughts and actions entirely my own? And that sometimes I'm right and you're wrong?"

I sucked in my breath. In the best of circumstances, challenging Borgia the Bull was madness, but to do it now, when he was pushed to his limits and perhaps beyond— I could not begin to think what Cesare hoped to accomplish.

But perhaps he had reached his own limits in trying to deal with his father's implacable determination to regard his children as nothing more than extensions of himself.

For a horrible moment, I feared the two men—so alike in some ways, yet so different in others—might fall to blows. Any real conflict between them would severely undermine our chances of prevailing against the dangers closing in on *la famiglia* from all sides. I was certain that they both knew that, but even so, something had to be done quickly before either acted unforgivably.

"Cardinal Giorgio da Costa is *titulus* of Santa Maria, is he not?"

The vaulted brickwork ceiling and stone walls amplified my voice loudly enough to distract them, or perhaps they welcomed an excuse to step back from the precipice. Whatever the cause, father and son both shifted their attention away from each other and onto me.

"What of it?" Borgia demanded. He looked ill-disposed to hear anything I might say, yet he was listening all the same. I took courage from that.

"Da Costa is no friend to you. On the contrary, he is well known to be della Rovere's ally."

"You think he is supporting Morozzi?" Cesare asked. "Are you saying that madman is actually sheltered within Santa Maria?"

"Da Costa is too wily for anything so obvious. But priests in service to the Cardinal could be pardoned for thinking that they would win his favor by offering at least some degree of aid to one opposed to His Holiness."

"She has a point," Cesare said.

"She *may* have a point," Borgia corrected. He looked at me more closely as though deciding whether I might merit some small degree of trust. "How did you intend to kill Morozzi?"

"My knife was coated with a contact poison. When he realized that, he ran away."

"But you killed someone?"

I nodded. "One of the Brotherhood who I mistook for Morozzi. Next time, I will be certain before I strike."

Borgia considered that. I awaited his judgment, certain that I had made my case as well as I could but in no way confident of its persuasiveness.

After what seemed like a very long time, my master said, "See that you do."

I let my breath out slowly but my curiosity did not evaporate with it. Despite my better sense I asked, "May I know what interests you here?"

"A book of prophecy," Cesare said, ignoring his father's quelling look. "It describes the visions of a hermit monk living five centuries ago in a monastery in Carpathia. The book has been kept here under seal because its contents are disturbing in their detail . . . and in their seeming accuracy."

I am of two minds regarding the nature of prophecy. All good Christians are required to believe in it, as the coming of Our Savior was no less than the fulfillment of prophecy. Yet most of it seems to fall somewhere between outright fraud and the ravings of lunatics.

I kept my skepticism to myself, knowing as I did that Borgia sought glimpses of the future that he believed would give him an advantage against his foes. He even went so far as to claim that I was capable of such visions. Thus far, I had failed to disabuse him of the notion. To be fair, I had not managed to disabuse myself of it entirely either.

"In what way are they accurate?" I asked.

"Do you want a list?" Borgia demanded. Without waiting for a response, he proceeded to give me one.

"It warns, among other things, that the followers of the king of the world will perish at the hands of the innocent; that the son of France will destroy the sons of the temple; and that the mother will be rent twice over, bathing the world in tears."

By which I assumed he was referring to the massacre of the Cathars, followers of the one they called Rex Mundi, by Pope Innocent III in 1210; the destruction of the Templars by the French King Philip IV a century later; and the two schisms that had torn the Church apart and unleashed so much suffering throughout Christendom.

I will admit, all that gave me pause.

"Does it say anything about the present circumstances?" I asked.

Cesare nodded. "It warns that in the time of resurrection, the red bull will perish at the bidding of the unborn killer."

Were we in the time of resurrection? I supposed that a case could be made that with the ending of the most recent schism, the Church was experiencing a rebirth. Certainly, Borgia could be seen as the red bull. But who was the unborn killer, and if he hadn't been born yet, why would anyone be concerned about him?

"Our people in Ferrara have been making discreet inquiries regarding a certain friar," Borgia said. "I sent Cesare there to confirm what I was hearing."

It took me a moment to realize what he meant. Savonarola, scourge of the Medicis and lately of such concern to Borgia, had been born into an affluent family in the duchy of Ferrara.

"Reliable sources have informed us that Savonarola had a twin," Cesare said. "The other child, also a boy, was born first but emerged dead from their mother's womb. The dead baby bore marks indicating that he had been stabbed."

"Stabbed in the womb?" I tried to imagine how such a thing could have happened. Women sometimes resort to desperate measures to end an unwanted pregnancy, but if that had been the case, how could Savonarola have survived? For that matter, how could his mother?

"You think he stabbed his twin?" I asked. "Before they were born?"

"So it appears," Cesare said. He seemed to accept the possibility without question. "The family hushed it up, of course, but my men found an old nurse who revealed the truth."

For proper payment, I assumed. Wave enough gold in front of people—sometimes it takes surprisingly little—and they will say anything.

"How would a babe in the womb manage to stab another?" I asked.

Borgia shrugged, as though the details were of no importance. "Who knows what demonic means he used. What matters is that we have confirmed where the greater threat to me will come from."

Not from Spain with all its might, nor Naples, nor della Rovere and his ally, the French king? Borgia truly believed that the greatest danger he faced was from a fanatical monk railing against the decadence and corruption of the church? Now that I thought of it, that made a strange kind of sense. All the rest—Spain, Naples, France— was politics, a game Borgia had long since mastered. But the call to purification on the lips of a man who truly believed that he was guided by God . . . that was an entirely different matter.

"Savonarola would never dare to strike at my father directly," Cesare said, "not even through Il Frateschi. But he wouldn't hesitate to make use of someone who could not be linked directly to him. It is vital that Morozzi be dealt with at once."

Since I desired nothing on this earth so much as the mad priest's death, I could hardly disagree.

Even so, I was unprepared when Borgia said, "Cesare has convinced me that the two of you should join forces to dispose of Morozzi."

I stared at my dark lover. He returned my look with all the youthful sincerity of a devoted son wanting nothing more than to serve his father. Cesare and I had known each other most of our lives. I had few illusions about his character and I doubted that he had many about mine, yet I liked to believe that we were allies, perhaps even friends.

Why then the unease that stole over me as a dank mist from the river will, bringing hints of buried secrets and dangers as yet ungrasped?

23

While I was still mulling over my doubts, Cesare did not hesitate. He took a lamp in one hand and seized mine in the other.

"We will begin at once, Papa. Have no fear, Morozzi is not long for this world."

Borgia's only response was a grunt as he settled heavily into his chair. He appeared in no hurry to return to the world above. I could hardly blame him but neither could I deny Cesare's urgency. We were through the corridor and back in the papal office before I caught my breath.

Once there, he set the lamp on a table, grabbed me around the waist, and pressed me down onto the vast expanse of the desk. His dark eyes gleamed and his arousal, pressed against me, left no doubt as to his intent.

"I am going to kill him," he said as he drew the bodice of my gown down to further expose the welts around my throat. I felt his breath hot and strong against my abused flesh. A long tremor ran through me.

"Slowly and with enormous pain," he went on, sliding a hand down my thigh to grasp hold of my skirt and drag it upward. "Perhaps I will flay the skin from him and display it somewhere appropriate. What do you think?"

What did I think? Of Rocco standing in the sun in Saint Peter's Square, refusing to meet my eyes as he told me of Carlotta d'Agnelli? Of Sofia holding me in her arms as I wept in terror of the unknown? Of Morozzi, calling me *strega* and gloating as he contemplated my suffering in the flames? Of my father, bloody fragments of his smashed skull washing away in the filthy water running down the gully of a Roman street.

"You can do that after I've killed him," I replied, and tugged at his lacings.

You will think me mad or damned, although both would be the fairer guess. Borgia could change his mind and return to his office at any moment. Anyone might peer through the *spioncino;* Rome would drown under the wave of gossip that set off. Worse yet, we were in the inner sanctum of Christ's Vicar on Earth, surely a place that called for a modicum of decorum, although I had heard stories about Borgia and La Bella frolicking there.

I could claim that we were helpless victims of passion swept away by the moment. I could swear that we would never have engaged in such sacrilege had we been in our right minds. But the truth is that the sense of danger and sinfulness spurred our lust to even greater heights. Had we not been naturally shameless, we would have become so.

Even so, do not think for a moment that I am proud of what we did. The great men of the Church have no respect for Her but we lesser mortals, even those plagued by doubts, still honor our Mother. Eve, Isis, Aphrodite, Venus, she had many names before she was transformed into the Eternal Virgin, her purity insisted upon after countless years unmissed. Perhaps she understands and forgives us.

Cesare laid me across the desk with my skirts bunched around my waist, spread my legs, and entered hard and fast. I was more than ready. Breath rushed from me in a gasp of pleasure and fast-approaching release. I had been too long without him. As for my dark lover, I did not fancy that he was chaste when we were apart, far from it, but we shared a physical affinity that drew us together time and again. Our coupling was swift, rough, and eminently satisfying. When, very shortly, he lay sprawled across me, the rasp of his jaw a pleasant torment against my bared breasts, I could not restrain my laughter.

He raised his head and looked down at me, his dark eyes alight with challenge. "I amuse you?"

"Among other things, you do." I pushed him off—catching him by surprise so that he stumbled a little—and stood, straightening my skirts. Later, I would be glad to bathe, but just then I did not mind the lingering feel and smell of him.

Redoing his laces, he cast me a look that might have given another woman pause. Young as he still was in years, he had a man's pride and more. By no measure was he to be trifled with.

Nor was I.

"A Carpathian monk?" I asked, trying in vain to coax my hair back into some semblance of order. "Five hundred years ago? However did you conceive of that?"

Imagine Cesare, if you will, all liquid-eyed with a disingenuous smile, disclaiming all knowledge of whatever mischief he had just committed. Or more likely blaming it on younger brother Juan. The tactic must have worked well for he still pulled it out whenever he was otherwise at a loss.

"What are you talking about? Conceive of what?"

"The book of prophecy. That perfect book that spells out events we cannot fail to recognize, all the while encouraging your father to believe what you want him to believe."

I had come to the conclusion that the book was a fake while we made our way back from the Mysterium; it had taken that little time to realize what had likely happened. For all their differences of opinion, Borgia had long recognized that his eldest son possessed a brilliant mind. He had ensured that Cesare received the finest possible education, perhaps not entirely considering what that might equip him to do, including connive at a highly skilled forgery.

"Honestly, Francesca, such cynicism is not attractive."

That from the man who had just drained himself in paroxysms of passion because he couldn't wait to possess me.

I smirked. "What else is in the book? Something such as 'The firstborn son shall go forth as he will, following his own star, and reward the bull tenfold with his daring'?"

Cesare could admit defeat with surprising grace. Shrugging, he said, "That's good. I didn't put it quite that eloquently but close enough."

Opening the door a crack, I peered into the antechamber. It was empty. I slipped through and hurried across to the door giving access to the corridor. Cesare followed. Startled clerics moved out of our path, pressing their backs to the walls as they gaped at us. We were barely past when the steady clucking of tongues erupted.

Halfway down the marble steps, Cesare said, "You aren't going to tell him?"

"Of course not, so long as we agree that Morozzi dies by my hand."

"It means that much to you?"

The sun had reached its apex while we were below in the Mysterium. The day was warming rapidly; torpid air heavy with the overripe smell of the river barely stirred. Even the pigeons couldn't be bothered to do much more than hunch in the scant shade, drowsing. The entrance to the Curia was crowded with petitioners, clerks, prelates, and the usual hangers-on of every description, sweat beaded on their foreheads and their heavy black garb hanging like shrouds around them. Heedless of the ado our presence caused, I stopped and looked at Cesare.

"It means everything."

He met my gaze unflinchingly. "Morozzi must not be allowed to escape again. I'll give you one more chance but if you can't take him, he's mine."

I won't say that I liked that but I was honest enough to admit that Cesare was right. I had struck the best bargain I could hope for.

"Fair enough. I have matters to see to in the kitchens but we should meet as soon as possible to decide our course."

I had to hope that while I inspected the most recently arrived supplies, Cesare would not seize the opportunity to go after Morozzi alone. If he did, I feared he would succeed only in driving the priest ever deeper into the labyrinth beneath Rome and make finding him even more difficult.

"I have business to attend to myself." Without offering any hint of what that might be, Cesare added, "If I'm free before you are, your *portatore*—Portia, that's her name, isn't it?—will let me in."

I was quite certain that she would, nor could I really blame her. But to assure that he didn't have the upper hand entirely, I said, "Just take care not to touch anything unless you're certain that it's safe, all right?"

We were at the bottom of the stairs by then and about to part. Cesare could not resist having the last word.

"I'll bring supper. We both know you can't cook." He strode off, leaving me hard-pressed not to laugh again, this time at the unexpected domesticity cropping up between us, absurd yet somehow pleasing.

My mood sobered as I worked my way through the piles of supplies that had arrived while I was occupied hunting Morozzi. Mercifully, since the attack on Lucrezia, Borgia had decreed that all wedding gifts and other items meant for her use would be sequestered until such time as I could examine them with greatest care. Given the sheer quantity involved, I had to wonder if the marriage would still be in effect before I was done.

By the time I finished, I was tired, sticky, and regretting—just a little—my excesses with Cesare. Being laid across a desk and thoroughly . . . is there a polite term for what we did? Never mind. I told myself that the twinges I felt were merely a reminder that I was alive.

Slipping through an archway next to the kitchens, I passed through a short tunnel before coming out into the Piazza San Pietro. By then it was mid-afternoon. The day had turned even sultrier, the air hanging wet and limp. Most anyone with an ounce of sense had taken shelter out of the sun, as I intended to do myself.

Even so, the square was crowded with pilgrims moving like schools of gap-mouthed fish. Several, seemingly attached to each other at the hips, walked into a ruddy-faced priest who clearly did not relish being out and about in the heat. He dropped his ledgers and emitted a stream of invective that appeared to impress them mightily.

I dodged around the priest and his new admirers while avoiding a pile of manure fresh enough to still be steaming. I had it in my mind to pay Nando a visit, and perhaps enjoy a goblet of Donna Felicia's excellent homemade cider, when I stopped suddenly. Up ahead, no more than fifty or so feet in front of me, a tall, slender friar in a hooded robe emerged from a side door of the basilica. Something in the set of his shoulders . . . the way he moved . . . his haste despite the heat and the general languor of the hour caught my attention.

A group of visitors from the Low Countries in their distinctive peaked hats and tasseled capes stepped into my path. I went right, then left, then right again before I was able to evade them. By the time I had done so, the monk had vanished. Telling myself that I was jumping at shadows, I was continuing on toward the barracks when I caught sight of the same man near the main gate leading out from the Vatican. The distance separating us was greater by then, being easily a hundred feet or more, but when he turned his head in my direction, there was no mistaking the gleam of golden hair beneath the hood of his habit.

My breath left me in a rush. For a horrible moment, I froze, uncertain of what to do. If Morozzi really had penetrated the precincts of the Vatican, I could not let him escape. But what if he was not alone? His accomplices among Il Frateschi could be nearby, going about his bidding unrecognized. I had promised Rocco that I would keep Nando safe. Where was the boy?

I looked around frantically, hoping to spot Vittoro or one of his lieutenants but although more guards than usual were present throughout the square, they were all common soldiers unlikely to understand my concern, much less respond to it. Any time I spent pleading with them would be wasted.

I had two choices—go after the monk myself or find Nando.

Before I could decide, a two-wheeled carriage, the roof and sides of sturdy leather unmarred by any insignia, drew to a stop just beyond the gate. Without pause, the monk opened the carriage door and stepped in, shutting it behind him. The vehicle, connected by ox-hide straps to the wheeled chassis, bobbed with his weight. Before it could settle, the driver lashed the pair of horses. The carriage disappeared rapidly in the direction of the Ponte Sisto.

I had no illusions about the clergy's fondness for luxuries but I knew full well that it was not the custom of monks to ride about in carriages, such comfort being reserved solely for the wealthiest and most powerful, or those who enjoyed their patronage. Any doubt I had as to the identity of the man I had seen vanished.

Gathering up my skirts, I raced for the barracks, heedless of the startled, censorious looks that followed in my wake.

24

I found Vittoro near the stables and gasped out what I had seen. Mercifully, he did not doubt me but instead barked an order that sent a dozen men running hard in the direction the carriage had gone. I nurtured little hope that they would find it. Bent over, my hands on my knees as I struggled to regain my breath, I said, "Tell me Nando is safe."

I take it as a measure of his intrinsic honesty that rather than offer reassurances he feared might be false, he grasped my arm and, supporting me, moved swiftly in the direction of his residence. I held fast to him, weighed down by dread that threatened to crush me, but sometimes God truly is merciful. Before we reached the tidy house, we caught sight of Nando. He was sitting out in front, his tousled head bent over a flat board holding a sheet of paper. He was busy sketching.

I took my first full breath since glimpsing Morozzi and gathered up the shreds of my composure. With a smile I could only hope looked genuine, I approached the child.

"What is that you are drawing?" I asked.

He glanced up and, seeing me, smiled. Holding up the notebook, he said, "Moses receiving the Commandments. It's supposed to look like the one in the Chapel but it doesn't really, does it?"

In fact, it wasn't a bad copy, especially not considering the extreme youth of the artist. Yet it troubled me all the same.

"When were you in the Chapel?" I asked. It had been in my mind to take him but the opportunity had not presented itself. I doubted that Vittoro would have thought of doing so.

"This morning." Nando replied. He continued to regard his sketch critically. "The monk took me."

As though from a great distance, I heard myself ask, "What monk?"

"Papa's friend. He said we could go again and you could come with us."

Vittoro and I exchanged a quick glance. I saw that he was as taken aback as I.

With as much calm as I could muster, I asked, "Do you remember the monk's name?"

The boy shook his head. Belatedly, he seemed to realize that perhaps something was wrong. "But he has golden hair, like an angel."

I could say that my blood ran cold and that I was filled with dread. But all that is mere words, incapable of conveying the rage that consumed me. Morozzi had come into this place where Nando—and Borgia—were supposed to be safe. He had moved at will and in so doing, left an ummistakable message. He could strike where and when he chose. We were helpless before him.

"How could this happen?" I demanded under my breath lest I

alarm the child. My instinct was to blame Vittoro but the misery writ clear on his face made me reconsider. Without doubt, the condottierre was profoundly shocked. There was no mistaking his misery.

"I don't understand . . . I have men everywhere—"

"What were they told? To look for a golden-haired priest? They'd be too busy doing that to see anything else."

It is the way of people to see only what they expect to see. Most everything else in this vast, roiling world passes by uncomprehended. A monk, not a priest, striding with confidence rather than going surreptitiously would be all too unlikely to draw attention.

"Should I not have gone with him?" Nando asked. His voice was very small and filled with remorse. "He said he was Papa's friend and he knew your name, too, Donna Francesca." He ducked his head, staring at the ground. "I thought it was all right."

Of course he had. No doubt Rocco had warned his son never to go with a stranger, but how to prevent a child from trusting one who seems to be a friend, and moreover a figure of authority?

"It's not your fault," I said, trying as best I could to soothe him. A sudden thought occurred to me. "Do you think you could draw his face?"

Nando nodded eagerly. "Yes, of course." At once, he chose a fresh page in the notebook and went to work. Very quickly, a recognizable portrait of Morozzi began to take shape.

"I will make sure the drawing is shown to all my men," Vittoro said after we had watched for several minutes. "They will be warned that this devil may come in any disguise." He hesitated. "Donna Francesca, I don't know how to tell you how sorry I am. The boy is here on my pledge to keep him safe. If Morozzi had—" The man who was both father and grandfather paled.

What need I had felt for recrimination left me as abruptly as it had come. "You are not alone. I, too, have underestimated him."

Vittoro glanced around, then gestured to me. We walked a little way from Nando to a place where no one could overhear us.

"I thank you for your forebearance," the captain said. "Forgive me but under the circumstances, I have no choice but to raise another matter. Will you tell me how you stand with our master?"

"I seem to be forgiven, if only for the moment."

"I am glad to hear it. His Holiness is hard-pressed on all sides. He needs his friends close to him."

"He trusts no one outside *la famiglia*." I spoke without rancor, confident that Vittoro understood that truth as well as I did.

"His trust may be misplaced."

I looked at him sharply, wondering how he possibly could have learned of Cesare's deception. But it was not of him that the captain spoke.

"When Senor Juan is drunk, as he often is, his tongue rattles around in his mouth like dice in the hand of a man compelled to risk all even when he knows he cannot win."

"What are you saying?"

"He hates and fears his brother, believing as he does that Cesare will go to any lengths to take for himself the life that Borgia intends for Juan. Further, he is convinced that you and Cesare are in league against him."

I shook my head in dismay at my own failure to see the danger Juan could pose. Our few encounters should have given me ample warning.

"You don't think he would do something foolish, do you? Not now of all times?"

"I have no idea what he might do. I am only saying that he is increasingly agitated and bears watching."

"Does Borgia know?" Surely, a few of His Holiness's "eyes" could be dispatched to shadow the errant son?

"If he does, he seems unprepared to admit it. Juan frequents certain taverns in Trastevere. Last night, before all the trouble started, he was heard declaiming that his father is in thrall to a witch. There can be no doubt who he means."

"He called me that—a witch?" It seemed to be the fashion. Morozzi had called me the same.

Vittoro nodded. "*Strega*. He said that you will burn."

My throat clenched so tightly that I could not breathe. I looked away, hoping that Vittoro would not see the depth of my fear. It raged through me, a fire unto itself that could not be quenched.

I gasped, dragged in air, and forced myself to remember who— and what—I was. "He is a fool."

"Fools are dangerous." Vittoro paused, looked at me, and said, "He must be stopped."

"I cannot kill Borgia's son." The very idea was outrageous. Vittoro had to know that. He had to realize that were I to lift a hand against Juan, Borgia would lop it off, then remove the rest of me at his leisure. Mine would not be an easy death.

"I am not suggesting that you kill him."

Then what was the purpose of him telling me—? Too quickly, I realized what he intended. I could confide my troubles to my lover and let him deal with them. And why not? Cesare truly did want the life Borgia planned for Juan, and if anyone had a chance of surviving Il Papa's wrath, it was the son he wanted to follow him onto Peter's Throne.

"Why are you telling me this now?"

Ever practical, Vittoro replied, "Because you had to survive Borgia first. Now you have to find a way to survive the next threat."

"And the next and the next and the next. There will never be an end." I was only just beginning to understand that; it terrified me but it also filled me with more sadness than I could bear.

Vittoro sighed, as though called upon to instruct a pupil who had not quite grasped the lesson, yet who still showed promise.

"That is the nature of the lives we have chosen."

"I did not choose! It was not my choice that my father be murdered. Nor my choice that I should be the only person concerned with finding justice for him."

I was outraged that Vittoro should think otherwise. Surely any person who knew me understood that I had no choice in what I did?

"We all make choices, Francesca. You are no different from anyone else in that regard. If you truly think otherwise, you are deluding yourself."

I could not remember Vittoro ever speaking to me so directly or so harshly. He seemed intent on sparing me nothing. For a moment, I could think only to walk away before I said something irreparable. The look on my old friend's face stopped me.

"You think the danger is that great, that you must strip away my pretenses and force me to confront it?"

He looked so uncomfortable that I thought he would not answer, but finally he said, "I had a dream last night."

Vittoro, that man of straightforward action and no nonsense. The man who believed in nothing he could not see, touch, and kill.

"A dream?"

"A very unpleasant dream. Felicia insisted that I tell you of it."

"What was its nature?" I was not entirely certain that I wanted to know, the matter of dreams touching too closely on the nightmare lurking always just on the edge of my awareness. In the light of day, I did not wish to think of such things, but under the circumstances, I would be the fool if I ignored whatever it was that troubled Vittoro so.

He looked away, embarrassed.

"I was standing in front of a great pile of faggots set around a stake in a square somewhere I did not recognize. The fire was already lit, smoke rose from it and flames licked deep within. Ravens circled in the sky, cawing to each other. A man—I suppose he was a monk because he wore a habit with a hood pulled down, obscuring his face—held out his arm, pointing. I looked where he was looking and saw you coming out of a church. You were distracted by something in the other direction and were unaware of the danger."

"What happened next?"

"I tried to call to you but you couldn't hear me. Then I woke up."

"That was all, the monk was just pointing?"

"I know it doesn't sound like very much but the effect—"

He had been terrified for me. That good, brave man had awakened so worried about my welfare that he had confided in his wife and steeled himself to warn me.

"You really are concerned about Juan."

"My concerns go far beyond him. If Borgia falls—"

He did not have to explain what the consequences of that would be. If Borgia fell, his enemies would not stop until they had destroyed everyone close to him. Vittoro, Felicia, their daughters and grandchildren, all would be lucky to escape with their lives. So would I. It is the way in Rome, where the rise and fall of great men has meant blood in the streets since time immemorial. I had accepted that risk when I entered Borgia's service, seeking the power I needed to avenge my father's death. But now Vittoro forced me to consider that although I was without family, I was not without friends, and they, too, would be in danger. Rocco, even little Nando, could be hunted down and put to the sword. As for Sofia and David, and the Jews in general, suffice to say that they might well be doomed.

"Borgia will not fall," I said. "He is the wiliest, most ruthless, and most determined man of our time. Moreover, he has us to help him. It is his enemies who should wake in dread in the night."

"That is very loyal but—"

"Loyalty has nothing to do with this." Borgia was a means to an end for me. I fulfilled my duties to him diligently but only for my own purposes.

But Cesare was a different matter; I truly did not want to see him come to harm. That being the case, I could not think of encouraging him to commit fratricide. Juan was a problem beyond my ability to solve. I would have to hope that his father succeeded in negotiating a grand marriage that would send him far from Rome.

Only later, after I had parted from Vittoro with assurances that I would take his warning seriously, did I remember what he had said about my looking in the wrong direction. I turned the notion over in my mind, trying to understand why I could not let it go. Had I truly overlooked some possibility in searching for Morozzi? Was he hiding someplace that I had not thought of? Luigi and his army of *portatori* had discovered nothing. Alfonso and the smugglers had caught only his trail, not his lair. Similarly, David, Sofia, and Benjamin had found no sign of him, even though he seemed able to move at will throughout the city and even into the precincts of the Vatican itself. Guillaume had not been heard from since sending word of divisions within the Dominicans. Most puzzling yet, even Borgia's "eyes" seemed blinded.

How could a man render himself invisible in a city where the best of friends spy on each other and gossip runs as lifeblood?

For just a moment, the fear that Morozzi was something other than strictly human stirred in me. I had known that fear before and had successfully defeated it, or so I had thought. Yet there it was again, tormenting me.

That was nonsense. Morozzi was a man, nothing more or less. As Borgia said, he had to eat, sleep, piss, and perhaps even fulfill other needs.

Crossing the Ponte Sant'Angelo, I resolved to redouble my efforts to find the mad priest. Every tunnel and passage, every church and brothel, anywhere and everywhere he might hide had to be surveilled, but quietly so as not to alert him. At the same time, I could not simply sit back and wait for the results. I had to find a way to draw Morozzi out even if that meant I put my life once again within his reach.

25

I did not look forward to telling Cesare what I intended. Fortunately, Portia offered me a small reprieve. Seeing me come in through the loggia, she waved me over to where she stood on her stool, keeping an eye on all the comings and goings through the open half door. Her arm was out of the sling and she appeared fully recovered from the attack the previous month, for which I was grateful.

"He's upstairs," she said without preamble. "Arrived a few minutes ago."

I nodded, having seen Cesare's men-at-arms on duty in the street. Without doubt, they all knew who I was, but none had dared to so much as glance in my direction. I wondered what they made of their master's dealings with a woman of my dire repute.

"Servants carried up baskets of provisions, then left," Portia added. "I smelled chicken."

So did I; the aroma of it along with traces of rosemary and olive oil lingered in the loggia. Chicken prepared that way was one of my favorite dishes, as Cesare well knew. I wondered what else he had planned to distract me from asking what business had taken him off for so many hours.

I thanked Portia for the report but she was not done yet.

"About that matter you mentioned—"

I needed a moment to remember that I had asked her to find out whatever she could about Carlotta d'Agnelli. Embarrassed that I had done so, I tried to brush aside my interest but she went on all the same.

"She's a paragon, so it seems. Golden hair, skin like cream, a very nice figure. And she's the soul of virtue, devoted to her family, not a whiff of a rumor of a hint of scandal to her name. She goes to Mass daily, gives alms to the poor, is kind to her servants, and has the voice of an angel."

"She sings?" I seized on that particular detail rather than acknowledge the ache exploding in my chest. Rocco's wife-to-be was lovely, trustworthy, honorable—exactly the sort of woman he would fall in love with. And everything I was not.

"Exquisitely, so everyone says. Her neighbors try to be at home when she is most likely to sing so as not to miss it."

"Such a great talent must have made her vain," I suggested in desperation.

Portia sighed and shook her head. "Apparently not. She is unfailingly modest in both dress and manner." The *portatore* leaned a little closer, her brow wrinkling. "Which raises the question why a man like that"—she cast her eyes toward the floor above—"would be interested in her."

I could hardly blame Portia for misinterpreting the reason behind my curiosity about Carlotta d'Agnelli. She might know that I was acquainted with Rocco but she had no way of suspecting my true feelings for him. I kept those too well hidden, even from myself.

"Yes, well . . . there's no accounting for taste, is there? At any rate, thank you. I'll just—" I gestured vaguely in the direction of my apartment.

"Make him forget she exists," Portia advised. "Leave him so wrung out he'll barely remember his own name, much less hers."

I assured her that I would show no mercy and backed out into the loggia. From there, I quickly took the steps to my apartment. Cesare was stretched out on one of my Roman couches with Minerva perched on his chest. He had removed his boots and wore only breeches and a loose shirt. The ease with which he was making himself at home in my home took me aback even as I could not muster the will to object.

"I'd begun to wonder where you were," he said as I entered.

"I came as quickly as I could." Rather than give him a chance to ask what had kept me occupied, I went on quickly. "Portia said she smelled chicken."

He grinned, bounded to his feet, and with Minerva still tucked under one arm, took mine and maneuvered me toward the pantry.

"I'm thinking of asking her to come work for me."

"Are you? Why?" It actually wasn't a bad idea for Cesare to begin acquiring an intelligence corps of his own rather than rely on his father's, but I doubted that Portia would be interested. By all evidence, she liked working for Luigi d'Amico, who valued her skills and paid her correspondingly well.

"She's sharp-eyed, has all her wits, and she's a good judge of character."

"You only say all that because she has a soft spot for you. Have you ever met a woman who didn't?"

He caught my gaze and smiled, a little ruefully. "Perhaps one."

Before I could reply, Cesare tucked Minerva into my arms and turned his attention to the chicken. The vast staff of servants who tended to his every whim would have been surprised to know that he could carve quite credibly. He even went so far as to drop a pretty garnish of parsley on each of our plates.

We ate at the pedestal table, seated in the curved chairs, and washed the chicken down with a rich Tuscan red very lightly chilled in a stone ewer filled with ice water. Minerva nibbled delicately on morsels we fed to her, then fell asleep nearby.

We were licking our fingers when I said, "Do you want to tell me what you did this afternoon?"

Cesare was no more inclined to do so than was I. Later, perhaps, I would tell him what Morozzi had done, but just then I did not want to undermine his confidence in Vittoro or, for that matter, remind him of anything to do with Rocco.

"Not yet and perhaps not ever," he said. "But if you're worried, I didn't go after Morozzi, not directly anyway. We need a plan."

I already had one. When I told him of it, he scowled. "I don't like the idea. It's all well and good to want to flush him out, but he could take you unawares again."

"No," I insisted, "he could not. Besides, you will be there . . . or at least somewhere nearby."

That was the compromise I was willing to offer, that Cesare be on hand with however many men he thought necessary but that I still have the opportunity to kill Morozzi myself. I thought it both fair and sensible.

Cesare was of a different mind. "All this rests on getting a message to Morozzi telling him that you want to parlay. Leaving aside for the moment the question of whether he will believe you and allow himself to be drawn out, how do you intend to contact him?"

"I don't know . . . yet. But my guess is that your father has a spy in Il Frateschi, someone not deep enough in to have knowledge of Morozzi's whereabouts himself but still able to get information passed along. That's the likeliest explanation for how Morozzi learned that I would be at the villa."

"Wouldn't Papa have told us already if there was such a person?"

How to put my answer in a way that would give the least offense? "Your father keeps a tighter hold on what he knows than Saint Agnes of Rome kept on her virginity."

Cesare gave a shout of laughter and reached over to refill both our glasses.

"It's true, gold pours through his hands, but try to get a straight answer from him and you'll find yourself wound tighter than the Gordian knot. If he has a single failing, that is it."

Privately, I feared that Borgia had a good many failings, chief among them his obsession with the advancement of *la famiglia* at all costs, but wild horses could not drag that from me. For my own part, I was singularly inept at the time-honored practice of flattery, shockingly so for a Roman. I took a try at it nonetheless.

"Your father trusts you above all others. Surely, if you approach him on this matter, he will reveal what we need to know?"

A look of such yearning passed across his face that I had to avert my eyes.

"You think he trusts me?"

I could have thought so provided that I overlooked His Holiness's wild ramblings about Cesare plotting against him. Borgia had come as close to apologizing to me for that as he had ever done for anything but it was impossible to be certain of what he really believed. Sometimes I wondered if even he knew.

"Yes," I said without hesitation, "of course he does. You are his eldest son, the one he has chosen to follow in his footsteps. Clearly, he trusts you above all others."

Cesare twirled the stem of his goblet between his fingers and sighed. "He has been spending a great deal of time with Juan."

"Isn't he arranging a grand marriage for him? He may be trying to steady him for that." As volatile as Juan was, he could easily disrupt the delicately balanced negotiations needed for the sort of marriage Borgia no doubt contemplated, a union at the highest levels designed to serve his own interests above any other.

"That's possible," Cesare allowed. "Perhaps there is some princess in the Indies or wherever it was the great Colombo returned from who wants him for a husband."

I smiled and raised my glass to him. "That's a splendid idea. I think you should propose it."

"Alas, it seems the fortunate lady is King Ferdinand's cousin, Maria Enriquez de Luna."

It was to be a Spanish union then, sensible enough given Borgia's need for the support of Their Most Catholic Majesties but no help at all in reconciling matters with the French. I considered asking Portia to put a little money down for me. Of late, I was becoming too well recognized in the city to place my own bets.

"He has another meeting with de Haro this evening," Cesare said. "I'll speak to him after that, but in the meantime—"

He set his glass on the table, rose, and came round to stand behind me. I felt the warmth of his breath on my neck. His hands slid across my shoulders and along my arms. He bent and with disturbing ease lifted me from the chair. I was reminded, in the last moments while I was still capable of coherent thought, that for all his ability to play the courtier, Cesare was a man trained to war, honed in muscle and sinew, and implacable in will.

Unlike our hasty coupling in Borgia's office, this time my dark lover seemed intent on going slowly, much to my frustration. I wanted to lose myself—and all thoughts of what Portia had told me—in heedless passion, but Cesare was having none of it. When he was in such a mood as he was then, he was a connoisseur of passion, displaying skill many an older man would have envied. We made it as far as the bed, if only just. Once there, he removed my clothing piece by piece, lingering over each revealed expanse of flesh. For a young man, his control truly was remarkable but, as I have said, he had set himself to cultivate patience. Much as I resented being used as a tool to that end, I could hardly quarrel with the results. How else would I have learned that the arch of my foot is particularly sensitive to deep stimulation or that the stroking of fingertips along my ribs makes me tremble? Or that there is a particular very small area to the right and left of my pubis that is so exquisitely responsive that the mere flutter of his breath there sends me reeling?

Never mind how I reacted to the strength and power of him above me, the heat of his manhood against my thigh, the smoothness of his skin under my touch. The thick murmur of my name on his tongue was enough to almost push me over the edge as I clung to the sweetly strange need to hold him safe within my arms. Even, dare I say, within my body. Is it the conceit of every woman that she can provide such a haven? Is it the dream of every man to find it?

My back arched. I cried out, hearing my own helplessness, and rebelled. Without thought, being far beyond any such thing, I tightened my thighs around his torso, dug my elbows into the mattress and, using all my strength, flipped him onto his back. I had a moment to savor his surprise before I mounted him smoothly, smothering any objection he might have made with the swift clasp and release of inner muscles.

He laughed—the devil!—and succumbed with grace. I rode him hard but he won in the end. Release shattered me so wildly that I could not resist when he turned me, holding me fast with an arm around my waist, and drove into me with power that eclipsed the very world.

Some time later, when I had caught my breath, I turned my head to look from the bed toward the tall windows through which I could make out the slanting light of early evening over the nearby tiled roofs, glowing gold and red in the dying sun. Flocks of starlings were arcing in long, undulating curves toward their roosts. Here and there, an owl called tentatively from nests high up beneath the roofs of churches. The air smelled of wood smoke and the river, with just a lingering hint of the olive and lemon groves beyond the city.

I thought Cesare was asleep and was startled when he propped himself up suddenly on one elbow to look at me. Twisting a link of my hair between his fingers, he said, "You still haven't told me what troubles you so."

"You know the situation as well as I—"

"I don't mean that. I mean why you wake sometimes with tears on your cheeks or why I find you sometimes huddled in a chair looking like monsters from Hell have been chasing you."

Such is the trap of intimacy, exposing as it does that which we wish to keep most deeply buried.

I was about to lie—again—to assure him that he was imagining things, when I remembered Vittoro's embarrassment in speaking of his dream, and his determination to do so anyway for my sake.

I turned on my side, looking again toward the windows and the slowly gathering dark. Cesare tucked himself around me so that we lay like spoons. I slipped his hand beneath my cheek and said, "I have nightmares . . . really just one but it comes again and again."

"Will you tell me of it?"

"There isn't much to tell. I am behind a wall, there is a hole, I can see shards of light and blood, an extraordinary amount of blood. I am drowning in it."

"Nothing else?"

Oh, yes, something else. "A woman . . . screaming."

"Who is the woman?"

"Mamma." The answer came from me without hesitation or thought. Yet it made no sense whatsoever. "But that cannot be. My mother died when I was born."

His arm tightened, drawing me closer against the warmth of his body. "Then perhaps it is about something that hasn't happened yet."

"No, that cannot be, either. In the nightmare, I am very small and powerless to save myself or anyone else."

"That is not who you are."

I blinked back tears and shook my head. "No, damn it, it is not."

To the contrary, I was a woman capable of provoking the greatest fear and dread. People averted their eyes from me and went in terror of my enmity. I knew a thousand ways to kill and would deploy any of them without mercy or hesitation, or so I wanted people to believe.

I was Francesca Giordano, the Pope's poisoner, and my very life depended on making sure that no one ever forgot it. Least of all myself.

"Where are you going?" Cesare asked as I rose from the sea of rumpled sheets.

I answered over my shoulder. "To find out how to reach Morozzi."

He sighed dramatically but a moment later I heard the bed creak as he rose and came after me. Catching my arm, he said, "This is not a good time to approach my father."

I was honestly puzzled. Granted, the hour was late but His Holiness was notorious for working—or otherwise occupying himself—far into the night. He seemed to thrive on no more than a few hours' sleep augmented by short *sieste*.

"You did not hesitate to go to him at once when I told you that Morozzi was in the city."

"That was different. After yet another encounter with the Spanish emissary, Papa will not be in the best of moods. We have to wait."

"For how long and for what? I am doing my best, as is Vittoro, but even with all the effort in the world, Morozzi could still get past both of us. Every day, every hour increases the odds that he will succeed."

I did not overstate the danger, as I believed Cesare well knew. But after the briefest hesitation, he said, "I am . . . making inquiries. It is important to have all the facts. When I do, then I will—"

"What are you talking about? What facts?" Frustration overwhelmed me. Morozzi's escape and my own brush with death at his hands had affected me far more than I wanted to admit. Without thought, I lashed out at Cesare.

"You Borgias are all the same! Everything is intrigue, conspiracy, plotting. Nothing can ever be straightforward. But this is! We must act now!"

"You forget to whom you speak!"

A woman with the smallest degree of sense would have stopped then and there; indeed, she would have gone further and asked his pardon. No matter how long we had known each other or the intimacies we shared—my bed had not yet cooled from our latest excesses—Cesare had been raised as a prince by a father who saw himself as the equal or better of kings and emperors. He would not tolerate being spoken to in such a fashion other than by Borgia himself, and only possibly by God.

It was not too late. I could still soothe him with soft words and a touch. But anger hardened me, that and the sense that something lay beneath his otherwise inexplicable behavior. Something he refused to tell me.

And for that he caught the sharp edge of my tongue. "I am speaking to a boy who needs to be a man! Stop fearing your father and be the leader you claim to be!"

Before he could respond, I yanked fresh clothes from a chest and strode in all my naked glory to the pantry, where I steeled myself to bathe in cold water, being unwilling to wait long enough for it to heat. I washed as best I could and dressed, all the while expecting to hear the slam of the door as Cesare departed in a rage.

The possibility that there could be an irreparable breach between us made me feel hollow inside but I could not dwell on it. Whatever deep game Cesare was playing, the stakes were simply too high to indulge him. Finally, having no conceivable reason to linger in the pantry, I stepped out into the salon. To my surprise my dark lover was waiting for me. He had dressed and was pacing back and forth impatiently. Seeing me, he scowled.

"For a woman in a hurry, you took long enough."

I struggled to hide my relief. "I didn't know you were still here."

"I almost wasn't," he said, striding over to open the door and wave me through it. "But my father expects us to work together. To that end, I suggest you curb your temper in future lest I curb it for you."

I had to hope that my silence would be taken as contrition sufficient to assuage his pride, for my own demanded that I offer nothing more. Outside on the street, we waited while his men brought up his horse. Cesare mounted and reached a hand down, grasping mine and drawing me up into the saddle behind him. We set off at a trot. Behind us, several of the guard scrambled to mount up and follow us. Men ran alongside bearing torches to light our way. Dogs, alerted to our passing, barked in chorus. Here and there in upper windows where the shutters had been left folded back to admit the torpid air, I caught a glimpse of heads poking out to see who was causing such a commotion at that hour. But mostly, I concentrated on holding tight to Cesare rather than disgrace myself by tumbling from his cursed mount.

Being a city dweller at heart, I am not naturally fond of horses. They smell, they are too big, and they can wreak havoc in a crowded street. Donkeys are useful, as are asses, and the small ponies we see from Brittany seem harmless enough. But whenever I am forced onto the back of a horse, I take refuge in some pleasant thought intended to distract me. As we neared the Ponte Sant'Angelo, I was preoccupied trying to decide where best to lure Morozzi in order to kill him when a shrill shriek pierced the night air.

The horse shied but Cesare stilled him at once. He would have ridden straight on had I not pressed a hand to his arm.

"Wait." Despite the warmth of the night, my blood chilled. I recognized the sound. A second whistle took up the call, followed by a third, and then too many for me to count, all sending out the same urgent message:

Come running.

26

The fire was sputtering out by the time we reached the Piazza di Santa Maria. Smoke and the peculiarly sweet stench of burned human flesh hung heavy in the air. The body had been pulled from the stake and doused in water that ran in rivulets between the paving stones, reflecting the flames of torches illuminating the grisly scene.

Having dismounted, Cesare and I pushed our way through the gathering crowd. I was not too proud to cling to his arm, being overwhelmed with horror at what lay before us. She was young, so far as I could tell, dressed in a plain white shift, the bottom half of it burned away, along with most of the skin from her limbs. What was left was seared and cracked, still oozing blood and other fluids. From the waist up, she was almost intact save for the stain of black smoke around her nose and mouth where she had breathed in the fumes that had killed her, but not quickly enough to prevent her features from being contorted in agony. Incongruously, her golden hair still fell smoothly over her shoulders as though someone had brushed it before consigning her to the flames.

Alfonso knelt beside her, cradling her body in his arms. Huge, gasping sobs came from him. A guard of young smugglers stood in a circle, all wide-eyed and stunned, several looking as though they were about to vomit. I fought the urge to do the same and pressed closer.

Despite my revulsion, I knelt down beside Alfonso and stared at the girl. When I saw past the horror of her last moments, I recognized her as one of the two young blondes decorating the smuggler king's dais when Benjamin and I visited his lair. For a moment, I tried to convince myself that she could have been the victim of a dispute between Alfonso and a rival smuggler, but the circumstances did not fit. Particularly not when I gently drew aside the top of her shift to find the word that had been carved with the point of a knife into her small breasts: *Strega*.

Morozzi had avenged the attack on himself and at the same time sent the clearest possible warning of what he intended to do to me. I thought of Vittoro's dream and fought for breath.

"She never hurt a fly," Alfonso gasped. Tears poured down his face. He clasped the girl to him and rocked back and forth, moaning. "Not even a fly. She was the kindest, gentlest . . ." He broke off, so overwhelmed with grief that he could not speak.

Behind us, a scream pierced the shocked silence hanging over the piazza. I turned to see the girl's twin, for truly she did appear to be identical, running toward her. Several of the young smugglers gathered around moved to head her off but not before she saw what remained of her sister. Her howl threatened to rend the sky.

Cesare helped me to my feet. I had never seen him so grim but surely I looked much the same. Buildings surrounded the piazza on all sides, the largest and most impressive being Santa Maria and the three-story residence directly adjacent to it where the priests lived. Next to that was the smaller but no less luxurious guesthouse available only to the most honored visitors. At a quick glance, I guessed that several hundred people called the piazza home. Yet not a light shone anywhere. No single member of the clergy had come out to see what was happening, to pray over the dead or to offer comfort to the bereaved. The only people gathered in the square were Alfonso's young followers, and Cesare and myself.

"Bastards," Cesare murmured, looking toward the church. I followed his gaze, thinking the same. No one could have come into the square, set up a stake, tied a girl to it, and burned her alive without at the very least dozens of witnesses being aware of what was happening and doing nothing whatsoever to stop it.

As painful as it was to think, I understood why ordinary men and women living in the shadow of Santa Maria might have hesitated to thrust themselves into a situation that must have terrified and sickened them. They would have deferred to the authority of the church in such a hideous matter. When no one came from there to stop the assailants, the chance of help being offered from any other quarter would have disappeared.

But perhaps there had been more involved than simply a failure to offer help. Perhaps the crime had taken place with the approval of those within Santa Maria, the same men of God whom I suspected of aiding Morozzi.

Still staring at the church, Cesare said, "He could be in there right now, watching us. The only way to know for certain would be to take the church, the residency, all of it apart stone by stone."

I gathered that just then he would relish such a task, but I shook my head. "He has come and gone. We are no closer to finding him than we were before, and we will get no closer unless His Holiness tells us all he knows."

The reluctance Cesare had shown earlier to confront his father had vanished. He cast a last look at the remains of the girl, and called for his horse, ordering several of his men to remain behind to offer what assistance they could. Once more mounted, I leaned my head against his broad back and concentrated on breathing in the relatively clean air beyond the piazza. But the stench of burning flesh lingered in my nostrils all the way to the Vatican. I feared that it would follow me into my dreams.

We went at once to the Palazzo Santa Maria in Portico. The guards appeared considerably more alert than previously. They sprang to attention as Cesare passed. What they thought of my presence I cannot guess.

A sleepy servant on duty in the antechamber of La Bella's apartment went to alert her mistress to our presence. Giulia emerged, looking far too awake for the hour and with a hint of shadows beneath her luminescent eyes. She was, as you surely know, considered to be the greatest beauty of our age, that rarest combination of physical attributes and personal manner that will turn the most stalwart man into a besotted fool. Borgia was no exception; he adored her, cosseted her in every way, and, if rumor was to be believed, was poised to rain down ever greater riches on her family the moment the child she carried was safely born.

Even that night, when she was plainly harried, she looked exquisite with the long fall of her golden hair tumbling almost to her feet, her mouth small but lush, and her complexion as pure as cream. I have no idea how she managed that extraordinary hair in particular, aside from the obvious use of willow leaves, root of vervain, and pos-

sibly barberry bark for lightening, but I have heard that she had two
servants devoted solely to its care.

Giulia cast me a wary look, for which I truly could not blame
her. I had saved her life the previous year but she had lost a child in
the process and had no reason to think overly kindly of me. Still ty-
ing the sash of her robe above the swell of her new pregnancy, she
bestowed a smile on Cesare and said, "Thank God you are here. I do
not know what to do with him."

To my surprise and secret pleasure, he brushed right past her and
into the inner chamber. Giulia hurried after him. I followed at a discreet distance. Borgia was sitting slumped on the bed, naked save for
a sheet wound around his lower half. In his prime, he truly had been
a bull of a man, with broad shoulders, a barrel chest, and muscles
kept honed by long hours in the saddle and at the hunt. But age and
the excesses of his life were taking their toll. His skin was mottled by
brown spots and sagging a little where it was not puffed out by fat
that softened his belly and gave him a hint of womanish breasts. Of
more concern to me at that moment, his face was alarmingly red and
he was sweating profusely.

"He is ill, I fear," Giulia said, a little breathlessly. "He will not
speak to me. I offered to send for the doctor and he threw a vase at
the wall." She gestured to the bits of porcelain lying on the floor.
Clearly, she was shaken by the incident, understandably enough, as
Borgia had never so much as raised his voice to his adored.

Cesare knelt down in front of his father and put a hand on his
shoulder. Steadily, with no hint of the concern he must have felt, he
said, "Papa, tell me what is wrong. I will do whatever is necessary
but I must know what you need."

When Borgia did not respond, I began running down in my mind the list of substances that might help him. You may find that odd given my profession, but there are many ways to kill that can also cure. Like so much else in life, it is often a matter of balance. I was debating whether to trust my own experience or summon help from Sofia when His Holiness finally bestirred himself.

"Water."

I seized the carafe by the bed, filled a goblet, and handed it to Cesare, who gave it to his father. Borgia's thirst must have been considerable; he emptied the goblet in a single long swallow.

When he was done, he wiped the back of his hand across his mouth, sighed deeply, and said, "La Bella, most precious, tell me you did not summon my son and"—he glanced in my direction—"his constant companion at such an unseemly hour out of worry for me?"

Giulia clasped her hands together just below her bosom, blinked moistly, and flung herself at Borgia's feet. "My lord! My darling! How could I not be overcome with concern for you? Truly, the burdens you bear would crush any other man. How fortunate we are that Our Father in Heaven has endowed our father here on earth with such wisdom and strength to see us through this difficult time."

What amazed me—and still does—is that men actually believe that sort of drivel. Even a man as worldly, as brilliant, and above all as cynical as Borgia will nod complacently and take it as his due. Nor did Cesare so much as raise an eyebrow. I supposed he heard the same sort of thing often enough himself.

It was left to me to ask the obvious question. "Are you in pain, Your Holiness, or experiencing any other symptoms of illness?" Or had he merely, as I hoped, overexerted himself with La Bella, as a sixty-two-year-old man with more lust than sense would do?

He waved a hand impatiently. "I am fine. A momentary lapse,

nothing more. Giulia, sweetest girl, have no fear, I am still your bold bull."

While La Bella simpered and Cesare stared at the ceiling, I lost an admittedly brief struggle with myself. The Pope's pleasure bower might seem a world unto itself, but no amount of sensual extravagance and indulgence could alter the hideous reality pressing in around us.

"A girl was burned to death in Piazza di Santa Maria tonight."

La Bella gave a little cry and stared at me in wounded horror, as though trying to understand why I would wish to upset her. Il Papa shook his head wearily.

Cesare stood, looked at his father, and said, "Whoever is protecting Morozzi must be powerful indeed for the priest to act with such boldness."

Something flickered behind Borgia's eyes. It was there and gone so quickly that I wondered if I had imagined it.

"He is protected by Il Frateschi," he said. "We already know that."

"Then your man inside the Brotherhood can tell us how to reach him," Cesare replied.

Borgia held out a hand to La Bella, who took it and rose gracefully to her feet. He smiled at her gently.

"*Amore mio,*" he said, "do me the kindness of arranging for a carafe of that excellent peach juice you like so much. I have a sudden thirst for it."

Giulia must have understood that he wanted a few minutes to speak with us alone but she was far too adept to show any resentment at being excluded. With a pretty smile and a toss of her head, she hurried to do his bidding.

When she was gone, Il Papa gave a great sigh and heaved himself off the bed. I averted my eyes lest the sheet that was his sole cover slip away but he hitched it more snugly beneath his broad stomach and strode over to the windows where a slight breeze offered some relief from the sultry night.

With his back to us, he said, "My man in Il Frateschi was pulled from the Tiber several weeks ago. His eyes and tongue had been cut out."

A memory stirred. I recalled what Guillaume had told Rocco. "The Dominicans are in an uproar about just such a death."

"He was one of them," Borgia acknowledged, turning again to face us. "Ordinarily, I would be happy enough to have the Hounds at each others' throats but under the circumstances—"

"Are you saying that with your spy's death, you truly have no hint as to Morozzi's whereabouts or any way of reaching him?" Cesare asked.

"What do you think?" Borgia demanded. "That I have such knowledge but keep it from you? What are you, *pazzo?*"

Cesare's face darkened at the suggestion that he was crazy but he held his temper and his ground.

"Morozzi stages an attack on a villa owned by one of our leading bankers. He kills a Dominican friar. He stalks the Pope's own poisoner, then disappears like smoke. He sends minions out to defame my sister, and you as well, in the vilest terms. He goes so far as to burn a girl alive in the middle of Piazza di Santa Maria. And yet no one has any notion where he is. Truly, it is a marvel!"

"Do not mock me, boy!" Borgia exclaimed. "By all that is holy, you will regret it!"

I moved to try to calm Cesare but the look on his face stopped me. I saw there a combination of such pain and anger that I had no notion what to make of it, much less what to do.

"You are blind," Cesare said, but softly, as though the effort to speak had become too much for him. "Willfully blind."

He turned on his heel and strode from the room, almost walking into La Bella, who chose that moment to return with a beaded carafe of peach juice. Her startled smile turned quickly to a frown when she beheld her beloved even more upset than when she had left him. She murmured something about the brains of men being no larger than their testicles.

Catching up with Cesare at the bottom of the stairs, I asked, "What do you mean, your father is willfully blind?"

He brushed me aside and strode out into the piazza, where he called for his horse. As his men scrambled to obey, I seized his arm.

"Tell me what you know!" It was inconceivable that Cesare would hold anything back at this point, yet he seemed intent on doing exactly that.

He brushed me off and summoned a condottierre to his side.

"Escort Donna Francesca home and make sure that she does not leave. Put guards in front of the building, in the back, in the garden, in the loggia, and in front of her door. Do you understand?"

The young man nodded so vigorously that the mulberry plume of his helmet jerked back and forth like the tail of a great bird trying to flick off danger.

Cesare was not yet done. "I realize that you are afraid of her; any sensible person would be. But remember, you have much more to fear from me. Is that clear?"

Again, the plume jerked. The officer barked an order and half a dozen men formed up around us. Within moments, I was effectively encircled and trapped.

"You cannot do this! I will not be able to protect your father if I am shut away!"

A page brought the big ebony steed up. The horse shied but Cesare put a foot in the stirrup, took hold of the pommel, and swung easily into the saddle. He made short work of reining the animal in, then spared a glance at me. The same pain and anger I had seen in his eyes earlier remained there, and were still as inexplicable.

"I will not hunt Morozzi while worrying that he will get to you first."

And then I saw, off to the side watching us and making no move to intervene, Vittoro. A look passed between him and Cesare—two men of different ages and situations in life but both warriors and of one mind. Some understanding lay between them, some agreement as to the course they would follow. Apparently, it did not include me.

"You mean while worrying that I'll get to him before you do!" I shouted, but it was to no avail. Man and horse surged forward, the clang of iron-shod hooves on stone echoing sharply across the broad expanse of the piazza until the sound faded away into the night.

27

Riding back to my apartment surrounded by men-at-arms, I did my best not to give them any cause for alarm. The chances of lulling anyone into complacency regarding my intentions were negligible but I felt compelled to try, if only because I could think of nothing else to do just then. Despite the late hour, Portia was in the loggia as I arrived. She raised an eyebrow at my escort but held her tongue until I had slid to the ground and walked over to her.

"What have you done now, that he sends you back under guard?"

"It is for my own protection, don't you know? I am a mere woman who must be sequestered so that she does not come to harm."

Portia snorted. "Why is he really doing it?"

I wondered myself. It was not completely out of the question that Cesare wanted to protect me; he had saved my life the previous year. But the extraordinary possibility that had popped into my mind when I saw the look he and Vittoro exchanged could not be ignored.

I told myself that I had to be wrong—or *pazzo,* as Borgia would say—but the idea would not loose hold of me.

"I will need for you to do a little shopping for me while I am so confined," I said loudly enough for the guards to hear. "Come upstairs and I will give you a list."

"Of course, Donna Francesca," Portia said at equal volume. She bobbed her head in seeming deference while scowling at the men-at-arms as though they were so much offal beneath her shoe.

Alone together in my apartment, with a pair of guards directly on the other side of the door, I hurried to my small writing desk to find paper and ink.

"I must get a message to Signore d'Amico. Will you take it?"

"Certainly, but if those goons outside decide to search me—"

"Don't worry, it will appear entirely innocent."

My dear Signore d'Amico, I wrote, *I am desolate that I will not be able to join you and our friends this afternoon as we planned. Please give my regrets to Sofia and Guillaume, as well. I remain, affectionately, Francesca Giordano.*

I showed the message to Portia, as much to reassure her as to save her the inconvenience of having to open and reseal it. She grasped its meaning at once.

"Of course, he will understand that you want to meet and with the others present as well, but how are you to get there? It will be daylight soon and this building is surrounded by guards."

"I'll think of something." I could only hope that I would. Weariness weighed so heavily upon me that my wits, such as I have, scarcely could stir beneath it.

When Portia was gone, I took off my gown, intending to lie down for a short time. As I disrobed, my fingers brushed the packet Sofia had given me. For a moment, I considered taking a small amount of the powder in the hope that I would sleep without dreams. Only concern that I would miscalculate the dosage and be unconscious for longer than I dared stopped me. That and the lingering knowledge that Sofia likely would be reluctant to give me any more of the drug I increasingly had come to depend on for sleep.

I did not expect to do so then, at least not deeply. Rather, I thought to doze, balancing on the boundary between sleep and dreams as I have seen acrobats do on corded lengths of rope suspended in the air across the piazza on the Corso where Borgia lived until he ascended to the papacy and where it was his pleasure to host entertainments for the citizens of Rome. If the nightmare came, I could leap awake. But I had misjudged how drained I was by the events of recent hours. Scarcely had I returned to the bed where Cesare and I had lately cavorted than consciousness slipped from me.

I have never been able to explain why the nightmare came under some circumstances but not others. By any reasonable measure, it should have come then. But instead of finding myself helpless and terrified behind the wall, I was walking in a vast piazza, the boundaries of it somewhere beyond my ken. I walked on until I heard singing, the voice high and pure. Only then did I stop and turn, seeing in the near distance a young blond woman in a long white gown who smiled at me and held out her arms, as though beckoning me to join her. A sudden wave of coldness moved through me. I tried to withdraw but was frozen in place. Flames curled at my feet but were held at bay by the wall of ice surrounding me. I watched the first drops of water herald its melting and cried out, my voice harsh against the song of the young woman. From nearby, I heard a man laughing and watched as Morozzi unfurled his wings and flew over a city that was cast by them into deep shadow.

I woke drenched in sweat. Minerva slept beside me, oblivious to my distress. Sunlight slanted between the chimney pots. I stumbled from the bed to splash water on my face, hoping it would chase the phantoms away. Below in the garden, I saw Cesare's men on watch. They were not, as I would have hoped, lounging in the shade provided by the slender plane trees but instead were on their feet, weapons to hand, and clearly vigilant. Whether inspired by loyalty to their master or fear of him, their attentiveness to duty cut off any chance that I could escape through the garden. But then I had not expected to do so.

In the pantry, I found a little bread and cheese, and forced myself to eat. The plan that had formed in me while I slept required strength. Having dressed in boy's clothes with my hair pinned under a felt cap, I went into the salon and stared at the wide fireplace built into one wall. Luigi d'Amico prided himself on including all the latest innovations in his buildings, hence the water piped in from a collecting tank on the roof and the latest model fireplaces that carried away all smoke.

But it was summer now and I had not lit a fire for months. I had to hope that the same was true of my neighbors.

On my hands and knees, I examined the dark passage leading upward from the fireplace. It appeared just wide enough to accommodate me. Cursing Cesare—for he had driven me to such desperate measures—I slowly inserted myself headfirst into the chimney. The bricks lining it were reassuringly cool, if a bit damp, and had been cleaned scant weeks before by the boys kept for such work. Moreover, the fit was as snug as I had hoped.

One floor lay between me and the roof. Taking the ceiling heights into account, I estimated that less than thirty feet. Not an insignificant distance but surely not insurmountable either. I wedged myself into the chimney and began, by dint of pressing my hands, feet, and knees against the surrounding walls, to climb using the hand- and toeholds built in to aid the sweeps. Inch by careful inch, I squirmed and squeezed my way upward. Had the chimney been any wider, I would have had no chance whatsoever of success. As it was, I had gone perhaps six feet—far enough not to be eager to fall—when it occurred to me that I truly was mad. Who does such a thing? A normal woman is at home with her husband and children. She cooks, sews, directs her servants, and the like. She does not resort to desperate measures to escape her guards in order to conjure dark schemes with people as liable to be burned as she is.

I kept going. At about ten feet, I told myself there was no turning back. If I released the pressure that kept me in contact with the walls of the chimney, I would fall and likely be injured. Never mind the pain stabbing through my arms and legs, or the frantic beating of my heart and my labored breath; high above I could see a faint ray of daylight. That strengthened my resolve when nothing else likely would have.

Twenty or so feet above the floor of the fireplace, I paused for a moment to gather myself for the final effort. Belatedly, and I have to say rather ridiculously, it occurred to me just then that the condottierre might have had the foresight to put men on the roof. If he had, all my effort would be for nothing. I might as well give up then and there and make my way back to the safety of my apartment as best I could.

I continued on. My knees, shoulders, and hands were rubbed raw but I scarcely felt them. I could see a growing sliver of sky above where the flue was topped by a copper brace holding a terra-cotta chimney pot, its span considerably narrower than the chimney itself in order to reduce the effect of wind on the draft. Gathering my courage, I pressed my knees against the chimney walls and freed my right hand. The steel mallet I had used to pulverize Borgia's diamonds would have to serve me well now. Gripping it, I struck the brace. At first, it would not budge. I was just beginning to consider the possibility that having come so far, I could be stopped by a sheet of copper, when anger filled me. By God, I would not be defeated by such a paltry thing! With all my strength, I struck the brace again and again. Copper is a soft metal, easily malleable, and the brace was never intended to take such abuse. Gradually, it yielded enough for me to work the edge of the mallet under one corner and pry it loose. The terra-cotta chimney pot, being no longer secure, shifted to the side and broke free. I winced as it struck the roof tiles and shattered. If any of the guards below heard the sound or if pieces of the pot fell toward them, all eyes would be on the roof.

Even so, I had no choice but to go on. With the opening of the chimney no longer blocked, I pulled myself out as slowly as I dared while keeping crouched as low as possible. To my great relief, the roof was empty, and there was no sound of alarm from below.

Bent almost in half, I skittered across the narrow span at the top of the roof, ever mindful of the steeply sloping sides covered with smooth red tiles that would give me no purchase if I fell. Mercifully, the water tank was behind me, otherwise I would have had to find some way to maneuver around its wide bulk. My palms were slick with sweat and my stomach so tied in knots that I could scarcely breathe. I am no fan of heights but I had learned the simple lesson of not looking down. It afforded me no great comfort but it did keep me moving.

I dropped several feet onto the roof of the adjacent building and crossed it quickly, still taking every precaution not to be seen. The street below was filled with the usual crowd of merchants, shoppers, beggars, pickpockets, and wide-eyed travelers all jostling amid the crush of carts and horses. At any moment, someone might look up and see me. I scurried on, across another rooftop and another before finally reaching the building at the end of the street. It was one of many structures thrown up in haste in recent years to take advantage of the burgeoning population of the city. Rather than spend the money to install an interior staircase, the landlord had contented himself with a ramshackle wooden affair attached to the outside of the building. I spared a moment's thanks for his penury as I hurried down it.

Once on the street, I moved swiftly to lose myself in the crowd. Several times, I stopped and pretended interest in something or other in order to gauge if I was being followed. When I was finally convinced that I was not, I turned in the direction of Luigi d'Amico's palazzo.

The banker must have given instructions that I was to be admitted without delay for scarcely had I stepped into the loggia than an unctuous servant whisked me away to a room on the upper floor, well removed from the bustle that fills any great man's domain. I entered a small study to find Sofia and Guillaume waiting. Luigi joined us moments later.

"Dear girl," he said as soon as the door had closed behind him, "we have been worried sick about you. The terrible event last night . . ."

"How could such a thing happen?" Sofia was very pale, her hair in less than its usual good order, and her hands, when she clasped mine, were cold. "It is horrible enough when those madmen in the Church decide to burn someone, but for anyone to do so on his own authority—"

I took it as a measure of her trust in Guillaume that she did not hesitate to name his fellow clergy as what they were. That good friar showed no sign of disagreeing. On the contrary, his usually bright, eager gaze was dimmed with sadness.

"It was Morozzi, was it not?" he asked. "There are whispers in the chapter house that someone very powerful here in the city is protecting him. I have tried to find out who that is but without success."

"Have you been able to discover anything else?" I asked.

"Only that six members of Il Frateschi are in residence at the guesthouse adjacent to Santa Maria. They are disguised as visiting merchants from Florence come to discuss renovations for the church."

This was potentially useful information but I could scarcely stop to absorb it. "It was Morozzi last night," I confirmed. "I tried to kill him earlier but, alas, I failed."

"And in the process almost lost your own life," Sofia said.

Luigi did not look particularly shocked, leading me to suspect that he had already known about the incident inside Santa Maria. But Guillaume was horrified.

"We are blessed that the Lord God protected you," the good friar said. "You must take greater care as to your safety."

It was not in my heart to disabuse Guillaume of the idea that God protected such as I. Instead, I said, "There can be only one reason for Morozzi to risk returning to Rome. He wants to ensure that Borgia falls not to the French king or to della Rovere or to any enemy save himself. Control the circumstances of the Pope's death and the chances of controlling who succeeds him are greatly increased."

"Savonarola." Sofia spit the name.

Luigi paled. For a moment, I thought he meant to cross himself, but he said only, "Heaven and all the saints forbid that man gain such power over Christendom."

Guillaume nodded. "Truly we live in wicked times, that men of God would engage in such an enterprise." He did not seem surprised.

"You have a plan to stop him?" Luigi asked.

If the desperate, not to say bizarre idea I had conceived in the boundary between this world and the world of dreams could be called a plan. I half wished it had evaporated upon waking but instead it had clung in my mind, growing more solid by the moment, even as I scaled the chimney, made my way across rooftops, and alit finally in Luigi's private study where all three looked at me expectantly.

"Let us sit and be at such ease as we may manage," I said, bidding for just a little time to get my thoughts in order.

The problem with friends is that they are so much more difficult to lie to than enemies. Scarcely had we sat down than Sofia asked, "Is there a reason why Rocco is not here?"

"He would not approve of what I am about to propose."

On the other hand, honesty has its own advantages, chief among them being the element of surprise.

"All I ask is that you hear me out," I said quickly. "Sound reason lies behind my intent. Only give me the chance to make that clear."

As Luigi hastened to pour wine and pass it round, I continued, "You no doubt know by now that Cesare has seen fit to lock me away under guard." I was confident that Portia would not have hesitated to share that juicy bit of information, nor was I disappointed.

Despite her attempt to maintain a stern demeanor, Sofia chuckled. "Which explains, of course, why you are here?"

"Of course. Cesare may do as he pleases but he makes a serious mistake when he imagines that I will simply fall in with his wishes."

"Yet, if he is acting to protect you—," Guillaume ventured.

I took a sip of the wine—a good Piedmont vintage, if I was not mistaken. "I believe his motives are more complex than that. By locking me away so publicly—men in his livery surround my building, after all—he thinks to convince Morozzi that Borgia is more vulnerable and thereby lure him out."

"What are you saying?" Luigi asked. "That he is using his own father, Il Papa himself, as bait?" He could not disguise his shock.

For my part, I wasn't above taking a little pleasure at the thought of His Holiness being staked out on the board like one of his own pawns. Which is not to say that I underestimated the difficulties inherent in any such plan. But then I had a great deal more experience with going up against Morozzi and losing than did the son of Jove.

"Trying to use me as bait failed at the villa and again at Santa Maria. Indeed, all it has done is provoke Morozzi into what he did last night."

This was a hard truth for me to accept but I had no choice. I had played a part in bringing about the terrible death of the young girl.

"That being the case," I continued, "there is nothing left but to use Borgia."

"But the risk—," Guillaume began.

"Cesare overbrims with confidence. I am certain he has convinced himself that he can prevent any real danger to his father. To that end, I believe he has enlisted the help of Vittoro Romano, head of the Pope's own guard."

Such was the conclusion I had come to when I saw Vittoro make no effort to intervene as Cesare ordered me detained. To the contrary, it appeared to me that the two men were of one accord.

"But this is madness," Luigi protested. "Cesare cannot hope to predict what Morozzi will do in such circumstance. The attack against Borgia could come from any direction. No one can protect against every possibility."

"That is true," I agreed. "I believe that Cesare is relying on Morozzi—having learned that I am off the board, as it were—becoming overly confident and therefore careless. But Morozzi is cleverer by far than Cesare wants to acknowledge. He will not be fooled so easily."

"Then what do you propose?" Guillaume asked.

I had considered carefully what I would say to convince them, mindful that they would not be easy to persuade. Scarcely had I begun than Luigi choked on his wine and had to spit it out into his goblet. He turned bright red, whether from the effort or embarrassment I could not say, and looked at me in horror.

As for Sofia, she had gone pale as the alabaster statues that decorate the inner sanctums of the Vatican.

Only Guillaume appeared interested. His dark gaze on me, he asked, "How exactly do you intend to die?"

The experience of arranging one's own death has a certain macabre appeal. An event in which we generally have no control whatsoever suddenly becomes susceptible to the most exacting manipulation. But before I became too absorbed in the details of the affair, there were practical matters to be considered, chief among them the disposal of the body.

I proposed that Luigi serve as executor of my estate and in such capacity arrange for my internment within his family crypt.

From Guillaume, I requested that he stand as witness to my wishes and give his support to Luigi in all proceedings.

From Sofia, I needed the means to exit this world.

"Absolutely not," she said. "The risk is too great. You are mad to even consider such a thing. Do you truly have no notion of what—"

"I will do it without you if I must."

For a moment, I thought she would storm from the room. Only with the most visible effort did she regain control of herself. Even then her hands gripped the arms of her chair as she stared at me across the table.

"If Morozzi really has come to Rome to kill Borgia," she said, "he will act regardless of anything to do with you. When he does so, he will expose himself to capture or death. There is no reason for you to take such a terrible risk to bring about what will happen anyway."

I reminded myself that the apothecary, in addition to being my friend, was a woman of true intelligence and wisdom. I could not simply disregard her concerns.

"Cesare is underestimating Morozzi," I insisted. "He believes that when the priest learns that I've been locked away, he will be emboldened to strike at Borgia and in the process be lured into a trap. But Morozzi is far too clever for so clumsy a maneuver. He is much more likely to assume that there is a trap and take every precaution to avoid it."

"Whereas you think that if he believes you are dead, he really will become careless?" Sofia asked.

"He has been trying to kill me since last year. If he thinks I am dead, he will be elated. He may even take it as a sign that God favors his enterprise. He will feel safe enough to strike at Borgia and in so doing, please God, fall into the trap Cesare has laid for him. But beyond that, I will be alive, able to move against him without his awareness. He will not see me until it is too late."

"If you are wrong—"

"I am not. Nothing less than what I propose will do."

Sofia hesitated, weighing my argument. I knew that I had won when she attempted to redirect her opposition.

"The slightest miscalculation in the amount of the dosage or the potency of the ingredients and you will never wake."

"I have considered that and I am confident it can be done safely."

Despite my morose musings a few weeks before on the bridge spanning the Tiber, I truly did not want to die. Not then. But if Cesare overbrimmed with confidence, I was no stranger to it myself. So great was my faith in my abilities, augmented by Sofia's good sense and experience, that I believed the risk could be all but eliminated.

We need not dwell on the extent of my foolishness. In my own defense, I will say that I was still quite young.

"Is there truly a drug that can accomplish such a thing?" Luigi asked. He had followed the conversation between Sofia and me intently, but had not disputed my conclusions. Even so, he appeared to hope that the answer would be no.

"There are potions that suppress both heart and breath," Sofia acknowledged. "But as I just said, the risk—"

"Should not be exaggerated," I insisted. "All that is needed is for me to be seen to be dead and declared the same by people who will be believed. Borgia will try to conceal my death, of course, for his own protection. Therein lies the real danger to me. He is perfectly capable of smuggling me away to burial in an unmarked grave as he did with my father."

I had not forgiven Il Papa for that. After I killed Morozzi, I would demand as a sign of Borgia's gratitude that I be allowed to see my father properly interred.

To Luigi, I said, "You will have to act quickly to take possession of my remains and then stand firm against Borgia's demands. Wave the testament I will sign giving you authority to act for me in front of him and insist that I be interred as I wished."

"It will be my pleasure to frustrate His Holiness in such a matter." Clearly, the banker had not forgiven the destruction of his villa.

"Then we have only to determine when it will be done," I said. My eyes met Sofia's across the table.

"If Borgia falls to Savonarola," I said, "there will be no future for any of us who believe in a world of light and reason. We will die in any case and so will tens of thousands of others, perhaps more. Everything we have been working for will be destroyed. Surely, any risk is justified in order to prevent that?"

I knew that I had her when she blinked back tears and looked away.

The details took over. We trundled down to the cellar beneath the palazzo where Luigi kept a strong room complete with scales. There the men courteously absented themselves. Under Sofia's supervision, I removed all clothing save for my shift and submitted myself to being carefully weighed. When that was done, Luigi returned with a trusted secretary, who took down my last testament. After designating funds for a simple—and I hoped speedy—funeral, I divided most of my wealth between Sofia, who protested that I should do no such thing but who I knew would use it to care for the truly needy, and Rocco to hold in trust for Nando. My books would also go to Sofia, who I knew would treat them well. I left a sum to Portia along with the request that she look after Minerva. On sudden impulse, I decided to leave my mother's wedding chest to Lucrezia. She had many items of far greater value and yet I believed she would take good care of it. My puzzle chest would go to Cesare, who would appreciate its cleverness. Guillaume witnessed my signature with his own, after which I saw the testament locked safely away in Luigi's vault.

All was in place, save for one remaining matter. I am not a sentimental woman, believing as I do that such emotion breeds folly. But having been forced by Sofia to at least consider the possibility that I might truly die, I had a call to make.

Careful to avoid the patrols roaming throughout the city, I made my way to the Campo dei Fiori. Rocco was in the courtyard behind his shop. I watched in the shadows near the back door while he clipped a perfect sphere of crimson glass streaked with gold from the blowpipe and set it carefully on a rack. When I stepped forward, he looked surprised but, to my relief, not displeased to see me.

"I thought Cesare Borgia had you locked away."

"He has, can't you tell?" It was a feeble attempt at humor, to be blamed on my nerves. I will not say that I was suddenly anxious as a girl, though you may conclude that for yourself.

Rocco stripped off his thick leather gloves and set them aside. "The boy lord has some misconceptions about you, doesn't he?"

As I had no particular desire to discuss exactly how well Cesare did or did not know me, I said only, "He can believe what he likes. I don't actually have much time—"

Every moment I stayed away increased the risk that the young condottiere would take it into his head to make sure I was still under lock and key.

"I only came to say that . . . I've been thinking and . . ."

"It's all right," Rocco said. He came forward quickly and took my hands in his. I felt their warmth, saw the look in his eyes, and forgot to breathe. His stiffness dropped away from him and he looked suddenly young and eager.

"I'm sorry that I mentioned what I did," he said. "Nothing has been decided. I have no particular desire to ally with the d'Agnellis. In fact—"

"But you should." I spoke in a rush, suddenly fearful that I would lose my courage if I let him say another word. Rocco was everything I yearned for—life, love, a chance to step out of darkness into light, all temptations before which I feared my brittle resolve would crumble.

Before that could happen, I said, "Carlotta d'Agnelli is a wonderful person, everyone thinks so, and this is a great opportunity for you. You deserve it."

As he most surely did not deserve a woman roiled by inner darkness and driven to kill. A woman who, one way or another, might be dead herself before much longer.

He went very still, his gaze so intent that I had no choice but to look away or risk him seeing the twisted black knot that was my heart.

"That's why you're here, to tell me this?"

Why had I come? Because if my grand plan went wrong and I really did die, I wanted to leave Rocco free to go on with his life without feeling any guilt at having been unable to change mine? How extraordinarily presumptuous, even for me. No, the truth was I had come to free myself. Whatever I was about to face, I wanted to do it without clinging to false hope for a future that could never be.

"We live in perilous times," I said. "No one knows from one day to the next what will happen. You should not hesitate to do what is right for you. Carlotta d'Agnelli—"

He dropped my hands and took a step back. For the first time since I had known him, his eyes went cold.

"I don't need marriage advice from you, of all people. Really, sometimes I think you are the most thick-skulled woman in Creation."

Under the circumstances, I really had not expected compliments. But neither was I prepared to hear his complaints regarding my character just at the moment when I was trying, for whatever purpose, to rise above my baser urges.

"Perhaps I am, but that doesn't change the fact that—"

"You are out, wandering around like this"—he gestured at my boy's garb—"after the atrocity at Santa Maria. I never thought I'd have any sympathy for Cesare Borgia but I'll give him this, he's right to want to lock you up. You're at least as much a menace to yourself as to anyone else."

I opened my mouth to utter a withering reply only to stand mute and gaping. His sudden alliance with Cesare of all people—hadn't they almost been at blows not long ago?—seemed a betrayal of the worst sort. Rocco was supposed to be my patient, stalwart friend, the one who never gave up on me. Yet he seemed to be doing exactly that.

Fine, then, the Devil take him.

"Why don't you tell him that yourself?" I asked. "The two of you can get drunk and complain to each other about the folly of women. I'm sure you would both enjoy that."

"Francesca . . ."

"No, no Francesca! I came to you out of decency after you suddenly announce, at the worst possible time, that you've found the perfect helpmate. I think you're right, she is perfect! So marry her, for pity's sake, and be done with me!"

"If it weren't for Nando—"

"Nonsense! She is beautiful, sweet, pure, kind, she sings like an angel and she will set you on the path to make your fortune. Of course you want to marry her! Admit it!"

He looked down at his feet, then up again at me. "She is not entirely objectionable."

Do not be misled by so seemingly tepid an endorsement, for surely I was not. Rocco did not act but for looking first, and again, that lesson having been hard-earned in his youth. If he could consider marriage to Carlotta d'Agnelli at all, he knew himself willing to bed her, keep faith with her, and build a life with her.

Well, then.

"I have said what I came to." I turned to go with as much dignity as I could muster.

He reached out to stop me but I jerked away and kept going, out through the shop, into the street, and quickly along it, around the corner and beyond, intent on losing myself in the anonymous crowd. Behind me, Rocco shouted my name, but perhaps it was only the wind, which, after several days of calm, had begun to blow hard again.

By the time I had retraced my steps and regained my apartment, the last of my strength was gone. I fell the last few feet down the chimney and emerged from it on my hands and knees. I crawled out of the fireplace but got no distance at all before I bumped into a sturdy pair of legs topped by a startled frown.

"I was wondering when you'd be back," Portia said. "I've been rattling around here for hours, talking to myself so those idiots outside wouldn't think anything was amiss." She held out a hand to help me up.

I blew out soot, wiped my nose on my sleeve, and said, "Thank you. I'm sorry to put you to such trouble."

That was as close as I could come to apologizing in advance for the burden I was about to lay on her. If my plan worked, it would be Portia who found my body. Her reaction, not to say her absolute belief that I was dead, was crucial. To that end, I could not breathe a word to her of what I intended.

"No need to apologize, Donna," she said cheerfully. "You're far and away the most diverting tenant I've ever had. I got the food you wanted. Are you hungry?"

I was starving, and since I wasn't entirely clear on when—or if— I might enjoy another meal, I agreed readily when Portia announced that she would be cooking.

"Come along then," she said as she headed toward the pantry. "I've news as well."

I followed her willingly. After my encounter with Rocco, not to mention the strain of planning my own death, I preferred company over the solitude of my turbulent thoughts. When Portia directed me to wash my hands before chopping the fennel, I obeyed. Minerva joined us, no doubt in search of some treat. Already, she looked startlingly different from the bedraggled kitten I had adopted. I began to wonder exactly how big she would become, and whether I would see that happen.

Simple domestic tasks have a way of driving off such moroseness. As Portia set purposefully about the business of preparing us a meal, I whittled away at the stack of fennel until there was scarcely anything left of it. My skills with a knife did not extend to vegetables.

"Everyone is talking about you and Cesare," Portia said as she set water to boil over the small pantry stove. To it she added thin strips of dough made from durum wheat and a little water. There are some who claim that this dish was introduced to Italy by the revered Marco Polo, but that is nonsense. Whatever he saw in faraway China merely reminded him of what he had already enjoyed in his homeland. Some say we always knew how to make such delectable and versatile noodles; others say that we acquired the skill from the Arabs when they invaded Sicily. Whatever the source, it is good, filling food that, in the hands of a Portia, can transcend all expectation.

"The general opinion," she added, "is that you have had a lovers' quarrel."

"For God's sake."

"I'm only reporting what I hear. You know how people love to gossip."

"Love to invent things out of whole cloth, you mean. People should tend to their own affairs and leave mine alone."

As they surely would the moment human beings ceased to be human and became angels.

A little olive oil, a handful of sardines from the Adriatic, whose cool waters produce the most flavorful fish, all tossed with what was left of the fennel, and we were ready to eat. Portia even produced a fragrant white wine from Umbria redolent of just a hint of honey.

My stomach growled.

Lest you think me entirely unfeeling to be so moved by base needs at such a time, let me say only that my appetite—for food, at least—was always capricious, seemingly vanishing on a whim only to reappear without warning like a wolf emerging from a winter cave.

As we ate, Portia regaled me with tales of the hapless men-at-arms assigned to guard me. They appeared trapped between terror at what Cesare would do to them if they failed in their duty and excruciating boredom made all the worse by the antics of the neighborhood children, who, with each passing hour in which nothing of interest occurred, became bolder, darting out from around corners to taunt the guards before disappearing again.

"I could almost feel sorry for them," Portia said. "They're in full armor in this heat and they don't know who to be more frightened of, you or Cesare."

"Me, definitely," I said, leaning back to pat my stomach. My plate was empty but Portia had kept my glass full. The bleak sorrow that had dogged my heels all the way back from Rocco's still lurked, but at sufficient distance for me to pretend to ignore it.

"You should become a chef," I said. "Borgia would hire you. I'd make him."

"I wouldn't work for that man if he offered me a job on bended knee," Portia scoffed. She hadn't stinted on the wine either. "He's a lech, you know, and that's hardly the worst of it."

"You don't have to tell me about Borgia. I'm the one who's supposed to keep him alive."

"That can't be easy. Does he get up every morning intent on making yet more enemies? The French, most of the princes of the Church, the Spanish if he doesn't do what they want, the Sforzas if he does. Tell me again, why was he elected?"

"It was the will of God."

We both fell to giggling. You will conclude that I was drunk and you will not be far wrong. In my own defense, I will say only that I am far from the only woman—let us not even attempt to count the men—who has found relief from death's shadow in the arms of kindly Bacchus.

"The real question is why Borgia hasn't sent his own men to release you," Portia said. "What could Cesare have told him to make him accept your absence?"

"If I had to guess, I'd say he told Borgia I'm being used as bait to lure out an enemy."

"You seem to have more than your fair share," Portia observed.

I shrugged. "On the other hand, perhaps Il Papa thinks that being forced to work together has caused us to fall out. Perhaps that is even what he wanted to happen."

"You aren't making sense. Why would he want that?"

I waved the hand that held the goblet in airy explanation. "He has a dark side, our pope. You might not think it to look at him but it's there all right. It whispers that Cesare and I are in league against him."

Portia looked shocked but not surprised. The higher a man climbs in this world, the more keenly he feels the wind. Even so, such things are not to be spoken of, and she knew it.

"I'll tidy up, Donna. You need to rest."

Perhaps so, but what I wanted was more wine and company to hold my thoughts at bay.

"It's scarcely evening. I can't possibly sleep at such an hour."

"Then just lie down," she said, and led me, like a fractious child, to my bed, where she lingered until my boy's garb lay discarded on the floor and I was tucked between cool linen sheets with Minerva on watch beside me.

Despite my protests, sleep was about to claim me when I grasped Portia's hand.

"I'm so sorry. Forgive me."

Her broad face creased in a frown. "For what, Donna? What have you done?"

If I tried to answer her, I have no memory of it. Whether because of the wine, the food, or being tucked into bed like the child I had never been, I slept heavily, and mercifully without dreams, waking only to the calls of the street sweepers and night soil collectors that came with the dawn.

Two days passed. Portia came regularly to take Minerva to the garden, to bring me food, and to keep me company. If she thought at all of my drunken attempt at apology, she did not mention it. I suspected that Luigi had told her to keep an eye on me but I was also confident that he would not have breathed a word to her of what I planned. My guilt regarding her remained even as we chatted, cooked together, and played cards.

Portia brought a set of *carte de trionfi* that she claimed was copied from a deck made for the Sforzas themselves by a great seer. The family into which Lucrezia was about to marry were notorious card-players and never stinted when it came to providing themselves with the best. They were also rumored to seek glimpses of the future in the arcane deck but I cannot say whether this was true or not.

Portia and I played a simple version of the game, acquiring and discarding cards in search of the most profitable combinations. She was better at it than I, or luckier. Hand after hand, I was left with the infelicitous pairing of Jove and Mars, father and son, the two ever vying for power across the cosmos. Worse yet, brother Mercury kept appearing, that clever god so skilled at placating Jove and thwarting the ambitions of his sibling, Mars. Had I been so inclined, I might have imagined that the cards carried a portent of events well beyond a simple game. As it was, I was merely glad of the diversion, for the hours weighed heavily as I waited for Sofia to do what was necessary.

29

At mid-morning on the third day of my incarceration, Portia was off tending to her other duties when a clamor erupted below. Bored and anxious, desperate for diversion, I opened my door in time to see Sofia bustling up the stairs with a red-faced guard hard on her heels.

"Your pardon, Donna," he called after her. "I meant no discourtesy—"

"You cannot recognize your own master's seal," she said without a backward glance, "or be bothered to read his orders until they are thrust under your nose. Who would expect otherwise?"

Before he could reply, she reached the top of the stairs. Her gaze went straight up and down me before she nodded.

"You've been eating at least, that's good. I shudder to think what will happen if I report back to Signore Cesare that you lack for care."

"She does not," the guard protested. "The *portatore* comes several times a day bringing the finest food, wine, everything imaginable.

The greatest attention has been given to—" He broke off, looking at me fearfully. Clearly, it was not prudent to refer to me as *strega,* but what else fit? "—to the prisoner's care."

"Prisoner!" Sofia exclaimed. She shook her head in disgust. "So much for your master's claim that he only seeks to protect Donna Francesca. How long does he think such a lie will be believed with you spouting off the truth at every opportunity?"

The guard's face turned redder yet and his eyes began to bulge. I watched, well diverted, until Sofia caught my arm and drew me inside, slamming the door behind us.

When we were alone, she let go of me and heaved a sigh. "That man's an idiot."

She tossed the paper she carried on a nearby table. Out of curiosity, I picked it up and scanned it quickly. The document directed that one Sofia Montefiore, Jewess, be allowed admittance into my presence and further be permitted to converse with me privately. But careful examination showed that the paper had been bleached to erase an earlier message, faint traces of which could be seen underneath. As for the seal and signature, so far as I could tell they were Cesare's.

"What did it used to say?" I asked, holding the paper up to the light. Anxious though I was for the waiting to end, Sofia's arrival had taken me by surprise. I needed a little time to rein in my nerves and get my thoughts in order.

"Something about authorizing Luigi to transfer funds from one bank to another. No matter, it served well enough. How are you really?"

I set the paper aside and produced a smile. "Without complaint other than being bored to distraction. You?"

"I've scarcely slept, what for arguing with David while trying to determine how to see you safely through this. We have racked our brains seeking an alternative."

"And have you found one?" It was not an idle question. Even then, I would have considered any other option save what I believed to be necessary.

"No," she admitted. She held her hands clutched at her waist, the knuckles white. "There is something more that you should know. In the last few days, rumors have been spreading that are clearly intended to discredit Cardinal della Rovere. People are saying that his lust for power is so vast that he does not care if the French make war from one end of this land to the other so long as he is pope in the end. David believes that Il Frateschi is encouraging such talk in anticipation of the papacy becoming vacant very soon."

"You mean in anticipation of Borgia's death?"

Sofia nodded. "Every sign points to the attack against the Pope being imminent. Della Rovere has badly miscalculated the matter. When he does try to claim the papacy, the mob will erupt in fury and come out into the streets to stop him."

Roman mobs had a great history of rioting upon the death of popes, including looting the properties of anyone thought to be a candidate for the papacy, as a flagrant reminder that the collective will of the people could not be trampled upon. In such uncertain times, it was entirely possible that the outraged citizenry would place the College of Cardinals under such threat that no member of it would dare to stand against it.

"If worse is possible," she added, "there are also rumors that the Spanish envoy de Haro has instructions from Their Most Catholic Majesties that, in the event of Borgia's death, their support is to be given to the Hound of God and not to any friend of the French."

Which suggested that Ferdinand and Isabella had at least some inkling of what Savonarola planned. Truly, we lived within a nest of vipers with the only wonder being that they did not swallow themselves whole.

"There are other candidates—," I ventured without conviction. Excepting a few pious old men, every prince of the Church believed himself amply well endowed to mount her. But I doubted there were any who would have the courage to put themselves in the way of a rioting mob backed by the might of Spain. While they dithered, Savonarola would prevail.

I caught the sheen of tears in Sofia's eyes just before she looked away, but when she looked back again, she showed only resolution. We both knew what had to be done.

"I should stay with you."

"You cannot. A Jewess is too easy a target. No suspicion can fall on you."

"What of the *portatore?*"

I pointed to the maze of glass tubing, retorts, crucibles, and the like that I had set up on the large table in the salon. It was all to no purpose, but to the untutored eye I thought it would appear suitably sinister.

"Does not it look as though I have been producing something nefarious, possibly even with the intention of taking my own life?"

"Is that how you want to be perceived, as a suicide?"

"I want matters to move along quickly. What better way to guarantee that?"

No priest will pray over a suicide, no Mass can be said. After an interval sufficient for me to be seen to be dead by people who would spread the word, Luigi would be free to spirit me away to his family crypt with what would be considered unseemly haste were I to die in the grace of Our Lord.

"I must ask you again to reconsider."

"Even after what you have just told me? You know there is no other way."

"If I have made even the slightest error—"

"I have every confidence that you have not. Now for both our sakes, let us delay no longer."

For truly, I did not think I could bear much more. A great urgency to be done had sprung up in me. I felt a wind at my back, pushing me forward to whatever fate awaited me.

Sofia's lips moved without sound. I wondered if she prayed to the God of Abraham, beseeching his guidance. For a moment, I envied her, for I, too, would have liked to pray. I am no good at it, I never have been, but there are still times when I feel a great yearning that pulls me beyond myself toward something I can scarcely glimpse and surely cannot comprehend.

She slipped a hand into a pocket of her gown and withdrew a small glass vial no longer than my thumb. I stared at it in wonder that so ordinary an object could be fraught with such momentous intent.

"If I have misjudged the dosage—"

The vial contained a black liquid that appeared to absorb all light. I took it from her carefully, finding the glass cool to my touch. Or perhaps the chill was in me, for terror lapped at my feet, a thick and unforgiving tide that threatened to pull me under.

Even so, I said, "I would trust no one to manage this so well as you. If I may ask, what did you use?"

I will not repeat what she told me, for God forbid that I give you or anyone else occasion for sin. However, I will say that the ingredients are rare and difficult to work with, which is all to the good lest some fool be tempted to try.

"It will take effect almost immediately," she said. "Everything I know assures me that it will be painless. However, I cannot say with certainty how much you will be aware of what is happening to you. You may be conscious on some level for at least a little while."

As much as I did not relish that possibility, there was no turning back. "It doesn't matter," I said with false bravery. "I must do this no matter what is involved. How long will it be before I give the appearance of death?"

"No more than a few hours. Your body will cool and your skin will become pale. Your heart will beat so slowly and faintly that no one will discern it. Nor will you show any evidence of breathing."

"And all that will last—?"

"I cannot say for how long. Hours certainly, possibly a day. Enough time, please God, for Luigi to spirit you to safety." She took a breath and I saw her throat working as though she wished to take back every word, spin time on its heel, and set us all on a different path. We both knew that there was none.

"I will be in the crypt," she said. "And I will do everything possible to revive you—blankets, restoratives, everything. I promise I will not give up no matter what."

"I know you won't," I said, and hugged her quickly before either of us could think better of what was about to happen. "Go now, before the guards become suspicious."

"Francesca—"

"Truly, there is nothing more to say. You are my friend, I trust you absolutely. But if anything goes wrong, know that you are not to blame. This is my choice and mine alone."

We embraced in farewell, hopefully only temporary. I thought she was about to speak again, as though there was something that still needed to be said. But whatever it might have been, she must have thought better of it.

She stepped back, touched my cheek lightly, and was gone. The door closed behind her so softly that I scarcely heard it. I was left once again alone, the vial nestled in the palm of my hand.

I waited until Portia had come and gone on her last visit of the day; until darkness descended and the sounds from the street faded away. When I could hear only the hum of cicadas in the garden below and the faint creak of leather against metal as the guardsmen moved about, I made my final preparations.

Minerva had eaten earlier, but I put out more food for her, along with water. Portia would come in the morning, I knew, but I wanted to make sure that the cat did not suffer for my unavoidable neglect. With that done, I undressed and washed myself, then donned a fresh shift. Ordinarily, I slept in the comfort of my own skin but I preferred not to be found in that state. Such a concession to modesty would be taken as further proof that I had intended my own death.

Even then, I hesitated, making sure that everything was in good order, my books neatly arranged, the pantry tidy, any substances that could be dangerous safely locked away. When all that was done and more, I stood for a few moments in the center of the salon, looking around at the place that had been my home for a few scant months. It contained more of who I was than anywhere I had previously lived, yet already the impression of myself seemed to be fading, no doubt because of the excessive order I had imposed. A stranger could move in and with very little effort make the place his own.

But that was not going to happen. I was going to live. I would defeat Morozzi and preserve Borgia. Life would go on.

Or not.

Sitting on the side of the bed, I took a breath and considered, yet again, the list of all I had felt that I needed to do. Everything was complete. There was no reason for me to delay any further.

I took up the vial and stared at it. Sofia had said nothing of how it would taste. What if it tasted terrible and I retched it up? We would be undone before we had barely begun.

I went back out into the pantry, found some of the good Umbrian wine left over from one of Portia's visits, and swallowed half the goblet's contents before returning to the bedroom. Clutching the goblet in one hand and the vial in the other, I used my thumb to ease off the wax closure. My gorge rose and for a moment I feared that I would not be able to swallow.

Before I could think further, I threw back my head, put the vial to my lips, and drained its contents in a single gulp. Immediately, I emptied the remaining contents of the goblet down my throat and dropped it along with the vial onto the floor. My heart was pounding and a fine sweat had broken out over all my body. Pressing my lips together tightly, I laid down on the bed and forced myself to breathe deeply.

At first, nothing happened. I did not, as I had feared I might, vomit. Slowly but steadily, my heartbeat returned to normal. I was able to breathe more easily and even began to feel a certain sense of relief. This was not so bad after all.

Hard on that came the thought that, in her concern for my safety, Sofia might have mistakenly rendered the potion ineffective. I was debating how long to wait before deciding that was the case, and what I should do in such an eventuality, when I noticed a slight tingling in my hands and feet.

I wondered if my overwrought mind had conjured the sensation, but very quickly it spread up my limbs and throughout my body. I was in no pain and as yet I felt no cause for alarm until, that is, I tried to lift my head only to discover that I could not. Nor could I move a finger or toe. I was effectively paralyzed.

Panic surged through me but I forced it down, telling myself that I should have expected such a reaction. But the fact was that I had not considered how it would feel to lie utterly helpless, unable to bestir myself in any way, as the potion did its work. Over the next few minutes, I became aware of a great coldness moving over me. I could still see the wall directly opposite my bed and the window looking out into the night, and I could still blink, but my perspective grew fainter and more constricted with each breath. When my eyelids lowered and I discovered that I could not raise them again, I was plunged into darkness lit by strange red shards that seemed to have their existence only in my mind. Yet for all this, I remained entirely aware of what was happening to me.

With that awareness came terror that I could not control by any rational means. Had I been capable of movement, I surely would have thrashed about in my eagerness to escape. As it was, the paralysis seemed as a giant serpent constricting every inch of me. I tried to cry out only to discover that I had become mute. My sole remaining means of expression were the tears that slipped down my chilled face. I felt their passage, but only distantly. With the disconnection of my body, my mind seemed to leap forward of its own accord. Vivid images darted before me. I saw Cesare on his horse racing across Saint Peter's Square while the basilica still so filled with dread memories loomed above him; Borgia, wrapped in a sheet, suddenly old and palsied as La Bella knelt at his feet to perform an act I prefer not to describe. The world fell away and I was floating along the street where my father died. It was night; nothing stirred save the rats that fled at my approach. I saw a man in the distance and tried to call out to him but could not. Yet he turned even so and I saw that it was Morozzi, laughing.

I went on into a room I did not recognize yet felt that I knew, where a child lay in a bed. She turned her head toward me and I found myself looking into my own eyes. Voices surrounded me:

"I don't know what to do."

"She is possessed."

"Get out! I will not let you—"

"My own fault, dear God, my own."

A woman was singing very softly, the sound filling me with contentment. My fear dissolved and I reached up my arms to be lifted by her. I felt her breath on my cheek and heard the song she sang:

> *Firefly, firefly, yellow and bright,*
> *Bridle the filly under your light,*
> *The child of my heart is ready to ride,*
> *Firefly, firefly, fly by her side.*

"Again, Mamma, sing it again."

> *Firefly, firefly, yellow and bright . . .*

"I believe in one God, the Father Almighty, Creator of heaven and earth, of all things visible and invisible. And in one Lord Jesus Christ, Son of God, the only-begotten, born of the Father before all ages."

"*Converso!*"

"Filthy Jew!"

"*Mamma!*"

"Hush, don't make a sound. Please God, don't let her see!"

Terror beyond any I had ever known overwhelmed me. In my

mind, I screamed and clawed, desperate to escape, but I was trapped, utterly and completely. Behind the wall. Where I would most surely go mad.

But God is not without mercy. Even as I felt myself about to shatter into a thousand pieces, blackness swallowed me. I was pulled down into icy depths, engulfed, and held, intact and whole, in the shroud of my own being.

So I remained for an unknown time. At intervals my mind stirred sluggishly. I knew that I remained in this world yet I was no longer a part of it, floating as I did in the netherworld between life and death.

While I was in that state, much went on around me, but I would know nothing of what happened until later, when those who were most closely involved told me how events unfolded.

30

I t began as we had planned, with Portia's discovery of my body
when she arrived to bring me breakfast. She entered the apartment
under the eye of the guard and went directly to the pantry, where
she set down the basket she had brought filled with fresh bread, eggs,
and some of the good goat cheese from Veneto that she knew I liked.
When she did not see me or hear me stirring, she tiptoed into the bedchamber, not wanting to wake me if I was still asleep. Of course, it
was also in her mind that I might have slipped out again, in which
case she did not want to do anything that might alert the guards.

A few moments passed before her eyes adjusted enough to see
beyond the shadows surrounding the bed. At first, she thought I
really was asleep, but the unnatural stiffness of my posture alerted her
that something was wrong. She crept to the side of the bed and looked
at me closely. As she described later, "Your skin was pale as alabaster,
your lips were without color, and there was no sign that you were
breathing."

Portia screamed; she couldn't help herself, but she did manage to stifle the sound by clapping both hands over her mouth. As she stood looking at me, her gaze also took in the presence of the empty goblet and vial on the floor. Their significance did not escape her.

At once, she turned and, though her legs threatened to give way, left the apartment. She told the guard that I had a sudden craving for honey and that she was off to get some. Noticing nothing untoward in her manner, he let her go and maintained his position outside the door without alerting the condottierre that anything was wrong.

Portia went directly to Luigi's villa, where he was pacing up and down in his private study, awaiting word. Having been admitted to his presence at once, she broke down and wept as she told him the news.

Luigi instructed her to remain at the villa and went immediately to my residence. When the condottierre refused to admit him, he raised such a hue and cry that windows were flung open up and down the street and eager heads poked out to determine what was happening.

"I am telling you, I must see Donna Francesca at once! I have the gravest concern for her welfare. If she has come to harm and you do nothing, your master will have you drawn and quartered. And I will provide the horses to do it!"

The condottierre paled but he was not without courage. Insisting that Luigi go no farther than the loggia, he stomped up the stairs to my apartment, ordered the guard to open the door, and entered.

Moments later, he emerged looking like a man who had seen his own death rather than mine.

In the confusion that followed, Luigi managed to insert himself into my bedchamber. He confirmed for himself that I was, to all appearances, dead even as he said a quick prayer that I was anything but. He also unfurled the document he had brought with him, that being my last will and testament giving him full authority to order all matters concerning my estate.

By then, two of the men-at-arms had been dispatched to alert Cesare. He arrived as people were beginning to mill about in the street. Already, the rumor that I was dead was spreading. Cesare entered the apartment alone. Finding Luigi in the bedchamber, he ordered him to leave, only to be refused. As gently as he could manage, Luigi told him what had happened.

Cesare did not believe him. He insisted that I was only sleeping heavily, nothing more, and went over to the bed to see for himself. When he was unable to rouse me, he demanded that a physician be summoned. That worthy arrived and without delay pronounced me dead. Due note was made of the goblet and the vial on the floor.

With the arrival of the physician, the crowd outside had fallen silent. When he emerged again almost immediately, looking grim, and hurried off, the conclusion was unmistakable—this time the Pope's poisoner truly was dead. Most everyone had the sense to seek the relative safety of their homes but others rushed to spread the word throughout the city. Rocco heard it as he was opening his shop. At once, he dropped the shutters, bolted the door, and raced off in the hope of finding that it was a lie.

He arrived outside my apartment just as Cesare exited. The son of Jove came in a fury, one hand closed around the throat of the condottierre as he pulled him after him, uttering dire imprecations as to his fate while at the same time exploding in a stream of orders. Reinforcements arrived led by Vittoro, who directed that the street be cordoned off and attempted to calm Cesare while determining what had actually happened.

With his fears mounting as to my safety, Rocco tried to force his way into the building, in the process exchanging blows with several of the guards. Such was his desperate fury that he did them more harm than they managed to do him, only to finally be stopped by Vittoro, who got both arms around him and held him fast until he calmed enough to understand what was being said.

"She is gone," Vittoro told him. "We do not know how or why but that is the truth. I am sorry. There is nothing to be done save try to prevent this entire situation from spiraling out of control."

Cesare was back inside the building as this went on. He could be heard shouting at Luigi.

"You will not take her! I will not allow it! How dare you even suggest such a thing—"

He broke off as Luigi tried to reason with him. He pointed out what was by then already being said from the Palatine to the Capitoline and back again, that Borgia's poisoner had poisoned herself. Moreover, she had done it deliberately.

I like to imagine that by this time a mood of delicious horror was descending over the city. People are always inclined to enjoy the misfortune of others but never more so than when they believe such suffering is deserved. I was a woman who had risen above myself, shunned the life every woman is supposed to want, and become a figure of fear and resentment. Now I had been struck down in what must surely be a sign of divine displeasure. Moreover, I would go on paying for my sinfulness through all eternity. I am more than a little surprised that a celebration did not break out, at least among Il Frateschi, who must surely have believed that the way was now clear to send Borgia to his own damnation. But perhaps they were simply too busy laying their final plans and had to postpone their revelry.

Cesare and Luigi were still arguing over what was to be done with me, with Cesare refusing to allow my body to be removed on the grounds that obviously there had been some mistake; I could not possibly be dead, no matter what the idiot physician claimed. It was now the second hour since Portia's discovery of my remains and Luigi was, understandably enough, anxious to get me away. He thought he had begun to make some progress with Cesare when a note arrived from Lucrezia.

It was a tearstained and barely legible plea, first that what she had just heard be revealed as "the most scurrilous and vile lie ever told." But if it was not, I must be brought home at once so that those who loved me could mourn me properly and see me to a decent rest. "Home" apparently was the Palazzo Santa Maria in Portico, where I had lived briefly after Borgia's ascent to the papacy and from which Lucrezia declared that she intended to bury me.

So much for the best laid plans.

Luigi protested. He flung about the will, shouted at the top of his lungs, and pleaded and cajoled. Finally, he begged. Cesare was having none of it. His beloved sister was entirely right. Obviously, I had perished at the hands of that madman, Morozzi, who would pay for what he had done with the most excruciating and prolonged death ever seen in God's Creation. Indeed, a prize would be offered to whoever came up with an entirely new method of inflicting death so horrible that it would be whispered about for centuries. The entire city would be summoned to take part; people would come from hundreds of miles around; there would be feasting in my honor, and games. Yes, damn it, games. Cesare himself would sacrifice a bull.

In the meantime, lest the filthy rumor that I was a suicide gain any credence, I would be honored with a funeral Mass performed by no less than His Holiness, Christ's Vicar on Earth, Pope Alexander VI. I have no idea what Borgia made of this idea when he heard of it, which he must have very shortly. Perhaps he was willing to go along in the hope of soothing Lucrezia's grief sufficiently to get her through the wedding in a few days' time. He must have also been concerned about his own safety, fully expecting to see Morozzi pop out from behind any corner at any time. With such danger looming, he could not afford a rupture within his own family. When all is said and done, it does not matter why he agreed. Any hope I had of a quick departure to the safety of Luigi's family crypt where Sofia would be able to revive me died the moment that he did so.

Worse yet—the entire situation truly was going from bad to worse at a remarkable clip—Rocco agreed with Cesare. He informed Luigi that any suggestion of my having taken my own life was outrageous and that I would have what I had so regretted had been denied my father—a proper and decent funeral. Or there would damn well be hell to pay.

All of which explains, so far as anything that happened that day ever truly can be explained, how it was that at mid-morning, as a hushed crowd reassembled in the streets, I was borne on a stretcher down the stairs and out through the loggia to begin my solemn journey to Saint Peter's.

Actually to the Sistine Chapel. I was laid out there on the handiest catafalque—the same one, I believe, used for the funeral the previous year of Pope Innocent VIII. The irony hangs a little heavy, considering that I may have put him on that bier. Borgia was at the entrance to the chapel to receive me. Lucrezia stood beside him, crying piteously while outdoing her brother in vows of revenge. Juan was not in attendance but a remarkable number of other people were. Most were clerics, no more immune than common folk to the excitement caused by my demise. However, more than a few foreign ambassadors squeezed in, anxious to report to their masters what transpired. There was a handful of nuns who kept close to the walls out of the conviction that lightning would rain down the moment a *strega* entered the sanctuary, incinerating anyone standing too close to me. I assume they were properly disappointed when this did not occur.

Rocco forced his way in, meeting up with Vittoro, who had been joined by Felicia with Nando in hand. The entire rest of the family was also there, all the girls with their husbands and children, which I think was rather sweet. Renaldo was bustling about, doing his best to keep the proceedings organized while dabbing at his eyes with his sleeve. He broke down at one point and sobbed openly, but got control of himself quickly enough and soldiered on. Portia slipped in just as the doors were being closed and took up a position next to Luigi, who by that time was well and truly frantic. In his despair, he let slip the truth to her, fortunately in a whisper. She responded with such glee that at once the rumor sprang up that she must have had a hand in my demise.

About the only bright spot was Borgia himself, who had recovered from the shock of my death enough to realize that the situation was teetering out of control. People were far too excited and he was far too vulnerable. Accordingly, he made short work of the Mass but was still sufficiently shaken to deliver a brief homily in which he seemed to compare me to Esther, who saved her people from extermination in Babylon. Having caused more than a little shock with the suggestion that I was a secret Jewess being buried with the honors due the most devout Christian, Il Papa blessed all those assembled and sent them on their way. Barely had he turned from the altar than he ordered Vittoro to double the guard around the Vatican and dispatch every available spy into the streets to gauge the mood of the city.

Still in tears, Lucrezia approached the bier and kissed my forehead gently. Cesare gathered her to him and together they wept. She led him away finally, whispering that I was in a better place and that they should be glad for me while demanding at the same time that Morozzi die by inches and that she be allowed to help dispatch him.

Near to breaking down entirely, Luigi flung himself at Borgia and pleaded, "Let me take her now, for pity's sake! We're on the edge of the precipice here and you know it. Let me get her away before something terrible happens!"

Whether he truly believed that the citizenry of Rome was about to rise up in outrage at the presence of an apparently Jewish witch within the holy of holies, I cannot say. Perhaps he feared that I would be dealt with as was Hypatia, another woman who did not know her place, flayed alive and burned by the mob in ancient Alexandria for the sin of being a mathematician. But Borgia must have known that he had gone as far as he dared to keep peace in his family and, not incidentally, to placate my vengeful soul.

He waved a hand as though to be done with the whole frantic business.

"Take her then, but do it quietly. And make sure no one knows where you bury her or she'll be dug up by nightfall."

Vittoro suggested smuggling me out through one of the two tunnels he had left open when he closed all the rest. The intent was to get me as far from the Vatican as possible before concealing me in a wagon that would carry me the rest of the way to Luigi's family crypt.

A little procession formed up quickly—Vittoro; a dozen men-at-arms; Rocco, who was endeavoring to console Nando; Luigi; and myself, of course. Two of the guards were designated to carry the litter holding my body. The rest spread out in front and back to prevent any intrusion.

They had not counted on Cesare. He heard the clamor of the

guards clearing the way between the Sistine Chapel and the tunnel entrance, and turned back to see what was happening. The discovery that I was being taken away with such haste made him forget any thought of indulging his grief. He squared his shoulders and announced that he would be the chief mourner at my entombment. It was, after all, his right, as he was as close to a husband as I had.

I do not care to think what Rocco made of that but he could not have been entirely surprised. He had witnessed Cesare's possessiveness firsthand in Saint Peter's Square when the two almost came to blows because Rocco had dared to embrace me. Moreover, he had to know that I was a woman of unorthodox behavior and more than a little passion. Please God, let him have known and not found out that way, for all that he claims the past does not matter. He did, however, choose not to continue, apparently unwilling to watch the spectacle of Cesare mourning me.

And so we went, first by foot, then by wagon, until we reached the d'Amico family crypt set in a lovely little garden adjacent to Luigi's villa. There he had caused to be constructed a perfect jewel of a chapel and beneath it a resting place of polished brick with an arched ceiling, below which was set a series of marble biers rising from the stone floor. It was the custom then, as it is now, for the wealthy to be laid out in such circumstance so that time may transform their mortal remains into bones suitable for placement in an ossuary. Luigi being the first of his family to rise to such heights, the crypt had never been used, which was part of the reason why I had suggested it. I had no particular desire to wake among rotting corpses.

But enough of that. Sofia and David were waiting near the crypt, along with Benjamin, who had insisted on coming along. They had half concealed themselves behind a cluster of linden trees but were able to see clearly what transpired. The little procession arrived, Luigi led the way toward the tomb with Cesare walking beside the litter. The double doors were unlocked and opened. I was carried down a short flight of steps into the interior lit with torches. At Luigi's direction, my body was placed on one of the marble biers. A thin sheet of gauzy silk sent for that purpose by Lucrezia was laid over me, enshrouding me from head to toe.

Cesare dismissed the guard, ordering Vittoro and the others back to the Vatican to protect the Pope.

"Be assured, Lord," Luigi said when they were gone, "she will be safe here. Her life was not easy but she is at peace now. Let us leave her to it."

He turned to go, as did all the rest, all save Cesare. To Luigi's horror, the son of Jove announced with great dignity that he would pray alone for the repose of my soul, and ordered everyone else out of the crypt.

31

My memories of returning to this world are scant and fragmentary. I floated upward as though out of a deep pool. I had no idea as to my identity or any need to know. I simply was, a condition which filled me with inexpressible contentment.

Gradually, my awareness of myself became more distinct. I was separate, apart from wherever I was emerging from. Curiosity stirred in me, driving out tranquillity.

Where was I? What was happening?

I felt the rise and fall of my chest, and knew that I was breathing. With that realization came a rush of relief. I was alive! But where and in what circumstance?

Hesitantly, I opened my eyes but only barely, half afraid of what I would see. Had the plan gone terribly wrong? Was I buried, as I had feared that I might be if Luigi did not prevail? Or had I been laid in some catacomb surrounded by the truly dead?

At first, I saw only the flicker of torches set in brackets along the walls and the deep shadows between them. Only gradually did I realize that I was not alone. But instead of Sofia being there to help me, inexplicably it was Cesare who knelt beside the bier, his head in his hands. I heard a low murmur coming from him and assumed that he was praying. That he should do so on my behalf astounded me. I was on the verge of regretting how often I had thought him too vain to humble himself before the Almighty when I realized that he was berating God, demanding to know why He had done this to him.

Him? Disbelief rose in me, warring with exasperation. Belatedly, I remembered that for the Borgias life was what they saw in the mirror and nothing else. The purity of their focus was at once their greatest strength and their ultimate weakness.

After several moments listening to Cesare harangue the Deity, I felt compelled to respond.

"For heaven's sake—" My voice emerged as little more than a croak but it might as well have been a thunderclap. Cesare jumped up and leaped away from the bier, his mouth agape in horror.

"Aiyeeeh!"

I will not belabor the moment save to say that it was not his finest.

I sat up slowly, partly because I was still very stiff and weak but also, I admit, because I was enjoying knocking him sideways. Too great a sense of one's own exalted position in the Cosmos is not good for any man.

"Don't scream, it hurts my ears."

He backed up farther and stared at me. "Holy Mother of God!"

I winced. "For pity's sake, don't do that."

My head throbbed and the light in the crypt seemed overly bright but apart from that I felt better than I had expected. Already, the cold caul of death was slipping away, replaced by returning warmth and strength. Discovering that I could move, I swung my legs over the side of the bier and attempted to stand up. That was a mistake. Immediately, my knees gave way and I collapsed onto the floor. Cesare being frozen where he stood, I was left to haul myself back onto the bier, where I sat until I caught my breath.

"I'm not dead. I'll explain everything—" I wasn't looking forward to that but his presence in the crypt left me no choice. "But first, why are you here and where is Sofia Montefiore?"

He gave no sign of having heard me but he did take a step nearer, followed by another. "You aren't dead?"

"Obviously not, nor are you witnessing any sort of miracle." I added that last part lest he was befuddled enough to think that Almighty God would favor one such as me.

"Then what in Hades is happening here?"

I think he had figured out at least part of it already, for he had a brilliant mind and an even greater genius for intrigue. Even so, the sheer enormity of the deception I had engineered gave him pause. He needed a little time to believe what I had done.

"This is all a charade? You faked your own death?"

I nodded. "You want Morozzi to show himself and so do I. This was the best way."

Which made us coconspirators in the plot to use Borgia as bait. I had to hope that having joined him on the side of expediency in contradiction of all natural law, Cesare would be willing to overlook my little ruse.

"Damn it, why in hell didn't you tell me!" He strode to the bier, seized hold of me, and dragged me upright. "Do you have any idea how I felt? I thought you were dead. Dead! Even then I said you weren't, I told everyone that idiot doctor was wrong but you were still just lying there, not moving. I couldn't hear your heart or feel you breathing. You were cold as ice. Why didn't you say something! Why didn't you tell me!"

"Because I was unconscious! How else could I have looked like that? Blame me for not telling you before I acted, although I had good reason not to and make no apology for it. But don't blame me for failing to consider your sensibilities when I was hanging on to life by the thinnest of threads!"

The full enormity of what I had done finally dawned on him. He did not let me go, probably just as well, as I would have fallen again, but he did ease his grip.

"My God," he said, "you took something."

"It was perfectly safe." I saw no reason to mention that it might not have been or, for that matter, ever to think of that again.

"Are you mad? You could have been killed!"

"I *will* be killed if Morozzi disposes of your father and clears the way for Savonarola to become pope. A great many people will die. You're likely to be among them."

That possibility seemed not to have occurred to him but then he was still in the stage of his life when he thought himself immortal. Even so, he did not reject it out of hand.

"You may have a point."

Judging that to be as great a concession as I could hope for, I said, "Sofia and Luigi must be worried sick. Why aren't they here?"

"They knew, both of them? You told them and not me?"

I considered trying to explain that to him but it would have involved so much placating and soothing of his vanity that I simply could not muster the strength. Instead, I chose the more practical course.

With a soft moan, I sagged against him.

"Francesca!"

It was cruel, I know, to taunt a man so lately overcome with grief at the thought of my death. But as I said, I had chosen the side of expediency.

He swept me into his arms and was striding toward the doors of the crypt when they were flung open and Sofia entered. I peered at her surreptitiously as she railed at Cesare.

"That's enough! You put her down right now and let me take care of her! Luigi, bring the blankets. Binyamin, where is that tea I brewed? David, don't just stand there, take her from him!"

He stepped forward without hesitation. Unlike Rocco, David ben Eliezer had grown up brawling in the streets of Rome, where the greatest provocation was to be seen as a proud Jew. Never one to bow his head to any man, he went nowhere without a knife, a cudgel, a garroting wire, and the power of his own fists. Moreover, he was as adept at using those weapons as was Cesare himself. Both men were warriors to the bone. Let loose, they would have done each other a great deal of damage.

How fortunate that I was there between them.

"Stop!" I cried out. "We have no time for this. Cesare, for pity's sake, put me down. These people mean no harm. They care as much for your father's safety as you do yourself."

"They are Jews."

"They are my friends! And they will be yours if only you let them."

That was a bit fanciful but thankfully neither Sofia nor David contradicted me. Even better, Cesare must have realized the folly of dividing our forces, for he relented and sat me down on the bier.

Sofia rushed forward. I was draped in blankets, chafed with warm hands, fed the restorative tea, and generally made much of.

"How is your vision?" she demanded. "Can you see properly?"

When I assured her that I could, she rushed on. "Wiggle your fingers and toes. Good. Turn your head. The other way, too. What day is it? Who am I? What is the last thing you remember? Is there any ringing in your ears? Are you experiencing melancholia or any other morbid sensibility? Can you pass water? I would like to examine it to be sure that—"

"Enough! Unless you have found a way to stop time, we must be done with this."

She paused. Only then did I notice how closely Cesare was watching us. Looking at Sofia, he said, "Did you give her whatever it was that she took?"

Knowing full well the consequences of any such admission on her part, I spoke before she could.

"It was a potion of my own devising. Sofia tried to dissuade me and only agreed to go along so that she could be here to help me."

Cesare was clearly unconvinced, but in the face of my lie, he could hardly interrogate Sofia further. That being the case, he turned his attention to Luigi.

"What is your excuse?"

I thought that the banker, being a sensible man, would seek to soothe Cesare, but instead Luigi said, "Francesca risked her life to persuade Morozzi that the way is clear for him. Your own grief will help convince him that she truly is dead."

"You used me."

"We are all using each other," I said, my exasperation returning in full force. The chill of the crypt was beginning to penetrate the blanket I clutched. I had no wish to linger.

Turning to Sofia, I asked, "Did you bring clothes for me?"

Sofia indicated a basket. Together, we moved deeper into the crypt, where I dressed behind a blanket she held up. The breeches, doublet, and broad-brimmed hat that I donned were the uniform of a page in Luigi's service. The livery was both easy for me to move around in and likely to deter unwanted attention.

Dressing, I whispered, "None of us bargained on Cesare being here. He can be useful later but I need to elude him for some little time."

"Why?"

When I told her, she balked. "It is too dangerous. Surely, David can—"

"He wouldn't be believed, nor would Benjamin. I have to do this myself."

In the twilight sleep between life and death, it had occurred to me that tragic events had provided an opportunity to assure that Morozzi, never one to put himself at risk if he could avoid it, would not delegate the attack on Borgia to his Il Frateschi allies and slip away unseen. I did not add, although I suspected Sofia knew, that I also needed to repay a debt of honor.

Reluctantly, she agreed. With an arm around me, she hustled us past the men, announcing loudly, "Enough of this terrible place. Francesca must have fresh air."

A quick look passed between her and David. That smoothly, he stepped in front of Cesare and Luigi, delaying their own departure from the tomb.

At the first touch of the sun on my face, unfettered relief flowed through me. Despite the desperate gamble I had taken, I was alive. For that I was truly thankful, but any expression of my gratitude would have to wait.

With a quick nod to Sofia, I slipped away through the screen of trees and out onto the busy street.

32

It was mid-afternoon when I set out to cross the river to Trastevere. In body and mind I was still more fragile than I had admitted to the others. The dark pool in which I had floated for so many hours had not entirely loosened its hold on me. I moved through the waning light of day while behind me trailed wisps of the strange contentment I had felt, lightly tethering me to that sense of oneness that I would never entirely forget.

In my page's garb, I attracted no notice whatsoever. As I walked, I listened to snatches of conversation from passersby. Most of what I gleaned was of no import but here and there I heard references to the death of *la strega,* to Borgia's chances of survival—not considered good—and to the terrible war that he and della Rovere seemed determined to bring down upon simple people who wanted nothing more than to be left alone to get on with their lives.

Mulling over all that, I crossed the Ponte Sisto and had a sudden uncomfortable moment when I spotted Vittoro on horseback patrolling with several condottierri, including the hapless fellow that Cesare had set to guard me. I was glad to see that he had not suffered for my "death," but thought his pardon likely due less to any act of mercy than to the simple need for as many armed men as possible to shore up Borgia's defenses.

Vittoro was another to whom I would have to explain and hope for forgiveness, but rather than worry about that, I found myself thinking about the kindness of his family in coming out to mourn me. To do that for someone whom most others condemned as a witch took courage as well as genuine feeling. With the realization that I truly was less alone in this world than I had thought, the dark pool lost a little more of its appeal.

Within the warren of narrow streets that fanned out from the larger avenues where the wealthy had their houses, I found the vine-covered entrance to the netherworld that Benjamin had revealed to me. Using the flint and tinder I had acquired from Luigi, I struck a light. The passage leading downward was as uninviting as I remembered but I did not hesitate. This much I owed to Alfonso and to the nameless girl Morozzi had turned into a living torch.

I had barely stepped into the remains of the buried villa where I had first encountered *il re dei contrabbandieri* when various of his acolytes took note of me. At once I was surrounded by a motley crew of red-eyed, angry boys and a few girls who looked ready to tear any intruder limb from limb.

Without delay, I whipped off my cap, let my hair tumble about my shoulders, and announced, "I am Francesca Giordano. If you think to harm me, be prepared to die."

I was taking a risk revealing myself to them but I considered that I had no choice. Further, I believed that given all that had occurred, they would keep my secret rather than risk giving benefit to the vile enemy who had killed one of their own.

Even so, their reaction was everything I expected and more. Scant hours before, they would have learned not only of my death but of the honors afforded me at my hasty but well-attended funeral by no less than Il Papa himself. Truly, one cannot get much more dead than to be sent to eternal rest under the auspices of Christ's Vicar himself.

Yet there I was alive. Orpheus returned from the underworld could not have been received with greater awe and terror. They drew back, wide-eyed and gasping, and made no attempt to impede me as I crossed the space to stand before Alfonso's throne.

Il re sat slumped in the gilded chair, his raw-boned features suffused with grief. The dead girl's twin knelt beside him, weeping.

Glancing up, he saw me and for a moment I thought he might be overcome with horror. But any such capacity had been leached out of him by what he had witnessed. He simply shrugged.

"Have you lost your way to Hades?"

"No, although I can understand why you might think so. I am very sorry for what happened."

"It would not have if I had not made common cause with you."

There was no denying the truth of that. I had, however inadvertently, had a hand in the girl's horrible death. Yet another sin for which I could never make amends.

"There being no consolation for such grief," I said, "I have brought you something else that I hope you will find useful."

He looked at me with his better eye. "What would that be?"

"Morozzi did not act alone. He had help from six members of Il Frateschi who are resident at the guesthouse adjacent to Santa

Maria. They are disguised as merchants from Florence come to discuss renovation of the basilica."

Alfonso stirred a little in his chair and looked at me more closely. "How certain are you of this?"

"Entirely certain. It should be a simple matter to confirm that."

"Yes," Alfonso said, "it should be. What about the priest?"

"Leave him to me."

"I would rather not."

"I understand that but you have no choice. I do not presume that my claim on him is greater than yours but he is mine nonetheless."

Alfonso considered that. Finally, he said, "Do you think she suffered long?"

"I think the smoke suffocated her before the flames could do very much."

It happened like that sometimes, but burnings can be done with green wood, the better to stretch out the torment of the condemned and be sure that death comes only after great agony. I could only hope that the girl had been more fortunate than that.

"I want him to suffer," Alfonso said. Just then he sounded very young, a child's voice coming out of one who seemed aged far beyond his years.

"He will," I promised, and knew that within the ledger of my soul, the torment of the girl and the grief of her compatriots had been added to all the other harm Morozzi had done and sought to do. The reckoning, when it came, would have to be very great indeed.

I left the way I had come, confident that Alfonso would act to eliminate the allies who might yet help Morozzi. As I emerged back into Trastevere, the fading rays of sunlight were turning the rooftops red-gold. Cesare's house was on a corner near the river. Not much smaller than the building where I lived, for all that it was home to only one man and his servants, it was also three stories tall, with a sloping, tiled roof and small barred windows facing the street. Only the fineness of the carvings around each window and beneath the roof, as well as the presence of armed men at the ornate entrance, declared it to be the residence of a great lord.

I approached it by a circuitous route and stood for a little while deep in the shadows of a doorway on the other side of the street, from which I could watch the house. Servants came and went through an entrance to one side. I waited until a page went in, then slipped quickly behind him before the door could shut. Scarcely had I taken half a dozen steps inside than I was seized from behind by the nape of my shirt and lifted off the floor.

"What do you think you're doing, brat, prancing in here like you're the lord's own get?"

"Begging your pardon, sir," I gasped in as servile a tone as I could manage. "Message for Signore Borgia from Signore d'Amico." For good measure, I added, "To be delivered personally, sir."

I was dropped, only just managing to land on my feet. The guard pointed a beefy arm toward the stairs. "Present yourself to the sergeant-at-arms next time, whelp, instead of skulking around. Not everyone here's as patient and kind as myself."

Pursued by guffaws, I scrambled for the stairs and quickly made my way to the main floor of the house. The loggia bordering lush interior gardens was elegantly designed with paneled walls, marble columns, and a selection of statues I recognized as having been taken from some of the many excavations going on all over the city. I walked past a naked warrior with a bow strung across his back, a youth strumming a harp, and a young woman bare-breasted in all her glory who might have been Venus herself.

A steward, accepting my claim to come from Signore d'Amico,

brusquely directed me up another flight of stairs, where I proceeded down a hallway. My eye caught a door designed to blend in with the wall and meant for use by servants. I opened it and found myself in a narrow corridor running the length of the house. Steep steps led to the uppermost floor where half a dozen doors led off the passage. Opening one, I discovered what was likely Cesare's private office. Another led to what I assumed was his bedroom.

The spurt of energy that had carried me along since the discovery that I was still alive was waning fast. I stared at the bed in longing only to decide that a message boy making himself at home so daringly was likely to earn himself a beating from outraged servants. Glancing around, I spied another door, which upon examination led into a small chamber with windows facing the garden. An immense silvered mirror in a gold frame took up one entire wall. The others were lined with floor-to-ceiling shelves and finely carved wardrobes. The room was filled with clothing, everything from velvet doublets, wool capes lined with silk, fine linen shirts, brocade collars, soft leather jerkins, hose of every description, and a truly astounding quantity of footwear from shoes to boots and back again. In addition, several locked chests held what I assumed to be jewelry—chains, rings, and the like. No wigs, though. Cesare had a marvelous head of hair and would never have dreamed of concealing it.

Too weary to do more than sigh, I slid down onto the floor, leaned my back against one of the walls, and was about to close my eyes when I heard shouting.

"Where in hell is he then, this boy you say brings a message from d'Amico?"

Murmur, murmur, placating sounds . . .

"For God's sake, I'm surrounded by incompetents!"

347

The door to the closet was flung open and Cesare strode in. He took one look at me sitting on the floor and slammed the door shut.

"You are going to be the death of me," he said.

"No, I'm not. Your terrible security will get you killed long before I can."

Something unfathomable moved behind his eyes. He sighed deeply.

"Do you ever, even once," he asked, "consider the price of caring about you?"

I opened my mouth to tell him that I was not so foolish as to take that seriously, but no words came. For whatever reason—my wayward nature, the darkness within me, whatever—I simply could not comprehend that he might be speaking from the heart. After another long look in my direction, he threw off his cloak, leaving it where it fell, and turned toward the mirror. I scarcely had time to wonder what he intended when he pressed a concealed latch, causing the glass to swing outward.

"Up you go," Cesare said, and hauled me to my feet. Before I could think to protest, he thrust me through the opening behind the glass and followed swiftly.

I found myself in a gracious salon lit by the faint gray light filtering through small windows near the ceiling that were covered with tilted wooden slats. As I looked around, trying to take in my surroundings, Cesare lit several candelabras. I realized that I was in a cleverly concealed apartment.

"One of two in the house," he said in response to my startled observation. He reached behind me to close the mirror, which on our side was an unremarkable door.

"A hidden stair leads to a passageway that comes out behind a stable near the river. There are horses always on hand as well as several boats."

Still trying to take it all in, I said, "Your father thought of everything."

Or at least everything needed for a fast escape should the unhappy day come when that proved necessary.

"Actually, I did. He had the notion to build the houses but I suggested that privacy and security both would become even greater issues when he achieved the papacy. Fortunately, he agreed." Cesare paused. "Of course, that was in the days when he didn't imagine me to be his enemy."

"He doesn't really believe that." Never mind that Il Papa had said as much in what surely must have been no more than a bad moment.

"He at least entertains the notion. Turn around."

Already, his hands were on the laces of my doublet. I could not deny the sheer carnal pleasure that welled up in me at his touch. I lived, I breathed, I felt, and in that moment, nothing else mattered so much. That in acquiescing to his sexual demands I would also placate him did not enter my mind, or only very slightly. Even so, I did take a faint stab at reason.

"Your father—"

"Decamped for the *castel* immediately after your funeral. Vittoro has him under heavy guard there. Hold still."

The news that Borgia had been inspired by my "death" to take shelter in the city's ancient fortress where I had almost perished the previous year while doing my utmost to usher Pope Innocent VIII to his eternal reward gave me pause.

"If Morozzi realizes where he has gone—"

The mad priest knew the *castel* well, having lived there for a time as part of Innocent VIII's inner circle. If anyone other than myself could penetrate the fortress with deadly intent, Morozzi could.

"He went by the *passetto*," Cesare said, naming the passage hidden within what looks like nothing more than an old city wall between the Vatican and the *castel*. "Every effort is being made to make it appear that he is still within the Vatican. We have left the way open for Morozzi there, not too obviously to arouse suspicion but enough for him to be tempted by it."

"All well and good but Il Papa can't remain in hiding for long. Pesaro is due in the city tomorrow."

With the wedding scheduled to take place two days after the Sforza bridegroom's arrival. Borgia would have to be present for the welcoming ceremonies as well as all the other events leading up to and including the actual marriage.

My breeches fell to the floor, the laces having been undone by his too-clever hands while I scarcely noticed. His shirt followed swiftly, as did the remainder of our clothes. Finding the knife in its leather sheath across my breasts, Cesare removed it with great care, tantalizing me as he brushed his thumbs across my nipples.

"Are you never without this?" he asked as he dropped the blade onto the pile of clothes.

"I keep it as a remembrance of you."

He laughed, far too wise to take me seriously, and yet there was something fleeting in his eyes that made me think he wished that my sally was true.

As I watched, he hopped on one foot, then on the other, to remove his boots; he considered it the mark of a gentleman to do so before coupling, although by his own admission—and my experience—that level of civility sometimes escaped him. We did not make it so far as the bedchamber but fell together onto the floor of the salon. I had a moment's appreciation for the thick, soft carpet covering it before passion blotted out all else.

After my sojourn in the dark pool, my senses were acutely heightened. I was vividly aware of the salty tang of Cesare's skin on my tongue, of the weight of his thigh pressing between mine, of the hard length of him driving into me in response to my heated urging. The muscles of his buttocks tensed under my hands, his heart beat powerfully against mine, and I caught, like a fluttering echo, the deep current of that oneness in which I had drifted free and at peace for too little time.

Cesare rose above me, holding my hips, and drove harder, deeper, faster. The fury of the day with its pain and fear, its tumult and risk fell away and I soared on a current of near-unbearable bliss into the heart of a burning sun.

And then it was over; I mean no criticism of Cesare, he never lacked for stamina. It was my own impatience that drove us to a hasty completion. In the aftermath we lay side by side, struggling for breath. I reached out, brushing my fingers lightly down his arm. He seized my hand and pressed it to his lips. We remained like that as slowly the world righted itself.

I became aware that naked cherubs were grinning down at us as they cavorted across billowing white clouds on the ceiling.

"Pinturicchio?" I asked.

Cesare propped himself up on his elbows and nodded. "Do you like it?"

I squinted, considering. "Honestly, it's a little romantic for my taste. The frescoes he's painting in your father's new apartment are better."

With a laugh, he bounded up and held out a hand to help me rise. "Truly, Francesca, if all women were like you, I would become a Turk for the sole purpose of assembling a harem."

"A harem of poisoners? You do like to live dangerously."

Looking around for our clothes, Cesare said, "No more so than you. Have you considered how my father will react when he discovers that you deceived him?"

"Perhaps he will have greater concerns."

I do not pretend to understand the workings of my mind, roiled as it was by the darkness that was never still for very long. Why I should ricochet from the heights of passion into the depths of suspicion escapes me. I could only conclude that even as I took Cesare into my body and drained him of the pleasure he offered so unstintingly, some part of me remained aloof and calculating, weighing what he had let slip.

He dropped his shirt over his head and began lacing it. "What does that mean?"

I finished dressing swiftly and eased the knife from its sheath, holding it behind my back. As I did so, the darkness stirred within me, a reminder of what could happen if I was not very careful to keep myself in check.

With my fingers closed around the hilt, I asked, "Who is in the other apartment?"

My timing was poor, to say the least. I would have done better to put the knife to his throat while yet we lay in postcoital bliss, for that is the best time above all to take a man by surprise. A woman less susceptible to passion might have managed that. As for myself, I had to do the best I could.

He peered at me in what gave every appearance of honest bewilderment. "What are you talking about?"

"You said there were two apartments hidden here. Who is in the other?"

"No one. Why would you think—?"

Given a choice, an intelligent man usually is preferable to a stupid one, but on that particular occasion, I wished that Cesare wasn't quite so swift of mind.

Not taking his eyes from me, he reached for his breeches and pulled them on, then stood, his arms loose at his sides, ready to move with lightning speed if he thought it necessary.

"What are you suggesting, Francesca?"

"You seem unconcerned that very shortly Il Papa must leave the safety of the *castel* to officiate at the wedding celebrations. Since that doesn't worry you, you must think that this will be over before then. The only way you could believe that is if you already know Morozzi's whereabouts."

Did I truly believe that my dark lover had been sheltering Morozzi all this time, providing succor to the man who had caused me such unbearable anguish? Recall, I had not yet had any opportunity to learn of Cesare's reaction to my death, apart from what had transpired since my return to the world. I knew nothing of his frenzied vow to kill the mad priest, but even if I had, I would not necessarily have been swayed by it.

Cesare was a true Borgia, capable of spinning plots within plots to dizzying effect. Moreover, he could tell himself that so long as Morozzi died in the end, using the priest to win favor with Il Papa was no sin.

Of course, I saw the matter differently.

"For God's sake," Cesare said. He thrust a hand through his hair in the manner of a man pressed to exasperation and beyond. "You don't trust anyone, do you? Not a single soul."

What could I say? He had me to rights. "No."

"Not even that glassmaker, Pocco—"

"Rocco."

"You didn't tell him what you were planning, did you, when you plotted your death?"

How exactly had we gotten on the subject of Rocco when all I wanted to talk about was Morozzi? Did Cesare truly care so much about my relationship with another man, or was he merely seeking to distract me?

"I did not want him involved. He's getting married."

Cesare raised a brow. He stood only a few feet from me. I could see the shadow roughening his jaw, the thick lashes shielding his eyes, the soft pulsing of the vein in his neck along which I had pressed my lips. I kept my gaze on the beat of his life's blood as the darkness stirred again inside me.

"Is he? Who to?"

"Carlotta d'Agnelli. It is a good match for him. He will have a chance to be happy."

Cesare heaved a sigh and came a step closer.

I took a step back, uncertain which I dreaded more, that he would try to disarm me or that I would lose control and attack him.

"Tell me what you are concealing," I said.

He pretended not to have heard me, absurd given how close we stood to each other, so close that I could watch the steady rise and fall of his chest and imagine how easy it would be to put a stop to it. There would be blood, of course, the same blood I hated and feared, and desperately needed. The darkness was growing stronger. I had to end this quickly but Cesare seemed disinclined to do so.

"What is happiness?" he asked. "You win or you lose, in between you struggle. That is the essence of life. Anything else is a tale told for children."

"And I am supposed to be the cynic?"

In truth, the teachings of the ancient Cynics elude me. The notion that life should be lived free of all desires and possessions because none have any true value seems absurd. We are in this world; therefore we must accept our hungry, striving selves as best we can. Claiming that we can be other than what we are is self-deception at its worst.

"Tell me, Cesare! What are you hiding? Or is it who?"

"You think too much of my abilities. I am the son my father means to make into a puppet following slavishly in his steps. Such a creature counts for nothing."

"When you are pope, you will think differently."

"When I am pope, the world will be in ruins for there will never have been so vast a violation of nature. Or do you really believe that Juan has it in him to be a true duke, a leader in battle and in a peace of his own shaping?"

"I scarcely know Juan." What I had seen of him was not impressive, but to be fair, his belief that I was a witch in need of burning tainted my opinion.

"I know him all too well," Cesare said. "He is a fool, plain and simple. But our father loves him and will believe no ill of him unless I can present him with irrefutable proof of what he has done."

I heard what he said clearly enough but my mind reeled from the implications. I needed a breath and then another before I could begin to come to terms with what he seemed to be telling me.

"Juan? Your brother, Juan, is sheltering Morozzi?"

That hot-tempered dullard of a second son who still managed to be Borgia's favorite by virtue of his willingness to do anything Il Papa wanted of him? *He* was conspiring with his father's would-be murderer?

"What possible reason would Juan have for doing such a thing?"

"I have no idea," Cesare admitted. "But I don't pretend to under-stand the workings of what passes for my brother's mind. Morozzi is sheltered within Juan's own residence, in one of the hidden apart-ments much like this. He has access to a tunnel, again like the one here, which means that he can come and go by the river or through the streets, including the underground passages he knows so well. That's how he's been able to move around the city at will while re-maining virtually invisible."

"How do you know this?"

"I have a man in Juan's household. A few days ago, he reported that someone might be hidden in one of the apartments there but he couldn't be sure. Early today, he finally got a glimpse of him. The moment I heard the description, I knew that it was Morozzi."

"I am so sorry."

Really, what else could I say? I was sorry to have come close to drawing a knife on him, true enough, but that was as nothing com-pared to the sympathy I felt for his being saddled with such a brother and a father unable to see his sons in their true light. While he lived, my father knew me as I truly was and, incredibly, loved me all the same. Borgia could not see past his own interest to perceive his sons for the men they were.

"What are you going to do?" I asked.

"Every means of egress from Juan's house is under watch. As soon as Morozzi is on the move, I will know. We will close in, take him—alive if possible, dead if we must—and Juan will be made to account for what he has done."

And then what? Borgia would awaken to the true nature of his sons, perceive Cesare as he really was, and allow him to live a life of his own choosing? As much as I wanted to believe that, I had my doubts.

But I said nothing of that as I slipped my knife fully back into its sheath and tucked both into a pocket of my breeches. As I did so, the darkness subsided, if only sullenly.

Cesare didn't even pretend not to notice what I did. He watched my every move and shook his head when I was done.

"Pocco could never have managed you, surely you know that?"

"I don't want to discuss him."

"Fair enough, but if you ever think to pull a knife on me again, you had better be prepared to use it."

"I'll just slip something into your wine."

He didn't take me seriously, of course, which was as I intended. I had to hope that he would never again come so close to discovering what I was truly capable of doing.

"Speaking of," he said, "I'm hungry."

We dined on roasted quail accompanied by crusty bread; carrots drizzled with honey; fresh greens topped with oil, a dash of vinegar, and a sprinkling of chopped herbs; and what may have been the best duck paté I had ever tasted. Cesare poured a fruity Tuscan red that carried a hint of plum.

"How long have you suspected Juan?" I asked as I dipped a morsel of the bread in the quail sauce, then spread a little of the paté on it. Any concern that my stomach might not be up to such rich food had dissolved with the first bite.

"All my life, I think, although that may not have been true when we were very young. It's hard to remember exactly when I realized that he was doing his damndest to turn our father against me."

"Yet Il Papa has given you great responsibilities."

Juan might be the recipient of noble titles and the lands that went with them, as well as having a grand marriage planned for him, but it was to Cesare that Borgia turned on matters as sensitive as the dispersal of family funds or the gathering of intelligence. Surely, that could be seen as a sign of paternal favor?

Cesare twirled the stem of his goblet between his fingers and looked at me over the rim. "He regards experience in finance and diplomacy as essential for a future pope. But it is Juan who will be given armies to lead, if in name only. My brother will win glory he does not deserve."

"And is that what you want, glory?"

"What else is there in this world? It is through glory that our names ring down through the ages. It is our immortality."

I waved a hand dismissively. "You've spent too much time reading Homer. Glory didn't do the Greeks much good in front of Troy, or afterward, for that matter. Their temples are cast down, their alabaster cities buried, what are they but memory?"

"What is there but memory?" Cesare countered. "Achilles, Odysseus, Ajax, Patroclus . . . we know their names and their deeds. When we speak of them, they live again."

I did not see it but neither did I expect to dissuade him. He had a vision of the heroic life that overrode anything Il Papa could intend. The only question was how far he would go to achieve it.

"What do you think should happen to Juan?"

Cesare hesitated. I could see that the subject was a sore one, for all that he must have contemplated it at length.

"For the sake of the family, nothing public can be said, of course. He would have to retain his honors, even proceed with the Spanish marriage. But apart from that, he cannot be allowed to do any more harm."

"He will blame you. Have you considered that he will seek vengeance?"

"I will deal with that when I need to."

Which left me wondering how far exactly Juan would be able to go before Cesare sought a more final solution to the problem of his brother.

I was mulling that over when there was a soft knock at the door leading to the dressing room. Cesare got up to answer it. He returned, frowning slightly.

"There has been an incident at the guesthouse next to Santa Maria."

I leaned back in my chair and pretended renewed interest in the cherubs.

"What sort of incident?"

"A fire, apparently."

"Were there injuries?"

Cesare remained standing. He refilled both our goblets and handed mine to me.

"Oddly enough, the flames spread so quickly that no one was able to escape. You wouldn't think that a stone building would go up like that, would you, but apparently it did."

"Perhaps it had some help." There were any number of flammable liquids that Alfonso could have used—tar, pitch, lamp oil, to name a few—that thrown through the windows and ignited would have done the job effectively.

"That could be." Cesare drained his goblet and set it down on the table. "Mention is being made of Florentine merchants in the city to consult on renovations for the church. None of them has been seen since the fire broke out."

"Oh, dear."

"Perhaps we need a papal commission to investigate fire safety in the city."

"An excellent idea," I agreed. "Juan could head it."

That wrung a rueful grin. I finished my wine and managed to grab a bit more of the paté on the way out the door. Morozzi would hear of the fire almost as quickly as we had. With his allies gone, my nemesis would have no choice but to make his move.

33

Juan's residence was less than a quarter mile away. Cesare had a cordon of men surrounding it, all drawn well back into the shadows of nearby buildings, all heavily armed. We slipped in among them, saluted by a young condottierre who snapped to attention at first sight of Cesare. He scarcely noticed me, which was exactly as I wanted it.

"Sir," he said, "there has been no activity since Gandia"—he referred to Juan by his ducal title—"returned approximately an hour ago. No one has entered or left since then."

Cesare nodded without taking his eyes from the house. "Has there been any activity on the roof?"

I understood what he was thinking, that someone might have caught a glimpse of the flames coming from the guesthouse next to Santa Maria and gone up for a better view. A pall of smoke, heavier than usual for a June night, hung in the air, sure warning of a large fire somewhere nearby.

But the condottierre shook his head. "No, sir, no activity at all."

"Then we wait," Cesare said. To me, he added, "It can't be long."

We waited all night. As the hours dragged by, Cesare's frustration and impatience grew. Twice, he stalked away from the house, through the streets that led to the hidden exit near the river where the tunnel from Juan's house came out. The guards on watch there were as alert and vigilant. They swore, and I believed them, that the only sign of life came from the ubiquitous rats who emerged at first hint of darkness, scurrying back and forth between the river and the shore.

We heard the same at the nearby stables where the horses slept undisturbed by the careful vigilance of hard men who stood in the shadows, ready to move in an instant.

We returned to the street near the house and continued waiting. My legs grew stiff and the small of my back ached. Had our quarry been anyone other than Morozzi, I would have found a reason to seek my bed. As it was, I sat down, leaned against a wall, and dozed lightly.

Dawn approached with no sign of Morozzi. Cesare was beside himself.

"This makes no sense," he insisted. "He has to know that with each passing hour, the risk that he will be discovered increases. And once Pesaro is here, security will be even tighter. He has to realize that, too."

I stood stiffly and brushed myself off. "Perhaps he suspects that you're watching. Why don't you just go in and take him?"

I thought I already knew the answer but I still hoped that Cesare might be persuaded to do it all the same. It was the simplest solution, at least so far as I was concerned.

"In case you haven't noticed," Cesare said, "my brother has his own household guard. If I try to enter without his permission, there will be a battle. In the confusion, Morozzi could get away."

I considered that unlikely, though not impossible given the mad priest's wiliness. The more probable reason for Cesare's restraint was his knowledge that his father would blame him if blood was shed at Juan's expense. Cesare's goal in all of this was to emerge elevated in his father's eyes, the son who had proven himself a man of action, capable of defeating a deadly enemy, a true *dux*. He would not risk giving Borgia any excuse for believing that he had acted only to defame his brother.

My goal was simpler; I wanted Morozzi dead.

The previous year, I had thwarted the mad priest, but only barely and only at the last minute. I had underestimated him but I also had, without even realizing it, made certain assumptions that had proven to be false. I wondered if I might be doing the same again, as might Cesare.

A trap had been laid, baited with nothing less than Borgia himself. By all rights, Morozzi should have been lured into it. Yet he seemed content to wait. Because he had a plan to kill Borgia designed to unfold during the wedding itself? But that would mean acting in public, in the presence of both the papal guards and Pesaro's own men. With the portrait that Nando had done of him being circulated among all the condottierre, his capture would be certain.

What then was his thinking? What did he intend?

If I were him, what would I do?

You will understand that I shied away from trying to put myself into the mind of the mad priest. I could not bear the thought that the evil in him was akin to what dwelled in me. Yet there was no denying that both of us were killers, driven by dark forces beyond the ken of those fortunate enough to live in the light.

Even so, though I did try, I could not discern Morozzi's plan. It continued to elude me.

With the coming of day, Cesare had no choice but to pull his men back farther or risk discovery. They took up positions in buildings surrounding Juan's residence, careful to keep out of sight. The ordinary activity of the street began, people coming and going seemingly without noticing that anything was amiss. I was encouraged by that but still preoccupied with wondering what Morozzi planned.

Red-eyed and unshaven, and far too anxious to stand still any longer, Cesare withdrew to his own residence with me in tow. There he hastily bathed, threw on clean clothes, and ate standing, without, I believe, noticing what he chewed. I contented myself with a restorative tea and a pitcher of cold water splashed on my face.

"I'm going out," I said when I was done.

"Where?" Cesare demanded.

"I want a look at the guesthouse. The men who died there were Il Frateschi."

"I suspected as much."

"They're the only link we have to Morozzi. They may have left some clue as to what he intends."

We went, Cesare reluctantly but desperate for something, anything to do that might prove helpful. The piazza in front of Santa Maria was less busy than usual. The combined effect of the girl having been burned there followed by the fire at the guesthouse kept people away. Only a few women were drawing water from the fountain, going as quickly as they could and scurrying away swiftly with their buckets sloshing from their haste.

There was little wind, meaning that the stench of fire hung heavy in the air. Cesare and I approached slowly. I suspect that he was as struck as I was by the utter devastation of the guesthouse.

Fortunately, because all the buildings surrounding the piazza were built of stone with tile roofs, the fire had spread no further. But the guesthouse itself was a virtual ruin. The building stood open to the sky, the floor separating the two stories having fallen in along with the roof. Blackened timbers lay in heaps against scorched stone.

I stepped over the threshold gingerly and took a quick look around. If any remains had been present, they were not in evidence. So far as I could tell, the ferocity of the fire had been intense enough to turn bone to powder. It might be that the fate of the "Florentine merchants" would never be known precisely.

"What could have such an effect?" Cesare asked.

I straightened and slowly shook my head. "I don't know. I've never seen anything like this."

The fountain was less than fifty feet from the building. It stood to reason that a genuine attempt would have been made to extinguish the fire. Yet it had raged so fiercely that even the stone of the outer walls appeared to be in danger of crumbling.

"It will have to be pulled down," Cesare said.

I nodded. The devastation of the guesthouse posed a mystery that I could not begin to solve, yet neither could I bring myself to walk away. I turned in a circle, trying to comprehend what I was seeing. Where had the fire started? How quickly had it spread? No one had been seen to escape so it must have been swift indeed, but not even that accounted for what I saw all around me.

Hesitantly, I bent and ran my fingers over the charred surface of a fallen beam. The wood disintegrated under my touch. A heavy, wet smell rose from it—the scent of fire dampened by water, but under it there was something else.

I lifted my hand to my face and inhaled deeply.

"What are you doing?" Cesare asked.

I did not answer him at once but exhaled slowly and breathed in again. Fire, yes, flame on wood and less familiar, probably flame on stone. But underneath all that . . . what was it?

"Trying to determine what happened here," I said finally. "There is something—"

I got up, dusted off my hands, and walked farther into the destroyed building. Cesare followed.

"Be careful," he said. "The floor could give way."

It remained in place only by virtue of being made of slate, but I saw his point. In all likelihood, there was a croft beneath. If the beams under the slate had been touched by the fire, they could crack. Indeed, as I looked more closely, I saw a large, gaping hole off to one side of the house.

I made my way to it cautiously and bent, peering down into the darkness.

"Something happened here," I said.

Cesare joined me, staring into the croft. "The floor collapsed."

I supposed that he was right, but something about how the shards of slate were lying around the hole gave me pause. So, too, did the faint smell that rose from it.

"We have to go," Cesare said. "Pesaro is due at noon and I must be on hand to welcome him."

No doubt Borgia had ordered that he be in attendance, and on his best behavior as well. I shot him a sympathetic smile.

"You go ahead. I want to look around a little more."

He agreed reluctantly, really because he had no choice. If he was late, or worse yet did not appear at all, there would be hell to pay with his father.

Once he was gone, I took my time slowly surveying the ruins.

What I saw puzzled me deeply. From what I could tell, the fire had started near both the front and back windows, which was believable given that Alfonso and his confederates could have thrown flammable liquid in from both sides. But that did not explain the hole in the floor, much less the dark stain of smoke darkening the wall behind it.

Or the fact that the slate shards were lying a few feet away from the hole, as though they had been thrown out of it rather than falling into the undercroft.

"What happened here?" I murmured.

Scarcely had I spoken than I heard off in the distance the blare of trumpets announcing Pesaro's entry into the city. How excited Lucrezia must be. I imagined her standing at the windows of Palazzo Santa Maria in Portico, straining for a glimpse of her betrothed. Would he be everything she hoped for? Could any man ever fulfill the dreams of a woman?

What was that I smelled?

I knelt again and plunged both my hands into the debris on the floor, then raised them and inhaled. At once, I coughed and regretted my impulsive action. And yet, there was something—

Cannons roared in honor of the Sforza heir. Startled pigeons rose into the air and I, losing my balance a little, tumbled back onto the slate floor hard enough to feel it crack under me. Scrambling to my feet, I moved quickly toward the street. Once safely outside again, I stared into the ruin. It revealed nothing more than what I had already discerned. The fire had been swift and terrible; the likelihood of anyone escaping being virtually nil. But something else had happened as well.

What was that smell?

I closed my eyes and raised my fingers cautiously toward my

nose. At the same moment, I wondered why I was wasting so much time. Morozzi had not come out of Juan's house. Either he had not been there to begin with, no matter what Cesare believed, or—

He was too afraid to come out?

That did not agree with anything I knew of the mad priest. He was a true fanatic convinced that Almighty God favored his cause. He would fear nothing.

What if he did not need to come out?

How could that be? How could he remain safe in Juan's house and still manage to kill Borgia?

Poison. In food, in drink, in something intended for use during the wedding celebrations. But I had checked everything once, twice, and again. No round of cheese, or tun of wine, no chicken, pig, cow, no carrot, turnip—nothing had escaped my scrutiny. After the attack on Lucrezia, I had redoubled my vigilance. What had I missed?

Panic coursed through me but hard on it came blessed reason. Sternly, I reminded myself that Morozzi was no poisoner, though he might aspire to the alchemical arts. He had no particular skill in compounding deadly substances. But he could have acquired something from one of my profession in Florence or elsewhere.

Something that could have escaped my notice? I did not think so, especially given that after Lucrezia—

After the attack on Lucrezia, I had redoubled my vigilance. The strange episode of the soaps, tainted but not in any way that could kill, had left me more convinced than ever that Morozzi would strike at Borgia with poison.

But what if all that had been a diversion? A means of making me look where the mad priest wanted me to and not where I might better have done so.

What was that smell?

Again, I closed my eyes. Again, I breathed, and finally I caught the scent under smoke and wood, fire and stone . . . the dry, sharp, but unmistakable bite of . . . sulfur?

With salt and mercury, it is one of three alchemical principles, denoting the expansive force, dissolution, and evaporation. I had worked with it myself in a variety of experiments and understood its capabilities.

Did Il Frateschi harbor alchemists? Holy Mother Church is conflicted as to our activities, being uncertain about whether we plumb the mysteries of the divine or invite the worship of the demonic. In either case, our curiosity is not encouraged.

But why else would I find sulfur in the ruins of the guesthouse?

Off in the distance, I heard cheering and realized that Pesaro was on his way to Saint Peter's Basilica, where he was scheduled to be received by a Mass welcoming him to Rome and into the embrace of *la famiglia*. Borgia would be officiating with Cesare and Juan no doubt in attendance, the youngest, Jofre, would be there as well, I assumed. Only Lucrezia would be barred from attending, forbidden as she was from meeting her betrothed before the wedding.

In addition, the basilica would be filled with those princes of the Church who still allied themselves to Borgia. There would be wealthy nobles and merchants, foreign ambassadors, and—

Sulfur!

I may have cried out; I do not know for certain. What I do know is that I turned and ran, as fast as I possibly could, through the piazza, along the streets where startled passersby leaped out of my way, over the Sisto Bridge and into the Piazza San Pietro. Directly ahead stood the one place on earth where I most dreaded setting foot. A guard tried to stop me but I darted past him and raced on, my breath coming in gasps, my heart pounding so fiercely that it threatened to explode from my chest, up the steps to the basilica crowded with honored guests, past the banners of the great houses of Sforza and Borgia, and into the ancient nave.

Where the Mass had just begun.

34

Confíteor Deo omnipoténti . . . I confess to Almighty God . . .
The instant I stepped inside the basilica, terrifying
memories of the events of the previous year swept over me.
So, too, did I brace myself for the divine retribution I feared must
surely fall upon one of my dark calling daring to enter so holy a
place. Only the knowledge that I came to do good—surely God
would take that into consideration?—kept me going. That and the
fact that I truly could see no choice. Grasping such courage as I possessed, I plunged on. A pair of guards near the entrance to the nave
moved to stop me. They were big and clumsy whereas I was fueled
by stark terror that lent wings to my feet. I darted under the outstretched arm of one and around the other.

. . . *beátæ Maríæ semper Vírgini* . . . to blessed Mary ever Virgin . . .
The basilica was fragrant with the perfume of incense. Down the
length of the nave, I glimpsed Borgia, garbed in red, standing before the altar, his arms raised as he conducted the holy liturgy.

. . . *beáto Michaéli Archángelo* . . . to blessed Michael the archangel . . .

Several noble guests—not too noble, for they were positioned toward the back of the basilica—noticed my presence. A little flurry of activity ensued as they hesitated, uncertain whether to try to stop me or pretend nothing was amiss.

. . . *beáto Joanni Baptístæ* . . . to blessed John the Baptist . . .

I raced on, down the aisle adjoining the nave toward the pillar that I knew concealed a staircase leading to the garret that stretched the length of the basilica above the ornate ceiling. I had almost died there the previous year, but please God, I would not think of that.

. . . *sanctis Apóstolis Petro et Paulo* . . . to the holy apostles Peter and Paul . . .

A man stepped out suddenly to intercept me, his face first stern, then abruptly wreathed in confusion.

Vittoro!

. . . *ómnibus Sanctis, et vobis, fratres (tibi, Pater)* . . . to all the saints, and to you, brethren . . .

"Francesca?"

. . . *quia peccávi nimis cogitatióne, verbo et ópere* . . . that I have sinned exceedingly in thought, word and deed . . .

He looked torn between shock and sudden joy at the discovery that I was not, after all, dead. That he could be glad for my continued existence given how I had deceived him struck me to the core. Surely, I did not deserve such good and true friends.

. . . *mea culpa, mea culpa, mea máxima culpa.* Through my fault, through my fault, through my most grievous fault.

"Help me," I pleaded, reaching out to him. "Something terrible is about to happen!"

To this day, I do not know how Vittoro managed to react as

quickly as he did. In a heartbeat, he assessed the situation, accepted it for what it was, no matter how bizarre, and made his decision. Explanations could wait for later. Action was called for *now*.

"What do you need?" As he spoke, he took me by the arm and drew me quickly into the shadows beyond the pillars where we would not be seen.

Gasping, almost bent double from the effort to breathe, I said, "I think Morozzi has placed gunpowder here in the basilica."

You will wonder how I had come to such a conclusion unless, of course, you already know that sulfur is one of the key components of gunpowder along with charcoal and potassium nitrate. I had used all three together on a very small and limited basis in my own experiments. More important, I was well aware of the effect of gunpowder in any real quantity. It had been responsible for bringing down the walls of Constantinople only a few decades ago, the same walls that had made that city invulnerable for centuries. Its presence in the guesthouse would explain the devastation I had seen there.

Its presence in the basilica, if I was right about that, raised visions of an apocalyptic nightmare at the very heart of Christianity.

Not to mention the destruction of *la famiglia*.

Savonarola would ride to the papacy on a wave of conviction that God Himself had struck down his princes in their corrupt palace to prepare the way for the purifier of Holy Mother Church. Heaven and all the saints help us.

"Where could it be?" Vittoro asked.

I shook my head in near despair for truly I did not know. The basilica was immense and filled with a warren of crypts, not to mention the vast derelict garret above. The gunpowder could have been hidden anywhere.

"I'm going up. Send men into the crypts, but for God's sake, hurry!"

At once, I mounted the stairs to the garret, taking them two at a time. It was not, unfortunately, a single open space in which I might have had a chance of swiftly spotting what I sought. Instead, the immense space above the ceiling was a maze of cubbyholes and cubicles alternating with long aisles.

Seeing them, I was swept by remembered terrors that threatened to overwhelm me—images of a madman bent on ritual killing, a child about to suffer a hideous fate, and my own self, plunging to my death only to be saved at the last possible moment by a quirk of fate. With the greatest difficulty, I managed to retain control of myself.

At some time in the distant past, the garret had been used for storage. But time and neglect spawned by the chaos that had afflicted Holy Mother Church and the world in general had taken their toll. The building erected a thousand years before by the great Justinian had deteriorated to the point where most of the floor of the garret was too weak and unstable to hold anything heavy.

Which raised the question of where Morozzi could have placed barrels of gunpowder in a building notorious for its soft floor and leaky roof.

That last thought, so mundane, came as purest inspiration. If I was right, the gunpowder could have been put in place weeks ago, even before Morozzi's arrival in Rome, by confederates acting on his behalf, and certainly before the increase in security around Saint Peter's after the mad monk's presence in the city was detected. In that time, it had rained on several occasions, enough to create the possibility that the gunpowder might have become too wet to fire.

Unless it was properly protected. At once, I stopped looking for the telltale rounded shapes of barrels and instead began probing through the dim light for some sign of a canvas-covered heap.

I was moving toward the farthest end of the garret, almost directly above the main altar, when I put a foot down too hard and almost went through a soft spot in the floor. Stumbling, I only just managed to right myself without falling. As I did so, I thought I heard a faint but insistent hiss.

Like most people, I associate that particular sound with snakes, but if any such lived within the confines of Saint Peter's, I did not know it. Rats there were in plenty, enough to keep a bevy of rat catchers constantly employed, but I had never heard of a single serpent daring to enter the holy precincts. Except, you may argue, the human variety, and I will give you that for they came in droves.

What else hissed? Vapor of any origin escaping through a narrow pipe can make that sound. I had heard it or very similar during certain of my alchemical investigations. But this was different. Under the hiss, something crackled softly.

Cesare would have recognized it immediately; I realized that later. But he was a warrior, trained in battle, the man who stole time to be with the army his father was determined not to let him lead, to share their hardships and to learn from them.

Oh, yes, Cesare would have known what it took me a heartbeat or two to recognize.

I had never had reason to use a fuse but I knew of their existence and how they worked. A length of hemp cord treated with potassium nitrate in such quantity as to control the rate of burn is used to fire the matchlock guns some say will revolutionize warfare. The same arrangement is used for controlled explosions in the construction of buildings, dams, and the like. Some even rely on the technique for help in mining, although that is considered extremely dangerous.

It was also, of course, the perfect means for igniting barrels of gunpowder.

I stopped breathing. If I had been able to cease the beat of my heart as well, I would have done so. With all my strength, I strained to hear the sound and identify where it was coming from. Slowly, praying that I was correct, I followed it.

The sound grew louder. I saw up ahead of me a faint spark moving away at a rapid rate. Quickly, heedless of the danger from the soft floor, I hurried toward it. In the faint light filtering through the holes in the ceiling, I saw a red unblinking eye.

And beyond it, under canvas, what I could only assume was an enormous quantity of gunpowder. Enough to bring down the crumbling roof of the basilica and several of the pillars that supported it onto the unsuspecting heads of the crowd gathered below. Pope, cardinals, princes, ambassadors, Borgias . . . all dead and with them all hope that Savonarola and what he represented could be defeated.

I leaped, my arms outstretched, on the wings of a prayer I did not even know I uttered, I who cannot pray. Flying through the dim, dust-moted light, my fingertips straining until, just as the red serpent's eye was about to vanish beneath the canvas, I seized the slender length of hemp and pulled with all my might.

It came loose so suddenly that I fell backward, landing hard enough for the wind to be knocked from me. Still the fuse continued to burn, singeing my hand. I gasped, jumped up, and threw it onto the floor, where I stomped on it with both feet until at last the red eye winked out and there was only the rasping of my breath and the pounding of my heart in the vast, crumbling heights of Holy Mother Church.

Gloria in excelsis deo. Glory to God in the Highest.

I must have slumped onto the floor, for some moments later, I was aware of Cesare lifting me. His embrace was fierce, his grip hard. I savored both. Absurdly and improbably, I was alive. *We* were alive.

"What in the name of God is happening here?" he asked. "Vittoro said something about—"

"Lift the canvas," I urged.

Still holding me, he bent down and eased the covering away. At once, we both gasped. A dozen or more barrels of gunpowder, each small enough to be carried by a single man concealed beneath a cloak but large enough to contain a lethal quality of explosive, were piled against one of the main supporting piers holding up the roof and by extension, the entire eastern side of the basilica. Had they gone off, at the very least that side of the building would have collapsed and likely its sheer weight would have brought the rest of the dilapidated structure down. The death toll would have been in the hundreds, as virtually no one in the basilica would have had a chance to escape. The toll on Christendom itself was unimaginable.

"How did you—?" Cesare asked.

"The smell in the guesthouse. I had trouble placing it but finally I realized that it was sulfur. I think there must still have been a quantity of gunpowder stored there that went off when the fire was set. Il Frateschi may have planned to stage other attacks around the city in the aftermath of the destruction here. That would have ensured complete chaos and the likelihood that the College of Cardinals would have accepted anyone as pope who could put an end to it."

Cesare nodded slowly. He set me on my feet but continued to stare at the barrels. "Did you see who lit the fuse?"

I shook my head. That part still puzzled me. "There was no one in the garret when I got here, at least so far as I could see."

It was possible that someone could have escaped by a staircase other than the one I had used, but to do that, he would have had to run the length of the garret. That was well over three hundred feet, a distance I did not think anyone would try to cover while a burning fuse raced toward enough gunpowder to bring down the basilica.

"Vittoro is about to interrupt the Mass and order an immediate evacuation," Cesare said. "We will have to stop him."

We went then, quickly down the curving stone steps. I remained at their foot while Cesare went to tell Vittoro that the danger had been averted. They returned together. My old friend looked at me narrowly.

"You appear no worse for your sojourn in the afterworld," he said.

"I am sorry—," I began, but he dismissed my effort at apology with a wave.

"Later, Donna. If what Signore Cesare has just told me is true, you have earned yourself a large measure of forgiveness."

I was humbly grateful for his understanding even as I remained uncertain that I truly deserved it. Once again, I had embroiled my friends in my own search for vengeance, and although this time I had not outrightly put any in harm's way, that was only because the need to do so had not arisen. Next time, who knew what I might do?

Unless I could put a stop to it all right then.

"Morozzi," I said, and Cesare nodded. We left Vittoro to handle the inevitable questions from Il Papa and any of the other notables who might have perceived something amiss, and hurried down the aisle. Before we had gone very far, I stopped abruptly.

We were passing the great water clock that has stood in that aisle off the nave of Saint Peter's since shortly after the basilica was built, all that time measuring the passing of the hours that control the great canonical wheel of prayer from lauds to vespers and at every point throughout the day. The water clock is a marvel of engineering, being half again the height of a tall man and consisting of two reservoirs of carved stone, one raised above the other. A small opening in the higher reservoir allows for the measured drip of water into the lower. As the water level shifts in each vessel, rising in the one as it falls in the other, cylinders rotate to display the day, month, phase of the moon, and the astrological sign. The water clock is considered by some to be a vestige of paganism, as it is well known that the ancients used such devices for their own worship, therefore little is made of it. I had walked past it more times than I could count, and had found it fascinating enough to ask my father to explain its workings. Once he had done so, my curiosity was satisfied and I took little further note of it other than to wonder occasionally what other marvels had come down to us on the river of time, if only we had the wit to see them.

It had been in my mind to wonder why I had not encountered either Morrozi or one of his allies in the garret. Surely, someone must have lit the fuse? Now I was struck by a sudden, seemingly absurd possibility. Staring up into the shadows directly above the lower vessel, I thought I saw something that did not belong. A small but unmistakable hole drilled into the wall.

"Boost me up," I said to Cesare.

He frowned but did as I bid. In an instant, I confirmed that a hole had been drilled a few inches above the top of the lower water reservoir. Moreover, the size of the opening was familiar, being slightly larger than the diameter of the fuse I had stamped out. With proper preparation and given the decrepitude of the basilica, it could well have been possible to extend a fuse up through that hole, along one of the many interior pillars, and through the crumbling floor into the garret. But to what purpose?

Grasping hold of the top of the vessel, I peered inside. What I saw sent a jolt of shock through me. Leaning against the stone to balance myself, I reached in with both hands. As Cesare watched, I removed a long, shallow pan still holding a quantity of oil at the center of which floated a coil of slow-burning wick.

"What the hell is that?" Cesare asked when he had lowered me again to the ground. Together we stared at what I had found.

"The explanation for how Morozzi lit the fuse," I said. "The clock runs on a seven-day cycle with water flowing out of one vessel into the other. We are at the point now when the lower vessel is near its fullest. At some point in the past few days, he or one of his confederates set this pan to float on the water with enough oil in it and a long enough wick to remain burning as the vessel filled. The water level rose, lifting the pan and bringing the flame finally into contact with the fuse that must have extended out from there—" I pointed to the hole in the stone. "With sufficient planning, it would be possible to know exactly how fast the vessel would fill. Then the moment when the fuse would ignite could be timed precisely."

"To occur during the Mass." Cesare looked grim, but at the same time, I could see that he was as fascinated and unwillingly impressed as I was myself. "It is ingenious," he said.

We do not like to believe that brilliance can march hand-in-hand with evil yet I suspect that happens more times than we know.

"It is," I said, and felt the first stirrings of despair as I realized what my discovery meant.

35

Morozzi was gone, vanished from Rome as though he had never been. Later, we were able to confirm that the mad priest had been seen departing through the Septimian Gate leading northward out of the city along the Via Cassia, from which he could reach Florence or, for that matter, any number of other towns and ports. That knowledge came too late to matter.

Whether he had been responsible for the other attacks against Borgia remained to be determined. Certainly, he could have used Il Frateschi to that end but, loath though I was to admit it, other parties might have played their part. The Spanish, the Sforzas, the French, della Rovere—truly my master possessed an embarrassment of enemies. How fortunate that he had his family to count on—or not, as the case may be.

Juan was defiant at first when Cesare confronted him, then denied everything and finally sought refuge in outrage.

"How dare you question me?" he demanded. "I serve our father far more loyally than you have ever done! You would see him at war while all I want is peace."

"What kind of peace?" Cesare demanded. We were in one of the many antechambers scattered through the Vatican Palace, where Cesare had cornered his brother in between the conclusion of the Mass and the beginning of the other welcome ceremonies for Pesaro. I was doing my best to fade into the background as any good servant should. That may have been unnecessary, as I doubted Juan would have recognized me under any circumstances. The notion of a woman daring to dress as a man was simply beyond him.

Besides, everyone knew the *strega* was dead.

"The peace of Saint Peter's in ruins and all of us buried under it?" Cesare went on. "Is that what you're talking about? It's what the man you protected and helped was intent on doing. How could you possibly have allied with him? *How?*"

"You are lying! He never meant any such thing. Father Morozzi is an emissary from Cardinal della Rovere bearing messages of friendship and peace. All he wanted was to convince our father that there need be no enmity between them, no war! But you have destroyed the hope of that. He warned me that you might have a spy in my household but I didn't believe him. The moment he realized he'd been seen, he knew that he had to leave or risk being killed by you."

"You are an idiot!" Cesare roared. "Christ's breath, how do you even have the wit to live? He left because he had accomplished what he came to do, or at least he believed that he had. What do you think, that angels put the barrels of gunpowder in Saint Peter's and rigged a fuse to set them off while we were all at Mass?"

"No," Juan said. His glared at his brother sullenly. "If any such thing happened, the witch did it, perhaps with your help. Thank God and all the Saints that she has perished."

"It's going to be an awful shock to him when he discovers that I'm still alive," I said after Cesare had stormed out of the room with me on his heels. Later, I would have to come to terms with my own feelings about Morozzi escaping—again. But just then I was intent on calming Cesare. After all, I needed his help in dealing with his father.

Borgia had been informed of my deception. Vittoro had no choice but to tell him and I think it was better that he heard it from him, as that gave him an opportunity to work through the worst of his rage without my being present. Or at least I hoped that he had done so. I was not looking forward to speaking with him.

Yet with each passing moment, my attitude hardened. I considered the lengths to which I had gone to save Il Papa, including risking my own life. True, he would believe that my real motivation had been to kill Morozzi but the effect was the same—Borgia lived and with him all his vast plans for *la famiglia*. That had to count for something.

"Are you going to tell him about Juan?" I asked as I followed Cesare up the grand stairs toward the papal office.

"What's the point?" he replied over his shoulder. "He'll never believe me. He'll just think that I'm trying to undermine my brother out of jealousy. The best I can do now is make sure that he doesn't take any of this out on you."

I had mixed feelings about Cesare fighting my battles for me—on the one hand, I recognized that I could benefit from his help, on the other my damnable independence wished otherwise. That being the case, I kept silent as I tried to decide how best to handle the situation.

Borgia was not alone; several of his secretaries were with him, as was Renaldo, who was going down the list of events planned for the remainder of the day. When the steward saw me, he broke out in a smile so broad that I feared his face would crack. Such was the extent of his unalloyed relief at discovering me alive that I could not help wonder if, despite all evidence to the contrary, Renaldo might not have placed a side bet in favor of my surviving. In his position, I likely would have done so, for surely the odds would have been highly favorable.

With a quick nod in his direction, I concentrated my attention on Borgia. Christ's Vicar did not appear at all pleased that one of his faithful servants remained among the living. To the contrary, he looked prepared to order me to Hades posthaste.

By all rights, I should have been filled with fear, but instead a great calm possessed me. Its source was no mystery. I had faced my greatest dread, the near certainty that I was too dark a creature to stand in the light of God. I had entered the holiest of holies and survived. Beside that, Borgia seemed scant challenge.

Even so, he made a good show of it.

"Explain yourself!" he demanded after the other men had prudently fled the room and only Cesare and I were left. "What in God's name did you think you were doing to stage such a spectacle? We had a Mass for you, for pity's sake! Christ weep, you truly are mad!"

"And you are alive," Cesare shot back. He faced his father squarely and did not flinch even when Borgia purpled with anger.

"The two of you have been in league all this time," Il Papa declared. "A faithless son and a treacherous poisoner. What have I done that God should burden me so?"

Really, how could anyone even begin to answer that? Before Christ's Vicar could further proclaim how abused and mistreated he was, I said, "Only say the word and you will not have me to concern you any longer."

For the second time, I had failed to avenge my father's murder and rid the world of Morozzi because I felt compelled to save Borgia. I had wrested the job of poisoner for myself because I believed that the power it brought would enable me to kill the mad priest. So far all I had done was leave him alive to strike again.

"I will gladly resign from your service," I declared. "Then I will be free to find Morozzi and kill him. Nothing else matters so much to me, as you should know."

It was no idle threat; at that moment, I truly meant what I said. Despite my feelings for Cesare, the thought of being done with *la famiglia* held an almost irresistible appeal. They were so fiercely focused on themselves, so all-absorbing and demanding that wherever they were, they seemed to leave very little air for anyone else to breathe. I was becoming very tired of that.

"Francesca," Cesare began. He looked appalled and I could not blame him. At the very least, I might have given him some warning. Yet surely by now he must have known not to expect such consideration from me.

Borgia, by contrast, appeared suspiciously less alarmed. He calmed enough to look me up and down, as though confirming that I truly was no ghost, then said, "Nothing else matters? Is that so? Then what about Lux?"

"What is Lux?" Cesare asked with a frown.

Borgia shrugged. "That depends on who you ask. Some would say that it is a coven of conspirators intent on using alchemical and other means to undermine Holy Mother Church and open the way for the Devil to come into the world. Others would say that it is a group of dedicated natural philosophers striving to grasp the underlying truth of God's Creation."

He looked at me and said, "The first explanation will get you burned. As for the second—" Again, he shrugged. "I'm sure you've noticed that so much in this life is a matter of interpretation."

One thing that can be said for Borgia, I never had any difficulty understanding him even when I did not want to do so.

"You would go to such lengths to keep me in your service, despite how I deceived you?"

"Despite and because of it. As I said, you have a gift for finding fresh solutions and I have need of that, at least for the moment. Behave yourself, cause me no further upset, and you and your friends may do as you like, discreetly, of course. Otherwise—"

"That is not good enough." Cesare sucked in his breath at my daring but I did not hesitate. If I was to be coerced into remaining with Borgia, there would be a price to pay.

Facing him squarely, I said, "You will not simply tolerate Lux, you will afford us your full protection, which means never again trying to use us to your own ends." Before Il Papa could respond, I continued. "And that is not all. You will give me unfettered access to the Mysterium so that I may pursue my own studies and report back whatever I find to the other members of Lux."

Borgia's gaze narrowed. He was not a man to accept demands from anyone.

"Is there anything else you want? My papal crown, for instance, or perhaps I should vacate Saint Peter's Throne two, no three days out of every week and let you sit there, giving out rulings on all and sundry matters?"

"No, thank you," I said properly. I would not let him make light of my sacrifice in not going after Morozzi at once. The thought of doing so still tempted me almost unbearably, yet I knew that my father would have wanted me to protect Lux and to make the most of the extraordinary opportunity presented by the Mysterium. Was it a measure of my healing heart that I could think of his hopes for me rather than my own need for vengeance?

Reluctantly, Borgia agreed, or so it seemed. As always when I had dealings with him, I was left to wonder if he had not plotted it all out ahead of time, deciding how best to manipulate me that I could be of further service to him.

Cesare, on the other hand, seemed to believe that I had scored a great victory.

"You beat him," he exclaimed when we had left the office and were making our way back down the grand stair. "You stood right up to him, dared him to do his worst, and you won!"

"Not precisely," I said. "I have traded away pursuing Morozzi for what I admit are important concessions. But if I did not believe that the mad priest will be driven to strike at your father again, thereby coming once more within my reach, I would never have done so."

He waved that off as though it were of no account but he also warned me, "Accept your victory, Francesca, and savor it, for believe me, my father will exact full price for it."

I was left to ponder that as, after a brief, hard kiss guaranteed to scandalize everyone passing through the entry to the Curia who saw the son of Jove apparently *intimo* with a page boy, Cesare took himself off to prepare for the remainder of the welcoming ceremonies.

With no thought left in my head save that of a bath and bed, I made for home, ignoring the shocked whispers that accompanied me. Cesare had managed to knock my hat off as he kissed me and I had not bothered to put it on again. Without it, I was all too recognizable. Already, word was spreading that Borgia's *strega* had returned from the dead.

Portia was in the loggia when I arrived. She dropped the basket she was carrying and stared at me, open-mouthed. A moment later,

I was kneeling in front of her as she flung her arms around me and hugged me fiercely.

"Praise God you truly are whole and well!" she said. "But Donna, if you ever do such a thing again, I swear by all that is holy I will—"

"If I ever plot my death again," I assured her hastily, "you will be the first to know, I promise. Now tell me, is that chicken I smell, by any chance?"

Fed, bathed, and at rest finally in my own bed, I slept without Sofia's powder and without nightmares. If I dreamed at all, I do not remember it, but perhaps I chose not to. I woke with thoughts of Rocco already uppermost in my mind. By all rights, I should do no more than send him a brief note apologizing for my deception, then leave the man in peace. He had every right to the chance for happiness that I was convinced Carlotta d'Agnelli could bring him. So, too, did Nando.

Imagine then my surprise when I opened the door to a knock and found an ashen-faced messenger quailing at the prospect of facing an undead witch who was, as I shortly learned, the talk of Rome.

The poor man thrust a package into my arms, declined any payment, and fled with such alacrity that I waited to make sure he did not fall headfirst down the steps before stepping back inside my apartment.

I set the package on a cleared space on my worktable and slowly unwrapped it. My breath caught when I recognized the crimson sphere streaked with gold that I had seen Rocco creating. He had crafted it into a lamp inscribed across the base with the words: *Ex obscuritate lucem fers*—Out of darkness, you bring light.

I did not weep, so I told myself, but I did sit for a long time, my hand on the lamp as I considered what the faith of such a man meant to me. So many struggles still lay ahead—to protect Lux, to keep Borgia alive, to deal with the matter of della Rovere and the looming threat of war, to discover whether Morozzi or someone else entirely had been behind the earlier attacks on Il Papa. Above all, I had to find a resolution within myself for the terrible darkness that still threatened to devour me. Yet on that day, sitting beside the table where I pursued my investigations, in the home of my own making, I felt the stirrings of confidence that I might, when all was said and done, come out a better person than I was.

On the cusp of that hope, I rose and lit the lamp. As the first rays from it fell upon me, my heart lightened and I smiled.

Reading
Group
Gold

THE BORGIA
BETRAYAL

by Sara Poole

About the Author

- A Conversation with Sara Poole

Behind the Novel

- Historical Timeline
- "The Hinge of History"
  An Original Essay by the Author

Keep on Reading

- Recommended Reading
- Reading Group Questions

*A
Reading
Group Gold
Selection*

For more reading group suggestions,
visit www.readinggroupgold.com.

🦁 ST. MARTIN'S GRIFFIN

 *A Conversation with Sara Poole*

Could you tell us a little bit about your background, and when you decided that you wanted to lead a literary life?

I grew up in a family of journalists who were taken aback when, at the tender age of twelve, I announced my intent to write fiction. I immediately set about doing so and have never stopped. Along the way, I've worked in advertising, public relations, and publishing, but fiction has always been my lodestone drawing me home. I can't imagine a life without it.

"Fiction has always been my lodestone drawing me home."

Is there a book that most influenced your life? Or inspired you to become a writer?

As a child, I read everything from Lewis Carroll to comic books (*Little Lulu* stands out in particular). I loved it all indiscriminately and gobbled up anything that fell into my hands. Somewhere along the way, I encountered Jean Plaidy in one or more of her various incarnations and became hooked on historical fiction.

What was the inspiration for *The Borgia Betrayal* and its heroine, Francesca?

Several years ago, I became interested in the wild plants on my doorstep that in one form or another are poisonous. One evening, I mentioned this to my family at dinner, setting off a round of teasing about what I'd put in the food. Two words popped into my head: *woman poisoner*. In the strange way of such things, Francesca appeared shortly thereafter, virtually fully formed. I've had to run to keep up with her ever since.

The Borgia Betrayal is your second book featuring
Francesca. How many books do you plan to include
in the series? And how do you plot Francesca's
growth in each book?

I know where and how Francesca's story ends, and
I have a fair idea of how she gets to that point from
the moment when we first meet her as a young, desperate woman about to enter the employ of *la famiglia* Borgia. I have a timeline of many of the important
events in her life that also tracks her development as
a character. Fascinating me as she does, I can easily
foresee a dozen books following this mistress of the
dark as she strives to bring light into her own life
and her world.

How much of the writing you did for book one was
based on your intention to write a sequel? How did
knowing this was a series affect your writing of
the first book, *Poison*?

In the beginning, I assumed that I was writing a single
book. As a rough framework, I thought it would cover
the eleven years from shortly before Rodrigo Borgia's
election as Pope Alexander VI in the summer of 1492
to his death eleven years later in 1503. I'd written
about thirty thousand words when I realized I was on
day four. About then I decided I was writing a series.
Writing a series is significantly different from writing
a single novel. Knowing that I don't have to try to
cram a sprawling, multifaceted story into one book
allows me to concentrate on short, intense periods of
a few weeks or a few months in which conflict—both
internal and external—compels my characters to
adapt and change.

Were you surprised at all by how your characters
grew from *Poison* to *The Borgia Betrayal*?

Francesca surprised me a great deal. I didn't anticipate

the lengths she would go to in order to do what she regards as her duty. In this book, she takes a desperate risk that illuminates her precarious mental state but which I think also makes her realize how much she values her own life. That discovery will turn out to be very important in the third book.

Your books are part of a series, but do you think readers who are new to them necessarily need to read the books in order?

Each of the books is a standalone work. While some readers may prefer to read them in order, they definitely don't need to be read that way. In fact, I think it would be interesting to pick up one of the later books, discover Francesca, and then go back and explore earlier events in her life.

"I can easily foresee a dozen books following [Francesca]."

What can readers expect from the third novel in the series? We don't want any spoilers, of course, but can you say anything about what lies ahead for your characters?

In the third book, something truly terrible happens to Francesca. This woman who believes that all that is worthwhile in life happens within the city limits of Rome is forced to endure an extended stay in the countryside. On a more serious note, Francesca will make a shattering discovery about her own past when she meets an adversary who plunges her into a nightmare confrontation with her deepest fears. From this, she will emerge as the woman she must be if she is to survive the deadly danger and conflict that is about to tear her world apart.

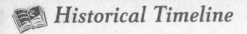

March 4, 1493

La Niña, the flagship of Christopher Columbus, limps out of a fierce Atlantic storm bringing word of the discovery of vast new lands to the west.

Spring, 1493

Intent on increasing the wealth and power of his family, Rodrigo Borgia, Pope Alexander VI, seizes lands previously belonging to the Kingdom of Naples and grants them to his second son, Juan, newly created Duke of Gandia.

Ferdinand I, King of Naples, warns of war if his rights are not respected by the papacy.

Rumors spread that the Pope plans to make his first son, seventeen-year-old Cesare Borgia, a cardinal, laying the foundation for a dynasty of Borgia popes that will rule all of Christendom.

Fear of Borgia's intentions increases opposition to his papacy among many of the great families of Italy as well as the prelates of the Roman Catholic Church.

From his base in Florence, the fanatical Dominican friar Girolamo Savonarola preaches against the corruption of the Roman Catholic Church and the rule of Pope Alexander VI.

April 25, 1493

In answer to challenges to his papacy from the Kingdom of Naples and other opponents, Pope Alexander VI formally begins preparations for war. Borgia's great rival for the papacy, Cardinal della Rovere, withdraws to his bishopric at Ostia and begins fortifying it.

Behind the Novel

May 4, 1493

Rodrigo Borgia, Pope Alexander VI, signs the papal bull *Inter Caetera,* granting all the newly discovered lands a hundred leagues west of the Azores to Spain. In doing so, he seeks to buy the support of Their Most Catholic Majesties, Queen Isabella and King Ferdinand, against his enemies.

Mid-May, 1493

Cardinal della Rovere withdraws to his family seat at Savona. He enters negotiations with the French king, Charles VIII, with the intention of overthrowing Pope Alexander VI.

June, 1493

The Spanish emissary Don Diego Lopez de Haro arrives in Rome, bringing more demands from Their Most Catholic Majesties in return for Spain's support of Borgia.

June 12, 1493

In fulfillment of his pledge to the Sforza family of Milan, by which he secured their support for his papacy, Rodrigo Borgia marries his thirteen-year-old daughter, Lucrezia, to Giovanni Sforza. The marriage signifies a hardening of positions and makes war all but inevitable.

Rodrigo Borgia

Lucrezia Borgia

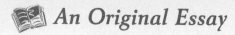

The Hinge of History

The Borgia Betrayal begins at a moment when Europe dangles in the grip of stunning news. That crazy fellow, Christopher Columbus, who deluded himself into believing that he could reach the Indies by sailing west, didn't die at sea as every right-thinking person was certain that he would. He's back and he's claiming to have succeeded. Moreover, he's brought proof in the form of exotic people, plants, and animals unlike any ever seen before.

For a civilization exhausted by centuries of war, famine, and plague, in which oppression rules and the tentative rebirth of learning risks being smothered in its cradle, no news has ever been more exhilarating or more challenging. The moment the battered caravel *La Niña* limps out of an Atlantic storm into the port of Lisbon on March 4, 1493, everything changes.

Columbus's return sets off a series of rapid-fire events as everyone from merchants to monarchs and the Pope himself—Rodrigo Borgia, Pope Alexander VI—struggles to determine how to exploit whatever it is that has just happened. But beyond that, it inspires people from all walks of life to think of possibilities that have never occurred to them before. Within thirty years of Columbus's return from his first voyage, dozens of European explorers will remake the map of the world. For the first time in history, the Spanish scholar Juan los Vives will be able to report accurately: "The whole globe is opened up to the human race." The end of isolation will have a devastating effect on indigenous people, but it will also propel humanity into the modern era.

"Within years of Columbus's return…the 'whole globe is opened up to the human race.'"

Caught at this moment as the hinge of history swings wide and the door opens on a new age, we see the Borgias, their world, and their poisoner, Francesca Giordano, enmeshed in the challenges of their daily lives yet aware that just beyond, vast, transformative forces are at work. Like us, they struggle to ride the wind carrying them toward a destination both alluring and unknowable.

Christopher Columbus

Behind the Novel

Recommended Reading

Sarah Bradford
*Lucrezia Borgia: Life, Love,
and Death in Renaissance Italy*
Cesare Borgia: His Life and Times

Johann Burchard
At the Court of the Borgia

E. R. Chamberlain
The Fall of the House of Borgia

Ivan Cloulas
The Borgias

Sarah Dunant
The Birth of Venus
Sacred Hearts
In the Company of the Courtesan

Clemente Fusero
The Borgias

C. W. Gortner
The Confessions of Catherine de Medici: A Novel

Christopher Hibbert
The Borgias and Their Enemies

Marion Johnson
The Borgias

Jeanne Kalogridis
The Borgia Bride: A Novel
The Devil's Queen: A Novel of Catherine de Medici

Michael Edward Mallett
*The Borgias: The Rise and Fall of
a Renaissance Dynasty*

Reading Group Questions

1. Francesca Giordano lives at a time when civilization is being revitalized by new perceptions and ideas that threaten the existing power structure. How does the struggle between the two shape this story and the challenges that Francesca faces?

2. As official poisoner serving the House of Borgia, Francesca has saved Rodrigo Borgia, Pope Alexander VI, from numerous attempts on his life, but the threat against him continues to grow. What are the consequences of living in such an intense, high-stress situation where life and death constantly hang in the balance?

3. In the course of this story, Francesca takes a desperate gamble with her own life. What does her willingness to do so say about her mental state? Is she genuinely tempted by suicidal thoughts?

4. While she yearns for the glassmaker, Rocco, and the life she could have had with him, Francesca does not hesitate to pursue a relationship with Cesare Borgia that is sexual and more. Why is she unable to give up her feelings for Rocco even as she tells herself that there is no possibility of a future with him? What continues to draw her to Cesare?

5. In modern terms, Francesca suffers from post-traumatic shock related to an event early in her life. In a time before psychoanalysis, she can understand her condition only as the act of a supernatural agent, either God or the Devil. What factors in her life may prompt her to look elsewhere for the true cause of her distress as well as the path to resolving it?

Keep on Reading

6. Francesca belongs to a secret group of scholars and alchemists known as Lux. Like other such groups of the time, they are forced to work in secret. Why did the Catholic Church—which had nurtured such scholars as Thomas Aquinas, William of Occam, and Roger Bacon—resist new scientific discoveries? Was the new learning really a threat to the authority of Rome, or could the Church have chosen to embrace it?

7. Francesca regards the priest Bernando Morozzi as the embodiment of evil, yet she also fears that they are alike in some ways. Is she right in either regard? In both? What does this story reveal about how far each is willing to go in order to stop the other? Can conclusions be drawn about which of them is ultimately more dangerous?

8. Lucrezia Borgia claims to be resigned to being used by her father as a pawn to further his ambitions. Yet she also seeks ways to have at least some control over her own life. Is she deluded in thinking that is possible, or did women of her time find means to circumvent the oppressive traditions under which they lived?

9. As Rodrigo's son, Cesare Borgia has access to great power, yet he cannot use it to claim the life he truly wants. Instead, his younger brother, Juan, receives all that Cesare believes should be his. How dangerous is the rivalry between the brothers likely to become? How far may Cesare go to supplant Juan in their father's love and trust?

10. Throughout this story, poison appears as a
    metaphor for the stain of corruption running
    through the highest levels of society. Is a similar
    metaphor appropriate in our own time, and
    if so, where?

11. What role do you think the corruption of the
    popes and other high-ranking prelates of this
    time played in triggering the rebellion against
    Catholicism that we know as the Reformation?
    Were there internal reforms the Catholic
    leadership could have taken that might have
    prevented the Reformation from happening?

12. If Rodrigo Borgia's dream of a papal dynasty
    controlled by his family had succeeded, what
    would have been the implications for his time?
    For ours?

Keep on
Reading